BIG
GIRL

BIG

GIRL

A Novel

Mecca Jamilah Sullivan

LIVERIGHT PUBLISHING CORPORATION

A Division of W. W. Norton & Company

Independent Publishers Since 1923

Copyright © 2022 by Mecca Jamilah Sullivan

A portion of this work originally appeared in *Palimpsest: A Journal on Women, Gender, and the Black International* under the title "Christopher Cat," Copyright SUNY Press, 2013.

For information about permission to reproduce selections from this book, write to Permissions, Liveright Publishing Corporation, a division of W. W. Norton & Company, Inc., 500 Fifth Avenue, New York, NY 10110

For information about special discounts for bulk purchases, please contact W. W. Norton Special Sales at specialsales@wwnorton.com or 800-233-4830

Manufacturing by Lake Book Manufacturing
Production manager: Julia Druskin

Library of Congress Cataloging-in-Publication Data

Names: Sullivan, Mecca Jamilah, author.
Title: Big girl : a novel / Mecca Jamilah Sullivan.
Description: First Edition. | New York, NY : Liveright Publishing Corporation, 2022.
Identifiers: LCCN 2022011911 | ISBN 9781324091417 (cloth) | ISBN 9781324091424 (epub)
Subjects: LCGFT: Novels.
Classification: LCC PS3619.U4435 B54 2022 | DDC 813/.6—dc23
LC record available at https://lccn.loc.gov/2022011911

Liveright Publishing Corporation, 500 Fifth Avenue, New York, N.Y. 10110
www.wwnorton.com

W. W. Norton & Company Ltd., 15 Carlisle Street, London W1D 3BS

1 2 3 4 5 6 7 8 9 0

This novel is dedicated to all the teachers
who told me I could always amount to anything,
and to my family and friends.

Breaking as blessing. Why do we forget this
has always been the way?

—KAMILAH AISHA MOON, *"Eulogy"*

I

Saturday

THE TRUTH WAS, Malaya Clondon had been thinking of French fries since last night. She craved them as she ate Chinese food in secret with her father while her mother worked late at the university. The thought of French fries stayed with the eight-year-old through the canned laughter and blond-headed family tableaus of the Friday night sitcom lineup each week, and helped her push herself from bed the next morning. She thought of the shiny fried strips, nestled together, boasting countless shades of yellow and gold, from the time she cleared the front steps of the family's brownstone at 8 a.m. each Saturday until she felt, at last, the film of hot grease on her face after African dance class, so much later in the day.

On the walk to the Meeting on Frederick Douglass Boulevard, other foods did drift to mind. Malaya and her mother, Nyela, passed at least eight bodegas, plus the McDonald's, the Kentucky Fried, and the Woolworth's on Broadway, where the smell of hot popcorn seeped out in slow waves from beneath the glass doors. On 145th Street there was Copeland's Restaurant and Reliable Cafeteria, where they made crispy smothered chicken with gravy as thick as pudding and potato salad that was perfectly sweet and salty at once. But by the time the Clondon women pushed through the heavy green doors of AME Mount Canaan Church and went down to the basement community center—by the time

Malaya took her turn on the scale and watched red numbers blink and multiply beneath her, feeling Nyela's eyes fixed on the number panel from behind—Malaya thought only of the potato-and-ketchup crunch-crusted mush she would have later. She did not think of the hour of dance she would have to get through beforehand, or what lie she would tell as to how her allowance had been spent.

"Well, don't everybody speak up at once now!" Ms. Adelaide, the Meeting leader, laughed over the collar of her lavender suit.

Malaya sat in a sea of fat women on folding chairs and watched Ms. Adelaide walk to the front. Ms. Adelaide caressed the plastic easel, flipping back a page marked EMOTIONAL TRIGGERS PIE CHART and exposing a sheet as clean and white as the face of a new tub of Cool Whip. She stood there, her hip sloped prettily out before her, arms loose and easy along her waist.

"Come on, ladies. Don't be shy." Ms. Adelaide shifted into another breathtakingly casual pose, resting her weight on one tall plum-colored high heel and letting a hand float up to stroke the paper. "I want you to think about your favorite food. You know we all have that one food that always gets us in trouble. I want you to think about it. Call it out!"

Malaya listened, catching a few coughs, small squeakings of the metal seats. The rustling of a paper bag somewhere in the back of the room brought salt water to Malaya's mouth as she thought of removing the fries from their paper bag. She imagined the strips bending over one another in their red-and-white-striped dish, salt crystals hitting them from all sides and sparkling like glitter.

"Alright, now. I know it can be embarrassing."

Ms. Adelaide leaned back, posed, then moved slowly toward Malaya and Nyela, who sat a seat away from each other—to leave room for both their hips, Nyela always said. Malaya thought nothing of Ms. Adelaide's first steps, except how nice it was the way the tapping of the woman's heels seemed to punctuate the soft rub of her shimmery pantyhose: *gzhhh-TPP, gzhhh-TPP*. But within seconds Malaya could smell Ms. Adelaide's perfume in her face and found herself staring directly at the silver buckle on her purple suede belt.

Fear frothed up in Malaya's chest as the synthetic cherry stink of Ms.

Adelaide's uncapped marker prickled the insides of her nostrils. She would lie, she decided. She would disclose a passion for yogurt, welcome and unusual in a girl of eight. Her face puffed with earnestness, she would tell the woman that she was "Centered, Committed, and in Control"; that she'd take fat-free frozen yogurt over cookie dough ice cream any day. She would make her mother proud and force this lean purple creature to go back and check her scale—those red numbers could *not* be right. This girl could not weigh one hundred and sixty-eight pounds, committed as she was. It was Malaya's specialty, this kind of invention. It was how she helped other children pronounce her name: *Ma-LIE-ya. Like I don't tell the truth.* She parted her lips, prepared to declare her fidelity to the Program.

Ms. Adelaide's mouth was plump and her red lipstick looked like jelly sliding over her lip line into her deep brown skin. She tugged at the empty chair between Malaya and Nyela, gently easing it from between them.

"I'm sorry, baby," she cooed. "Did you want to say something?"

Malaya's mouth went dry and mealy. She paused, wondering if her lies were worth telling now that it was clear she wasn't being asked to give up anything more than an empty chair. She shook her head no.

Nyela looked at her over the empty space where the chair had been, then turned to give Ms. Adelaide a stiff half-smile. Malaya knew this smile. It was the Professor Clondon smile, the small talk of her mother's facial lexicon, used to assert her presence and to make vague reference to Malaya, as if to say, sighingly, "Yes, that's my daughter." Nyela Clondon did have real smiles, of course. Malaya had seen them on weekend afternoons when she, her mother, and her father, Percy, adventured through the city together, before the family moved to Harlem. But these public smiles were a matter of etiquette for Nyela, like knowing what shoes to wear with a winter-white suit with black buttons, or how to deadhead flowers without compromising the symmetry of a bouquet. Ms. Adelaide smiled back.

"Well, everyone is so shy this morning!" She pushed the chair to the center of the room and glided into it like a goose into a familiar pond.

"So I'll tell you-all first. Mine was corn with butter. Anytime there was corn around, I knew I would not be able to control myself. I used to be a corn *junkie!*" A few ladies along the wall chuckled. "And I don't mean just a little pat," she continued. "I'm talking about *butter*, okay?"

At this, Ms. Adelaide changed shape before Malaya's eyes. She uncrossed her legs, hunched over, filled her cheeks with air, and made smacking noises as she ran her fingers back and forth in front of her mouth, mimicking a wet and unsightly battle with an ear of corn on the cob. The room roared. Fat ladies shifted massive thighs in their chairs. Thick ladies clapped their hands and crashed against each other like waves.

"And let me tell you something," Ms. Adelaide said, leaning forward and pointing a finger at the group in a gesture of sistagirl confidence. "I *know* I'm not the only one."

The whole room laughed again, and one woman leaned her head back and opened her mouth so wide Malaya thought she might freeze in that pose, turn to stone, and begin to spout water like a fish in a fountain. Then Ms. Adelaide returned to herself, just like that—left leg draped over right, shoulders straight, manicured hands with their red-tipped nails resting coolly on her lap.

"Well," another woman said from the fourth or fifth row, "I do have a weakness for pasta."

"I heard that!" someone shouted. "What kind?"

And they were off, talking about food. Malaya tried not to listen, except when Nyela murmured in testimony when the women mentioned foods she herself liked, like oxtails and pistachio ice cream. As food names began to appear on the easel, Malaya imagined each item rising from a plate before the woman who'd claimed it as her "trigger." Squares of lasagna and tall Styrofoam-cupped milkshakes with cartoon eyes and gloved hands cuffed these women to their chairs in Malaya's imagination, dancing and singing devilishly as they leapt down their throats. The women, helpless victims, dragged themselves sadly to these meetings each week as their only hope.

Quietly, in her mind, Malaya considered what this "trigger" might be for her. But each food she thought of suddenly lost its appeal among these women who seemed to feel guilty for putting too much gravy on their grits. She thought of the dulce de coco candies she ate on the school bus with Shaniece Guzmán, the little butter-colored girl from Amsterdam Avenue, whom she played with, and the chocolate chip cookies—as big as her face—that she bought every day at school with money stolen from her mother's coat pocket. These foods seemed unspeakable among the Meeting women. Even imagining them stung her with guilt. Malaya planned to eat her fries and enjoy them as soon as she could leave the women's sight. She would not ruin that moment by thinking of it now.

Instead, she let her mind float to thoughts of Daundré Harris, the fourth-grader who was the only good reason she could think of for coming here every Saturday, or for trying to stay on-program at all. Each week as she waited for the numbers on the scale to stop climbing beneath her, she thought of Daundré and how much closer she might be to becoming Amandra Wilson, his pretty, thin girlfriend, who had a face the color of sawdust and long hair that curled like lo mein. Malaya had lost two pounds a year ago, when the family first moved to Harlem. She was in the second grade then, and had beamed all week, convinced that it was the beginning of a new life for her. She told Shaniece and marked it in her Hello Kitty diary, along with the news that Daundré had noticed her weight loss and asked her to be his girl, which was a lie. She had even given her grandmother, Ma-Mère, the good news in a letter she wrote and mailed to Philadelphia all by herself. She gained three pounds the following week, but the letter had already arrived.

"My daughter and I like pie." Nyela's hand fell into her lap once the sentence was out. Malaya felt a force field of eyes on her.

"I don't keep anything like that in the house, of course," Nyela continued. "And when we go out I try not to order dessert. But sometimes, on the weekends, I'll order an apple pie . . ." Malaya anticipated the fancy syllables she knew would come next. "À la mode."

"I try not to eat all the filling," her mother went on, shifting her weight and pulling her African mudcloth jacket around her shoulders. "My favorite part is the crust. My daughter likes the filling, so if I do have a craving, rather than deprive myself, you know, I always suggest we share." The room emitted a wave of supportive *mm-hmm*'s. "But you know children. They want their own. I don't usually let her order anything, but once we've eaten that pie we're out of control. We're Off-Program for the rest of the weekend, sometimes the whole week."

Ms. Adelaide added PIE to the list, which had grown to cover the entire page, leaving only a tiny diagonal of space between SALMON CAKES and PLÁTANO CHIPS for the three letters of the Clondon women's apparent trigger. Malaya wished to liquefy and slide from her seat, find herself gone from the basement into that word PIE, curled into the lower nook of the *E* as though it were a shaded ground below an apple tree. She wished for spots of sun to heat her sandaled feet as the leaves of her *E* tree rustled, and for the cool of an afternoon to raise goose bumps along her legs. In truth, Malaya was not so compelled by pie. She would eat the filling because it was there, and because it was the only chance she'd have all week to indulge herself in plain view, right next to her mother. And besides, Malaya knew, Nyela would feel better if she herself ate only the crust.

What her mother did not know, what could not be written on Ms. Adelaide's board for lack of space and limitations of language, was that Malaya would have preferred an endless plate of potatoes over pie without question. Mashed, salted, swaddled in gravy or butter or both, and served in a bottomless mixing bowl—that was how Malaya wanted to eat. She rarely had the chance: even when her mother and father weren't there to watch her, Giselle, the babysitter, usually was. But Malaya found her ways, sneaking single-serving bags of breakfast cereal from the kitchen in the sleeve of her nightgown and volunteering to dispose of her friends' leftovers at lunch.

And by now, Malaya had noticed in herself a tendency to choose quantity over quality—pools and pools of potatoes over a shared slice of fancy pie. She had not yet learned words like *abundance*, or *profusion*, or *glut*. The only word she could find to describe her true trigger was *MORE*. Of all the women in the room—thirty at least—only two seemed to share her passion: the loud woman who had broken the silence what now seemed like ages ago, and a smaller woman in the corner, who raised a hand only inches above her shoulder and said, almost in a whisper, "I have trouble with plain white rice."

AFTER THE MEETING, Nyela decided they would take the long route to the Harlem Arts Academy, walking along Seventh Avenue to 145th and then up to Sugar Hill. It had begun to rain, and wet air stuck to Malaya's face as she held her mother's hand at the stoplight on St. Nicholas. Women moved across the wide spans of pavement, before the limestone stoops and busy storefronts, gliding in a flurry of hair and shoes and eye shadow and wonderful outfits blaring more shapes and colors than Malaya could count.

"Malaya"—Nyela squeezed her hand in the drizzle and pointed her chin toward three women crossing the street in trench coats and umbrellas—"you see those women? Big as houses, over there? I hope you don't ever get that big."

Malaya looked again, confused. Each woman could have looked like a house—she supposed it was true. The largest one sort of sprawled like a mansion, and the shortest was tight and round like a shack. Still, Malaya was more interested in their elaborate angled hairdos, which fanned and swirled about their heads.

"I won't," she said.

It was sweetly obvious. Malaya would not become a house. She could not imagine how those women got that way, and it had not occurred to her, before that moment, that this might be a way to *become* at all. It seemed to her that either a woman was born a house or she wasn't. Malaya wasn't.

"I hope you don't," Nyela continued. "People like that are very unhealthy. They lead very unhappy lives, and usually they die."

It angered Malaya that her mother could doubt her on so sure an issue as this. Nyela had always seemed to regard her own weight as an irascible young sibling, something to be managed to the point of exasperation in private, and then, in public, defiantly ignored. But lately Nyela had begun to monitor Malaya's eating with a hawkish fastidiousness, and to harp on it in conversations like this. Malaya nodded again, emphatically this time. She imagined her ears stuffed with cotton balls, blocking out her mother's voice, leaving space in her mind only for sweet things and French fries.

WHEN THEY REACHED the Harlem Arts Academy, Nyela stooped to give Malaya her allowance and a kiss, instructing her to hold on to the money in case of an emergency. "I know. I will," Malaya said. She tucked the money into the pocket of her backpack, with the change from last night's Chinese food, which Percy had let her keep. She took a breath and readied herself for class.

Entering the dance hallway, Malaya stepped over the narrow, breadstick legs of ballet and jazz girls whose straw-colored tights stopped abruptly at their ankles, exposing different shades of bony brown feet as they stretched. Silently, she pushed further, weaving through a group of girls in her African dance class whose black leotards spanned their flat torsos like gift wrap over book covers, and whose red, yellow, and green kente-printed lapa skirts hung merrily around their waists like Christmas garlands.

No one spoke to Malaya as she undressed at the back of the flock. Facing the wall, she pushed herself into her leotard and tights, then pulled her lapa from her bag and wrapped the fabric around her middle, tugging the ends hard in a tight half-hitch so that the skirt held her belly in and made a waist for her hips.

She pulled out the bra she had stolen from her mother's bureau earlier that week, which still smelled like her father's cigarette smoke. This was the subject of one of her parents' many fights, which they recently seemed to call up at will as though from a Rolodex. Percy had been born with a lung condition that made smoking especially dangerous for him, but he refused to quit. Nyela said this was evidence of his carelessness and indulgence, but Malaya liked the smell. It reminded her of the time before the brownstone, when the family lived on the Lower East Side in three small rooms and seeing her parents touch was common as weather. She tucked the bra under her chin and stretched the elastic around her back as she'd seen her mother do. By the time she had finished dressing, the hallway was empty and the drums had begun to play.

Dance Studio One was a huge room with a wall full of mirrors and floors so smooth that if you ran on the panels in pantyhose and stopped short, you could slide and slide for what felt like miles. Some girls did come to class in pantyhose, and on the first day Malaya had been one of them. Having found nothing in Malaya's size at the fancy Capezio dance store on 110th Street, Nyela dragged her to Woolworth's after the Meeting and bought a black bathing suit in a women's size 14-Plus and a pair of Queen Size pantyhose in black.

"Can't y'all read!" Mrs. Breeves, the trunk-legged dance teacher, had yelled, holding a copy of the class description in the air. " 'Footless Dancin' Tights'! I don't want to see none of y'all in here in stockin's! This is about respect!"

Malaya went home crying that afternoon, and by Thursday of the following week Nyela had brought home two pairs of Extra Large footless tights from who-knew-where. This was a mother's magic. Nyela often said no to what Malaya wanted, but when something was truly needed, she could make it appear out of thin air. Now, toward the end of the season, the only girls in pantyhose were the ones whose families, Nyela had said, couldn't afford dance tights.

Malaya stood in the back of the room and watched in the mirror as the other girls warmed up, bending and stretching just enough to avoid drawing Mrs. Breeves's attention as they chatted in their rows. Almost all of them were long and thin. Unlike Malaya, whose body was the shape of a potato, the other girls her age had bodies that made her think of what an ostrich might look like before it grew its big behind. But the older girls had the kinds of bodies Malaya dreamed about—hips that curved and sloped with dazzling symmetry, legs that shone like strokes of wet ink in the iridescent black tights. Though she was much wider than the oldest of those girls, the bra and tightly tied lapa gave Malaya a taste of that body, a hint of what it might feel like to be only a little loose at the top, cinched in the middle, and round and full at the bottom. She parted her legs slightly, raised her left arm over her head, bent her torso to the side, and explored this curve in the mirror.

Soon, Mrs. Breeves instructed everyone to gather in the corner of the room while she demonstrated the day's dance. The girls clung there in clusters and watched the drummers play, pointing at the ones they thought were cute and laughing at the ones with messed-up teeth. Some watched Mrs. Breeves and tried to mimic her as she went over the first step of the day, a simple side-to-side march to grab hold of the rhythm. Malaya stood in the back and listened to the chorus of drums, playing games with the sounds in her head. She studied the steady *bum-bum-bap!* of the lowest drum, pulling it apart from the *shhka-shh-shh* of the gourd rattles and the *brrrap-dap-dap* of the djembe until she could hear each sound separately.

The dance was always easy enough at first, and it was normally not until the third full trip across the room that Mrs. Breeves threw in some twist, so Malaya had learned to start paying attention after the second step of the day. She watched brown feet tap and fly, trusting that her own body would do the same when her turn came. She was standing in the middle of the floor with Mrs. Breeves crouched down like a gargoyle in her face when she realized that, today, the twist had come too soon.

"You! What's wrong with your arms?" Mrs. Breeves shouted, spreading her own arms out across the room. The two girls in front of Malaya were reaching into the air and pulling their elbows down in syncopation with their feet in the step. Malaya glanced at her partner, whose arms hit her sides just as Mrs. Breeves's voice faded into the sweat-thick air. Malaya had forgotten to raise her arms.

"I said, why you not moving? What's wrong with your arms?"

No response came to Malaya's mind, other than *Nothing, what's wrong with your face?* which, of course, she couldn't say. Her throat filled tight with breath and her eyes stung.

"The step is *ba-ba-da-DA!*" Mrs. Breeves pounded the floor with her heels and toes, reaching up at the ceiling with her arms and neck, grabbing what could have been a coconut from the air and tucking it down toward her stomach in time with the beat.

"You got to be in your body, girl! Move your arms! Your feet!"

But Malaya had been moving. She had not gotten the arms right—that was true. And her footwork may not have been as quick as everyone else's, but still, she had moved.

"You want to be in my class, you got to learn to be in that body of yours!" The woman's hand shot out and pinched Malaya's belly hard on the side where the lapa was knotted. Then Mrs. Breeves looked past Malaya at the rest of the class. "You have to disciplint yo mind, ladies!"

Malaya imagined "disciplint" as a vise on her head, a metal sheet clamped and soldered over her mouth and eyes like in the cartoons. The word made her think of pain worse than too-tight pantyhose and Ms. Adelaide's marker, worse than the sound of her parents arguing downstairs first thing on a Saturday morning.

She and her partner repeated the step, the other girl moving with a fresh vigor, Malaya floating through the movements without the vaguest commitment to the dance or the drums. Even the hope of salt-showered fries slunk silently from her mind. She spent the rest of the class daydreaming about sleep, wishing for a life into which she could wake up happily, a life of which Daundré Harris could be a real part, or in which one could actually crawl quiet and alone into the bottom nook of a letter *E*, curl up, read a book, eat an apple.

MALAYA STILL FELT the dance teacher's pinch in her side late that night. She sat alone in her room with the light off and Friday's leftovers in her lap, spooning hard heaps of rice and cold, congealed gravy into her mouth.

There had been other kinds of Saturdays once, before the move to Harlem. Malaya could remember those mornings still, if she squinted hard. Leaving her mother in the small yellow kitchen to work on her dissertation, she and her father would climb from the high-rise tenement apartment down into the funk and dampness of the subway and ride the few short stops to Columbus Circle. He would buy her something—an Italian ice in the summer or a pretzel if it was cool. Then he would let her lead them in any direction she wanted to go. In the afternoon, her mother would join them, and the three would wander around Central Park for hours, watching mimes whose faces and bodies were part man and part woman, so that they looked like a new kind of person entirely. Sometimes they would sit with Dr. Testudine, a ruddy-faced man who raced baby turtles by the pond, taking bets on which would win. Nyela's favorite was a little runt named Arnold, whose shell was marked with a bright smear of green. Nyela would clap and cheer for Arnold during the races, spilling into laughter on Percy's shoulders when Arnold lost, which he always did. Malaya liked remembering those times, but the idea of climbing and racing did not appeal to her as much now, though she couldn't explain why.

There was a feeling Malaya Clondon imagined, one that grew in her on nights like this and stayed with her long after. It was the heart-pounding feeling of sliding loose from good dreams, glad to be in reality. She imagined waking one day, not sad and slow and praying to crawl back up into sleep, but quickly, with a lightness, a spring. She had tasted this feeling in the predawn hours before trips to the park with her father, or during the first short breaths of a holiday. On those mornings, she would leap out of her dreams like a splash of water from a boiling pot, ready for what the day might bring her.

But most mornings, she lay stiffly in bed, wishing for the sun to fold up into the clouds so she could be swallowed back into her dreams. To be nice, she thought, she might consider visiting this real life she'd left, so long as she wouldn't have to stay. She might float out of her dream and back over these steps for a while, hover above the Meetings, watch calmly as the dance teacher pinched her flesh. In a show of grace and generosity, she might even reach down from her elsewhere and touch this body, listening from an easy distance to her mother's voice on the stairs as it crackled its first chords of the day:

"Malaya, get in the shower! You have to wake up!"

Hooky Day

THE NEXT MORNING, Malaya awoke to the sound of her father's favorite Stevie Wonder record, *Songs in the Key of Life*, playing from the family room. She climbed out of bed, planning to stop by the kitchen to sneak a few mouthfuls of leftovers on her way down. The brownstone had three narrow stories, plus a garden floor used for storage and a small backyard whose brick-colored concrete slabs had cracked outward in all directions like the hands of a compass. On the first floor was the foyer, where the family hung their coats and laid their bags and briefcases each day, plus the parlor, which was full of brightly colored African masks and Ma-Mère's old piano, sent from Philadelphia to celebrate the family's move uptown. Percy and Nyela's room was on the second floor across from the family room, and Malaya's was on the third. This was one small gift that came with the move up to Harlem. The kitchen was a skylit room right next to Malaya's, and her parents were a whole floor away.

When she opened the door, she was surprised to find Percy in the kitchen, his back to her. He stood at the stove in his plush burgundy bathrobe and his favorite gray track pants, his Afro shiny under the skylight.

"Morning, My Laya," he said, turning to face her.

He was tall and lean, the color of church pews. His smooth features were impressively symmetrical, and they gave his face a placid look that whipped quickly to life when he was excited or upset. Now his eyes flickered as he looked at her, smiling, a can of low-fat cooking spray in his hand.

"What do you think about pancakes?" he said. "Your mother had to go to campus to pick up some books. I thought we'd surprise her."

He gestured to the table, where there was an impressive array of ingredients: sugar, pancake mix, heavy cream, a bunch of bananas, and a large bag of chocolate chips, slumped tantalizingly against a mixing bowl.

"Okay," she said, trying not to seem too excited. She went to her room for her colored pencils and sketch pad, then settled in at the table to draw as Percy shuffled around the kitchen. He poured and measured, spilling pancake mix and bopping to the beat of "Sir Duke." The song named several jazz musicians she'd heard her father talk about, and she filled the page with images of what she thought they might look like, though mostly they ended up looking like Percy. When everything but the chocolate was in the bowl, he pulled a spoon from the cabinet and stirred, the mix and the milk swirling into a thick cream. He extended the spoon toward her, then swooped it up and held it below her mouth like a microphone.

"I bet you've never had Percy Clondon Jr.'s world-famous chocolate chip and banana pancakes, have you?" he said in a fake, nasal voice, like an announcer on a TV game show.

Malaya giggled and shook her head no. "I don't think so."

He took the spoon back and continued without missing a beat.

"Sweet, fluffy pancakes like you've never known. A time-honored family recipe perfected in the finest kitchens of Harlem." He made a sweeping gesture for emphasis as he spoke and batter began to drip down his wrist, onto his robe and the table. She laughed again.

"Okay," he said, stirring, "they might not be world-famous, but they are good. I used to make these for your Uncle Book when we were kids. It was a real treat for us. We didn't get chocolate often. Stuff like chocolate was an *occasion*." He grabbed a handful of brown morsels from the bag and released a cascade of chips into the batter.

Percy had grown up in Harlem, moving between its various tene-
ments and projects from the time he was born until he met Nyela in college. Once in a while, he talked about the government bread, canned
meat, and big blocks of cheese he ate with his brother, Malaya's Uncle
Book, and their mother. He didn't tell these stories often, but when he
did, they always ended on a note of defiant, if somber, celebration.

"The powdered milk and stale bread and all that. That'll get you
through. But you want to really live, you need the good stuff, right?" He
popped a handful of chocolate chips into his mouth and sprinkled a few
into her palm. "Who says today's not an occasion?"

The chocolate sweet and soft on her tongue, Malaya mouthed the
word: *occasion*. It sounded fancy. This was one of Percy's talents: without
much effort, it seemed, he could make something fantastically special
out of an ordinary day.

He turned to the stove and began ladling batter into a frying pan,
then laid a few strips of bacon in another. When some of the pancakes
began to burn, Malaya watched as he cut the darkened edges from the
stack and kept ladling. The stink of burning lingered, even after he
threw the charred scraps in the trash. But it didn't matter. The bacon
smelled good and a few chocolate chips still winked from the leftover
batter. He must have seen her looking, because he smiled and nudged
the bowl toward her with his elbow, averting his eyes dramatically, as if
to say "You didn't get this from me."

While Percy finished cooking, Malaya happily licked the bowl. After
a while, the record stopped and the only sounds were a beat-box-heavy
rap song playing from the block outside and the sizzle of bacon on the
stove. Soon, the front door slammed open downstairs, its old wood
smacking through the tight doorframe.

"You home?" Nyela called. Malaya ran a final finger along the mixing
bowl before putting it in the sink, licking her hands clean of the choco-
latey batter. Percy covered the food with foil and turned off the stove as
Nyela's bangles chimed up the stairs.

"Smells good in here." Nyela appeared in the doorway, her briefcase
strapped across her chest and a bulky tote bag in either hand.

"We thought we'd make you breakfast," Percy said. He sat the dish of pancakes on the table and unveiled it, looking at Malaya. "A Sunday surprise, right, My Laya?!" She loved his nickname for her; it made her feel grown-up and capable, but still somehow small enough to fit in his hand.

He passed Malaya three plates from the cabinet and she began to set the table, folding the napkins as neatly as she could in triangle shapes to make the meal fancier.

"This is a surprise," Nyela said. She was smiling, but she seemed uneasy. She stood quietly in the doorway as Malaya fiddled with the napkins. Finally, she sat the tote bags on the floor.

"Malaya, do you have enough points left?" she asked. She looked at the bags of sugar and chocolate, still sitting on the table. "Pancakes are a lot of bread points. Let alone the sugar. Is this the first thing you've eaten today?"

Malaya's face went hot. She had crept into the kitchen last night as she always did, spooning heaps of cold leftovers in the narrow light of the refrigerator and pushing the empty cartons deep down in the trash to hide the evidence. She had felt full and warm right afterward, but now regret sank in her belly.

Malaya looked up at her mother, unsure how to answer, but Percy spoke first.

"It's eleven a.m., Ny," he said. "This is breakfast."

"Okay," she said, "but I'm asking Malaya. You didn't have anything between when we went to bed last night and now?"

She shook her head no.

"Are you telling the truth?"

Malaya's eyes began to sting. "Yes," she said. "I promise."

Nyela looked at her again, then sighed. "You can't lie to the scale, Malaya. You know that, right?"

"That's enough, Ny," Percy said in a loud voice that startled Malaya. "She said she didn't eat, she didn't eat. Can't we just have breakfast? Shit."

"You don't need to curse at me," Nyela said. "You don't have to talk to me that way. I'm trying to help her. Somebody has to."

Malaya shifted her weight on the stiff kitchen chair, wishing she could vanish as their voices smacked back and forth across the room.

"You know what? I try to do something nice for you, and instead I get this shit. Next time I won't bother."

"Still with the cursing, Pra? I asked you not to—"

"No. You're not gonna make this about me. I had a week of hell at work, but it's the weekend and I'm here, trying to do something nice for my wife and my kid. Some men wouldn't bother." His voice was louder now. "I'm here, and this is what I get. So yeah, I'm fucking angry."

"So I should be grateful?" Nyela said. Her voice was swirling, rhythmic, like an alarm. "Is that it? Grateful that I have a man who's here, a woman like me?" She opened her arms and looked down quickly at her middle, the briefcase still strapped across her chest. "Like I don't go through hell at work, too. I should just be grateful that you're here, never mind how you talk to me? Never mind what you feed our daughter?"

"I'm done." He picked up the napkin from his place setting and grabbed a handful of bacon strips with his fingers. "Enjoy breakfast," he said, biting into the meat as he strode out of the room.

Soon the music was back, louder, the Commodores blaring up through the halls from the family room. Nyela pulled her briefcase off and sighed as she sat down at the table. After a few seconds, she reached down into one of the tote bags and retrieved a stack of books and folders, piling them on the kitchen table. Then she sighed again. Malaya watched her stare at the table, there and not there, her body deflated as though she herself were an empty bag.

After a few seconds, Nyela got up, pulled two light strawberry yogurt cups from the refrigerator, and reached for spoons. Malaya watched as she cut a banana into neat pale yellow disks and passed half of them to Malaya on a saucer.

"Here you go," she said. "It's better with bananas. I know you like them."

Malaya pushed the slices into the yogurt one by one until each was submerged in the pale pink cream. She watched as her mother cleared the pancakes from the table, the chocolate chips still blinking from the stack as she slid them into the trash.

THAT TUESDAY, Malaya shuffled down to the brownstone foyer, ready to swipe a few dollars from Nyela's coat pocket and prepare for their walk to the bus stop as usual. But when she reached the bottom of the staircase, Percy was there waiting for her. Her father rarely took her to the bus stop, unless Nyela had to be on campus early for some presentation or talk. His presence this morning could mean only one thing, Malaya thought excitedly: Hooky Day. One day each winter, Percy took off work and Malaya took off school and they took the subway together to eat honey roasted nuts and explore the Christmas windows on Fifth Avenue. After a few hours, Nyela would meet them, and together the three would catch the matinee of the Rockettes Christmas Spectacular at Radio City. This word, *spectacular*, was the essence of Hooky Day, and the thrill of cold city air, the salty steam from the pretzel carts, and the dazzle of candy-colored window displays defined the word in her mind.

"Morning, My Laya," Percy said. He wore his long, tailored wool coat, its shiny black buttons already fastened almost to the lapel. He seemed distracted as he wrapped a flat gray scarf around his neck and handed her a jacket. "Come on, we have to go."

Malaya fastened the snaps on the puffy pink jacket, luxuriating in a fantasy of hot cocoa filled with a constellation of tiny marshmallows and everything else Hooky Day would bring. Percy took her hand and led her down the brownstone steps toward Amsterdam Avenue. His long limbs made it difficult for Malaya to keep up when they walked together. Still, she was proud to walk with him, her handsome father. She wriggled her mittened hand in his so he would notice she was lagging behind.

"I'm sorry, My Laya," he said. His voice warmed a little, and he slowed down for her. As they neared St. Nicholas Avenue, he made a game of keeping in perfect step with her, left leg then right, as though they were characters from *The Wiz*, easing on down the yellow brick road.

When they reached the fading burgundy awning of St. Nick's Pub and the subway entrance beside it, Malaya veered toward the stairs, ready to hop the D train and head to Radio City, but Percy kept walking. It had snowed the night before, and the pavement on St. Nicholas was slippery.

He looked at his watch and sailed forward. Now, as she scuttled behind him on the slick ground, he only seemed to speed up.

"I'm sorry we have to rush, but we're late."

"We're walking?" Her breath was short, but she tried to hide it. She wasn't sure how many blocks it was to Rockefeller Center. She imagined the city's icy streets stretching out before her, ready to swallow her up.

"Of course, My Laya." He looked down at her. "Dr. Perior's office is right on Edgecombe. You know that."

If Malaya had to name one place on earth that was the full and singular opposite of Radio City—the opposite of *spectacular*—it was Dr. Perior's office. Where Radio City gleamed with color and magic that transported you to galaxies of delight, Dr. Perior's office was a small, shadowy box of dull grays and browns. The examining table was covered with a rough strip of what felt like construction paper that was never wide enough to protect Malaya's thighs from the cold plastic cushion, and the scratchy paper gowns were always too small for her, so that to keep them closed in the back she had to suck her stomach in and try not to breathe. Worst of all was the scale, a wobbly, pointy metal contraption that looked to her like a monster from a fairy tale, with a tall neck, thick black eyebrows of numbers and lines, and a heavy hunk of a nose that always pointed too far to the right.

Malaya wondered if Percy was playing a joke. At Galton Elementary Academy for the Gifted, where Malaya went to school, every Wednesday was Opposite Day, which meant at lunch and recess, the children agreed to say the opposite of what they actually meant, and everything anyone said could possibly mean its inverse. On Opposite Days, Rachel Greenstein, her best friend in the white world of Galton, would come up to her after class and say, "Malaya, I would *hate* to have a sleepover with you this weekend, and I would *really, really hate* to play GirlTalk phone with you, so *don't* ask your mother, okay?" and Malaya would say, "Ew! No way. That would really suck!" and the two would laugh and go home to arrange the playdate with their parents. Turning toward Edgecombe with her father now, Malaya wondered if somehow he was in on the joke of Opposite Day, if by "Dr. Perior's office" he really meant "the Radio City Rockettes Christmas Spectacular," and if by "walk" he meant "take a taxi." But he wasn't laughing, and it was Tuesday. Percy pressed the buzzer and pushed open the heavy doors of the office building, ushering her in before him.

The doctor's office smelled like sickness and cleaning liquid, a combination that made Malaya's stomach flop. Percy hated this smell too. Malaya understood that her father's aversion to doctors' offices had to do with his lung condition. The condition was called pulmonary sarcoidosis, which, as far as Malaya could understand, meant that his lungs worked slower and with more difficulty than other people's lungs, contracting and expanding in slow motion as though he had an accordion in his chest. He had developed the condition in utero, the result of a fire in the building where his parents lived at the start of the 1950s, just above the Top Flight Ladder Company, which had made ladders, stepstools, and safety equipment for homes and businesses as far as Westchester since the 1920s. After months of withheld wages, the story went, the company's black workers had protested, first with their voices, then with flames. His mother went into labor early, her lungs full of smoke. Percy was born the next day, smaller and yellower than any baby the family had ever seen. He stayed at Harlem Hospital for weeks, and returned many times during childhood. He always said the smell of doctors' offices was "repulsive," and ever since then, the smell and the word and even the idea of doctors' offices made Malaya feel she might vomit, but the fact that her father shared the feeling lessened its weight.

Malaya stood on the T-shaped scale, blinking up at Dr. Perior, whose palm rested on her shoulder. He pushed the large hunk of metal along the scale's balance until it slid into a notch. He nudged the smaller piece of metal along its track tentatively at first. Then he ran it quickly to the end of the balance. Another notch for the big hunk of metal, another run of the small one. As the process went on, the scale began to feel unsteady under her body. She reached out an arm from under her paper gown and grabbed the pole in front of her for balance.

"Don't touch, Malaya," the doctor said, moving his hand to her back. His palm was rough and heavy, like his voice.

"Malaya, please don't touch that, baby," Percy added from the corner of the room. His voice was softer than the doctor's. Malaya lowered her hand and looked higher up on the pole at the frowning metal face of the scale, her beaded braids stuck in the neck of the tight paper gown as it clung to her skin.

"Okay," Dr. Perior said. His eyes were still fixed on the scale. Malaya looked at Percy, who smiled back at her.

"Can she get dressed now?" he asked.

"I want to listen to her heartbeat again," Dr. Perior said. He had the look of an old basset hound, his long face shrouded in plush folds. He gestured toward the examining table, and once she'd managed to climb up, he pressed a cold stethoscope into her chest.

"Inhale."

Malaya closed her eyes and sucked in her stomach, straining to keep her gown closed. She tried to send her mind away from the office, from the scale, from the scratchy paper and the cold metal and the rough, heavy hands pressing into her skin. She reached down to pinch the gown away from her belly, then looked back up at the doctor to check whether he'd noticed her panic, which he never did.

"Exhale."

She let her body deflate a little.

"Okay, Malaya," the doctor said. "Me and your dad are going to talk right out here for a minute. Do you need Angela to help you get dressed?"

"No, thank you."

She looked at the chair where her sweatpants and sneakers were draped, waiting for the men to leave.

When they had disappeared, she pushed herself off the table, put on her clothes, and leaned against the wall to listen. Every time adults talked about her weight, it ended in a fight. Two years ago, when Malaya was six, she and Nyela went to a birthday party for LaSondra, an older cousin on her father's side. The party was enjoyable enough, with pizza and nachos and the kind of music that played from the cars outside her window, rap songs with elaborate story lines, lyrics like riddles, and beats that sparked her heart alive. The party was at a roller skating rink, and after the cake, which was butterscotch, the DJ played one of Malaya's favorite songs, about a boy alone in his room imagining the love of his life. The song was sad, but it also made her laugh, because at one point the rapper looked for a girlfriend under his bedroom carpet and sang, "*Damn sure ain't in my closet, or under my rug. This love search is really making me bug!*" This image made her giggle from her belly every time she thought of it. How silly it seemed to look for a person under a rug. How silly the man, or how tiny the girl. It made her laugh either way.

When this song came on at the party, Malaya strapped up her laces, ready to hit the rink, but LaSondra stopped her. "Uh, Malaya, ain't you hear?" she demanded, looking at Malaya as if she were a large insect that had invaded her party. "This is a *couples'* skate. Obviously you ain't got no boyfriend, big as you are." This made Malaya cry, and she had not yet learned to hide these kinds of tears from her mother. Nyela was sitting with a group of aunts, and when she told them what happened, her Aunt Ro raised her eyebrows and said, "You see you need to do something about that girl's weight. We *been* tried to tell you that," to which Ro's twin, Aunt Augustine, added, "And they say whoopin's is child abuse. This here is child abuse. It really ain't right," and slurped the last of her soda. When they got back from the party, Nyela told Percy what had happened, and later that night Malaya could hear them arguing about it for hours from her bedroom.

Now, through the doctor's office door, Malaya could hear only crumbs of the conversation: Dr. Perior's deep voice saying "Yes," and "It's important," and "I've told your wife," followed by silence from Percy. Then, finally, clear as glass, the strange phrase: "Malaya is morbidly obese."

Malaya moved back to the examination table and made a game of tracing imaginary doors and windows along the side of the table with her finger. She pictured herself shrinking with a *pop!* to microscopic size, then crawling through one of the windows and hiding there in the sky until the appointment was over. She thought of her father's favorite song, a smooth, soaring melody he'd been singing in the shower that morning. The song was "Can't Hide Love," by his favorite group, Earth, Wind & Fire, which sounded to Malaya like the name of a fantastic superhero team, a soul music version of the Super Friends or the ThunderCats. She couldn't understand most of the lyrics, but her favorite part was when one of the men sang in a voice like steam, "*Hoo . . . I know the truth, now so do you.*" Malaya hummed the song to herself in the office, tracing patterns on the paper and waiting.

Eventually Percy emerged. She studied his face, but all she could tell was that he looked drained. He wrapped her fuzzy pink scarf around her neck a few times as they left, promising the doctor she would return in two months.

In the elevator, he smiled at her, his eyes tired. "That wasn't so bad, was it?"

"I guess not." She fastened the snaps on her coat and dug around in her pockets for her teddy bear earmuffs. "Can we take a cab?"

"No, My Laya," he said. "I think we should walk."

"Why?" She stretched the earmuffs out in front of her.

"Walking is good for us," he said. "I know it's cold, but it's important. Anyway, if we take a cab, we might speed past the perfect Christmas tree. We have to walk around and look for the right one."

"Okay." She sighed and snapped the earmuffs over her ears, then tugged the ends of her coat together. He bent to help her, pulling the coat tight around her middle, forcing the zipper into place.

As they walked home, he told Malaya stories about growing up in Harlem. He loved to tell these stories. When he did, his face brightened, and his knobby cheekbones shone like the crests of an apple. He pointed out the places where he had lived, played, and worked when he was young, many of which, he noted delightedly, were still around. He even pointed out the places where he and Book, whose real name was Sammy, got into various kinds of trouble, like the corner of 134th and Lenox where Book got hit by a drunk driver one summer, and the playground on Seventh Avenue where he got into a fight defending Book against a boy who said he'd stolen his watch, which he later learned was true.

"That's how your uncle got his name," Percy said, adjusting his scarf against the cold as they waited to cross on the corner. "He loved to make things up. Our dad used to say as soon as Sammy learned to talk, he learned to lie. But our mother, your grandmother, just called them 'tall tales.' Like in a storybook. And of course your uncle liked that. It made him feel important."

As they turned onto the avenue, he pointed downtown toward the St. Nicholas projects. "That's where we all lived growing up. One of the places, anyway. Me, your Uncle Book, and your grandmother. That's where we stayed after our dad left. Before this was Adam Clayton Powell Jr. Boulevard. When it was plain old Seventh Avenue." He said it matter-of-factly, but his voice was heavy.

"How old were you?" she asked.

He looked uptown, toward the hill. "About your age. Maybe a little older. Nine or so. But I was supposed to be the man of the house, after he left. And I really thought I was." He gave a sad chuckle. Malaya had never met her paternal grandmother—she died a few weeks before Malaya was born. But she always imagined Emanuella Clondon as a tall, brown, billowing woman with a smiling face as round as a penny. Not like Ma-Mère, who had the stiff, broad build of a skyscraper and who only seemed to smile under extreme circumstances such as a baptism or a wedding. Percy's mother had been a bookbinder, but she'd never learned to read. Malaya wasn't exactly sure what a bookbinder was, but she liked the way the word sounded, and it seemed a perfect job for the beaming, bosomy grandmother of her dreams. She wondered what it meant to take care of a woman like that, how that task could be left to somebody her own age, and how it would feel.

When they passed the empty lot between the chicken spot and the check-cashing place on 139th, Percy jutted his chin and said, "That used to be Book's favorite candy store. You know how your Uncle Book likes to talk? Well, he did back then, too. Wild tales about fighting fires and beating up robbers. He would talk to anyone who would listen. Made the stories up off the top of his head and told them like they were the God's truth. We all got tired of it, but the store owner, Mr. Phillips, he liked Book's stories. He called him an 'entertainer.' He would give him Turkish Taffy and Dum Dums, just 'cause he liked to hear him talk." Malaya looked at the lot, past the layers of trash and glass, trying to imagine what had once been there. She pictured a store full of sweets, Uncle Book hamming it up for free candy, her father strong and patient, keeping watch. It was stunning to think that what she saw now could once have been something else entirely—that the empty lot before her could once have been a candy store, or that her father was once a boy. The stories made her feel time was so real she could hold it in her hand, as if anything could become anything at all.

As they walked up the avenue, Percy told her about the United House
of Worship, the church on 135th where his father had been a pastor.
Malaya had been to the House of Worship several times on Easter, and as
Percy talked she remembered sitting in the rows of folding chairs that
filled the wide white room, the smells of yams and collard greens simmering from the church's storefront kitchen while the organ and tam-
bourines blared insistent rhythms that burrowed so deeply and soared
so high she felt they might lift the whole building into flight. She imagined little-boy versions of Percy and Book busting free from the church
after these services, crawling through these same blocks and stores and
neighborhood playgrounds with a gaggle of little boys like them. Percy
told her about games like It and Desperado, in which they pinned pil-
lowcases to their shoulders and skydived off the neighbors' brownstone
banisters while shouting superhero creeds. He talked about games with
no names, like racing through the hallways of the Harlem River projects or the Polo Grounds to see who could collect the widest variety of
colored glass bottle shards, or running wildly after the girls at St. Cath-
erine's Catholic School, then kissing them in an alleyway or throwing
a piece of trash from the ground, turning, laughing, running back to
the group.

Malaya had not lived Harlem this way. When the family moved into
the brownstone in 1988, children on the block still ran the streets, and
at first Malaya was allowed to play outside, too. But this changed one
day during their first summer in the neighborhood. She brought home
a handful of the red, yellow, and blue plastic tube caps that studded the
pavement. The colors had fascinated her, so she made a game of collecting them with some girls from the block. She showed them to Percy,
hoping to impress him with her haul. Instead, he swiped the plastic
quickly from her hand. "These aren't toys, Malaya," he said. His voice
was sharp, unsteady. "These are crack vial caps. They're dangerous. You
don't touch them. Okay? And you don't talk to kids who do." He made her
wash her hands with hot water and hydrogen peroxide. After that, she
wasn't allowed to play outside again.

Malaya was only mildly disappointed by the decision. There were
other people she could play with. She enjoyed playdates with Rachel

Greenstein, who would sometimes come home with her and Giselle after school to make magazine-clipping collages and invent dramatic skits to show their parents. But one day while they were choreographing a dance to the latest Paula Abdul song, there was shooting on the block. Malaya turned off the lights and closed the curtains, as Percy always did when this happened. Then, when the commotion outside quieted, she turned the stereo back on and they finished what Malaya thought was a pretty good dance, complete with dips and a pas de bourrée. They performed it when Rachel's father came to pick her up. Malaya felt it had gone well, but after that, Rachel's parents wouldn't let her come up to Harlem.

Shaniece Guzmán, on the other hand, loved coming over to the brownstone. The kids at Galton regarded Shaniece as strange because she was quiet and brought bodega foods to school for lunch. But Malaya liked her voice, which was soft and gravelly at once, as though she were perpetually waking up. She was one of a handful of black girls at Galton, and Malaya had always been curious about her. She hadn't known her well before the move, but now that she lived nearby, it was easy for her to come over after school. She lived in one of the big tenement buildings on Amsterdam. Malaya had never been inside Shaniece's house, which Nyela said was probably because the apartment was small, or messy, or both. Whenever she came over, she seemed content simply to sit with Malaya, gazing up the brownstone walls at Nyela's books and paintings while Malaya drew. There was no running, no labored dance routines with Shaniece. Instead, they would talk about school or television or boys. Sometimes, they played touching games in the family room while Giselle made dinner upstairs, calling down to them occasionally, "You girls not makin' nuh mess in your mama's nice house, right?" After the crack vials and the gunshots, Percy and Nyela determined that Shaniece would have to be neighborhood gaggle enough for Malaya, and Malaya did not complain.

As she and Percy neared the hill on 145th, Malaya saw a group of girls jumping double Dutch on the sidewalk. Their breath made curls on the air as they chanted:

"I like coffee, I like tea! I like your boyfriend and he likes me!"

Malaya watched them command the rope, their wrists and shoulders whirling with rhythm as they cheered for the girl jumping in elaborate patterns at the center of the crowd.

This was one thing she did long for: the chance to jump double Dutch with the older Harlem girls. She had only gotten to jump in one time, the summer after the move. Two girls she didn't know called her over one day, saying "Hey, big girl!" They invited her to jump in in exchange for a box of prized banana Now and Later candies from Mr. Gonzales's bodega on the corner. It was a generosity, and Malaya was grateful. The girls stood on the sidewalk with a white clothesline wrapped around their waists, their hips and arms bouncing to the beat as they chanted a song about boyfriend love Malaya pretended to understand. A line of other girls stood nearby, and as the rope twirled they took turns leaping in, hopping over and under the whirling whip. When Malaya's turn came, she did not leap in. Instead, she asked if she could start in the rope. She walked to the center of the clothesline as it lay limp against the pavement. They counted a chant and the rope came alive, and only for an instant Malaya sprang up, her braids floating on the air. Soon the whip hit hard against her ankles and clattered to the pavement. She tried a few more times before giving up, her feet hopelessly tangled in rope.

"Daddy, can we get Chinese food?" she asked as they crossed St. Nicholas. There was a dirty hunk of ice near her foot, and she kicked it as they walked, nudging it this way and that with her pink boot as they trudged up the hill.

"My Laya, I don't think that's a good idea. Maybe Mommy will cook tonight."

But when they passed the Twin Donut on Amsterdam, he surprised her by popping in and buying her two old-fashioned doughnut holes as a treat.

The chunk of ice was still there when they came out of the store, and so Malaya kept kicking it up the avenue, munching happily on the soft, sugary dough. And when, closer to home, she lost control of the ice and it flew over to Percy's side of the pavement, he kicked it back to her and sang:

"I know the truth, now so do you / You can't hide love . . ."

THE NEXT MORNING, Malaya awoke to Percy's voice loud in the hall.

"What the hell does that mean?"

She pulled the covers up to her nose and tried not to listen.

"I don't know, Pra," Nyela wailed softly, like a siren far away. "Pra" was the name he'd gone by in college, when he was a poet and Nyela a girl in love with him. Nyela had two names as well: Nathallie, the name Ma-Mère had given her; and Nyela, the one she took in college, in an effort to connect herself and the family she dreamed of to their African roots. Nyela never referred to him as Percy except in the third person, when giving his name to school administrators or bill collectors on the phone. When Nyela talked to him, he was always Pra. Her voice seemed to soften with breath when she said it, even when she was angry. This made Malaya think of who they must have been all those years ago, though sometimes it was hard to imagine.

"She's sneaking food, Pra. I don't know what's going on at that school. And it's clear you don't know either."

Fast footsteps creaked along the hardwood floor.

"Don't you think you're blowing this out of proportion? Let's be honest."

Nyela's voice grew jagged. "Don't patronize me! 'Out of proportion'? Are you kidding? She has to be held responsible for this. We can't fix this problem if we don't know what's going on!"

Malaya pushed herself out of bed and walked to the doorway as quietly as she could, then quickly to the kitchen. She opened the refrigerator door only a few inches and wedged her body into the cool, bright crack to muffle its murmur while she peered into the thicket of yogurt cups and leftover containers.

"Nyela, I know my daughter! I know the only help she needs is us letting her be a fucking child! Nothing is wrong with her. She's a kid. A kid who likes dessert. What the fuck is wrong with that?"

Malaya shook the peanut butter loose from its shelf and picked up a spoon. She tiptoed to the top of the staircase in quick, wide steps she hoped her parents wouldn't hear. There, she twisted the lid off the jar and stuck the spoon deep into the soft brown paste, the rich smell floating sweet and smoky toward her face. She sat at the top step and hunched down, sliding her slippered feet to the wall so they were out of view.

"If you didn't make such a big deal of it, she probably wouldn't even eat as much." Percy's shadow stretched down the hall below her. "You see how she lights up when she's painting or drawing or whatever. She's happy. She's young, Ny, and she could lose that spark real quick. I'm not going to let that happen."

"*You're* not going to let that happen? *You?*"

Malaya dug into the jar and brought a heap of peanut butter to her lips, scraping the cold metal of the spoon with her teeth and tongue, sweetness clinging to the roof of her mouth.

"What are you going to do? And when?" Nyela leaned on the words as though she wanted to fight them. "You're not even here. She does need help. She's struggling. You just don't know. *I'm* the one who's with her, Pra. The one who's trying. Where the hell are you?"

"Oh fucking come on!" Malaya heard Percy move in heavy steps toward the bedroom. "You're not talking about Malaya now. You're talking about us. I'm not doing this with you. Malaya does not have a hard time following directions! She has a hard time following a diet, *your* diet, made for insecure grown-ass women! She's a fucking child!"

A pause.

"'Insecure,'" Nyela said. Her voice was clear. "She's a child with a problem. The girl is out of control. Have you even noticed? You went to the doctor yourself for god's sake. Can you at least listen to him? What did he tell you?"

"Fine," he said. A beat. "But how much fucking control do you want her to have? She just learned to count a couple fucking years ago, and now she's supposed to be calculating calories? She can't do it, Ny! Shit, you can't even do it, and you're pushing forty!"

A breath chilled the air, and the walls said nothing. Malaya gripped the spoon, listening for her father again, waiting for him to say something that would make it better, but it was quiet and his shadow was still.

"Look, I know you don't want her to struggle," he said finally, softer now. He walked toward the bedroom, out of Malaya's view. She tried to imagine him sitting down beside her mother and putting his arms around her as he spoke, but she knew he was probably on the opposite side of the room. "I don't want her to struggle either. Later in life, but also right now. She's a kid. I want her to be a kid."

"Sometimes children have to work. You want to give her what you didn't have. I get it. But I want the same thing. This is her life we're talking about. And I know that for her to be happy, she's gonna have to lose weight. She's gonna have to work. Work doesn't kill children. Fuck. *This*—what's happening now, what she's doing—this will kill her."

The squeal of the mattress, Nyela shifting her weight.

"What did the doctor say?" Nyela's voice was quiet now. Malaya heaped more peanut butter onto the spoon.

"What did he say?"

"You know what he said." Percy's voice neared and his shadow appeared under the hallway light. "He said what the school says. What these people always say. That she's morbidly obese. In danger. Okay? And yeah, I know what that means. I get it. But Nyela, do you really think you're helping?"

"What?"

"What you're doing, I mean—the meetings and the points, all of it."

"So it's my fault."

"No." The walls breathed and the shadows were gone.

"That's what you're saying. That this is something I've done. Even though I spend every minute of my life trying to undo it. Even though I'm scared to death."

Malaya closed her eyes and dug into the jar again. She scrunched her face and spooned more peanut butter into her mouth, then more and more, until the paste felt thick and solid in her throat. She imagined herself shrinking, folding and hardening inch by inch until she could

become the spoon and plunge deep into the soft, sweet brown. She saw
herself stuck there, tight, small, surrounded, eventually falling still.

"No. I'm just saying."

Another wide breath.

"What about the fact that it's not working? What about the fact that
things are only getting worse? What do we do with that?"

La Isla Bonita

As the streetlights went off and the day opened to the first sirens of the morning, Malaya lay awake in bed, humming her favorite songs. It was Christmas Eve, and Percy and Nyela had both taken off from work to clean the house and prepare for Ma-Mère and Uncle Book's arrival. Eventually, they would wake up, Percy would put on an old soul record, and Nyela would vanish downstairs to go through dusty boxes of flatware and rinse out the crystal punch bowl. Then Malaya would be safe to leave her room undetected, to find food and a place to draw undisturbed. But for now, it was quiet, save for the not-yet-memory of her parents' voices floating soundlessly in her ears: *Getting worse. This will kill her. Morbidly obese.*

There was a clear division in Malaya's mind between the family's life in the small, sun-steeped apartment on the Lower East Side and this new life in the big Harlem brownstone, which was drafty and held tight to the previous owners' dust. She imagined a thick black line between then and now. The old apartment was on the twentieth floor of a sprawling public housing development made up of several buildings joined by a wide playground that was always full of children. When they'd lived there, Malaya took the bus up to Galton every day, but in the afternoons she would play under the eye of Grandma Titi, a woman with a slow, jingly laugh and skin like crepe paper, who taught her words in Spanish and watched her until her parents came home from work. Malaya luxuriated in those endless afternoons, riding her bike on the playground, then eating instant oatmeal with extra brown sugar and napping on the plastic-covered sofa while Grandma Titi watched her telenovelas and smoked Marlboro Rojos at the kitchen table.

When they lived downtown, life seemed a breathless rush of sights and activities—flying kites and picnicking on Brighton Beach in the summers, weekend adventures in Central Park. Malaya's weight was mentioned only rarely then, usually by Ma-Mère, who, when she visited, could only scowl and make an inscrutable comment like "Least I know you-all ain't struggling too hard, big as this girl is," since she lived too far away to act on the issue.

Little was said to Malaya about the reason for the move. Nyela had gotten a new job as assistant professor of psychology at Drummond, the rich university on the Upper West Side, and Percy was quickly scaling the ranks at the glossy consulting firm where he worked as a programmer in Midtown. The move was a milestone for the young couple: Nyela had been born in Philadelphia to divorced parents, and though Ma-Mère prided herself on her upwardly mobile vision and taste, Nyela described her family of origin as "house poor," by which she meant that they were always a paycheck away from missing the mortgage and losing their home. Nyela's father had been an alcoholic who gave most of his boot factory earnings to the local bartenders and numbers runners. Percy's parents were divorced as well, and they had no house. He always said being born in the projects was a curse he'd had to recode into a gift: it introduced him to hunger, but it also taught him to hate hunger with all he had. He said this bitterly, as though tasting years of memories, pungent in his mouth.

Both Percy and Nyela were the first in their families to attend college. They had met as students at NYU, which may as well have been as far from Harlem as it was from Philadelphia. Quickly, they put themselves to conjuring a new dream of home. This seemed to have worked, and for most of Malaya's eight years of life, things had been happy enough.

Nyela was successful, and Percy was what everyone called a Good Black Man, present, supportive, and, as all the women Malaya knew seemed to agree, *fine*.

Before the move, when Nyela was still in coursework as a graduate student, she would pick Malaya up from Grandma Titi's and the two spent their evenings together reading stories out loud and talking about their respective days at school while Nyela cooked in the narrow apartment kitchen until Percy got off work. But now their time was spent reciting bread point values and going over the dangers of fat.

Sometimes Malaya thought back on the sun-dappled apartment days and wondered if that could really have been the same family—the same parents, the same her. Other times, she wondered if those memories could be real, and, if they were, what else in life could change without explanation.

LYING IN BED, Malaya looked at the cracked beige plaster on the ceiling. Her bedroom was big, with three tall windows and a sealed fireplace over which arched a wooden mantel, adorned with tiny wood-molded bunches of leaves and grapes. The brownstone's previous owners had covered the moldings with a chalky white paint that made it hard to see the details of the designs, partly because the paint was constantly covered in a layer of dust. The same dust covered the row of stiff, fancy dolls Ma-Mère had brought her from trips to places like Barbados and Oaxaca which sat atop the mantel, their thick fluffs of hair and delicately stitched dresses too pretty to touch. The dust swirled through the air of the wide room and clung to the glow-in-the-dark LOVE sign Malaya had brought home from Philadelphia last summer and pasted to her vanity mirror with Krazy Glue, even though Nyela had told her not to.

Malaya's room downtown had been much smaller, but it was large in her memory. It was painted a bright yellow and had a single window that seemed perpetually lit white with sun. When she thought about that room, she played over and over in her mind a song that was on the radio at that time, about a place called "La Isla Bonita." In it, a chirpy white woman told about this place, a glittery dream of sun and breeze, and though the woman said she'd never been there before, her yearning to go seemed to stretch and pierce through the notes so that Malaya felt she could actually see the island's clouds in front of her, feel its mist on her skin. The song was full of Spanish words, some of which Malaya recognized from her days with Grandma Titi, like *bonita* and *te amo*. Then there were other words, like *siesta*, that she didn't understand but wanted urgently to learn. The song ended in a delicious trail of *la la la*'s that you had to listen very closely to hear. Each time Malaya replayed the ending in her memory, she was overcome with a longing to go with the white girl.

MALAYA HUMMED the song as her parents' voices sprang up downstairs. When it became clear that they were arguing again, she sang the *la la la*'s louder. She pulled her sketch pad and pencil set from her vanity drawer and started drawing, imagining the gifts she might find under the tree tomorrow marked with "Happy Kwanzaa!" or "From Santa!" She had stopped believing in Santa in the second grade, after Rachel Greenstein told her he was made up by Christian parents to make their children behave, but she liked the idea of a big magic man flying through the sky with presents, so she said nothing.

This year, she had written to Santa, and left the letter on her parents' bed with a halo of stars and exclamation points around the item she wanted more than anything in the world: an electronic label maker called the Brother P-touch 3. The children at Galton had taken up label makers as their latest fad, after cinnamon-flavored dental floss, oily blue-green stickers that looked like they had oceans inside them, and erasers that smelled like cotton candy. This label-making trend had turned the third-grade classroom into a vista of colors and words: thin green strips announced students' names from their desks, phrases like @^KEEP OUT!^@ and *!DON'T!*!TOUCH!* glared in red from lunch boxes and notebook covers. One student, a box-shaped boy named Ben Heath, had printed all the words to the first part of Lewis Carroll's "Jabberwocky" in rainbow lettering, sticking the verses inexplicably on the bars of the class gerbil's cage. Malaya couldn't wait to spread her own blue and purple lettering across the classroom walls.

The daydream stopped short when Nyela called her from the stairs.

"Malaya? Come down. We have to talk to you."

Nyela was sitting on the bed in her shiny green nightgown, a half-folded piece of paper in her lap. Percy stood with his back to the door, leaning over the windowsill.

"Sit down, My Laya," he said, turning toward her.

"Do you remember what Dr. Perior said when you went to see him yesterday?" Nyela glanced down at the paper.

Malaya scanned her memory, her chest tight. She thought of the scale, the feeling of the cold stethoscope and the tight, scratchy gown. She thought the words: *morbidly obese*. She had heard them before, and she knew they mattered deeply. But she did not know what they meant, and suddenly this filled her with shame.

"Do you remember how much you weighed when he put you on the scale?"

"No," she said.

It was true. Even though she weighed in every week at the Meeting, it was as though a great gray fog came and wiped the number out of her head as soon as she left the room. She always remembered how much she had gained—or, especially, how much she lost—but she could never make the number on the scale itself stick. Her stomach tightened. She felt like she was on the examination table again, trying not to breathe.

"One hundred and seventy-two pounds," Nyela said, tapping her knee with the corner of the folded paper with each syllable. She looked nervous, too. "That's more than a lot of grown women, Malaya. Four pounds more than at the Meeting last week."

Malaya studied the curve of her mother's knee under the slinky gown. She tried to play the island song in her mind, but she couldn't catch the melody.

"My Laya," Percy said, "what we're trying to say is we're worried about you."

"Your teachers are worried, too." Nyela tapped the paper again, then unfolded it. "The school sent a letter about your fitness test scores. They're calling us in for meetings."

Nyela looked at her, waiting for something. Malaya knew this was serious. She had heard stories of black children being taken from their parents in the name of child welfare. This had happened to Aunt Augustine before Cousin LaSondra was born, and the few times Percy and Nyela mentioned it, both their faces cracked with pain. And though Nyela was always adamant that protecting children was important, it was clear that the white people's modes of protection were not to be trusted in this regard. Nothing good ever came of being called in for meetings with white authorities, and the idea of putting her parents through such a humiliation filled her again with shame. Her face got hot and tears began to trail down into her mouth.

"You're a smart girl, Malaya," Percy said. He moved toward her as though he was going to put a hand on her shoulder, but he didn't. "And you're beautiful. You know that, right?"

Malaya didn't know how to respond. It felt like something that was true to him, but was a complete fabulation to the outside world. In this way, beauty was twofold. There was the side of beauty Malaya knew deeply, the twin arcs of a passing cloud or the perfect yellow cast of a streetlight glowing in the rain. This was also the beauty of blackness, the unspeakable ember of timeless knowing that sat at the heart of Harlem's kente-colored life, powering its rhythms and tuning its flourishes to brilliance. But then there was the other beauty—the one that, in the outside world, was reserved for skinny white and light-skinned women, a beauty as distant as a meteor for Malaya. When Percy called her beautiful, it was this beauty she suspected he was talking about, and it confounded her. Any response would either be a delusion or, worse, a betrayal. She sniffled and nodded, not because she agreed, but because she wanted the conversation to end.

They asked a barrage of questions about Malaya's eating: Was she sneaking food? Was Giselle feeding her junk when they stayed late at work? *Where was she getting the food? How was she hiding it? Why was she eating so much?*

To each question, Malaya lied: no, no, no, no . . . I'm not. *I don't know.*

She looked at her parents sitting there on the bed, Nyela's face stiff and heavy, Percy's crumpled. She did her best to keep her breath from going off beat.

"You can be the smartest, most beautiful woman in the world," Nyela said, "but if you can't control your weight, you won't be happy." She looked at Malaya, first her belly, then her face.

"Do you think you understand what we're saying, Malaya?" she asked. Malaya nodded.

"Is there anything you want to say, My Laya?" Percy asked.

She shook her head no.

"I know you want to go back to your room," Nyela said. "We just want you to know that we love you. Are you going to work harder on this?"

She nodded again.

"Okay," Nyela said. "We have no choice but to believe you."

But it didn't seem true. Nyela placed the letter on top of the stack of papers on her nightstand, where she kept all the things she didn't want to forget.

CHRISTMAS MORNING CAME with all its familiar smells: the turkey, string beans, and collard greens simmering in the kitchen, the rich, woody prickle of the tree downstairs, which made the house feel like an enchanted forest. But it was the smell of Ma-Mère's coffee that truly meant Christmas had begun. Each year, Ma-Mère brought bags of roasted coffee beans from the trips she'd taken, rich blends from places like Guatemala and St. Kitts packed tight in plastic bundles and wrapped in fancy gold ribbons. Coffee always smelled stranger when Ma-Mère brewed it—stronger than when Nyela did, at least. This made sense to Malaya. Ma-Mère was like a more saturated version of her mother.

Malaya brushed her teeth and placed her slumber bonnet neatly under her pillow, shaking her braids loose and finger-combing them so they hung neatly at her shoulders, beads clinking. She made her bed carefully, propping her pillows just so, so that she would have a place to sit when she returned to pore over the coveted P-touch 3.

When she reached the parlor, she found it transformed. Brimming with red and green gift wrap and kente-print wreaths, the space seemed both bigger and smaller at once. The ceiling seemed to have stretched upward to make room for the tree, which towered in the center of the room, its branches spreading generously in all directions. The walls seemed whiter and the stucco left on the ceiling by the previous owners seemed to catch glints of sunlight from the window and shine as though frosted. The room was thick with gifts. Objects of all sizes filled the space from the tree to the doorway, some wrapped in red and green paper, some in small bags with sparkly ribbons curling festively from their handles. There were a few larger gifts in odd shapes, covered in plastic bags printed with candy canes, wreaths, and snowflakes. Malaya assumed these were from her father. Percy always bought large gifts, and Nyela had told Malaya once that this was because he had grown up poor, which meant he was liable to say yes to everything, as if the word *no* were a curse.

She pulled her backpack from the seat in the foyer and took out the gifts she'd made at school: a painting of a blue-and-green globe swirled with snow for her father and another of a purple sunrise for her mother, a clay ashtray for Uncle Book, and a picture frame decorated with fancy gold foil and brass grommets for Ma-Mère. She sat the gifts on the piano bench, pleased with how she'd wrapped them. Her parents were still sleeping, and Ma-Mère wasn't in the parlor, though the coffee smell filled the first floor. This meant she could explore the presents undisturbed.

She tore past the bags and boxes that filled the room. There was the art set she had wanted from the Harlem Arts Academy, the newest version of the GirlTalk game she and Rachel Greenstein played, with its pink telephone and a fake answering machine. There were several books, including the latest from *The Baby-Sitters Club*, featuring her favorite babysitter, the black one, Jesse. There were clothes that horrified her with their old-lady shapes and drab colors. With each gift she opened, she felt a wave of emotion that was delicious at first, as it seemed to bring her closer to the Brother P-touch 3. But soon she had gone through all the gifts with her name on them, and it wasn't there. She dug deep into the Christmas stocking, which Nyela always filled with papery shelled, unsalted peanuts, which the Meeting ladies called a Low-Guilt Treat. Still nothing. For a moment, Malaya wondered if she had gotten it wrong: perhaps there was a Santa Claus after all, a spiteful man who had decided to bring her hideous clothes and tasteless peanuts to punish her for her nonbelief.

"Merry Christmas, My Ly-Ly."

Ma-Mère appeared in the doorway, looking down at Malaya. She was a tall, thick woman whose body seemed to be made up entirely of straight lines. She had broad shoulders that suggested to Malaya what He-Man might look like if he were a grandmother instead of a superhero. Malaya looked down at her nightgown. One of the joys of Christmas was the chance to wear pajamas all day, provided that she brushed her teeth in the morning. But Ma-Mère was fully dressed in a prim green skirt and suit jacket. Under the suit was a shiny blouse buttoned so far up her neck Malaya thought it must have been uncomfortable for her to talk, but Ma-Mère didn't seem to have that problem.

"Well, look at you," she said, hovering over Malaya's face for an air kiss. She made a lipsticky smooch centimeters from Malaya's cheek. The family never hugged or touched skin, something Malaya hadn't thought about until a sleepover at Rachel Greenstein's when she saw Rachel's mother hug her little brother like a greedy bear and plant a big, smacking kiss on his mouth. Malaya was scandalized. But after that, she began to notice how much hugging and kissing went on in some families. She craned her neck and air-kissed Ma-Mère, who smelled of strong black coffee and lipstick.

"You still putting on weight, huh, My Ly-Ly?" Ma-Mère said. Malaya hated this nickname. It made her think of a small, squeaky animal, a hamster or pet pig. "Look at them ham hocks!"—Ma-Mère pointed to Malaya's thighs—"and all that belly. I suppose you're 'bout big as me at this point, huh? Hmh." Malaya imagined herself disappearing with a *poof!* into a feather and vanishing into the fabric of her nightgown. "Guess we're big as belugas, the both of us. And your mama too," Ma-Mère said finally. She sighed and shook her head. "I was hoping she'd get you under control by now. But not so." And then, as though to herself: "Some people can't see a problem till it pisses in their face."

Malaya didn't know what to say. Ma-Mère was full of these sayings, sharp little proclamations that didn't usually rhyme, but felt like they should. Malaya could never be sure what they meant exactly, but the tone always stung. She couldn't shake the feeling that, by talking about her mother, Ma-Mère was also talking about her.

"Well, did you see what Santa brought you this year, at least?" Ma-Mère asked. She sat her coffee down on the side table by the piano and pulled up a chair, her heavy gold rings clinking against the wood as she smoothed her skirt down and sat. Malaya pointed to the art set and the other gifts.

"No, My Ly-Ly," she said, "I'm talking 'bout the big one. That's it over there." She pointed to a large, angular shape wrapped in a pink African batik-print cloth in the corner of the room.

Ma-Mère watched in amused anticipation as Malaya tugged the fabric. Finally, she freed the gift from the cloth and stood back to look at it.

"It's a stationary bicycle," Ma-Mère said. "For exercise!"

She laughed in the way that adults often laughed when explaining things they thought were simple, a short, deep chortle whose slim cruelty was meant to go unnoticed.

Percy and Nyela soon emerged from upstairs, grateful for the chance to sleep in, and the day went on as Christmas always did. By afternoon, Uncle Book arrived with bottles of liquor, a doll for Malaya, and a barrage of ticklish kisses. There was food, plenty of it. But for Malaya, the exercise bike loomed over the day, souring everything. Even Christmas dinner was dismal, its parade of glistening yams and golden macaroni and cheese ruined by the misshapen hunk of metal.

At the table, Ma-Mère began to tell the story of the first time Nyela made Christmas dinner as a teenager in Philadelphia, but Nyela protested. "Nobody needs to hear that," she said between bites of turkey. She swallowed and gave a tight smile.

"Yes we do!" Uncle Book shouted as he poured himself some rum.

"She was no more than thirteen, if I recall correctly. But she was big, you know. Could have been eighteen or twenty, 'cept she's always been young in the eyes. Her father had left by then, so it was just us two. Well, somehow she got the idea of a Christmas goose in her head," Ma-Mère said, a smile stirring on her cheeks as she cut a shard of broccoli neatly on her plate. "She insisted on it. A Christmas goose. Went down to Reading Terminal and bought the bird herself with money from the little job she had folding blouses at the Strawbridge and Clothier. She was so proud. She turned up hugging that package like she was Julie Andrews holding her Academy Award."

Percy gave a quick chuckle and refilled his glass. Uncle Book laughed, leaning a muscly arm against the back of his chair. "Go on, Mrs. Smith!" he said.

Malaya looked at Nyela, who shifted her weight and took a sip of water.

"Well, I left her in the kitchen to make this dinner, you know, since she was so grown," Ma-Mère continued. "And it didn't smell half bad so I figured she was doing fine. Well"—she leaned back a little and cast a look around the table, then sat up straight again—"she brought that dish out, all garnished with celery and radishes and who knows what else. And her round face is just smiling like she's about to win the Nobel Peace Prize. And she sits that dish on the table and when I tell you that bird wasn't a goose at all! The poultry man had sold that poor girl a chicken—the skinniest one I've ever seen. He trussed it up like a goose and sent her on her way, with all her money in his pocket."

Nyela gave another tight smile and looked down at her plate as Ma-Mère continued.

"Now if you know anything, you know a goose don't lose its pink when you cook it, but a chicken's a whole different story. Pink chicken's liable to kill somebody. I'm no gourmand, but I do know that. Well! This girl called her big self making Christmas goose. I cut into that chicken and I swear I heard it still squawking! It was pink as a flamingo's tail. I tell you it about jumped off the plate and told me cock-a-doodle-doo!"

At this, Uncle Book smacked the table so hard the silverware shook. "No it didn't, Mrs. Smith," Uncle Book said, shaking his head. He laughed again and took another drink.

"If I'm lying I'm flying." Ma-Mère arched her eyebrows and dabbed at the corners of her mouth with her napkin, smiling under the folded cloth. Percy let out another chortle and Uncle Book raised his glass.

Malaya watched them, her mother, her father, and her uncle, laughing over the spread of half-empty plates. Then she looked at her mother. Nyela lifted her eyes toward Percy, her face heavy.

"What, Ny?" he said, his voice suddenly sharp. "Don't start! It's just a joke." After that, Nyela said nothing. She only nodded and swallowed a spoonful of greens.

When the meal was finished, Uncle Book carried the exercise bike up to the family room to set it up in front of the television. Malaya took a last sip of her Diet Coke and followed behind him, carrying his drink as he hefted the bike up the stairs. Uncle Book was shorter than Percy, and thicker, with a solid, muscly build and Jheri-curled hair that was perpetually wet with sweet-smelling oil. Like Percy, he always seemed to be moving, though his movements were smaller and heavier. She handed him the drink and watched as he took a gulp, plopped the glass down on the hardwood floor, and began to jostle the limbs of the bike, shoving its parts into place.

"You're lucky, My Ly-Ly," he said, whipping a handlebar free from its plastic wrapping. "We didn't have Christmases like this growing up. All the presents and all this food and everything. Your daddy loves you." He pushed the handle onto the display console. "He loves your mama too. And you know what? Even if he didn't, I bet he wouldn't leave. He's the type to stay for the child's sake. Keep the family together for the kid. They both are. So you're lucky."

Malaya watched as he leaned back and looked at the bike, taking another sip of rum. It had never occurred to her that, of all the things that made a family, the keeping it together could fall to the child. She thought of the word: *lucky*. Uncle Book pulled the resistance band tight across the wheel. He stood up and gave the bike a smack.

"You do thirty minutes on this every day, Ly-Ly, and you'll be skinny in no time! You'll look like Downtown Julie Brown!" he said, his face bright.

When everyone came up to the family room, Nyela instructed Malaya to climb onto the bike so she could take a picture with the new Polaroid camera Percy had given her for Christmas. Malaya did as told, hoisting herself up onto the ugly contraption, trying to hold in her stomach, refusing to give anything but a cheerless half-smile when the flash blinked its hot spark of light. Then, while Nyela and Ma-Mère cleaned up, and Percy and Uncle Book vanished to wherever it was they went after holiday meals, Malaya crept back up to the family room.

Alone, she kicked the bike, noncommittally at first, then harder, until her toes throbbed. She sat on the sofa and looked at the photo. She was bigger than the bike, two or three times bigger. She hadn't known she was this big.

She ran her finger along the Polaroid's plastic casing where the shoulder of the girl in the photo met her side. She traced the big bulge of her arms and stomach, imagining what it would look like if she cut those parts away. She covered both sides of the girl with her fingers, so that there were no handlebars and no bike seat and only a thin, narrow strip of Malaya at the center of the plastic square.

She tried to rip the photo there, but it wouldn't tear. She bent the plastic back and forth and pulled until her palms cramped, but still nothing. Her face flushed, she put it in her mouth and bit down, moving her teeth left and right over the plastic, slowly at first, then faster, until her jaw hurt. Soon, the plastic tore, and a too-sweet liquid oozed from the photo, stinging her tongue and dripping in a watery black trail down her chin. She spat it out and ripped the photo down the left side, then the right, tearing through the plastic until the thin strip of Malaya fluttered to the floor. She picked it up and looked at it: her head, her narrow, armless shoulders, her straight sides. She thought about what label she would give this picture. She imagined printing GIRL or FAIL or MORBIDLY OBESE in fat red letters below the photo, but she wasn't sure if she could spell these words correctly. Or, she thought, she might print something else—a funny poem, as Ben Heath had done with the gerbil cage, or one of the breezy words from "La Isla Bonita": *San Pedro . . . siesta . . . verdad . . .* But there was no label maker, and now there was no picture either. There was only Malaya, huge and stained and sticky, standing in a mess of plastic and ink.

When she heard footsteps on the stairs, she ran to her parents' bathroom. She stuffed the crumpled scraps of the Polaroid into the pocket of her nightgown and scrubbed at her face and neck with Nyela's washcloth. She spat hard, trying to get the chemical taste out of her mouth and the black juice off her skin.

Ma-Mère appeared behind her in the bathroom mirror. She caught her eye as she scrubbed, her face still stained with soap and black.

"What you been eating now, child?" Ma-Mère frowned in the glass above her. It was clear she didn't want an answer. She took the washcloth from Malaya and rinsed it off.

"Go up and get in the shower 'fore your mother sees you," she said. "No sense ruining her Christmas just 'cause you can't control that mouth of yours."

Ma-Mère pulled a rag from the shelf and began to scrub the trails of black that gathered in the sink like spiderwebs.

"Don't put that nightgown in the laundry. Leave it in the bathroom upstairs and I'll get to it later. Looks like a day of rest on Christmas would be too much miracle for me, but at least your mother can catch a break."

Malaya wiped her face again with the back of her hand and went upstairs to draw. Her room was still neat, just as she left it, but now, by the window, there was a tall wooden easel with thick, wide slats and an adjustable bench that rose almost as high as her shoulders. There was no wrapping paper, only a small tag with a glittery teal snowflake. The note read "Love Mom and Dad," but the choppy handwriting was her father's.

Malaya propped her sketch pad against the easel and pulled out her pencils. She tried to draw the narrow strip of her body from the torn photo. She made herself small and straight, covering the missing arms and bulges with sky and trees, soft blues and lush greens. The chemical taste still stung in her mouth as she murmured the glittery island song, trying as best she could to make up the words she didn't understand.

Freeze Tag

"My mom gave me extra dulce de coco today," Shaniece Guzmán said to Malaya after settling into the narrow school bus seat. The motor whirred beneath them as the bus rumbled down Broadway, past the Lin Fong Restaurant and La Caridad Billiard Hall, past the red and yellow awnings of the bodegas, blinking their lights against the gray sky. It was raining, and between the din of the motor, the wet rush of traffic, and the older children singing pop songs at the back of the bus, Malaya had to lean in to hear Shaniece's quiet voice.

"She gave me a lot extra. Like, even more than yesterday."

Shaniece hoisted her peeling Janet Jackson backpack onto her lap and produced an oily paper bag, its mouth crumpled to a close. She brought these bags every day to the coffee shop where the Northern Harlem children waited for the bus to whisk them across Manhattan to Galton on Park Avenue. Her lunch was always a collection of the most delicious Forbidden Foods from Mr. Gonzales's corner bodega—pork rinds and Doritos and cans of Hawaiian Punch; beef jerky and bulls-eyes with Now and Laters and quarter-water juice; deli sandwiches as thick as fists and fifty-cent bodega pies—always accompanied by a handful of dulce de coco candies wrapped in wax paper and grease. These lunches were unfathomable to Malaya, who was instructed every night to pack her own lunch: a tuna or turkey or reduced-fat peanut butter sandwich on light bread with light mayo or sugar-free jelly; a cup of light yogurt; a diet juice box; and a dry clementine. Thankfully, Shaniece was always willing to share her treats.

"Cool," Malaya said. It was January, and cold, but the sleeves of her puffy pink jacket pinched tight at her arms and shoulders. She tugged it off, left arm then right, and balled it up on her lap.

These morning rides with Shaniece were one of the few pleasures of the school week. They took the bus together every day, stuffing themselves into the small leather seats, feeling their thighs press against each other as they ate and talked. Shaniece was chubby—not as big as Malaya, but *heavy*, as Nyela would say. She was a yellow-skinned girl with hair the color of brown construction paper left out in the sun. Her straightened bob fell stiffly down from her head, swiping at the collar of her jean jacket almost like a white girl's, but with sharp, jagged edges that reminded Malaya of scissors. Nyela had vowed not to let Malaya relax her hair until her sixteenth birthday, despite her most enthusiastic protestations. Every day on the school bus, Malaya looked at the flap and flow of Shaniece's hair with envy, stealing pats and rubs of it when no one was looking, which Shaniece never seemed to mind.

She opened the paper bag of Forbidden Foods, and together they talked about boys and ate what was for Malaya the second breakfast of the day.

"We had butter bread and marmalade this morning," Shaniece continued. "Plus plantain and cheese. And mango juice. It was real good." Malaya imagined a sheen of butter seeping into a slice of toast thick as a textbook, dollops of sweet orange marmalade flecked with amber spreading over the bread in luxurious swirls. Shaniece's voice grew louder as she spoke, and she sat up a little in the seat. "My mom was watching so I couldn't bring you any."

Shaniece was normally quiet, with a distant expression that reminded Malaya of a bored or irritated adult. But each morning, Malaya watched Shaniece's face stretch wide and her cheeks flicker with light as she talked about her mother. Sometimes she got so excited her words tripped over themselves, like when she described the marvelous breakfasts her mother had made her—sausages, potatoes, guava bread, and all kinds of jellies. According to Shaniece, her mother was a beautiful woman with a name almost as fancy as pie à la mode, *Pat-RI-ci-a*, the *t* and *ri* of which stuck fabulously together over Malaya's tongue and slid into a delicious lace of soft *s* and vowel sounds when she said it. To hear Shaniece tell it, Patricia Guzmán was a miracle of motherhood. She came from a beautiful place called Santo Domingo, where, in Malaya's mind at least, the sweet dulce de coco candies grew in fields. Malaya had never met Shaniece's mother. Shaniece usually came to the bus stop alone, and it was her father who attended parent-teacher conference nights at Galton. Nyela had said that this was what happened when people tried to raise families without being married—one always got caught holding the bag. Still, Malaya appreciated the mystery of the woman. She imagined Patricia Guzmán tall and curvy as a tomato vine, her blond hair falling like a splash of lemonade behind her, her body ever sprawling forward to the rhythm of her name.

"My mom told me to share the dulce with Rodrigo from my building 'cause she—she knows he likes me." Shaniece smiled, revealing a missing canine tooth. She pulled the candy from its oily package and passed a mound of coconut to Malaya.

Malaya could not decide which part of the bus rides she liked better—the food or the talking. Shaniece was a year older than Malaya, and had been admitted to Galton from PS 153, the nearby public school, on scholarship only under the provision that she repeat the first grade. When Malaya got to the first grade, it seemed like Shaniece had been there for years, if not forever. Shaniece was what Nyela called "grown," and what Ma-Mère called "fast." Even at nine, she moved like someone who had lived a life and had stories to tell, though she rarely told them in their entirety, which made her even more like an adult. Yet there was a quiet sadness to Shaniece that Malaya liked, as though, beneath her fierce-set eyes and pudgy frown, what she wanted most was candy and a nap.

Sometimes, Shaniece's hair and skin and savvy scared Malaya. Every now and then she worried that she would one day become a pretty girl like Amandra Wilson, leaving Malaya behind. So she simply made a point of not talking to Shaniece much among the wealthy kids at Galton. Shaniece's father, Jerome Armistice, was a quiet, Jheri-curled man who worked long hours on the sales floor at the Home and Office Depot on the Upper West Side, which meant that her family was even further from wealthy than Malaya's. This idea comforted Malaya, though she knew better than to say so.

Shaniece told her boy stories with cool detachment, sighing as she recounted the bags of bodega candy and sunflower seeds they'd bought for her, or how they'd etched her name and theirs together, ensconced in a heart on the wall of her building's elevator. But for Malaya, Shaniece's stories about boys were delicious. She guzzled them excitedly, interjecting once in a while with stories of her own. Malaya had no real boys to talk about, so she made up imaginary boys on her block who liked her. She gave them names like Quentin and Romulus, which she had come across in books, though she had a hard time spelling them when she tried to write about them in her diary.

Malaya bit into the dulce, sweet bursts of coconut juice sloshing in her mouth as she chewed.

"This boy on my block likes me, too," she said, hoping to sound casual. "I mean he sweats me. His name is Matthias. He has hazel eyes and he's *fly*." She rolled her neck a little as she'd seen the older girls on her block do.

"That's cool." Shaniece fidgeted with the strap on her backpack and looked out the window as the bus neared the elevated train tracks on 125th.

"You wanna come over later?" Malaya asked. "Giselle said she's making Haitian patties and rice. My mom said you can come." She put another candy in her mouth, trying not to sound too eager as she waited for a response. Shaniece came to the brownstone after school several afternoons a week, which gave the two a chance to feel each other's bodies and touch each other's hair all they wanted. This was one of the few times Malaya's roundness worked in her favor. Shaniece's weight was concentrated tightly and evenly from her shoulders to her ankles, giving her body a banana-like bulge. Malaya, on the other hand, was round everywhere, and though she had no waist to speak of, she did have soft, deep cups of flesh around her nipples that could pass for breasts. This meant that when she and Shaniece played, Malaya got to be the girl.

They would sneak together into the family room on the second floor while Giselle cooked dinner upstairs, taking towels from her parents' bathroom and pinning the ends to the floor with her mother's Malian statuettes, sliding Ma-Mère's old rocking chair to the center of the circle to give their towel tent a shape. Malaya would lie beneath Shaniece, squeezing herself against her body until she started to warm. When the feeling got good, she would lock slick tufts of Shaniece's hair between her knuckles and wiggle her hand, letting the strands prickle the crevices between her fingers, sending little bolts of feeling down to her armpits and the folds of her legs. Sometimes, she would imagine Shaniece was Daundré Harris and she was Amandra Wilson. Sometimes, Shaniece would slide her arms into Malaya's sweatshirt sleeves and press her palms against Malaya's so it looked like the small, buttercolored hands coming out of the shirt were Malaya's own. They never talked about these games; outside the brownstone, the closest they came to touching was the press of one's leg against the other's as they ate on the school bus.

"Yeah," Shaniece said finally, "I can come over. My mom won't mind." She was still turned toward the window, distant, but it didn't matter. Malaya took another dulce, the crisp coconut shreds melting in her cheeks and leaving moist brown pads of sweetness on her fingertips.

As the bus turned east across Central Park, the older children began to sing a song Malaya had heard playing often on the street outside her window at night. It was a fast-clapping song about a pretty, dangerous girl who made boys fall in love with her simply by smiling.

Harlem was full of these songs—about love, about lonely boyfriends, angry girlfriends, and people who were so happy they could neither sleep nor eat, could manage only to sing. Malaya listened to these songs closely every night, repeating them to herself in the mirror and writing the lyrics in her diary so that when they cropped up in the back of the bus, she could imagine herself back there, too, next to Daundré Harris, belting a wondrous duet about the love they shared.

This song's chorus was a soaring lament about how the girl had driven the boy crazy, ensnaring his every thought with her butt and her inexorable charm. Daundré's voice drizzled over the whir of the bus's motor and the rain. While Shaniece talked about her weekend with her mother, Malaya danced with Daundré in her imagination, fast moves like in African dance class, then slower, closer, like in her towel-tent games with Shaniece. Caught in her fantasy, she did not notice when the singing stopped. She heard only Daundré's voice lingering in the air:

If I were you, I'd take . . .

He hesitated, and Malaya's chest fluttered as the next line pushed up in her throat. She sat up and looked over the back of her seat, jostling Shaniece with her hips and elbows, pressing her belly against the hard leather. Daundré was sitting alone in the last row, his backpack beside him, saving room for Amandra Wilson. A run of black curls sat neatly on top of his head, and the faded edges at either side of his face peeked out over the seat. Stretching a little, Malaya could see his smooth brown forehead, his mouth slightly open, his eyes straining to remember the next word.

"*Pre-cau-shuuuuun!*" Malaya sang, her own voice so loud it startled her.

Daundré raised his head up over the seat.

"*Before I step to meet a fly girl . . .*" Malaya murmured, shrinking back and lowering her eyes.

"*And it's a po-tion . . .*" Daundré sang. He wrinkled his eyes into a smile and nodded at Malaya. Then he turned to the sixth-grade boys across the aisle and sang the rest of the line to them.

He had gotten the lyrics wrong, but it didn't matter. Malaya settled back into her seat and luxuriated. He had seen her, had smiled at her. Malaya had become, for an instant, that fly girl to whom someone like Daundré would sing. The feeling would become familiar later—the nervous thrill of having something to offer. Her face felt lit with possibility.

She stuffed the dulce back in its bag, and for the rest of the ride, while Shaniece described the delicious empanadas Patricia Guzmán had made the night before, Malaya counted her breads. The sandwich she'd had would cost her one bread point, plus at least two proteins for the turkey, and one milk for the cheese. The dulce would cost her another bread, and she'd have to add it to her week's tally of Forbidden Foods. She would skip lunch, she decided, pulling her Hello Kitty diary from her backpack. She calculated her point values on a blank page. If she was careful throughout the day, she'd be left with two breads for dinner. Even if Giselle made her vyan bèf nan sòs, with its wondrous bursts of meaty juice, Malaya would eat only a little. She would find Commitment, Control. No matter what happened as the day went on, she would think about Amandra's popsicle-stick body, about Shaniece's boyfriends, about her own glorious song with Daundré, and she would make herself stop. Today, she would not mess up.

Malaya turned to tell Shaniece about her decision, but just at that moment Shaniece swallowed the last of the dulce, licking the sticky juice from her fingers. Malaya said nothing, unsure that her friend would understand.

THE CLASSROOM WAS under a hush as Randall Creighton, a tall girl with hair the color of fruit punch, walked around the clusters of desks, dropping a large white envelope in front of each student. Report Card Day at Galton was an event. The school prided itself on exceptional performances from all its students, nursery and pre-K on. Some parents were rumored to spank their children for grades less than "O," short for "Outstanding," which brought a frantic air to the report card ritual and led the teachers to treat some students with extra care. Malaya's third-grade teacher was an angular white woman who insisted that all the students call her by her first name—Brooke—which Nyela hated and which made Malaya love Brooke even more. Brooke sat at her desk cooing softly to Ben Heath, who had turned bright pink and begun to heave as soon as the report cards appeared. While Ben whimpered, the other children tore their envelopes open. After a few minutes of whispering and comparing grades, most of the children pushed the envelopes into their monogrammed L.L.Bean backpacks and ran to the courtyard for lunch. A few—like Ben and Sasha Westland, a tiny girl with a lisp who'd skipped the first grade—cried at the sight of their envelopes, hugging them tightly to their chests.

Malaya pushed her chair back to make room for the envelope on her lap. She opened it and pulled out the grid of lines and letters, checking it over quickly to be sure she had O grades in the only classes that mattered: art, music, Spanish, and English/language arts. She traced the O's proudly with her finger. This done, she sat at her desk and waited for Rachel Greenstein to finish reading her report card so that she could leap outside with her like a thin girl would and practice her new, skinny life on the courtyard.

"Ready?" Rachel said excitedly, sliding her report card into her L.L.Bean backpack, its embroidered monogram flashing her initials in sateen lavender.

Malaya tugged the straps of her own backpack over her shoulders. "Ready!" she answered, trying to match Rachel's tone.

While other children buzzed around the courtyard in a flurry of colorful jackets playing freeze tag, Malaya and Rachel sat under the jungle gym as usual. They invented a fantasy game in which they were glamorous teenage Witches-in-Training, conjuring potions and tirelessly honing their magical powers to help them slay the villainous Ben Heath.

"What is your pleasure today, Aryala, Witch-in-Training?" Rachel said in a low, crypt-like voice.

"Today we shall brew a gruesome spell to defeat the villains of the fourth form!" Malaya cackled. She leaned her weight against the jungle gym's splintering wood beams and gestured to the corner where Amandra Wilson and a group of fourth-grade girls sat, braiding each other's hair.

Malaya enjoyed these games with Rachel. Everything about Rachel's life seemed remote. She lived in an apartment off Fifth Avenue, with a sunken living room and a baby grand piano in the parlor. Her family kept cheesecakes decorated with fresh strawberries in the refrigerator, not only on birthdays, but at all times throughout the year. Despite this, Rachel was endlessly long and thin, with skin like an uncracked egg, and dark green eyes like the underbrush of a Christmas tree.

Malaya and Rachel shared an enthusiasm for imaginary worlds, and a proud disdain for the silly playground games children their age were expected to play. They turned down their noses at hopscotch and dodgeball, though Rachel expressed a distinct interest in learning the hand-clapping games Amandra and the Spanish Harlem girls brought to Galton's courtyard from uptown. For the most part, the two spent their playdates at Rachel's house making up elaborate choreographed dramas to perform for their parents at pickup time, usually inspired by whatever Broadway musical Rachel's older sister had discovered most recently. It was in this way that Malaya memorized the full soundtracks of *Fiddler on the Roof* and *Annie Get Your Gun*, which they remixed with choruses Malaya heard on her block, producing irresistible lyrics like: *Who must feed the family and run the home? The Mama-se, Mama-sa, Mama-koo-sa!*

As Malaya's hips and thighs began to numb, she shifted her weight again. Her stomach was growling. Nyela and the Meeting ladies always said that meant your body was on the right track. Malaya was proud. She had made it to lunchtime without a single mistake: she had eaten nothing since the bus ride, had not borrowed money for cookies or ice pops from the open pockets of the wealthy first-graders. She imagined her new self, thin and pretty, a vision tantalizingly within reach. She felt so changed, so hopeful, that when Rachel suggested they join the game of freeze tag forming on the other side of the courtyard—"to spy on the earthling children"—Malaya felt herself push up from the ground and heard herself say "Okay."

She felt her classmates' eyes on her as she and Rachel neared the huddle of small bodies gathered on the blacktop next to the basketball court. Rachel took her hand and led her to the center of the group, where they stuck their feet into the circle and sang along to the chorus of "Eeny, Meeny, Miny, Mo" as Maurice Orland, a math genius with deep freckles, poked each sneaker in succession. Malaya prayed silently that she would not be chosen *it*. Soon, the teams divided and the children began to scatter over the wide brick courtyard like a bag of spilled jelly beans, running quickly away from Jonah Burkman, the runny-nosed boy whose sneaker had been chosen.

Malaya ran, slow and stumpy at first. Then faster. She felt herself loosen. She closed her eyes and thought of her new body, lithe and quick, the smaller, better girl she would be one day, so, so soon. The courtyard softened into a blur beneath her. Air rushing at her face, she felt light but also marvelously full, not in the stomach, but past it, everywhere else. She imagined herself there but not there, transported to a world where her body could do wild things like dart forward and bob on the wind like an ice cube in a cup of soda, then fizz quickly upward like a flurry of bubbles. It felt good—better than ice cream and Cool Whip, better than French fries. The only thing that soured the moment was the fear that at some point she might fall, and that falling from a feeling like this would be infinitely worse than never having run at all.

"I got Malaya!" Ben Heath crowed suddenly. He swooped toward her out of nowhere with a greedy laugh. "I got Malaya! I got Malaya!" He dug his fingers into her arm. Now she was *it*. Now it was her turn to chase.

Children flew around like bundles of burst balloons, scattering over the open space so quickly Malaya had no hope of catching one. The courtyard seemed to expand with each step she took, and she felt her body growing heavier as the children zoomed away. She looked for Rachel, hoping she would be kind and let her catch her, but she was on the other side of the courtyard. She even looked for Shaniece, but she was nowhere to be found. Malaya began to lose her breath. Her shoelaces unraveled and her knee started to hurt.

Soon, a group of fourth- and fifth-graders circled her. Taking turns, they leaned in toward her, laughing, then retreated just out of reach when she lunged to tag them. "Catch me, Malaya!" Ben Heath shouted. He jumped in front of her, sticking out his tongue, then leapt back just beyond her grasp. Maurice Orland danced a ring around her, a silly grapevine, chuckling and oinking as he went. Jonah Burkman walked toward her with an exaggerated casualness, like a gentleman from a black-and-white movie, then sprang back cackling as she reached for his shoulder.

Panting, Malaya turned desperately, praying for Rachel or Shaniece to appear in the circle. Instead she found herself face-to-face with Daundré Harris, who opened his mouth into a gigantic O shape, pointed at her, and laughed.

"*Haaaaaaa! Haaaaaaa!* Faaaat giiiirl caaan't runnn!"

The words poured out of him and filled the courtyard. The children, the playground, the whole school itself seemed to open up and laugh with him. Amandra Wilson appeared, twisting her long hair around her finger, her lean face tilted to the side as she joined in the laughter.

"*Oh my god!* She's so fat! She, like, can't even move!"

Malaya lunged desperately for her backpack, struggling to push her arm through its tight loops. She pinched her eyes closed and tried not to hear the laughter that followed her into the school building. Her face tingling with heat, she shuffled down the endless hallway to the girls' bathroom to sit in the wheelchair stall, the only one big enough to hold her with room enough to move. There, she pulled out her Hello Kitty diary and flipped to the page she had marked that morning: 4 BREADS, 1 FRUTE, 2 PROTEENS. NOW I WILL EAT LESS, EXERSISZE MORE, AND LOOSE WEIGHT. She raked her pencil over the words until they were covered in shiny gray, bits of graphite dust smearing the page. She pulled out what was left of her lunch—the L-shaped sandwich crusts and a light blueberry yogurt. She stuffed the dry, tasteless crust in her mouth and swallowed. She tore the tinfoil top off the yogurt, licked it clean. Spoonless, she squeezed the plastic cup and brought it to her face, lapping the yogurt, the sweet cream mixing with the salty taste of tears in her mouth.

She shook the report card loose from the books, crayons, and candy wrappers that crowded her backpack. The science teacher had given her a grade of "Good," noting that she had shown some improvement. The art, Spanish, English teachers wrote praise that fell heavy on Malaya now. Physical education showed a grade of "Unsatisfactory," with only three words of written comment: "Malaya needs help."

As her mouth and stomach filled, she erased pictures from her mind. Shade by shade, stroke by stroke, she went back and undrew the past. She had not sung with Daundré, had not felt a thrill of warmth seeing the line of O's on her report card. She had not imagined herself becoming skinny, a fly girl. And she wouldn't. She would not play tag, would not try to talk to Daundré, would not share any of this with Shaniece. She would not dream of running ever again.

Instead, she would finish her yogurt in the bathroom, and all through science class she would stare at the walls. In art class she would draw a scape of deep purples and sincere blues. She would let herself eat at every opportunity, taking breaks in the wheelchair stall, chewing in rhythm and sending her mind away, far away, so that by gym class, last period, Malaya would be gone.

Ladyness

As THE YEAR PRESSED ON toward spring, the air in the Clondon home grew heavier and more tense, though Malaya was not sure why. No one spoke on this change, yet as the evenings warmed, Percy came home later and later, and instead of coming up to the kitchen to kiss Malaya on the forehead and talk with Nyela about their days as he had once done, now he called hello from the vestibule and trudged up to the second floor to soak for hours in the tub. Nyela responded by coming home later as well, though still usually several hours before Percy. Nyela and Malaya sat and ate dinner together, covering a plate of whatever Giselle had prepared and leaving it for Percy on the stove, though it often went untouched until Giselle threw it away the next day.

For Malaya, the only real escape from home was summer. The anticipation of summer was one of the few things she felt she had in common with her classmates at Galton, though she suspected their reasons were different from hers. At the first stirrings of spring, an air of excitement spilled into the classrooms, brightening even the dullest lessons—like Colonial History and Spatial Visualization. By mid-May, Galton children began chirping about their summer plans—trips to country houses in faraway places with glamorous names like the Berkshires and Rehoboth Beach. Some talked about the summer camps they attended each year, places where they lived different lives entirely and where anything was possible, where Randall Creighton could be the cool New York City girl instead of the jittery math nerd, and where even snot-nosed Ben Heath could have a girlfriend.

What Malaya looked forward to was the season's foods: plump burgers dripping with gooey cheese and ketchupy grease, fresh off the grill at the family reunion; impossibly cold icies from the Coco Helado cart that stuck to her fingers and stained her mouth deep shades of red and blue; an ever-presence of ice cream. Getting her hands on these summer foods wasn't easy under Nyela's vigilant eye. Nyela was home more often in the summer, especially in the early days, before the summer session on campus began, and so for Malaya, the thrills of summer eating were elusive. But that was the beauty of the season—it was long, an endless stretch of possibility, and Malaya was sure to sample its sticky delights at least once or twice. Most of all, Malaya looked forward to the brief *nothing* of summer: days without classes or report cards or terrible games of freeze tag, evenings unmarked by her father's absence from the dinner table, afternoons with nothing to fill them but space and the buzzing sun.

She usually had a week or so of this kind of summer before Nyela took her for her annual two-week visit with Ma-Mère. But this year, there were only three such days, right after school ended. Then Malaya was made to pack her hot pink She-Ra suitcase. Nyela knotted a fresh set of beads into her braids, and the two boarded the train for Philadelphia, where she would spend most of the vacation alone with Ma-Mère.

On the train, Malaya sat with her pencils and sketchbook while Nyela flipped through a fashion catalog, remarking on the dresses she liked. "This one is pretty, don't you think?" she said, turning the catalog toward Malaya to reveal an uninteresting sleeveless dress the color of papier-mâché. Malaya looked vaguely at the image and nodded. "We can buy it as a goal dress," Nyela said, folding the corner of the page. "Maybe it'll fit by the end of the summer. I can bring it when I come to pick you up. Ma-Mère will love it on you."

Malaya resented the idea of a goal dress. Two springs ago, Nyela had said the same thing about a dress she'd bought herself. She came home one day with three summer dresses—two pale lace ones with eyelets at the neck, and a wonderfully bright sundress that looked to Malaya like the inside of an orange. "I'm getting into these by the end of summer," Nyela declared as she hung the dresses on the towel hook beside the bathroom mirror. "Maybe I'll wear the orange one when I come to pick you up." But Nyela wore blue jeans and a loose gray cardigan when she showed up in Philadelphia that August, and the dresses were still waiting with the tags on when they returned home. They appeared again the following summer, and Malaya noticed them as she packed this year, too, hanging in a stalwart row along the shower curtain rod. The idea of buying a too-small dress and trying to impress Ma-Mère angered her, but she could not help but admire the way Nyela licked her index finger and mused at the catalog, her wrists arched elegantly before flipping back each glossy page, her bracelets tinkling in the air.

As the train rolled past the plush lawns and sprawling malls of New Jersey, Malaya thought about the Philly summer that lay before her: days spent slogging through the city to Ma-Mère's hair appointments and auxiliary meetings, returning home to eat bland, colorless meals and watch the news while Ma-Mère talked about Malaya's weight and criticized Nyela's failures in her absence. Malaya imagined leaping off the train and springing out onto the wide roads beyond the glass, rolling alongside the tracks in an endless cartwheel until she reached the nearest mall, where she would stow away all summer, eating candy.

"Malaya, you're gonna listen to Ma-Mère, right?" Nyela said, as though in response to a complaint Malaya hadn't made. She rested the magazine on her lap and looked at Malaya. "I know it can be difficult but she loves you."

At the station, Nyela arranged a ride from one of the neighborhood "hack" taxi drivers, men who gave rides around the neighborhood, making small talk and playing old R&B songs on their car radios. When they arrived at Ma-Mère's, she was waiting for them at the door.

"Well, there's my Ly-Ly," she said. Malaya followed behind Nyela, sucking her stomach in to make room for herself and her suitcase as she gave Ma-Mère an air kiss in the doorway.

Ma-Mère lived alone in the two-story townhouse where Nyela had grown up, yet Malaya had a hard time imagining a child had ever lived there. The walls were covered with grainy wood paneling that reminded her of a church, and all of the furniture was fitted with clear plastic covers that had gone brownish yellow with time, so that the long, fancy chair Ma-Mère called the "chase lounge" looked the color of a tea spill, even though Ma-Mère insisted proudly that it was "ivory white." Malaya didn't know what a *chase lounge* was: to her, *chasing* and *lounging* could not have been more different, and lounging was clearly the better of the two. But whatever a chase lounge was, it was obviously very special, because when Malaya stretched out on it to draw with her headphones on, bouncing lightly to Stephanie Mills on her Walkman while Nyela and Ma-Mère talked about the train ride, Ma-Mère darted her eyes at Malaya and said, "Don't sit like that on the chase lounge, My Ly-Ly. And stop that bouncing. Can't have you breaking up my good furniture. This ain't the demolition derby." Nyela gave Malaya a sympathetic smile but said nothing. After that, Malaya sat as stiffly as possible with both feet on the carpet, but still she felt Ma-Mère's eyes on her. Eventually, she gave up, collected her markers and pencils, and slid down the chase lounge to sit on the floor.

It was a Friday evening, and Nyela and Ma-Mère were perched on Ma-Mère's grand, brocade-covered chairs watching the stories. Malaya found these soap operas horrifically boring, an emblem of the slow pace and numbing predictability of Philly summers. After a few years of hearing Malaya complain of boredom, Nyela had convinced Ma-Mère to devise child-friendly activities for Malaya's summer visits. Ma-Mère began to prepare a "Bored Bag," in which she collected cartoons, puzzles, and word games she'd clipped from newspapers and fashion magazines all year in advance of Malaya's visit. The Bored Bag hung on a plastic candelabra next to the kitchen doorway, which Malaya saw as a useless ploy to keep her from eating, as though, distracted by the wonders of the daily Crypt-o-Quote, she would forget about food. She resented this underestimation of her, but she never said anything because, in spite of herself, she liked the Crypt-o-Quote. She enjoyed sitting at the kitchen table hunting through the newspaper for word clues while Ma-Mère fixed breakfast and read her magazines. Sometimes, they worked on the Crypt-o-Quote together, and Ma-Mère told stories about the books each message came from and the people who had written them. Ma-Mère had an impressive store of knowledge, particularly on topics related to black history. She loved words, loved philosophical musings, and Malaya admired this. There was no denying the thrill of arranging the letters on the mealy strip of newsprint Ma-Mère had snipped for her, watching the sentence emerge like a Polaroid until the message came together: INDEPENDENCE IS HAPPINESS, or LEARNING NEVER EXHAUSTS THE MIND. Malaya wasn't sure she knew what the messages meant, but sleuthing them out and collaging them into mouthfuls was one of summer's true pleasures. She looked forward to it every morning, though she would never have said this to Ma-Mère.

The next morning, Nyela gave Malaya an air kiss and said, "You'll be back home before you know it. It'll be okay." Then she vanished to the train. When she was gone, Malaya and Ma-Mère settled into their usual vacation routine. Every morning, they got up at 6 a.m., and Ma-Mère fixed a breakfast of plain instant oatmeal or Rice Krispies with skim milk and a single packet of Sweet'N Low. Then they did their morning exercises, an age of leg lifts and jumping jacks on towels stretched out on the living room floor. Sometimes Ma-Mère played an exercise video on the VCR, and Malaya stared at the host, a peppy, curly-haired white man with a voice like a New Year's kazoo. She watched as he bounced around the screen pinball-style to the beat of old dance songs, calling out phrases like "We're twistin' the fat away!" and "Let's scream! Let's shout! Shake those calories to the ground!" while Malaya panted, trying to keep up.

If Ma-Mère struggled with the exercises, she never let it show. When she started to breathe or sweat too hard, she simply stopped the video. "We have to be ladies," she would say, lifting a piece of sugar-free chewing gum to her mouth and biting down primly. "Even if we're big as men." Then she would make her second cup of coffee and go back to reading the fashion magazines before preparing for the day's appointments.

Malaya thought of this as "Ladyness." Ladyness was a way of speaking and sitting and moving, of somehow exercising without sweating, which Malaya worried she would never understand. It was an elaborate latticework of do's and don'ts that were never fully spoken, but that carried grave consequences when transgressed. The only thing that was really sure about these rules, from what Malaya could tell, was that they were impossible to follow.

Each time she thought of Ladyness, she imagined this: Ma-Mère and Nyela and her, all in a line, holding their breath, trying to be as still and small as possible. They could never quite do it, even in her imagination. Despite all their exercising and calorie-counting and stiff-sitting and not-eating, Nyela was rounder than Ma-Mère, and Malaya, at age eight, was the biggest of all. But there they were, three not-ladies holding hands, each one trying harder than the last. And as bad as it was to fail at Ladyness, to stop trying was unthinkable.

This summer, Malaya thought of Daundre and the freeze-tag humiliation, and she vowed at least to try. When she did a good job, Ma-Mère poured praise on her like rain. Whenever she left food on her plate after dinner or didn't finish all of the tuna and saltines Ma-Mère set out for lunch, Ma-Mère looked down at her as though her face was a sunrise and said, "I'm proud of you, My Ly-Ly." Malaya felt her skin glow all over, which propelled her to try even harder. She worked her way through the breathless exercise tapes, the mealy breakfasts, the slow Philadelphia days. Eventually, a few weeks into summer, Ma-Mère pinched her thighs, wiggled her flesh, and said, "Ham hocks getting loose, My Ly-Ly. That means the meat's getting ready to slide off. Soon you'll be lean as a light pole and pretty as Beverly Johnson!" Malaya had no idea who Beverly Johnson was, but she felt her future blooming in Ma-Mère's face.

These victories early in the summer heartened her, and she declared it privately in her mind: this year, Ladyness would stick. She would remember the Meeting ladies' guiding principle: *Nothing Tastes as Good as Being Thin Feels!* She imagined her new self emerging, narrow and sandy-skinned on the first day of class in September. She saw herself popping into the classroom with a bright smile, her hair in a frothy updo like Lisa Turtle from *Saved by the Bell*, chirping a carefree "Hey, guys!" before sliding in at the lunchroom table next to Amandra Wilson and her cool, skinny friends. *Nothing Tastes as Good as Being Thin Feels!* Through each bland breakfast, each grim lunch, each juiceless dinner, through Ma-Mère's appointments, the evening game shows, and the nightly news, she reminded herself to *Prioritize the Program!*, to tap into her *Well of Willpower!* and give herself over only to *Food-Free Fun!*

For the first full week, she didn't sneak into the kitchen at night even once. Instead, she looked for *Food-Free Fun!* in the Crypt-o-Quote, and in Ma-Mère's stories, which were like Crypt-o-Quotes come to life. Some of Ma-Mère's sayings made sense to Malaya and others didn't, but all of them made her mind dance with possibility. When Malaya told Ma-Mère that Percy had been working late a lot recently, Ma-Mère said he was giving her mother a warning, "like a cow sitting down before rain." And when they missed the Olney Avenue bus one day because Malaya couldn't find a pair of shorts that fit, Ma-Mère pulled her to the bus stop pay phone and said, "If I wanted to sit my own life out for a child that couldn't dress, I woulda stayed married to your grandfather!" Then she plopped in a quarter to call a taxi.

Ma-Mère sprinkled sayings like these into long, detailed stories as they bused around the city. She was a busy woman. She had taken up college classes in African American studies after her retirement from the Philadelphia city clerk's office, and spent her spare time on an array of impressive activities: going on cruises with her retired ladies' travel group, working part-time as a tour guide at the new African American History Museum downtown, serving on North Philadelphia's community garden council, and volunteering at the local community center, where she read books to the blind.

As they moved through the warm hum of the city's summer air, Ma-Mère talked about the trips she had taken with the Senior Sunbirds to exotic places like St. Lucia and Las Vegas, where, she said, "they got enough lights to put the sun out of business." She talked about the women in the Silver Sparrows Bowling League, about their hair and their husbands, who, Ma-Mère said, were "round as bowling balls and dumber than the pins." She talked about the classes she was taking at the local community college, courses in American Sign Language and braille because, as she put it, "The sighted don't half hardly see, and the hearing don't listen anyway. Better off talking with folks that have real sense."

Malaya liked learning about Ma-Mère's life. It struck her as big and surprising. Nyela often said Ma-Mère had become a different person after getting divorced, around the time Nyela graduated college. She said this with a doleful sigh, as though this new flare for unpredictability was a symptom of great loss. But listening to Ma-Mère's stories now, Malaya decided privately that if this was what being alone could turn a woman into, it might not be that bad after all.

ONE DAY, Ma-Mère brought Malaya on an interminable visit to the bank, where she said she had to take care of some business. She had received an envelope in the mail the day before, and after going through its contents she sat silently, staring the paper down as though it had tried to fight her. "It's about three years late and three fortunes short," she said as they boarded the C bus downtown. "Some insurance. All this ensures is that he wasn't worth a damn. But it'll have to do." She said nothing else. Instead she gripped her green leather purse tight in her muscly hand and stared straight ahead for the whole bus ride. At the bank, she pulled an envelope from the purse and removed a piece of paper. She signed the paper, took a few bills from the teller, and they turned around and left.

After the visit, they went to Woolworth's, where Ma-Mère spent thirty-seven dollars on four bright blue marble-printed vases the size of Malaya's torso and so many bundles of silk flowers they had to take a taxi home. As Ma-Mère stood at the kitchen table arranging the shimmery blooms, she shocked Malaya by saying: "Your grandfather would spit if he could see this."

Ma-Mère rarely talked about Poppa. What little Malaya knew about him she had learned from Nyela. Malaya knew that Poppa was an alcoholic, which meant that when they went to visit him when Malaya was younger, he carried an iced tea bottle that smelled like sugar and gasoline everywhere he went. Poppa had died two years before the move, but until then Malaya knew him as a warm man, who loved fishing and always laughed when Malaya read to him from the joke books Nyela bought her in the train station, no matter how ridiculous the jokes were. And yet, Nyela told stories about hiding in her room when he came home drunk on Sunday nights and beat Ma-Mère into Monday morning. Once, she told a story about a time when she had to call the police because he was beating Ma-Mère so badly she worried her face would be too bruised to go to work that week. In the story, Nyela was eight— Malaya's age now—and Malaya spent a lot of time trying to imagine what it would be like to watch one's mother fight for her life. She wondered whether she would know who to call and what to do, which bruises said *hide* and which said *call the police*. And if she did know all that, she wondered, what kind of girl would that make her?

Malaya couldn't imagine anyone saying so much as a mean word to Ma-Mère now. Watching her this summer, it occurred to Malaya that this was one of the mysteries of adulthood, the strange narratives that seemed to hide behind almost everything, puffing life's countless parts up with meaning—good and bad—that lay just beyond her reach. If it hadn't been for the slim gold rings Ma-Mère still wore on her left hand, Malaya would have thought she and Poppa were two different planets entirely, opposite entities whose orbits could never meet. Yet now, an image came together, and it fascinated her.

Ma-Mère shook a bundle of huge red flowers shaped like snowballs and placed them in the towering bouquets four at a time, among thickets of deep purple tulips closed tight like fists.

"This much money spent on me and some flowers. He would just spit," she said again. She clenched the plastic in her hand and stepped back to survey the brimming vases. "And you know what?" she said, her eyes clear as she stared into the swirling silk. "I wish he would."

ONE MORNING in early July, the VHS tape stopped abruptly during their morning exercise, just as the little kazoo man declared, "It's my party, I'll burn fat if I want to!" freezing him mid-leap at the center of the screen. Instead of finishing the exercise session with an endless run of leg lifts, Ma-Mère surprised Malaya by turning off the VCR and telling her to shower.

"We're going shopping," she said simply. "Even oversized parcels deserve nice wrapping once in a while. Let's get us some dresses."

She announced they were going the Strawbridge & Clothier, the large department store downtown where Nyela had worked as a teenager. This was also where she'd been working the summer she and Percy fell in love. Ma-Mère began to tell the story as they walked toward the bus stop. Malaya craned her neck to watch Ma-Mère's face.

"You might not know it now, but those two loved each other something fierce." She stood tall and straight at the bus stop, fishing tokens from her slick crocodile handbag. People shuffled in and out of Anita's Unisex Salon on the corner behind them, and the warm smell of perfume and hot-combed hair wafted out to Cumberland Street each time the door opened.

"When they were in college, they were close as green and grass. You couldn't keep them apart. Believe me, I tried." Ma-Mère peered out onto the avenue looking for the bus. "Your father was from what white people like to call 'the wrong side of the tracks.' Except wasn't any tracks to speak of between here and Harlem, where his people are from. My mother—your great-grandmother—used to say there's two kinds of black folks: the Negroes and the niggas. Now we'd say 'African Americans,' I suppose, but the idea is the same. There's those of us who know how to be, and those who either don't know or don't care. I tried to raise your mother on the right side of that line. Your father's people were different, far as I was concerned."

Malaya listened, scandalized and delighted. When the bus screeched toward them, she heaved up the three steep steps behind Ma-Mère and followed her to the narrow two-seater in the middle, eager for the story to continue.

"I always worried about your mother finding a decent man to marry. She was a heavy girl all her life—not big as you, but heavy," Ma-Mère said once they slid into the seat. "I tried everything to make her stop eating, all the diets and gadgets and reducing plans, but I couldn't. She kept on going, eating like her life depended on it. I don't know why the girl couldn't stop." Malaya pushed herself against the window, the glass cool on her skin as she tried to keep her thighs from touching Ma-Mère's.

"You can't turn a freighter into a Ferrari, but you can at least keep the chassis neat. I raised her to know that. Women like us, if we can't figure out how to stop eating, we have to at least know how to be. So when your mother called me from her dormitory in her first semester to say she'd met a boy from the projects in Harlem, I like to choke on my own tongue. You'll see when you're a mother: the last thing you want is to find your daughter wasted on a useless man. That's what I thought when she told me about some Percy Clondon. A poet, going by the name of 'Pra.' I thought to myself, *What the hell is a Pra?* Sounds like a word someone started and didn't bother to finish. Only black poet people talk about is Langston Hughes, and half these fools out here don't even know about *him*. What kind of mark is a poet named Pra supposed to make on the world?"

Ma-Mère leaned over and lifted her purse onto her lap. Her perfume smelled like a forest. It tickled Malaya's nostrils.

"But Pra Clondon sure did prove me wrong." Ma-Mère's voice warmed suddenly. "When your mother came home that summer, he wrote her a four-page letter every week and called her up every evening. Called so much I thought Alexander Graham Bell himself would have to get up out the grave and cut the telephone wire to make him stop. But every time Percy Clondon called, your mother's face lit up like Christmas. She spent that whole summer walking around just smiling. Like she hit the winning number. Like she *was* the winning number. I'd never seen anything like it before, not a day in her life or mine."

Ma-Mère looked down at Malaya and smiled, her eyes spreading open like the pages of a book. This was the best of Ma-Mère's smiles. Malaya imagined this unfamiliar version of her parents as she listened, eager for more.

"Your mother was working at the Strawbridge and Clothier that summer, ringing up the fat ladies in the Full Figure department. Everybody loved her there, always said she was so polite and so sweet. I was proud of that. The women at church and the white ladies at work, all of them went out their way to tell me about how lovely my Nathallie was, how poised. They talked about her pretty eyes, too, how shiny they were, even though they were black. The manager at the Strawbridge was a miserable old white man with a rabbit face, and sometimes he got on her case 'cause she spent so much time talking to the customers about their lives and so on, to the point where her line wrapped halfway around the store. He even threatened to fire her, the dumb old donkey. It was just his foolishness, mind you. The customers never complained. They were there to see her. That's how much they loved her." Ma-Mère fished into her bag and pulled out a stick of sugarless gum, then handed one to Malaya. Malaya chewed gratefully, letting the sweet juice well in her mouth.

"Well, one day she comes home from work just beaming. She tells me she won't have those problems with Manager Rabbit Face again because this Pra Clondon came down on the bus from New York City in his good business suit and surprised her at work. Says he marched right up to Mr. Rabbit Face, shook his hand, and gave him a full-out business presentation on retail sales and customer retention, right there between the racks. Had charts and statistics and everything. And I don't know if it was the presentation or just the sight of this chubby black girl and her skinny black boyfriend loving her so hard that tickled Rabbit Face's heart back to pumping. Whatever it was, your mother tells me the old white man laughed and shook this Pra Clondon's hand again, then got on the speaker and moved a girl from housewares to Full Figure with your mother so she would have some backup. He even made Nathallie Salesgirl of the Week. I started to see this Pra wasn't hopeless, he was just on the way. Self-made. That's when I stopped thinking of Pra Clondon as a nigga and started seeing him as a man."

Malaya breathed out and let her thighs spill against Ma-Mère's now. She leaned back in the seat and imagined the story whirling to life in front of her, Ma-Mère's words buzzing around her like fireflies: *boyfriend, winning number, self-made man*. She knew *nigga* was a bad word, but it seemed to mean different things each time she heard it, which made her like it, too. Most of all, she liked the idea of her father taking a bus from Harlem all the way to Philadelphia just to surprise her mother, the sight of him giving her a summer's worth of smiles. She imagined the scene in bright, sparkling color: Percy waiting for Nyela to leave work and the two of them walking through these same streets, holding hands, eating blue and red water ices, gliding through the steamy rush of Market Street until it was time for his bus back home.

"They went on like that for years," Ma-Mère said when they reached the Broad Street transfer stop. "Longer than most." She pulled a small square of paper from her bag and folded her gum neatly into it, then slid another piece quickly into her mouth.

"I know they're not like that now. If you asked me what happened between them," she said finally, "I don't know if I could tell you. But of course, nobody asked me." Her voice dropped low now, and she turned to look for the bus. "Your mother and father are both dreamers," she said, her back still turned. "That's what brought them together, and that's what's tearing them down. You'll always have to wake up at some point. And if you not ready for woke-up love, it'll break your heart.

"Your mother would say it was when he lost that bank job," she said as they boarded the second bus. This bus was crowded, and they had to stand. Malaya steadied herself on the handrail. Malaya had heard this story: around the time she was born, Percy was in line to be promoted to electronic data processing manager at the bank where he worked, but had been replaced without warning by a young white programmer whom he had hired and trained. "I'm sure that's part of it," Ma-Mère said, her arm draped neatly from the handrail strap, "but I try to tell her: when a man can't be proud of himself, he looks to the woman. If she's not something to be proud of, she'll pay double for both of them. I learned that the hard way." The bus lurched forward so suddenly Malaya almost lost her balance, but Ma-Mère only swayed as though to music and tightened her grip.

"Your mother don't believe beached whales bloat. She insisted on going to graduate school. And I was proud of her. I was and I am. But she suffered. He started spending money they didn't have on god-knows-who-or-what, and she buried herself in work and food. She had a stack of books in one hand, and a plate and a baby in the other. She put on thirty pounds at least, on top of the baby weight. That's never good news for a marriage." She looked down at Malaya, sliding her gum discreetly into its paper and folding another piece quickly into her mouth. "And of course, your problem doesn't help. We're working on that, though, aren't we, My Ly-Ly?" But she looked away before Malaya could respond.

WHEN THEY REACHED the department store, Ma-Mère pushed past the children's and Missy areas to the ladies' section. There, she picked out three plain dresses that looked to Malaya like the drab, shapeless smocks from shop class at Galton. Then she marched toward the fitting room.

The store attendant was a thin white lady with narrow teeth and wet eyes that reminded Malaya of a stuffed puppy. The woman gave Malaya a dreary smile as she opened the fitting room door. When the stall door closed behind them, Malaya put on each dress, and Ma-Mère leaned over her, pulling, tugging, zipping and unzipping, but nothing fit. Eventually, the attendant called to them in a saccharine voice: "Honey? Our Full Figure women's department is on the second floor. I'm sure they'd be able to help you."

Ma-Mère opened the stall door and frowned at the woman. "That won't be necessary," she said. She handed over a dark green dress that sagged shapelessly on its hanger. "Just bring us this one in the biggest size you've got."

To Malaya, the dress was awful. It was a tarp-ish size-16 ordeal the color of frozen spinach, with a run of pale pink flowers scattered over the neck and the hemline. It was heavy and scratched at Malaya's skin as Ma-Mère pulled it over her body.

"Well," Ma-Mère said, standing back and inspecting her in the mirror, "it won't win you no beauty pageants, My Ly-Ly, but it's the best we're gonna do." She handed the dress to Malaya and they went to the Career Wear section. This section was bright and colorful, filled with skirts, jackets, dresses, and pantsuits printed with tiny geometric patterns, whole worlds of pointed line and detail, ornamented with sleek, perfect trim at their lapels and hems. Ma-Mère strutted along a long rack of sharp-looking dresses and tailored skirt suits, thumbing through them as though they were folders in a filing cabinet, pulling a hanger here and there just far enough to appraise the item on it, wrinkle her face, and push it back into place. Malaya looked down at the dress on her arms, its dismal spattering of spring. Something lurched inside her, urged her to move.

Malaya excused herself, saying she needed to use the bathroom. She walked toward the corner of the store, where LADIES ROOM was printed in flowery pale pink letters. When she got to the escalator, she looked over her shoulder quickly and stepped on. She climbed the moving stairs as fast as she could to the second floor, where the escalator left her right in the mouth of the Full Figure section.

The dress was still draped heavy on her forearm, scratching her skin as she walked through the aisles holding her breath, past reams of drab, boxy skirts and rows of pants in dull grays and exhausted blues. In the Plus Lingerie section, large cone-like bras and girdles the color of Band-Aids protruded from the walls, and toward the back, where the registers stood, there were racks of coats that looked like parachutes and a row of T-shirts decorated with hideous glittery pictures of pastel cats.

Two large women with heaps of clothes piled on their arms looked in her direction and seemed to frown at her as she passed, but they said nothing. Malaya felt an embarrassment she couldn't name, but she kept walking, taking in the Full Figure section, wondering what it meant to belong there.

When she saw the register, she let the green dress slip to the floor and stared. She imagined Nyela standing behind the counter, her hair in a big, luminous Afro, her young face smiling and sparking while fat women lined up and waited for whole afternoons just to talk to her. She imagined Percy floating up on the escalator just as she had, gliding toward her mother, then standing up for her, putting the rabbit-faced man in his place.

She gazed at the register, wondering if she could smell her mother's perfume or hear the tinkling of her bracelets there if she got close enough.

"Do you need help, honey?" The wet-eyed woman from downstairs appeared beside her. She rested a cool, clammy hand lightly on Malaya's shoulder. The touch chilled her skin, and she wanted to wriggle loose, but that would have been impolite. She looked up.

"No," she said. "I mean, no thank you. I have to use the ladies' room. Can you hold this?" She picked up the dress and handed it to the woman, who smiled, her face breaking into an atlas of pink wrinkles. "Sure, honey," she said. "I'll be right here."

Free of the dress, Malaya moved through the aisles faster now, imagining Nyela there, presiding over the Full Figure section like a king. In the bathroom, she stood in front of the mirror and imagined her mother standing there too, smiling, fixing her makeup and smoothing her dress down while Percy waited eagerly for her outside.

When Malaya was done, she went straight to the escalator, leaving the horrible dress with the dog-eyed lady. She took the steps even quicker now, planning the lies she would tell about where she'd been. But heading down the escalator, she was blocked by the two women from the Plus Lingerie section, who stood one behind the other, each taking up the full breadth of the escalator stairs. "Oh, this is it!" one woman said loudly. "This is what I'll be wearing to tea with Princess Diana!" She held up a sweatshirt that featured a glittery pastel cat and held it to her chest. "You mean it's not haute couture?" The other gasped exaggeratedly and brought a bright red manicured hand to her chest. They were still frowning, but now Malaya could see that they were laughing too. "Dahling!" The second woman held out a garish T-shirt stamped with a winking unicorn. "Oh, love," she giggled, "it's *fashion*!"

Now, up close, Malaya saw that both women had long, fluffy eyelashes like peacock feathers, and both wore hot pink lipstick on their lips. "It's fucking awful!" the taller woman said, poking the other's fleshy side and pointing at a blue and gray dress that looked like a tablecloth as the escalator descended. The meat of her bare arm waved as she pointed. "Who on earth would wear that?!" she laughed. The other woman rolled her eyes and slung her head back dramatically so her double chins showed. She wrapped a huge taupe sweater around her neck as though it were a shawl. "Fucking horrendous!" she said, flipping the sweater dramatically. She poked her friend back and the two of them laughed again, bouncing on the escalator stairs as though the store belonged to them.

The dog-eyed attendant stood at the bottom of the escalator, hovering beside Ma-Mère, who frowned, the green dress draped over her arm. Malaya began to tell her lie, but Ma-Mère hushed her.

"Come on, My Ly-Ly," Ma-Mère said. She grimaced at the two laughing women as they passed, but they didn't seem to notice. She thanked the attendant and pushed toward the main register. "Time don't wait for no one but the tax man. I have to get dinner on. And we still have to finish our exercise."

THAT NIGHT, after the sweating, and the game shows, and the evening news, after Ma-Mère hung up the awful green dress and made a dinner of roasted skinless chicken and slimy okra, after Ma-Mère sat on the chase lounge and Malaya sat on the floor and they did the Crypt-o-Quote together while eating sugar-free lime Jell-O for dessert, Malaya thought of Ma-Mère's story. She replayed it in her mind—about how Ma-Mère thought Pra Clondon was one kind of man and discovered he was another. About defeating the rabbit-faced manager. About Nyela and Percy before their big jobs and their big house and their big child. About Nyela and Percy in love.

When Ma-Mère went up to bed, instructing Malaya not to "eat us out of home and headquarters while I sleep," Malaya nodded. Then she went to the kitchen and dug out the leftover chicken and a jar of fat-free mayonnaise.

Standing in the light of the refrigerator, she tore off hunks of chicken and dipped them into the yellowish-white cream, then chewed quietly. She ate until she had almost forgotten the look of the green dress, the chill of the store attendant's hand on her shoulder. She tried to forget the end of Ma-Mère's story, but she couldn't. Even when the food was nearly finished, she couldn't shake loose the question Ma-Mère had asked: *Why did the girl keep eating?*

When the chicken was gone and all that remained in the jar were a few streaks of white along the glass, Malaya went back to the chase lounge. She stretched out, letting her weight rest on the cushion. She opened her arms wide and propped her feet on the cover's hard plastic rim. It felt good, like freedom, like rest.

After a while, she picked up the scraps from the Bored Bag and fished out the day's Crypt-o-Quote:

A THING IS MIGHTY BIG WHEN TIME AND DISTANCE CANNOT SHRINK IT.

It was a quote by Zora Neale Hurston, whom both Nyela and Ma-Mère liked. Malaya liked the words. As with the best Crypt-o-Quotes, the message was a mouthful of meaning, and it changed each time she read it. At first it had seemed ominous, but now she looked at it differently.

She wondered for the first time if there could be something good about bigness, something mighty about not shrinking, after all. As the newsprint ink went shiny with grease under her fingers, the words comforted her. She read them again and again, first in her mind, then aloud, slowly, wondering if Ma-Mère could hear.

Theories of Class

As THE SUMMER THINNED AWAY and the fourth grade began, Malaya put herself to studying the ways of women: how they dressed, how loudly they laughed, what and how they ate. She studied the women around her, thin women glowering on sitcoms and grinning on toothpaste commercials, thick women shopping at the bodega in satin bonnets and scaling the streets of Harlem like they owned the world. Of course, the woman who blazed her curiosity most fervently was her mother.

Nyela's goal dresses hung faithfully on the curtain rod when Malaya returned to Harlem in August, and they stayed there into September. Every morning, Percy heaved the dresses off the rod and hung them on the banister before turning on the shower. One day, as she got ready for school, Malaya heard him downstairs saying: "You know you're never gonna wear these things. This whole huge house and the only place for your delusions is right here, in everybody's way?"

"I'm trying to lose weight," Nyela responded. "You know that. You don't have to insult me!"

They were still fighting when Malaya finished dressing and went down to the foyer, ready to walk to the bus stop. She zipped up her jacket and sat on the piano bench, waiting. As the argument got louder, she thought about what Uncle Book had said about her parents staying together for the child's sake. He had said it with a glassy admiration, as though it was evidence of a rare, noble quality in them both. But as she listened to them fighting now, Malaya could not help but feel this meant the blame fell to her. She pulled out her Walkman and her sketch pad and began to draw figures of women in all sizes, awash in color. She thought of the two fat women at the department store, poking each other and giggling, not a husband in sight, and it almost helped her forget.

MALAYA ENJOYED a good mystery. It wasn't the triumph of solving that compelled her. It was the sifting through—the discovering of new layers and textures, unthought-of twists and turns that thrilled her. One of the greatest mysteries in her life was her mother.

To Malaya, Nyela was like a good word, her meanings changing wildly depending on time and place. On Saturdays at the Meeting, she was prim and confident with a commanding air that seemed to set her apart from all the other women. But at home during arguments with Percy, she seemed small and vulnerable, like something just born. Sometimes she showed other faces entirely, surprising ones Malaya had no words for. Before the move to Harlem, the family often spent Saturday evenings at the South Street Seaport. They would walk down the dock in the salty gray air, her parents glancing in store windows while Malaya chased pigeons in the breeze. The seaport was host to a small indoor market that always smelled like rich ground coffee and fresh fish. The market was a softly lit cavern of stalls crowded with dried fruits, hanging meats, and gourmet spreads and jellies in hand-sealed jars. Near the entrance was a shop that sold coffee in exciting flavors like "Decadent Mocha" and "Sinful Cinnamon Swirl." It disappointed Malaya that these phrases referred to coffee and not dessert. Still, each time the family went to the seaport, she breathed the smells in deeply until they filled her, and let them transport her far away.

But even better than the smells was the way Nyela's face transformed when the family entered the shop. In her day-to-day, Nyela looked tightly wound, her back pinched forward and her neck tucked into her shoulders as though she was always about to flinch. But at the seaport, she unfurled. She would drift up and down the narrow aisles between the burlap sacks of coffee beans, lifting scoops of shiny brown gems to her face and breathing in, her eyes brightening, then closing in placid delight. Percy liked the seaport, too, especially a store called the Fullest Mind. It was a toy store for grown-ups, where they sold fancy high-tech gadgets, like office chairs that played music and massaged your back, and robotic car dashboard consoles that made missile and torpedo sounds when pressed in a fit of road rage. Percy loved these gadgets, and he would often spend nearly an hour in the store, pulling levers and pressing buttons while Nyela stood in the doorway looking distant and bored. Malaya liked the Fullest Mind, too. Its walls were covered with mysterious double-imaged posters that changed shape when you stared at them: a flock of birds transformed into a face; a chain of sketched hands held pencils that, as you watched, turned out to be sketching themselves. "It's brain magic!" Percy said when he noticed her staring at the posters once. He came up beside her and nudged her closer to the image. Then he touched her temple, his fingers falling gently on her braids. "You think it's the poster, but it's actually the magic of your own brain."

Her favorite poster was a huge gust of triangle and diamond shapes that seemed at first to be black and white, but if you stared hard enough, they sprang to life, full of so much color it claimed your breath. This was how Malaya thought of her mother. She was just this kind of mystery.

ONE MONDAY MORNING late in the fall, Malaya woke up with a stomachache. This happened often on Mondays; she usually spent Sunday nights alone in the kitchen eating her second and third dinner while she prepared her lunch for the week and Nyela graded papers downstairs. Then, on Mondays, she often woke up feeling sick. When Nyela called her from the banister that morning, Malaya's stomach was a churning knot of low-fat lunch meat and dread. Galton had a strict policy against children attending school while sick, referencing "the health and well-being of the Galton community" in a lunch-box memo sent home each fall. Percy referred to this policy as "a load of elitist garbage," and Nyela wondered out loud just how few Galton mothers worked a nine-to-five. But the policy gave Malaya an edge on these queasy Mondays, inclin-

ing her parents to accept her complaints of stomach flu, if only to min-
imize the risk of her being expelled. In the end, this was generally a
losing strategy, because in order to give an effective performance she
had to focus on the kernel of pain in her gut with such intensity that she
ended up actually feeling sick, and it sometimes took her the whole day
to return to normal. Before the move to Harlem, she would be brought
downstairs to Grandma Titi's apartment to convalesce and nap under
the tinny chords of the afternoon telenovelas and the dull blare of *The
Price Is Right*. But now, there were no titis or abuelas to welcome her, and
every adult the family knew uptown spent their daytime hours working,
or, in the case of Giselle, at school themselves. This meant that when
Malaya was sick the only option was for her to go to work with one of her
parents. This time, it was her mother.

Walking onto the campus of Drummond University was like walking
into a storybook. The trip there was the same as any trip through the
city. There were homeless people curled and sleeping next to steaming
manholes while briefcased and suited Upper West Siders stepped over
them like cracks in the sidewalk. There was the screeching of the M4
bus as it stopped on 116th Street and the constant rumble of the subway below, the thick perfumes of well-off white ladies clashing with
the salt-smoky gyro smells of Broadway. Yet when she stepped through
doors of Watkins Hall behind Nyela, Malaya felt like a fantasy charac-
ter clearing the threshold into a mystical world where everything was
supremely new and old at once. The walls of the building were high and
heavy with wood, but the bookshelves that lined them boasted a long
span of books whose spines were a dazzle of color, so that she felt she
was inside a kaleidoscope.

The Drummond Psychology Department offices were at the back of
the building, and Nyela's office was the smallest of these, tucked in a
tight corner behind a portrait display of several famous psychologists
who had taught at the university. All of these were pale, grayish men
with wrinkles lining their faces like maps. Just in front of Nyela's office
door was the desk where the department's secretary, Ms. Claire, worked.
Malaya liked Ms. Claire, not only because of the little yellow butter-

scotch candies she always kept on her desk, but also because watching Ms. Claire and Nyela talk was delicious evidence, morsel crumbs of the mysterious woman Nyela was when Malaya was not around.

"Mornin', Professor Clondon," Ms. Claire said as they approached the desk. Ms. Claire was older than Nyela, but she insisted on calling her "Professor Clondon." She said it warmly, as though she saw Nyela as both a younger cousin and a celebrity.

Nyela smiled and the two women chatted about their weekends—about Ms. Claire's husband's knee surgery and the renovations she was doing on her home in Brooklyn. She was a brown woman with a swoop of straight black hair and a smooth, broad forehead that bunched into ripples when she smiled. She smiled often, and sometimes Malaya wondered if it hurt her face to smile so much, but she didn't ask. Instead she slipped beside the desk and fingered the collection of small, colorful trinkets Ms. Claire bought on trips with her church group—a dancing palm tree with WELCOME TO KISSIMMEE! written on its trunk, a grass-skirted woman with ALOHA WAIKIKI printed at her feet. Malaya ran her fingers along the toys and imagined what these places might be like.

When the conversation was done and Nyela disappeared into her office to gather papers for her first class, Ms. Claire leaned over a stack of folders and smiled at Malaya.

"Well, it's always good to see you," she said, handing her a butterscotch. "Not feeling well today?"

Malaya shook her head and took the candy.

"They pushed back the faculty meeting, Professor Clondon," Ms. Claire called out, flipping through the large binder on her desk. "I can stay with Malaya if you need me to."

"Okay. Thank you, Claire," Nyela said, peeking out of the office. "I really appreciate it." She gave Ms. Claire a direct, lingering smile that reminded Malaya of the looks women gave each other on Grandma Titi's telenovelas when one was in trouble or needed help. It was a wordless look that both women held a second longer than they needed to, as though to confirm for each other what they'd said was real.

"You must be proud of your mother," Ms. Claire said when Nyela disappeared back into the office. It was a strange formulation, something

Malaya had never considered. But it didn't seem untrue. "There's not many of us around here, and none like her."

Percy and Nyela often talked about being the only black people at their jobs. Nyela was the only black professor in the department, and the youngest. She had one close friend at Drummond, a white woman in the Art Department named Karen who had wild hair and green eyes that flashed like firecrackers. But in the Psychology Department, it did seem that, beyond Ms. Claire, Nyela was alone. Malaya had only seen a few brief conversations between her mother and her colleagues. They were like transactions at the grocery store: the men would angle their faces toward Nyela and say something that was supposed to be funny, and Nyela would give a stiff laugh that sounded like a bodily function—more cough or hiccup than an expression of joy. Malaya could smell her mother's nervousness. The men would smile politely at Malaya and sometimes pat her head, which made her want to claw their hands, but of course she couldn't. Then the men would vanish down whatever hall they'd come from, tossing some instructions for Ms. Claire over their shoulders as they went. These exchanges added a sour taste to her mother's mystery, and made Malaya want to protect her.

After a few minutes, Nyela said, "Okay, Malaya, I'll be back in an hour," and went to teach her morning class, carrying her briefcase and a large plastic bag. This left Malaya to snoop through her office for clues. She had hoped especially for some evidence of what her mother ate when she was not around. But after half an hour, she found herself thumbing through pictures she had seen before of Ma-Mère, her father, and herself, completely bored and having to use the bathroom.

She crept out of the office and past Ms. Claire, who sat at her desk with the telephone receiver to her ear. Her face was knotted in confusion, but a milky "yes, sure, right" came from her mouth as she nodded and rolled her eyes. Malaya peered over the desk and whispered, "I'm going to the restroom!"

Malaya crept down the hallway, peeking into the classroom windows one by one. Soon she heard Nyela's bangles echoing in the long wood-paneled hall. But when she reached her mother's classroom, there was another sound, and it surprised her: laughter. She raised herself up on her tiptoes and stared into the square glass window on the door. A flock of students sat at small wooden desk chairs, leaning forward, their pens and pencils hovering in the air.

In all her visits to the university, Malaya had never seen her mother teach. But now, the sight unfolded wide and magical before her: Nyela stood at the front of the room, tall and straight, a monument come to life. Her face was lit up and her lips moved quickly, as though she had more to say than her mouth could make room for. The students leaned in, nodding their heads and pushing their pens across their notepads while she spoke. Then Nyela laughed, and the students laughed too, loudly, the silent tableau springing suddenly to life and tickling Malaya through the door.

Nyela was her same round self, but now she was brighter, better, her face gone electric with light. One of Malaya's favorite gadgets at the Fullest Mind was a big glass globe that shot volts of yellow and purple and pink when you got close to it, like a crystal ball that told all its fortunes in color. Looking at her mother now, she thought of those globes. The woman before her was different from the stern, quiet mother who sat a seat away at the Weight Watchers meetings, the woman who looked at Percy with pleading eyes, who laughed at her white male colleagues' jokes as though handcuffed, and sucked her stomach in constantly around Ma-Mère. This woman teaching was big and powerful, a wizard commanding the space around her.

When Nyela came back to the office to pick up papers for her second class, Malaya asked if she could come along. Nyela looked surprised, but she agreed. The class was preparing for exams, with review sessions to be held at the end of the week, and so this class meeting would be short. The plastic bag crinkled loudly in her hands as they walked together down the hall. Malaya wondered what was inside.

This classroom was a small, modern-looking space with a large table at its center, surrounded by wide, sleek plastic chairs with no desks attached. Nyela pulled a chair out from the table and pushed it to the back corner for Malaya, helping her arrange her sketch pad and pastels on a spare chair next to her. It was too hot in the room—Percy and Nyela had talked about this before, saying it meant the school had more money than it knew what to do with. Percy called it "project heat," the kind of dry warmth that invaded your lungs and tried to choke you from the inside. Malaya swallowed spit and began to draw candy and windows.

Soon, students filed in, greeting Nyela with "Hi, Professor" and sliding into the chairs. When Nyela introduced Malaya and said she would be joining the class for the day, a couple of students turned and waved at her eagerly. One ponytailed girl cooed as though at a baby duck. But most of the students simply nodded, pulling out stacks of books from their knapsacks and piling them on the table. Malaya eyed the bodega bag.

The course was called "Theories of Race and Class," which struck Malaya as strange, since almost all of the students were white. She couldn't say what a "theory" was, but she had an idea. She knew what "race" was—her parents talked about it frequently. This was another mouthful word with many meanings. When it came up over dinner after work, it brought exasperation, but other times, it was a word that meant responsibility, like at the Harlem Arts Academy, during Kwanzaa, and among her mother's Black Psychologists Association friends. Malaya wasn't sure what "class" meant, only that it was something Ma-Mère seemed to care a lot about. Nyela talked about it, too, though Malaya suspected she wasn't as invested. Either way, a class about "class" seemed redundant.

The bodega bag sat on the table, pert and tantalizing through the first several minutes of class. Finally, after a tedious string of announcements, Nyela reached for the bag. "You all did well on the paper, so I thought we'd celebrate," she said. One by one, Nyela pulled out packages of potato chips, popcorn, cheese puffs, and more, the kind of huge plastic packages with multicolored logos they always passed by at the grocery store. Malaya watched in awe as her mother heaped piles of dusty orange cheese curls and powdery white cheddar popcorn onto paper plates and passed them around the room to the students. She even took a napkin from the pile and kept a few kernels of full-fat popcorn for herself.

When the ponytailed girl passed a napkin full of barbecue chips her way, Malaya eyed her mother and smiled in grateful disbelief. Nyela wasn't even looking at her. Malaya put down her pastels and marveled at this version of her mother who came bearing Forbidden Foods by the armful. Malaya ate the chips carefully, savoring each burst of salty-sweet tang as the class continued, wondering what other surprises this Nyela might offer.

There were two black students in the class, a beefy boy with pinkish-brown skin who sat straight up in his chair at the front of room like a rubber eraser, and a short girl who wore thick, wiry glasses and the sort of boxy gold earrings Harlem girls liked, with shapes that made Malaya think of the talking door handles in her favorite movie, *Labyrinth*. The girl had a haircut like Cousin LaSondra, with a long, sharp bang pointing down over one eye and a spray of hair reaching up over the other side of her face, waving in all directions. She sat at the far side of the table, leaning slightly back in her chair and organizing the stack of books in front of her, while the class ate recklessly, as though she, more than the others, was there for business. Malaya watched her nibble her popcorn with elegant focus, never taking her eyes of Nyela.

"Professor Clondon?" A white boy shaped like a milk carton raised his hand over a faded baseball cap as the snacks circulated. It sounded like a question, but he didn't wait to be called on.

"Something's been bugging me," he said, "and I wonder if you'd be able to address it. All quarter, we've been talking about how race is, you know, a construct? That it's, like, more psychological than biological?" This, too, sounded like a question, but he kept talking.

"So," he continued, "then how do you justify this whole affirmative action thing, for example? Like, how is it okay for . . . you know . . . black people . . . to get more jobs if you're basically trying to say that race is not real?"

The ponytailed girl dropped her napkin suddenly and swooped down to gather the scattered popcorn, knocking her pen and notebook to the floor. The girls around her bent down to help her, their faces and necks flushing pink. The air in the room changed instantly as tension coursed quick and cool through the space. Malaya looked quickly to see if Nyela sensed the panic. But she only stiffened her back and looked at the boy as though he had just asked for the sum of two and two. "What do the readings have to say about this?" she said, her face perfectly relaxed. "Does the argument that it's psychological mean it's not real?"

The boy fingered the brim of his hat and said nothing. Malaya licked the barbecue dust from her fingers and shifted her weight in the chair, waiting for him to respond. A sharp tooth-sucking sound cut into the conversation.

"Schmth! I'm sorry, Professor, but what kind of question is that?" It was a breathy voice from the middle of the room. Malaya looked over to see the girl with the directional hair rolling her eyes.

"I mean, seriously," she continued, looking at the milk carton boy, "have you done *any* of the reading all quarter, or you just here for the popcorn?"

The room erupted in laughter, and even the people sitting next to the boy chuckled, their faces shining dewy pink. He sat up in his chair and darted his eyes around the room. Malaya felt a quick pang of dread, but then she turned to look at Nyela, who glided closer to the girl as though on a cloud and said, simply:

"LaTisha, do you want to point us to some of the readings Nick may have missed?" The girl looked up, smiled at Nyela, and rattled off a list of names with ease. As she spoke, some students nodded and took notes. Others sat, still reddish, the laughter staining their faces.

When the hour was over, the class clapped and the students filed out, some stopping to thank Nyela for a good quarter, to which she gave an radiant smile and said, "Good luck with your exams." Once they had all left, Malaya helped Nyela gather the empty plates and discarded napkins; she eyed the puffy cheese curls and crinkled yellow corn chips, but instead of swiping a few behind Nyela's back, she let them slide with the plates into the trash. She followed her mother back through the halls, which now seemed shorter and not as cold.

The day had been a triumph, as far as Malaya could see. Nyela had defeated the nefarious forces she and Percy fretted and argued over every night: racism, white boys, working life. Malaya, too, had succeeded in learning more about her mother's secret persona, and it was glorious. She expected Nyela to call Percy as soon as they got back to the office and propose that they all go to Copeland's for dinner to celebrate such a fantastic end to the course. But when they passed the portraits of the map-faced men, Nyela simply gave Ms. Claire an exhausted smile and asked her to hold any phone calls. She closed the office door behind

Malaya and, without saying a word, sank down into her desk chair, leaned her head back, and breathed out, deflating like a helium balloon. She gave a sigh as deep as a yawn and leaned back further, closing her eyes and letting her shoes dangle from the balls of her feet. She looked to Malaya like a woman in a painting, her body round and resting while a world of movement played on her face.

After several long breaths, she got up and led Malaya out of the building, across campus for what was sure to be a dismal lunch of tuna salad and Diet Sprite for both of them. But even that didn't matter to Malaya. As they walked, she thought of this new face of her mother, so full of spark she was almost airborne, her words doing dazzling battle from the head of the room. She was big, thick with power, heavy with movement and force. Malaya had never seen her mother this way, and now the thought occurred to her: *What else might a woman turn out to be?*

She let herself feel the weight of her hand wrapped in her mother's as they walked, the color and the shock and the possibility all still there, dancing in the skin.

Hurt It Back

"YOU WANT TO KNOW what to do when something hurts you?"

Giselle stood with her back to Malaya, shaking the water from a colander full of cauliflower under the kitchen skylight. The meat of her back and arms bounced beneath her long synthetic box braids as she washed the vegetables, the burnt ends of the braids catching on her bright red sweater. It was a cool Tuesday in March, and Malaya had been sent home with her mouth full of gauze after losing a molar in art class. Malaya greeted Giselle at the bus stop complaining of soreness where the tooth had been, hoping it would win her ice cream and an outpouring of sympathy. She told the story of the lost tooth with her eyes wide and her jaw in her hands. She had even cried, but Giselle was unmoved.

"You hurt it back," she said.

She switched the faucet off and dried her hands vigorously on the dish towel. Then she turned around and bounced down into a squat, her legs folding like paper clips in her jeans so that her deep brown eyes were level with Malaya's. Unsmiling, she looked her plainly in the face.

"When something hurts you, you hurt it back."

She picked up Malaya's hand, brought her pastel-stained index finger to the place where the tooth had been, and pressed. The pain was deep, and Malaya winced as real tears came to her eyes. But when

Giselle lifted her hand and left Malaya's own finger pressureless on her cheek, Malaya felt an unexpected relief and an immediate desire to feel the pain again. The feeling was exquisite.

"You see," Giselle said, returning to the sink, "your mama and papa not gonna teach you that, but that's the lesson you need. A woman knows—you have to hurt the pain back." Giselle turned the water on again and soon the smell of hot oil sizzled up from the stove.

Malaya sat with her finger on her cheek and added this to her growing stash of clues to womanhood. She observed women assiduously now, not only the ones on the street, but also—especially—the ones close to her. She filled her sketchbook with figures of women, some with curving breasts and hips like cellos, some with tall, straight backs and fiery pink hair, some with inky blue skin and boots that had heels as sharp as icicles. To each woman, she assigned a story. One was a rock star who ate Marshmallow Fluff straight from the tub; another was a glamorous mother who didn't bother to pick her children up from school. Malaya mined the women around her for details and suffused these stories with them, puffing them up with intrigue and life.

Now, pondering this latest lesson, she saw that Giselle was an untapped resource for her investigation of womanly possibility. She was nineteen, with skin the color of pancake syrup and bright red lipstick that made Malaya think of convertible cars. Malaya was never quite sure whether she liked Giselle, or whether Giselle liked her, but the way Giselle spoke made her want to listen. She was born in Haiti, and, along with English and some Latin, she also spoke a delectable blend of West African-inflected French that Ma-Mère called "Cray-ol," a word that brought to Malaya's mind a full color scale of undiscovered syllables. Giselle pronounced her words with r's that softened into w's and soft, lazy g's that sounded more like z's with full bellies, so that "problem" became "pwo-blem," "manage" was "man-azh," and "vegetable" became "ve-zhe-table." Giselle wasn't mean exactly, but she wasn't nice either. She spoke to Malaya in a direct, slightly agitated way, as though she knew several basic matters of great importance, and she couldn't believe Malaya hadn't learned them yet. Giselle had accepted the burden of teaching Malaya herself, and despite the lessons' sting, Malaya suspected she should be grateful.

THE NEXT DAY, the beloved fifth-grade teacher, Mr. Washington, announced he was leaving Galton. He was one of three black teachers at the school and the only black man. Malaya had never spoken to Mr. Washington, but he always smelled like a delicious blend of cedarwood and cake, and she loved the way his puffy brown hair made a halo around his deep forehead, which seemed to glow when he smiled. The fifth-graders all loved Mr. Washington, and so the whole of Galton was in mourning when Malaya went out to the courtyard for recess. The rumor on the school bus was that he was leaving because of discrimination, a vague presence the teachers mentioned during assemblies from time to time, often in connection to global issues like apartheid or the Holocaust. Discrimination was a shark circling ominously outside Galton's walls. Its mention sharpened the sting of Mr. Washington's departure, and added a profound but inarticulable sense of meaning to the students' grief.

Malaya walked out to the courtyard, looking for Rachel Greenstein. In the corner, a group of fifth-graders gathered on a single wooden bench, stacked as though for a class photo, crying. Daundré Harris stood at the center of the pack wearing an oversized Boyz n the Hood sweatshirt, his face slick with tears. Malaya had avoided him as best she could since last year, but something tugged in her now, watching him cry. Without thinking, she walked toward him. She wanted to say something, though she wasn't sure what. She still had a piece of Shaniece's dulce left in her backpack from the bus ride this morning. She let the strap of her backpack slide off her shoulder, ready to open it and offer the candy to Daundré as a comfort. As she got closer, his eyes went sharp.

"What are you staring at?" he shouted. She stopped walking and stood, stunned. "You fat bitch!"

He leaned forward and said it again: "You fat bitch! Fat bitch!"

Malaya felt her breath tighten and her body tense from bone to skin. He was speaking to her—she knew it, and yet she couldn't make sense of it. There was no circle of children taunting her, and no one even laughed, but somehow this struck deeper than the playground teasing. She was there alone, with all the courtyard's eyes on her. It was silent this time, except for those two words. *Fat bitch.* Her muscles said *run*, but that would only make things worse. She could not let them watch her try to run again. So she stood, looking down at her feet, the strap of the backpack dangling from her hand. When she couldn't think of anything else to do, she turned, eyes cast down, and walked back to the bathroom stall, where she ate the dulce, the words still ringing.

On the bus ride home, Shaniece gave her a Laffy Taffy and said Daundré was just upset. "Guys freak out when you see them cry," she said matter-of-factly, balling up the crinkly wrapper. "They think you'll make fun of them." But it baffled Malaya that Daundré would misunderstand her this way. She was usually the one stared at; it was a pain she knew well, and one she would never inflict on someone she liked. It had never even occurred to her that she could do her own staring, or that if she did, anyone would care. She took the candy and chewed it gratefully, but still the words radiated deep beneath her skin. *You fat bitch!*

For the rest of the bus ride, Malaya thought of Giselle's lesson—*hurt the pain back.* This wasn't a missing tooth or a sore elbow, nothing she could pin to a single spot on her body. But still, every time she thought of Daundré's morphing face and the words he had said, something sharp seized her. She wondered if that counted as pain, and, if it did, what it would mean to hurt that kind of pain back.

When Giselle picked her up from the bus stop, Malaya was looking forward to drawing in the peace and comfort of the kitchen as she waited for dinner. But instead, Giselle took her hand and led her toward the CTown grocery store on Broadway. It was time for another diet, Giselle explained, and Nyela had instructed her to prepare a pot of turmeric and cabbage soup, which was to serve as dinner for her and Malaya for the rest of the week. Malaya groaned on hearing this, but Giselle just tightened her grip on Malaya's hand. "Eh, come on. A little ve-zhe-table won't undo you," she said.

The CTown was a tight, dismal box of a store with low gray lights that hummed like tired houseflies, and bundles of wilted produce lining the shelves. It was the only supermarket in this part of Harlem, and whenever they went there, Giselle glided up the aisles frowning imperiously, picking up dull pieces of produce and putting them down with a suck of the teeth: "They call this a tomato? *Mtchhh*."

It was also cold in the CTown, and sometimes there was a mildew smell, but these minor annoyances were eclipsed by the illicit, tantalizing world of Forbidden Foods the store had to offer. While Giselle sauntered through the aisles selecting flavored rice cakes that tasted like Styrofoam dipped in Sweet'N Low, and frowning at the wrinkled plums and graying celery sticks, Malaya explored. Giddily she walked among all the foods she was not allowed to have: colorful boxes of sugar-sweet cereal, tall and towering on their shelves, bright packages of cakes and pies and cookies winking their chocolate chips from beneath their cellophane wrapping. Even the full-fat versions of regular foods like white bread and apple juice were special.

Giselle gave Malaya a strange look and told her to meet her at the cashier. "I have to pick up some feminine things," she said in an awkward half-whisper, before heading to the back of the store. Malaya nodded and went as quickly as she could to her favorite place in the store: aisle 5, the candy aisle. It was a universe of color, filled with great bags of caramel bulls-eyes as big as her torso and bundles of sugary striped Pixy Stix longer than her forearms. There were Mike and Ikes and Good & Plentys and Now and Laters, reams of sugar dots on narrow paper that looked like secret messages spelled out in neon Morse code. Walking down aisle 5, Malaya felt like she was alone in a courtyard tucked deep in a palace of sugar, the shelves stretching endlessly upward like enchanted trees that never bore fruit—only candy.

At the end of the aisle, there was a rack of smaller bags, all off-brand versions of the kinds of candy they sold at the movie theater—chocolate drops covered in white sprinkles like Goobers, colorful suckers hiding chocolate like Tootsie Pops, strips of gummy red coiled together and folded over like Twizzlers. Sometimes, Shaniece had brought these candies on the bus, and Malaya knew that they were always a little stale, a little powdery, nowhere near as good as the real versions. But they were small and cheap—two bags for fifty cents—and every time, Malaya was glad to have them. She had no money, but suddenly, she wanted candy more than anything.

She didn't even want it to eat—not right away. The day had taken something from her. Now she saw what she was to the kids at school: not a girl offering bodega candy, not a person who might be a friend. Not even a fat girl. A fat bitch. It struck her deep in the chest. She wanted the candy now, faster than now, but not to eat it. She wanted to take it, to carry it home and keep it close by, a reminder that something good was waiting for her.

There was no one in sight except for an old woman with a shopping cart at the end of the aisle, pulling a bag of marshmallows from the shelf. Malaya surveyed the rack. If she moved quickly, she could slip a package into her jacket pocket without getting caught. She wondered what kind of woman would do a thing like this. At the front of the grocery store, there was a large wall covered with photos of people who had tried to steal groceries. People of all ages were pictured in the collage of Polaroids, sometimes frowning, sometimes smiling and throwing up peace signs. In each picture, the person was made to hold up the steak or the bottle of bleach that had been their downfall, so that everyone in the neighborhood could see. In one photo, a slim girl with a face like a Benin mask posed, her cheeks sucked in and her head tilted to the side, holding a pack of baby bottles, looking directly at the camera. As if to say, *And what?* Malaya had always been terrified of ending up on this wall of thieves, but now the terror felt different, and having the candy seemed worth the risk.

She inched in toward the edge of the display rack and bulked her body up to hide her arms. Then she leaned down and swiped quickly, grabbing the closest package to her—a bag of chocolate-covered raisins. It wasn't the rack's best offering, but it struck her as a very reasonable choice. It was a Forbidden Food, but not *too* forbidden, which, she decided, made it less of a theft.

"Malaya, you know you can't have these things." Giselle's voice swirled up suddenly from behind her, just as her hand reached her pocket. Fear struck sharp in her stomach. She turned around, hoping the bag wouldn't fall. "I thought I said meet me up front. Is this the register now? The candy rack?"

"No," Malaya said, trying to sound normal. "I just wanted to look."

"Mmm," Giselle said. She looked down at Malaya's hands, which were wiggling aimlessly at her sides. Giselle bent toward her, and Malaya felt as though her heart would freeze on the spot and turn into an ice cube. Suddenly Giselle's shopping basket toppled over and a thick, puffy package fell to the floor.

Giselle let out a high-pitched noise, part gasp, part groan. A man appeared, moving down the aisle toward them. He stooped beside Giselle to help, but she lunged quickly and scooped up the package before he could reach it. "I'm sorry!" she said in an unsteady, saccharine voice. She waved the man away in a stumble of words: "Ha-ha. Oh no. Thank you. Sorry. Sorry!" She looked horrified and helpless, as though she, not Malaya, had been caught in some wrongdoing. Malaya thought of what Shaniece had said about boys freaking out when you happened to see them upset, and she wondered if this was something similar—if "feminine things" meant a shame that could change you. Giselle stuffed the cottony package down in the bottom of the basket, covering it with a bag of limp collard greens.

At the cashier, Malaya stood behind Giselle, still holding the candy tight in her pocket. She watched the bag of pale tomatoes, the parched baby carrots, and the mysterious fluffy package slide their way down the conveyer belt, trying not to look at the wall of thieves.

THAT NIGHT, while Giselle made dinner, Malaya hid her sketch pad and pencils inside her math workbook and drew under the kitchen skylight, waiting for her parents to come home. The skylight was her favorite feature of the brownstone. In the morning, it filled the house's hallways with a flat white haze like out of a movie. But at night, if it was dark enough, like tonight, she could stand under the glass and imagine herself sucked up into another world, a galaxy of blues deep enough to hide her.

Percy liked the skylight, too, and sometimes, if he came home early and in a good mood, he would stand under the glass as though beneath a spotlight and sing to her and Giselle with a soup ladle as his microphone. Malaya could tell this made Giselle uncomfortable, because when he did this, her face tightened up and she folded her lips over her teeth. In the apartment downtown, Malaya had once seen a photo of her parents on their honeymoon in Ghana, smiling behind a plastic table in a candlelit courtyard full of tall, floppy trees. The photo was made to look like they were sitting inside a champagne flute, and Malaya liked this idea—her two parents, surrounded by green, cozied together at the bottom of a glass. When Percy sang under the skylight, Malaya imagined that the photo had come alive, and that her mother was there instead of her, smiling and waving her head to the sound of Percy's voice.

By nine o'clock, her parents still had not come home. Huffing, Giselle gave Malaya her dinner of horrendous soup, which tasted like dirty water. When she finished, Malaya put on her nightgown and installed herself at the kitchen table with her pencils, waiting for the night to end so she could eat her stolen chocolate. She watched Giselle wash dishes, her long coppery braids jumping against her shoulders, their burnt plastic tips digging like claws into her sweater. Normally, while she waited, she would ask Giselle for an extra spoonful of rice and peas or an extra bite of sweet carrot loaf, to which Giselle would suck her teeth over her shoulder and say, "Nevamind that. You won't starve and neither will your parents. I know that for true." Malaya usually snuck a spoonful anyway, when Giselle went to the bathroom. But tonight, with the candy to look forward to, she tapped into her Well of Willpower and refrained.

By nine thirty, a thunderstorm had begun, and water hit the skylight with splashy thuds, then slid in thick sheets down the sides of the glass. Malaya watched water collect in the pot Giselle had set below the crack in the skylight, listening as each droplet hit with a *plink!* She imagined tearing slowly into the chocolates' flimsy plastic, pouring the sweet brown nuggets into her mouth like rain.

"Hi up there." Nyela's bracelets jingled downstairs. "Is Percy home?"

"No," Giselle called back, "not yet. Your dinner still hot, though. Rice and peas, stew meat, for Mr. Clondon, and cabbage stew for you, like you axe for. Malaya had hers already."

A few moments later, Nyela appeared in the kitchen and dropped her briefcase on the table, bending to give Malaya an air kiss.

"I'm sorry I'm so late," she said to Giselle. "We'll finish the dishes. Thanks for staying." She reached into her pocketbook and handed Giselle a few folded bills. "Just for tonight. The rest will come tomorrow. I promise."

Giselle gave a small smile back and dried her hands on the dish towel.

"Bye-bye, Malaya," she said in a voice much nicer than the one she used when Nyela wasn't around. "Don't forget to take the carrot babies we bought for your lunch, eh?" Malaya took a deep inhale of Giselle's perfume as she passed behind her—lemons. Bright yellow. She could almost see them.

When Giselle was gone, Nyela fixed herself a bowl of soup and sat at the table.

"Did your father call?" she asked between spoonfuls.

"Yes," Malaya said. She began to draw a woman shaped like the number 8 in the margin of her multiplication sheet. "He's working late again."

"Okay," Nyela said. "Then I'm going to need you to help me."

She explained that she was giving an important lecture the following day. She was nervous and needed an audience while she practiced. Malaya hated listening to her mother's lectures. It was like the Weight Watchers meetings, but worse, because although Malaya felt confused and lonely in both settings, at the Meetings she could at least hide among the other women. Here, there was no one. And though she didn't understand what was being said, she knew her job was to pretend.

"All you have to do is listen," Nyela said when she finished her soup. "And don't worry about making your lunch for tomorrow. We'll get you something good at the bus stop. Did you stick to your points today?"

"Yes," Malaya lied, but Nyela wasn't listening. Nyela rose and reached into the pot on the stove. She pulled out a heaping spoonful of rice and peas, swallowing it quickly before clearing her soup bowl.

"What time did he call?" she asked. Then, right away: "Never mind. We got this, right? Me and you." She dug in for another spoonful of rice. Malaya nodded.

While Nyela stood at the stove and ate, Malaya crept downstairs, past her parents' room on the second floor, down to the foyer to get the chocolate so she could bring it up to her room when the lecture was done. She tucked the bag between her legs under her nightgown and took the stairs back up to her parents' room carefully, one by one, clenching her thighs to keep the candy from falling.

The lecture was about African American families, Nyela's main research subject. Malaya couldn't discern much beyond that. She settled amid the books and papers at the foot of her parents' bed, careful to press her knees together so the chocolate didn't fall. Nyela sat at the head of the bed. She turned her bracelets nervously and launched into a string of sentences Malaya strained to understand. Occasionally she stopped to explain: " 'Adverse' means unhealthy," " 'Hereditary' means something family members share. You understand, right?" Malaya didn't understand, but she nodded anyway.

Nyela sat straight up in her silky green nightgown surrounded by books and papers, holding a wad of index cards like a black woman Statue of Liberty. As she glanced up and down from the cards, her eyes seemed to flash with light. They were deep brown, wide, and glassy. Sometimes, when Malaya stood in front of her, she could see her own tiny outline, clear as a photograph, across her irises. Percy used to comment on Nyela's eyes. He said they looked like the mosaic tiles that covered the lobby of Harlem Hospital, where he was born, little panes of dark glass glinting color. Everyone agreed Nyela's eyes were beautiful. Ma-Mère said people had talked about them since her childhood. When these conversations arose, Nyela turned her head down, uncomfortable. But Malaya wondered what it was like to be looked at that way, to have eyes on your eyes instead of on your body.

Now, the edges of the candy package dug deep into her thighs, poking so hard she worried they might leave a mark. She locked her calves together and squeezed as she listened, trying to keep the bag from falling, hoping the chocolate would not melt. She tried to pay attention: *addict, chemical, genetic, vice.* By the time Nyela reached the last of her note cards, Malaya's legs burned and her muscles had nearly given up.

"That's it," Nyela said finally. Her face looked tired and small, a shock. "What do you think?"

"It was good." Malaya pushed her palms into the mattress.

"Okay. You finished your homework, right?"

Malaya nodded, another lie.

"Good," Nyela said. She smoothed the nightgown over her stomach and glanced at the clock: 11:15. "Did Daddy say what time he'd be home?"

Malaya shook her head no.

"Well, look how good we did without him," she said, but she didn't seem to believe it. She packed her papers away and looked at Malaya again. "You're a good listener, Malaya. My daughter. My smart, smart girl."

Malaya felt her skin warm. She imagined the words pouring over her, thick and binding, a syrup. The shrill phrases of the day reduced to a hum in her mother's voice: *fat bitch*, *fat bitch*, *feminine things*, all simmering down, receding, sweetening into her mother's words. *My smart girl.* She thought of hands, never pointing or pinching at her body, only lifting to join in applause. Then, immediately, she felt ashamed. She had not really listened to her mother. She had sat and nodded, but she had not understood.

She said good night and squeezed her legs together again, climbing the stairs one by one again. She thought of Giselle's lesson: *hurt the pain back.* Even if the chocolate had melted by the time she got to her room, she decided, even if it was all just mess and goo, she would find a way to eat it.

LATE THAT NIGHT, Malaya lay in bed, chocolate staining her fingers, the sweet raisin mush soft between her teeth. She thought of Giselle and Ma-Mère, each with her grid of ideas about what a woman should be. She thought of Shaniece, who studied the rules of womanhood carefully, and the fat ladies at the Strawbridge & Clothier, who seemed not to notice them at all. She thought of Ms. Adelaide, the Meeting leader, with her sleek, elegant walk, and Mrs. Breeves, the dance teacher, pinching discipline into her flesh. She thought of her mother, who toggled

back and forth between womanhoods in a way that thrilled and frightened her.

A great business of body and heart seemed to join these women, and
only a few questions separated them: Did each understand the rules
of womanhood? Did she try to follow them? How hard did she try, and
what did it cost her?

As she drifted into a sugary sleep, Malaya wondered, with the urgent
clarity of new language, what kind of woman *she* would be.

II

Big Woman

THE SCENTS OF black coconut and African pear oils wafted toward Malaya from the tables that lined the street. As she walked, the smells of fried and jerk chicken, roti and rice pudding, plátanos and candied yams seeped from the storefront restaurants, mixing together like the ingredients of a gumbo. They spilled over Malaya as she moved down block after endless block, veering inward toward the stores to make room for a hurried dreadlocked man in a hoodie, then outward to avoid colliding with a cluster of children giggling in bubble jackets and scarves. She fingered the three purple braids that hung from her left temple and made games for herself as she walked, trying not to imagine what 125th Street thought of her, this double-wide block of black girl, streaked with color, bounding toward the Big and Tall men's section of Harlem Jeans.

The melody of TLC's newest ballad drifted across Eighth Avenue. In the alcove between the Apollo Theater and Tsitsi's African Hair Braiding, a cassette bootlegger pumped Shabba Ranks's deepest reggae bass line onto the street. Malaya could hear these songs blending with laughter, catcalls, arguments over the prices of African masks and homemade soaps. A Black Israelite man stood on the corner of Frederick Douglass, shaking a leather-wrapped arm at passersby as car horns and sirens rang somewhere around 123rd. Children snickered as Malaya pushed through the crowd, and an older man shouted "Whoa!" when she passed him, splaying his arms and making an exaggerated leap backward out of her way.

By 1996, Harlem was louder, its air sharper and more defiant. The changes came first in a trickle, then in a rush. That previous winter, a few idle chain businesses cropped up on St. Nicholas and Amsterdam, a lone Today's Man clothier and a Living Well Lady gym, perched close to the subway lines. Before, the street vendors had gathered on Adam Clayton Powell Jr. Boulevard and lined 125th from Broadway to Lexington, selling African print clothing, homemade soaps, bootleg tapes, and thick, sugary bean pies so good everyone bought them two at a time. But by the middle of this year, they were gone. A city rezoning project swept them up under a dusty tent on 116th with a dingy green and white plastic marquis labeled BETTY SHABAZZ SHOPPING PLAZA. This was widely regarded as an offensive display of city officials' ignorance; everyone knew the First Lady of Black Liberation would never have suffered such inelegance in her name.

The changes were massive, but the soul of Harlem seemed determined to fight. The restaurants and clothing stores that had been decades-long staples now pasted Xeroxed signs on their windows reading SUPPORT BLACK BUSINESS! They held regular events featuring African, Latin American, and Caribbean food, music, and fashion, a full geography of black cultures blaring out onto the streets. At times it seemed the entire neighborhood was lit in bold tones of red, black, and green.

For Malaya, Harlem's indomitable largesse was made all the more delicious by its new soundtrack. The staccato rap beats she once heard bumping from boom boxes outside the brownstone window now seemed to shake hands with the soul drags, funk riffs, and R&B synth sounds Percy loved to play on Saturday mornings. Together, they made a dazzling new confection, hip-hop, that seemed to charge the air with life. In her girlhood, she had had to lean against the window and catch snippets of other generations' music from car radios outside and beg her mother to buy bootleg cassettes to play on her Walkman. But now, at fifteen, she could push through the blocks on her own, her ears warmed by the foam pads of her CD player, listening to a music that seemed to have been made with her in mind.

Her favorite was a song she had discovered two years ago, in the eighth grade, and claimed as her personal anthem, an introduction to her newfound idol and kindred soul:

It was all a dream! I used to read Word Up! *magazine . . .*

The track was an irresistible tale of rags to riches, chronicling the rapper's rise from blinding despair to unfathomable, Technicolor hope. The artist was a big black man from Brooklyn with a lazy eye and a face as soft as chocolate frosting. His body puffed like a pouch of Jiffy Pop beneath his chin, and his voice was always thick and smooth, as though there was a scoop of ice cream perpetually lodged in his throat. Malaya loved the way the man told his success story, how he so prized the vestiges of hard living while casting the present as a gorgeous, unending feast. His album was full of all the things Malaya's mother hated and many of the things her father prized—sex and death and hope and fantasy, all mixed together like a compote, baked into a hard but secretly sweet crust. Malaya loved the paradox of the rapper's moniker—Biggie Smalls—how it was intimidating and diminutive at once, how it said so simply so many of the things she'd been feeling these fifteen years of her life. When Nyela saw the CD, *Ready to Die,* lying among Malaya's Sharpie markers and gel pens, she arched her eyebrows and asked, "So this is the message our artists are sending the youth now?" Percy only shook his head and said the album reflected a new generation's struggle, and that it was their job, as parents, not to understand.

For Malaya, the CD was a sixty-eight-minute eternity in which anger, violence, and all kinds of pain could coexist perfectly with a life of celebration and dream. Despite the album's undeniably morose theme, often behind the lyrics there were up-tempo beats and creamy-toned flute harmonies that struck her as dulcet, even happy. It reminded her of the apartment downtown—the sounds of Percy's Last Poets albums and the eighties children's shows she used to watch, their fray of humanlike puppets bobbing jovially before muted brown and orange backdrops while she sat in the little yellow apartment, awash in the smell of good food and close bodies. From song to song and from line to line, Biggie switched personas, painting himself as a proud father here, a homicidal drug lord there, here a gurgling child.

This mélange of pain and fantasy was hip-hop's hallmark, and the thing that made Malaya want to rise to it every morning. One of her favorite songs to wake up to was "Everyday Struggle." It was a quick-paced rhyme about things entirely alien to Malaya—crack slinging and money laundering and murder plots. The song's hook was "*I don't wanna live no more / Sometimes I hear death knocking at my front door*," but there was a brightness beneath the weight, if you really listened. Something strange and surprising—big and small, brash and vulnerable at once. Sometimes, when she listened to that song on the way to Galton or walking around Harlem, she let her arms unhinge and sway loose and wild, her body expanding across the pavement no matter who was watching. She would nod at neighbors as they passed her, and if they smiled back she would say something, compliment them on their hair color or their shoes. Sometimes she would laugh, quietly to no one, and let the laugh ring in her belly as she returned to the song. Other times, she would simply say whatever came to her: *There's nothing as good as the color blue*, or *One day I'll live a life of only oranges and orange juice*. Nyela would have flushed in embarrassment, and Ma-Mère might have fainted on the spot. But it didn't matter. There was something insistently unexpected in hip-hop, and it entitled Malaya to become unexpected, too. It meant she could be angry and tender, sad and hopeful, a black girl besotted, full of feeling, wearing lipstick and big men's clothes.

She turned up the volume on her Discman, and let the beat cover her as she pushed toward the Big and Tall.

> *How you livin' Biggie Smalls? In mansions and Benzes*
> *Givin' ends to my friends and it feels stupendous . . .*

"BIG WOMAN!" the cherry-colored man at the bag check counter exclaimed as she cleared the threshold. He rounded his arms into a sumo wrestler pose. The acrid stink of new plastic bags smacked forth as Malaya pushed her way into the store.

The man had become an uncomfortable acquaintance by now. He

always looked friendly enough, but he had wet, old eyes that seemed to catch on her body and drag away only full seconds after he spoke. He was short and squat, with a thin scar that curved along the side of his cheek. "I remember you. Do you have a husband?"

"Yes," Malaya said plainly, taking the bag check ticket. "I told you before."

The man acted as though she hadn't spoken. "So big!" he continued. "Healthy! But you have a pretty face. I'll call you 'Big Girl, Pretty Face,'" he concluded. But his eyes raked her stomach.

Each time someone told her, "You have such a pretty face," she felt as though they wanted to sever her head from her body, to discard the meat of her and leave the small round disk of her face as her one saving quality. She was supposed to be grateful for his attention. And in spite of herself, she was. This was what angered her the most—these conversations made her uncomfortable, even sad, but she needed them in a way she couldn't find words for. She imagined her foot uprooted from its plot on the ground, striking the man's cheek way above the counter with a cartoon-style POW! Instead, she smiled politely and said "thank you," and put the ticket in her pocket.

"You give me your phone number when you leave, okay?" The man's voice trailed behind her like a curl of stale smoke.

There were no mannequins in the Big and Tall men's section at the back of the store—only reams of logo-stamped cloth folded two or three times back, elbows pinioned together, hems rolled three times under to gesture at normal, man-sized forms. Malaya pushed past the Paco and Boss and Pelle Pelle racks toward the EMCEE labels, which she'd chosen as her favorite a year ago, when she made the twin discoveries that the brand both spelled out her initials with its logo and carried clothes in her size. When she heard the way Biggie used it in a chart-topping single, she considered it destiny:

> Throw down some ice for the nicest EMCEE . . .
> Niggas know the steelo, unbelievable.

She scanned the racks for a purple EMCEE sweater and a pair of size

50 jeans, imagining herself sitting casually in a room that glinted with color and lights like a Hype Williams video, swaddled in richly dyed denim. She thought giddily about how the cuffs of the jeans would fold into the tongues of her Timberland boots like waves of soft-serve ice cream into waffle cones, how tight and slick the look would make her feel.

As she thumbed through the racks, she imagined wearing these clothes, feeling this way, with RayShawn Carter. RayShawn was one of a handful of black and brown public school kids from Brooklyn, Queens, and the Bronx who had tested into Galton Prep in the seventh grade. The high school was just upstairs in the same Park Avenue building as the elementary, but these new students transformed the space, infusing the school with new language, logic, and fashion, evidence of an expansive world that made the cloistered life downstairs at Galton Elementary seem embarrassingly small. They wore the Jordans and baggy jeans everyone in Harlem wore, and brought the hood idioms of the city to Galton's corridors. When they saw each other between classes, one would call out *Eeeeeeyo!* regardless of who was around, and, without fail, someone else would would respond with a loud and rhythmic *A-a'ight!* from the other end of the hall, often followed by a barrage of Doug E. Fresh lyrics, or whatever song was most popular on HOT 97 that week. On papers and tests, the new kids outperformed most of those who had come from the elementary school, and for the few black and brown kids from the elementary, like Malaya and Shaniece, the new students were a beacon. Thankfully, Shaniece had made friends with the new kids in the seventh grade, and they had absorbed her and Malaya into what they all determined to call "LaFamille." Together, LaFamille talked about music videos and made fun of teachers and shared homework notes. They talked about sex, whatever they knew of it, and about people like Rachel from BET's *Caribbean Rhythms* and the thin, light-skinned singer Aaliyah, who everyone agreed was the height of beauty.

RayShawn Carter was LaFamille's patriarch and self-appointed prince. He was light and tall and seemed to have pulsed on the verge of manhood all his life. He was a year ahead of Malaya and Shaniece, with a broad, self-assured smile and a thick black sponge of hair that changed shape in perfect rhythm with music video fashion. When

Shabba Ranks's "Mr. Loverman" came out on HOT97, RayShawn boxed and faded his cloud of kinks into a sharp Gumby, just like Shabba. Then he grew it out and relaxed it into an S-curl when the pretty-boy Bill Bellamy became the face of *MTV Jams* later that year, and braided it into neat, long cornrows in time for "Nuthin' but a G Thang" and the *Doggystyle* album after that. When Malaya ventured a comment about his hair after Spanish lit one afternoon, RayShawn raised his chin at her and gave her a wink just this side of silly. "The question is," he said, "can the videos keep up with *me*?" Then he swept over his arrogance with a self-effacing laugh and returned to his lab report for AP bio. By now, he had started work on a crop of dreadlocks, little finger-widths of knotted hair screaming up from his scalp just like Busta Rhymes's. She imagined them together, the two sprawled over each other, he in his hip-hop high fashion and she in hers, a perfect curve at her chest and hips the only meaningful difference between them. Malaya had managed to craft a friendship with him over the past year, though she would never have admitted he was the reason for her trip to the Big and Tall today.

As she hovered by the banks of oversized denim at the back of the store, a slim saleswoman with skin the color of Ritz crackers approached. Her eyes were warm at first, but when Malaya asked for what she wanted, the woman looked at her as though she had requested a side of crème fraîche with her McDonald's Extra Value Meal.

"Um, they don't make big men's shirts in purple," she said, running a green acrylic-tipped nail over her hairline. "And the biggest jeans we got is a forty-eight."

The woman handed her the 48s and suggested she try on a dingy velour sweater that reminded her of tile grout. Malaya hadn't been weighed in years, but she knew she was at least three hundred pounds, because the last time she went to one of the many specialists Nyela had found for her, in the seventh grade, their scale stopped at three hundred when she stepped on and would go no further. She had willed herself not to feel defeated, bathing herself in the music she loved, braiding colors into her hair and matching them to her fashion to satisfy her own desire and whim. She had gone up in big men's sizes, from a 42 to a 46 to a 48. Now fear rooted heavy in her chest as she wondered if she'd finally outgrown even the big men's sizes. Malaya accepted the clothes, and the salesgirl gave a shallow sigh behind her as she walked toward the fitting room.

She squeezed herself through the fitting room doors. The walls were covered with graffiti tags, lewd drawings, beeper numbers, and fragmented rhymes. She slid her headphones off and examined the walls, reading limericks about girls named Chyna, looking at cartoon sketches of men with bulbous stomachs and sagging chests, learning which women the customers of Harlem Jeans thought were good for which kinds of sex.

She unlatched the button on her jeans and felt her stomach sigh into place. There was a strip of flesh around her middle that had been raked raw over the years by the constant rub of too-tight denim, and now she felt the skinless strip sting. She rubbed her fingers on her jeans and touched the raw patch, dabbing it dry with the back of her hand, wincing at the sting of contact. She pulled the 48s up, past her thighs and her hips, past her pillowy middle, the raw skin seething. She sucked in and tried to push the ends of the denim together, but they would not meet. She gulped breath, sucked in, tugged again, seethed again, over and over until water clung to her eyelashes and her face got hot. *The biggest jeans we got is a forty-eight.*

She fished a Sharpie from the pocket of her jacket and uncapped it, the sour smell boring into her nostrils. She angled herself against the wall and drew her tag—a sprawling letter *M*, blitzed with stars and topped with a crown cocked boldly to the side. She stood there for a while, her ink wet on the walls and her eyes stinging with heat as the salesgirl sighed again impatiently on the other side of the door.

"You good, ma'am?"

"Yeah," she said, "I'm okay."

She breathed in and tugged at the denim again. If the jeans would not give, she wished that they would take and take, until her body really became a separate thing from her smile, something she could leave there on the fitting room floor while she floated, above the clothes, above the noise, above the expectant whine of the salesgirl, away. She tried again, six times, until she couldn't take the pain around her middle anymore. Then she breathed in and let the denim fall, wishing she could suck up her skin, her fat, her muscle, and whatever it was that lay underneath those things, making her who she was: this person in this body, wedged between the too-tight walls of the Big and Tall men's section, wishing more than anything to feel small, and slight, and, somehow, like a girl.

"Big Woman!" the man said again as she slid her bag check ticket onto the counter. "You sure you have a husband?"

She stood there silently, trying to remember how to pretend. She tried to clear her eyes and brighten her face, to tilt her head and give the slight shrug someone small and carefree—a video dancer, maybe—might give.

The man introduced himself as Clarence Edgar. "I love big women," he told her, peering down at her belly from the bag check booth. "Nothing better than that. So what is your name?"

"Alya," she said.

"Oh," the man smiled. "Like the singer?"

"No," Malaya said. "Like that, but smaller. Al-ya."

"Al-yuh," he repeated. "Okay."

When he handed her a scrap of paper and asked for her number, Malaya planned to write a random spattering of digits, but she found herself writing her beeper number instead.

"Alya. Big Woman, Pretty Face," he said, his smile broadening. "You come to my house to eat. I'll treat you good, okay? Don't worry."

Malaya felt herself nod, heard herself agree.

That Monday, she slid her headphones over her braids and pushed up Park Avenue, through the heavy doors of Galton. The smell of the school rushed forward—aging metal and industrial cleaner, teenage bodies and sweat. It was lunchtime, and classes of elementary students streamed busily down the stairs to the basement exit and out toward the courtyard, their lunch boxes clacking behind them. A little girl with green marker on her face stopped walking and looked at Malaya as children often did, her eyes slowly climbing her body—the boots, the baggy jeans, the wide, billowing middle. As the girl looked up, her mouth opened and narrowed slowly as though she were saying "wow," but no sound came out. Then she turned to the child next to her and said, "She's fat!" The cruelty of children was commonplace for Malaya and she hated it. She had almost come to hate children in general, though when she thought of their absolute subjection to the rules and whims of adults, she felt sympathy. Soon the teacher, a new red-haired woman she didn't recognize, said, "Come on, Molly, let's all go play!" She flashed Malaya a brief apologetic look, her eyes narrowing in the corners. The girl scratched her cheek and the procession of children continued. Malaya stood at the bottom of the staircase, waiting for them to pass. She mouthed the lyrics to "Everyday Struggle," glad to be in her music.

When the children were gone, she took a breath and gripped the railing. She had skipped her morning classes, a habit she developed at the beginning of the year, when the grip of too-tight clothes and the threat of eyes on her body began to make mornings even tougher than usual. Today, she had gotten to school in time to hang out behind the auditorium listening to music with LaFamille before fifth period began. In the elementary days, Galton had been as bland as a pot of week-old grits left on the stove. But hip-hop brought its butter, smuggled in by LaFamille and the other new kids who enrolled in seventh grade. It was then that Rachel Greenstein begun to hang out with Randall Creighton, both of them dying their hair yellow-cake blond and falling in love with Jack Kerouac and Nirvana. That year, Ben Heath had had a growth spurt, pierced his tongue, and begun going out with a freckled girl named Mandy Prince, whom the halls of Galton dubbed "Chunky Mandy" to distinguish her from the three other Mandys in the grade, two of whom were her best friends.

Malaya heaved up the steps. She always chose the back stairwell because it was used mostly by the elementary school, which meant fewer of the people who mattered would see her struggle up the stairs. Still, a classmate jogged past her saying, "Hey, Malaya! We missed you in bio today." Malaya took a suck of breath and said something brief but, she hoped, friendly: "Hey! Thanks! I know!" She tried to smile as she pushed up the stairs and past the hallway where most of the other tenth-graders gathered, toward the backstage hallway behind the auditorium, which LaFamille had claimed as their territory.

"*Kaboom!* Guess who stepped in the room!" Eric Martinez called as she turned the corner toward the auditorium's backstage entrance. He was a round-cheeked and magnanimous science nerd from the Lower East Side, with short, sandy hair and a spattering of freckles. "MC Malaya Spits-the-Hot-Fiya!" He clicked his mechanical pencil and stuffed it into the pocket of his Karl Kani jeans, leaping from the stairs to give her dap and a hug.

"I didn't think we were gonna see you, Malaya," the trigonometry star Deanna Hillings said, her voice slow and lilting, a bottle of Mistic passion fruit punch in her hand. She sat on the auditorium stairs with a social studies textbook in her lap, her lips lined meticulously with deep brown pencil. "I have notes from logic if you need to copy them." She gestured to her JanSport backpack and fished for the straw in the bottle with a long burgundy nail.

LaFamille came to Galton with lives lived and stories to tell. They knew how best to cock one's Kangol hat or tie one's super-wide shoe-laces, which color bandanna signaled membership in which gang. They knew which labels to wear and where to find affordable knock-offs. They listened to hip-hop—loved it and studied it like Malaya did. Together, formed a critical mass of young brown anger and irreverent delight, right there on the Upper East Side. Malaya spent all her free periods with the group, spread together behind the auditorium. She would draw futuristic pastel sketches of Deanna and Lavar Hillings, math whiz twins from Jamaica, Queens, who spoke softly but blared like brass horns when they laughed. She went over Spanish homework with Shanté Scott, a Haitian cello prodigy from the Bronx with blunt roller bangs and a photographic memory. She freestyled and spat Biggie lyrics with Eric, who didn't own a stereo but could break down the scansion of any verse in any genre on first listen, and could beat-box like nobody's business. Between classes, Malaya drew everyone's portrait in bright pastels. She exchanged the portraits for lunch specials from the Chinese spot on Lexington, which sat at the bottom of a steep hill that winded her too much when she tried to climb it. Malaya appreciated the food, but the truth was, she enjoyed LaFamille as much as the lunches, and she would have done the portraits for free.

LaFamille gave Malaya a taste of what she imagined big black family life could be. As Percy and Nyela grew angrier and more distant over the years, it made less and less sense for the three of them to present themselves as the gleaming nuclear hope of the Black Family among the relatives. Gradually, Percy had begun to decline holiday invitations to Ma-Mère's, until it was no longer clear he'd be welcome if he did decide to come. LaSondra and Percy's other family members stopped visiting the brownstone, save for Uncle Book, who still showed up occasionally on Friday nights to pass out on the couch and sleep it off until Saturday morning.

"Thanks, girl," Malaya said to Deanna, who sat curved against a pile of rolled scrims and curtains with a copy of *Kindred* in her lap. Malaya opened the bag and pulled out the notebook. "This one?" she asked. Deanna nodded and slurped her punch, then turned the page.

With LaFamille, Malaya felt she was part of something huge and vibrant. It was a life of people dressed impeccably fly and laughing, dancing, singing familiar songs over plates of hot food, playing cards, and making art out of insults in playful, irreverent fun: *Yo mama so dumb, she brought a spoon to the Super Bowl! Yo mama teeth so yellow, when she smiles traffic slows down! Yo mama so stupid, I told her it was chilly outside and she ran out with a plate!*

Of course, there were fat jokes, too—*Yo mama so fat, she can't even jump to a conclusion!* These followed her through the streets of Harlem and popped up often on TV, piercing her each time. But LaFamille left the fat jokes alone around her. With them, Malaya was not the fat girl; instead, she was the smart, funny sister, protected and admired, loved in a for-real way.

Huddled behind the auditorium, the group joked about the rich white people of Galton, with their country houses, their Abercrombie outfits, and their Zima drinks, which Eric said cost a ridiculous $5.39 a bottle, though nobody knew for sure. There was power in their laughter, and they felt it. When Mrs. Ancil, the health teacher, pulled Shanté and Shaniece aside on separate occasions to tell them that they should probably get on birth control right away, based on their "demographics," LaFamille held a council behind the stage and told both girls that they were not wrong, that that *was* fucked up, that their anger was justified. The next day, Eric snuck into the health and phys ed office after class and poured exactly two and three-fifths ounces of piss on Mrs. Ancil's chair. No one asked how he transported it, or why he chose that measurement—the mystery heightened both the revenge and the glee. LaFamille conjured strength together. The strength sharpened their joy, and their joy turned into power and a limitless sense of what could be.

Malaya settled against a large prop chest in the corner behind the auditorium and began to copy Deanna's notes, waiting for RayShawn to appear. She pulled a bodega sandwich from her own bag and chewed as she copied, careful not to stain the notebook with the gooey cheese.

Eventually, Eric leaned out toward the hallway and called: "Yo-yo! S-boogie!"

Malaya watched as Shaniece walked toward the backstage steps. She wore a long black skirt, wedge heels, a white button-down shirt, and a black velour choker with a dangling silver charm shaped like a fang. It was video-vixen fashion with a goth edge, and it planted in Malaya an ember of envy mixed with a quiet want she couldn't name.

"Hey, y'all." Shaniece gave a small wave and smiled limply.

"Shaniece from Uptown! Miss 'I Like Your Smile' herself!" Eric said, hugging her. Deanna giggled and waved.

"Hey, Malaya," Shaniece said, turning toward her. She looked at Malaya, then darted her eyes away.

"Hey," Malaya said flatly. She glanced up at Shaniece and turned back to the notebook, just missing Shaniece's gaze.

Two years ago, in the eighth grade, Shaniece started wearing her hair in long, golden-brown micro braids, which gave her the look of an Amandra Wilson, but with a hood-style grit that only added to her appeal. This hadn't changed their friendship much at first, though some days looking at Shaniece made Malaya's chest draw tight with jealousy.

A few weeks into the ninth grade, Shaniece started a string of diets—first the Cabbage Soup diet, then the Cucumber diet, the Beet Juice diet, and so on—which she would clip from the tabloids at the CTown where she now worked after school. Shaniece didn't say much to Malaya about the diets in the beginning; she just let the clippings fall occasionally from her backpack down toward Malaya's feet while they rode the M4 bus back up to Harlem after school. But as Shaniece's weight loss quickened, she couldn't seem to stop herself from talking about it. Soon, she began to speak a different language—a dismally familiar idiom of grams and ounces and fat calories. Nyela had noticed Shaniece's weight loss and seized on it heartily, complimenting her on her figure whenever she came to visit the brownstone. Sometimes, the phone would ring and Malaya would pick up the receiver in her bedroom to find Shaniece and her mother chatting in businesslike tones about the newest brand of no-calorie sweetener, the best flavor of fat-free cottage cheese.

Shaniece stopped telling stories about Patricia Guzmán. Malaya still had not met Shaniece's mother, and she had begun to suspect that something about the woman in her stories wasn't real. She had seen a few old Polaroids of the woman when she and Shaniece were given a family tree assignment in the fifth grade. The photos, clearly taken before Shaniece was born, showed Patricia in a Harlem of the past, posed elegantly on corners and in restaurant booths, her hair a halo of curls and her eyes small and curious like Shaniece's. Jerome Armistice was in a few of the pictures, but in most of them, Patricia was alone. Shaniece had presented the photos reticently, handing them over as though to prove a point, then tucking them away before Malaya could ask questions. This intrigued Malaya. Once, when she was feeling mean, she asked Shaniece how her mother was doing. "You think she'll come to the Fall Family Brunch this year?" Malaya said, widening her eyes. She studied Shaniece's face for a reaction. Finally, Shaniece gave a blank look and said, "Probably not. She's busy." Then she took a sip of her Clearly Canadian, looking down into the bubbly water, her body slumped forward in a way that made Malaya feel far from her. After that, Malaya asked no more questions.

By the start of this school year, Shaniece had lost thirty pounds. She announced it proudly when Nyela picked up the phone in the kitchen one day, though Malaya was sure Shaniece knew she was listening on the line upstairs. Where once Shaniece had the doughy shape of an old-fashioned cruller, now a shoreline of dramatic curves emerged along her sides, giving her the look of an awards statuette. Malaya hated this. It made her nervous in a way she couldn't quite articulate; she only knew it brought to mind the terror of Amandra Wilson, Daundré Harris, and the playground days. Since the move upstairs to Galton Prep, Daundré had left for a boarding school in Connecticut, where, rumor had it, he had turned punk and was dating guys. But Amandra Wilson was glamorous and distant as always. She had begun to hang out with the rich Upper East Side white boys, smoking weed and cigarettes in the back courtyard of the posh Park Avenue high-rise next to the school. It was also well known that Amandra slept around, which only elevated her mystique.

Malaya let herself look at Shaniece, her narrow waist enfolded with each hug as she went around the group saying her hellos. Shaniece was not as pretty as Amandra in the prevailing view, but she was light-skinned, and her face bore an expression of constant curiosity that, in the right light, was more striking than beauty. Malaya had often wondered what it must be like for someone like Amandra—to have had all the world's favor so steadfastly and for so long, to have complete license to do what made your body feel good. It made Malaya nervous to think that Shaniece would soon know that feeling. Coldness seemed a reasonable protection for Malaya, especially among LaFamille.

But as obvious as their growing distance was for Malaya, Shaniece sometimes barely seemed to notice it. At least twice a week, she paged Malaya after her shift at the CTown with their code, 8008135: BOOBIES, ready to supply Malaya with foods forbidden in the Clondon home. She would appear minutes later on the brownstone stoop with bags of Utz potato chips and no-frills devil's food rolls. Until the start of her transformation, Shaniece and Malaya shared these foods and the closeness that came with them, laughing about the teachers at Galton, talking about what rappers and DJs they found cute. These days, Shaniece still came to the house, but now she didn't eat. Instead, while they talked and looked at music videos, Shaniece perched on the family room sofa and sipped from cans of Diet Sunkist while Malaya ate alone. Had Shaniece been anyone else, Malaya would never have let herself be seen that way. But the feel of Shaniece beside her calmed Malaya, lulled her into an ease that she knew could not be trusted. This embarrassed her, and made her want to be mean. So she let herself eat beside Shaniece at home in the evenings and regarded her as coolly as possible at Galton each day. But every once in a while, Shaniece said something there behind the auditorium that threw Malaya back to the towel-tent days, and Malaya felt guilt pierce her.

"I paged you this morning," Shaniece said quietly, after hugging Deanna. She dragged a small stool from the corner and pulled it toward Malaya, its metals clattering lightly against the floor. "Maybe you didn't get it. I wanted to see if you were down to take the bus. But then you weren't here either." She crossed her legs on the narrow stool and pulled out a cup of yogurt, swirling the cream around with a plastic spoon.

"Oh," Malaya said as coolly as she could. "Yeah." She pushed her sandwich aside to suggest she was finished, though she wasn't. "I just got here. I had a doctor's appointment." Then she added quickly, "Just a checkup."

Malaya shifted her weight on the hard floor and flipped the page in the notebook. Her hips were growing numb. She wanted the conversation to end, to retreat to the columns of numbers on the page, and not have to find words for Shaniece. But Shanice just looked at her with her same questioning eyes, as though they were still two chubby black girls up in Harlem, as though nothing had changed.

There had been many moments like this with Shaniece lately, when she seemed to be asking for a closeness Malaya could not let herself muster. Once, last summer, after Malaya woke up to hear Percy and Nyela in a bitter morning fight about his late nights away from home, Malaya called Shaniece impulsively. By then, they looked old enough to buy wine coolers from the bodega, and sometimes that summer they sat together on Malaya's stoop and drank from paper bags while her parents were at work. Malaya didn't know exactly why, but she was crying when she dialed the number after the fight that morning, hot tears leaking down her face with no words to explain them. Shaniece came over right away with a pack of Bacardi Breezers and the Mary J. Blige *My Life* CD.

Malaya felt embarrassed for the tears and the phone call. But Shaniece simply went into action.

"I get it, girl," she said, pulling the drinks from the bodega bag and rubbing the CD on the hem of her shorts. "For real." She brought out a pair of portable speakers from the Home and Office Depot and plugged them into her Discman.

The two sat together and listened to the album on repeat, sipping on the cold, sweet liquor, the stone steps hot under their thighs. They talked, first about the fight, then about Shaniece's father's drinking, then about nothing at all. They listened to each other until there was no more to say, then they just sat together, looking up at the streetlight as Mary's voice rolled slowly rolled from the speakers. When one of the speakers shorted, Shaniece said, "I'll be back," and disappeared toward Amsterdam. She returned five minutes later with a sticky package of dulce de coco candy and her headphones. They sat close then, each with one foam pad at her ear, and played the CD again. They stayed there until the sun disappeared, talking and eating and laughing so hard Malaya thought they might fall into the laughter and stay forever in its core, their thighs pressing together like in the school bus days.

Malaya looked at Shaniece now, pert and curvy, all crossed leg and thigh on the backless stool, eating her yogurt in slow, deliberate bites. She was even smaller now than she'd been in the summer, and Malaya felt further from her than ever.

"I'm glad you're good," Shaniece said. She raised her eyes to Malaya and then looked down, swirling her spoon slowly in the cup. "Let me know if you wanna roll out together later or whatever. I have work, but I can beep you after that, too."

"Yeah, maybe." Malaya pitched her voice flat. She leaned her weight against the prop chest. "Beep me, I guess. I'll call you or whatever. If I'm not busy."

Soon Lavar and Shanté appeared, complaining about a mishap one of the Mandys had caused that kept them in chemistry lab after class.

RayShawn blustered up behind them in a cloud of dreadlocks and cologne oil.

"No disrespect to Mrs. Webber," he announced to the group, peeling his worn leather backpack off his shoulder. "But this Western chemistry is just not the kind that appeals to me anyway. I'm more interested in Kemetic science. The chemistry that's felt, on a poetic level. Not just hypothesized. Of course, they won't teach that." He sat on the steps across from Malaya, his knees spread wide as he pulled a massive deli sandwich out of his bag. It smelled like pastrami and vinegar.

Eric broke out in a grand falsetto, singing the new Aaliyah song about "feeling chemistry." He shook his shoulders and jutted his hip out erratically as he moved across the backstage hall. Shanté chuckled, her glassy eyes narrowing beneath her bangs. Lavar threw his head back in a honking chortle. Malaya laughed, too, but when she saw RayShawn roll his eyes in annoyance, she stuffed her sandwich into her bag and nodded. "Word," she said to RayShawn, trying to sound serious. "You right."

When Malaya's mother first met RayShawn during the annual Fall Family Brunch in the seventh grade, she had remarked excitedly that he was like a young Huey Newton, whom she regarded as one of the handsomest and smartest men on earth. Though Malaya couldn't admit it, her mother's enthusiastic approval had only deepened her admiration. When she could not talk with RayShawn, she talked about him. She passed notes about him to Rachel Greenstein in art history class and made friends with Mei-Lin Rogers, a goth girl with a big chest and sad eyes who played Magic cards in the freak hallway. When Malaya passed the first note to Mei-Lin in social studies, about how she loved RayShawn's eyes, Mei-Lin had folded the paper neatly, sat it on her desk, and leaned over to Malaya across the classroom aisle. "Teenage love is an affliction," she said breathily in Malaya's ear. She passed back a note with RayShawn's name and Malaya's surrounded in thick black hearts and crossbones, a sign Malaya took to mean that she understood.

Malaya had considered it an act of divine grace when she passed the AP Spanish exam and ended up in RayShawn's Latin American poetry class. When she heard RayShawn struggle through a translation of

Neruda's twelfth sonnet, she saw it as an outright miracle and immediately offered her help. In this way, they formed a friendship apart from LaFamille. At first, he only called for help with his translation assignments, but soon they began to talk about other things, long back-and-forths about the three Toni Morrison novels they had read, the latest episode *of Showtime at the Apollo*, and what they knew about 1970s black social politics, which was, of course, less than either would admit.

"You good for the Spanish final?" Malaya asked. She closed her notebook and shifted her weight to one thigh, hoping to create a silhouette that obscured her belly and emphasized her breasts. "I can help you study if you want."

"That's wassup," he said, looking up from his sandwich. "Good looking out, Malaya." Malaya smiled. She felt Shaniece's eyes on her, but she looked away.

THAT AFTERNOON, RayShawn approached her after Spanish class, glancing over his shoulder.

"You got a second?" he asked.

Malaya had chemistry class the following period, and still hadn't completed the logic proofs due that afternoon. "Sure. Wassup?"

He scraped at his chin stubble and said he was going through some things.

"My moms is stressing me," he said. "I need to talk."

Malaya knew that RayShawn's mother had given birth to him at sixteen, that she struggled in the way that strong black women did, working several day jobs to stay afloat, going to night school to get ahead, waging fruitless court battles for child support, and relying on the help of her own mother—another strong black woman—to make it through.

RayShawn decided they would walk to the HMV record store down the steep hill on Lexington. The store was empty during school hours, and its basement classical section was like a nightclub lounge, with big plush sofas and low lighting. They left the building and crossed past Park Avenue, past the suited doormen standing before stately apartment buildings and the wide, pristine traffic medians that looked like gardens planted in the middle of the street. Malaya swallowed air as she moved behind RayShawn toward Lexington, trying to keep up.

The usual net of eyes caught on Malaya when they walked into the store. She looked up at the collage of album covers on the walls. A slim white man with sand-colored hair approached them at the escalator.

"Ma'am," he said to Malaya, "the rap section is over here, if that's what you and your son are looking for." He gestured to the back of the store.

Before Malaya could say anything, RayShawn cleared his throat and said, "Thank you. We're actually headed downstairs."

The classical room was empty as usual, but still RayShawn picked a sofa in the back. Malaya wedged herself in the corner beside him and smoothed her T-shirt over her bulges, waiting.

"She doesn't want me to see my father," RayShawn began. He took off his backpack and jacket and dropped them on the floor. "She doesn't even want me to call him. She can't understand why I'd want 'that nigga' in my life. That's what she calls him. 'That nigga.'"

Malaya shifted her weight. The springs of the sofa squealed beneath her, and her jeans gripped her middle like teeth.

"She doesn't get it," he said, leaning forward. "She feels like she's doing alright without him, so I should too. Like we're the same person and whatever she needs is what I need. She doesn't understand I'm trying to be a man."

Malaya tried to fix her face in a look of welcoming compassion. She could relate to what RayShawn was saying. Regularly, she had to hear Nyela talk about Percy's carelessness and irresponsibility, as though there was none of his blood inside her.

Malaya began to mention this connection, but when she opened her mouth RayShawn propped his back against her like a beach chair, and told the prehistory of his life to the room's vast walls. He talked about how his father had abandoned his mother as soon as he learned she was pregnant, how his brothers' fathers had done the same. How he had to raise himself and his brothers.

"Sometimes I worry it's not gonna happen," he said, looking at the rows of thick songbooks. He leaned back against her harder. "Like I won't be any better than him. Like I won't be any kind of man at all."

He pressed his shoulder against the meat beneath her arm. A whiff of imitation Cool Water cologne oil hovered from the coils of his hair. He pulled a book from his backpack—Eldridge Cleaver's *Soul on Ice*, which he had learned about recently on *Tony Brown's Journal*. He put the book on his lap.

"Being a black man is hard," he said. "The stress is unimaginable."

She felt his arm move against her side. He unfastened his belt, the buckle clinking. He took Malaya's hand and moved it under the denim.

"Do you understand?"

She nodded and raised her body slightly, angling herself toward him. He felt like a mound of old Jell-O, firm and squishy at once. She understood and she didn't, but it didn't matter. This was what she wanted. He wanted her to touch him. And he had touched her, too—a part of him had touched a part of her, at least. She was there and not there, as though she were seeing herself from a camera perched on her shoulder, watching herself move, hearing herself breathe. When it was over, she tilted her face toward him, but he wouldn't kiss her. "It's the refractory period," he said, zipping his pants. "Men don't like to be touched."

Malaya had a decision to make. She could fall into herself, collect in a puddle on the record store floor and stay there forever. Or, she could stand and console herself with the slim truth: There had been touch. That was something.

She could swipe money from Nyela's pocket to buy new boots, ask Percy to cover the cost of a new set of box braids, some purple, some electric blue. She could steal and save for weeks to buy more clothes, the best of what the Big and Tall had to offer her. She thought of the bag check man. However it had happened, she was a step closer to something important, though what it was she couldn't yet say.

As she drifted back up to Harlem alone on the bus, she did not think about what RayShawn had said, how he had looked, what she had felt. She erased the details from her memory as the streets scrolled by beyond the window. Block by block, she planned a translation of herself. She only wished she could tell Shaniece.

Christopher Cat

IN THE WEEKS THAT FOLLOWED, Clarence Edgar, the man from the Big and Tall, became a useful ruse for Malaya. Like most adolescents, she was reluctant to admit the tender truths of her life, constantly concerned that her secrets were somehow both more salacious and more pitiful than those of her peers. But unlike other teenagers' secrets, Malaya's carried a weight of mortal responsibility: every second lunch behind the auditorium, every grease-puffed snack Shaniece brought her, was a step toward an hours-long sit-down in which Nyela implored her to stop eating, to lose weight, if not for her health, then for what she called her "quality of life," a vision that, Malaya knew, included not only freedom and a successful career, but also, eventually, a man.

For this reason, Clarence Edgar was both an acquiescence to her mother's vision and a secret rebellion against it. He was a man, there was no doubting that. But he was an older man about whom Malaya knew little. He had told her that although his given name was Clarence, he preferred to be called Edgar. He hadn't gone by Clarence since he'd left Liberia at age twenty, some twenty years ago, he said, though Malaya wondered if he was older than that. "Clarence is a name from the past," he told her the first time they spoke on the phone. She let the name tumble over itself in her mind, trying to imagine this was not the bag check man from the Harlem Big and Tall, but a fantasy Clarence cooing to her from the other end of the phone. Occasionally, Edgar would page her, and they would talk about her made-up husband and all the things he wanted to do to her in the husband's absence, most of which involved food. One night, he said breathily: "When you let me take you out, you can eat as much as you want. You never have to stop. I like that." The skin on her neck went cool when he said this, but she gave a shallow laugh and said, as casually as she could, "I can't see you. My husband is sick. He needs me."

For Malaya, the conversations had the use value of a metronome. Clarence Edgar was a tool for marking the time and keeping her place in a fairy tale of her own devising. Where the real Edgar was awkward and insistent in a way that seemed to announce his loneliness, her fantasy Clarence gleamed with confidence and cool. The fantasy Clarence was a brilliant college student with long, golden dreadlocks like something out of a Janet Jackson video, who had fallen in love with her at a poetry reading at the last remaining black-owned bookstore on 125th. He had since consumed her afternoon hours so that she had little time for her waning friendship with Shaniece and was occasionally unavailable even to RayShawn. In the weeks after meeting Edgar, Malaya left class early and snuck to the pay phone on Park Avenue to dial his number and leave messages for her fantasy man, hoping that the real Edgar wouldn't answer, and that her classmates would see her making the call. If Shaniece asked if she wanted to hang out, Malaya would declare she was going out with Clarence. Then, most often, she would return home to put on music, sit at the easel Percy had given her, and eat before a blank canvas.

ONE MORNING IN DECEMBER, a blizzard hit Manhattan unexpectedly, and classes were dismissed after first period. On a nicer day, this would have meant taking it to the park or the two-dollar movie theater in Midtown to talk back to the screen and eat popcorn while Shanté and Eric made out in the back row. But the blizzard was serious, and the train schedules had slowed down, which meant that the kids from Brooklyn, Queens, and the Bronx had to start their treks home now. RayShawn,

Shanté, and the Hillings twins hit the trains, and Eric walked across the park in the snow to pick his little sister up from day care. This left Malaya and Shaniece.

Shaniece had lost at least ten more pounds in the last few weeks. She was somehow more of herself in her new body, like a lightbulb turned up on its dimmer. Now she always seemed to be *going*—to work, to class, to wherever it was that the men she met took her. As vague and placid as her face still looked, she now had around her an air of movement and certainty that overwhelmed Malaya. She had only come over to the brownstone a couple of times in the past few weeks, to borrow books about black family systems and Afro-Caribbean motherhood from Nyela's library. Malaya assumed this had something to do with the ongoing mystery of Patricia Guzmán, but this, too, was stuffed into the growing silence between them.

On the day of the blizzard, Shaniece surprised Malaya by suggesting they go downtown to a bar they'd discovered that summer. It was a tight hole-in-the-wall on Christopher Street, called the Fat Cat. Malaya loved this name. It reminded her of a Countee Cullen book her father used to read to her as a child. The narrator was a talking cat named Christopher, who mused with hilarious acerbity over the odd life of his owner, a ne'er-do-well poet who was hopelessly unable to handle his own life, let alone tame and manage the genius cat, despite the owner's best intentions. The book was called *My Lives and How I Lost Them*, and thinking of it gave Malaya a little thrill, because even on the title page, "Christopher Cat" was listed as first author. She imagined the orange cat hunched over an inky typewriter late at night, diligently preparing his manuscript to send to publishers behind his feckless owner's back.

The Fat Cat never checked their IDs, though whether this was because they actually looked grown, or simply because of Malaya's size, she didn't know. The best thing about the Fat Cat was the fact that it was on Christopher Street in Greenwich Village. This was where gay people hung out, which added to its appeal for LaFamille, making it a zone freer of expectation than Galton, or home. Malaya felt a particular appreciation for the Village because, though she never saw anyone close to her size, at any moment there was sure to be an impressive mix of human sights: painted, gregarious drag queens; break-dancing middle school-ers; crew-cut lesbians with tattoos covering their skin like murals. Theater types in elaborate astronaut and superhero costumes merged with all kinds of other strange bodies and walked the avenues, eating hot dogs, going to the post office, moving through their day like any-one else. If the spectacle of Malaya's body didn't fit in here, at least she wasn't the only one.

She had never spoken to anyone in her family about Christopher Street. Percy and Nyela had always considered themselves "tolerant," and Malaya had been raised to respect all manner of people, mostly by not asking questions. This included her godfather, Dee, a gay college friend of her parents who had died of AIDS when Malaya was two or three. Once, in the fifth grade, she had asked Percy what he thought of the shaggy-haired white singer who had just come out as a lesbian, and he looked at her ominously. "Watch out for lesbians," he had said. "They recruit." Their conversations never went beyond that.

The streets of the Village were covered in snow, and round, wet flur-ries whipped up on the wind and blew from all directions, blurring the colored glow from the traffic lights. Shaniece had suggested that they take the bus, probably to save Malaya the pain of subway stairs. Malaya noticed this generosity, and she was grateful for it. As they trudged from the bus stop to the bar, Shaniece also carried the conversation so Malaya could concentrate on each step and avoid careening into the slush. Malaya felt herself soften a little as she watched Shaniece and her S-shaped body lace along the snow-covered pavement.

The Fat Cat was surprisingly crowded, and the smell of fried food, gas heat, and smoky bodies welcomed them at the door. Malaya scanned the bar for the sturdiest-looking chair as she always did, and heaved herself up. Shaniece talked for a few minutes more, another kindness, while Malaya caught her breath. Marvin Gaye's "Trouble Man" played on the radio as Shaniece told about her latest man, whom she had met check-ing groceries at the CTown.

"They always think they're smarter than you just because they're older and they have penises," she said. She rolled her eyes and slid the large handbag she used for her books onto the hook beneath the bar.

Malaya kicked her backpack under her stool, out of sight, and propped her elbows on the bar. "Like having a dick boosts your IQ. I just let them think that. It's easier than trying to fight."

Shaniece ordered a house salad, and Malaya ordered a side of fries, though she really wanted a cheeseburger. When the bartender asked what they wanted to drink, Shaniece said, "I'll have a rum and Diet," and Malaya said, as confidently as she could, "Me too."

Shaniece rested her elbows lightly at the lip of the bar, her hips bulging perfectly just past the rim of the stool. She looked like a woman. Since the early days of her transformation, Shaniece had peppered their ever-brief conversations with stories about the men she was "talking to"—mostly friends of her father's who'd slipped her their numbers when he wasn't looking, and men she'd meet walking around Harlem. They bought her dinners from the chicken spot on Broadway and took her for drinks at St. Nick's Pub. Malaya hadn't believed her at first; usually she listened to these stories with a feeling of self-implicated suspicion, filing them away with the mysterious Patricia Guzmán and Malaya's own lies. But now, Shaniece stirred her drink and leaned in toward the bartender with an ease that shocked Malaya and made her breath quicken.

"Can we have another round?" she said, painting a lazy loop in the air with her finger. "You made them pretty good the first time."

The bartender smiled at Shaniece and said, "But of course, beautiful," in a stuffy, nasal voice.

As they talked, Malaya looked toward the door, watching people whirl in from the blizzard, snow coating their hats and jackets like sugar.

After more drinks, they were full and slightly dizzy, laughing first about Mrs. Ancil's ridiculous hairdo and Eric's latest hallway antics, and then about nothing at all. Soon the music changed, and one of Malaya's favorite songs came on. It was by Biggie's protégé group, Junior M.A.F.I.A. It had a burrowing bassline that transported her to a perpetual nighttime of deep mood and fast lights: *The only one thing I wanna do is freak you . . . You got ta hit me off.* It was about sex and success and longing, like all the best rap songs. Lil' Kim's verses stood for Malaya at the apex of irreverence and black girl raunch. In the video, the rapper faced the camera boldly in lingerie and multicolored furs, her bra and panties showing shameless as the sun beneath her bright green wig. Malaya imagined what it would feel like to be wrapped in nothing but luxury and a *what you gonna do about it?* look, making fearless demands for her pleasure in front of an infinite audience. Shaniece must have known what Malaya was thinking, because she sat her drink down on the bar and said, suddenly: "We're gonna dance."

Malaya hadn't danced in front of anyone since the Harlem Arts Academy. She had planned to spend the afternoon balanced on the barstool, mouthing song lyrics and waving her head to the beat. But now, there was the music and the snow and the heady wooze of the grease and drinks. And there was Shaniece's hand, leading her to the small clearing in the back of the bar.

Grown men watched as the two girls moved across the space, Shaniece winding her hips to the beat, Malaya sucking in her belly to swerve through the maze of tables and chairs. At first, it was hard to keep up, and Malaya wondered what the men were thinking as they watched. But then Shaniece put her hand on Malaya's hip and pressed herself so close Malaya could smell the rum on her breath and her African Pride hair oil. Shaniece turned around and pressed her body against Malaya's, bending down and rising up in the rhythm, dipping so perfectly to the beat that it lit Malaya's skin. Now, it didn't matter what the men were seeing, or that they were there at all. Shaniece turned to face her again and placed Malaya's hand on the slope of her waist, narrow but still full, a soft puff of flesh between her fingers. Malaya felt something pop inside her. She looked at Shaniece, who looked back at her for only a second before closing her eyes and dipping down once more. Malaya felt her arms melt, felt her body sink into the rhythm and the rapper's rasping voice. She let herself grab and sway and grip and feel. It felt like the towel-tent days, but better. It was a feeling so real she could almost hold it in her mouth— the wanting and the needing and the delicious having that all the songs talked about. She closed her eyes, breathed, and went in.

Shaniece seemed to feel it, too, because when the song's last chords faded out and the next one started, she turned around again and pressed her thighs into Malaya, grinding her hips so deep against her she felt they might catch fire.

As soon as they conjured a rhythm, a tall, narrow man in a red hat and scarf danced up in front of Shaniece, smiling.

"Is that your girlfriend?" he asked over the music. He pointed his chin in Malaya's direction as though she weren't right there, listening.

Malaya couldn't hear Shaniece's response or see her face, but soon Shaniece was dancing with the man, perched between his bent knees, winding to a reggae song Malaya had never heard before. She stood in the middle of the dance floor, hanging dizzily on the music for a beat too long. Finally, she pushed her way back toward the bar. By the time she turned around, Shaniece was facing outward, her behind sandwiched against the man's groin, her eyes on her own body.

Ma-Mère had once told Malaya: *A woman friend who leaves you drunk at a party is the worst kind of woman and no kind of friend.* Malaya hadn't understood it then, but she did now. She wasn't sure if it was out of duty to Shaniece or to her own grown woman self, but she couldn't move. Perhaps it was the thought of pushing through the bar, huge and alone, that stopped her. She looked back a few times to see if Shaniece was looking for her, but she wasn't. All she saw was Shaniece's waist in the man's hands, her head thrown back against him, her coppery braids threaded through the fringe of his scarf. Malaya lifted herself onto the stool again and ordered another basket of fries, this time with a cheeseburger, and dared herself to watch.

They spent the bus ride to Harlem in half-silence, Shaniece talking casually about the drinks and her salad and the bartender's strange voice. Nothing was said about the man with the red scarf. Malaya sat quietly, wedged in the two corner seats in the back of the bus, feeling the hum of the motor beneath her and eating the last of the fries, which she'd taken to go in a paper cup.

The snow had stopped, and now there was only wind and city, just as it had been before, only colder and covered in ice.

Soon, a silence fell and when Malaya tried to fill it with talk of Clarence, Shaniece paid no attention. Instead, she looked around the crowded bus, then fixed her gaze on Malaya's belly. Malaya looked down. A wide ketchup stain sat at the crest of her stomach. Her face grew hot. Embarrassed, she heaved the ends of her jacket closed, then looked back at Shaniece. There it was, plain as air: disgust. Malaya felt the moment like the last notes of a song, fading to completion.

As Riverside Drive scrolled past the window, Malaya told a new story about Clarence. She said that he had grown possessive, his attention gone bad. Her hands on her stomach to cover the stain, she turned to her friend.

"Sometimes I feel like it's not healthy," she said. She looked out the window, trying to swallow the desperation that lumped like a marble in her throat. "Sometimes I'm afraid."

She checked to see if Shaniece was listening, but her head was still tilted toward Malaya's belly, and her eyes were miles away.

WHEN HER PAGER SOUNDED with Shaniece's code the next day, Malaya didn't respond. In the afternoons that followed, she hustled down the stairs at Galton as quickly as she could to beat Shaniece to the bus. Sometimes, she left school early and spent hours at the Apple Leaf gourmet deli on Madison Avenue, eating room-temperature noodles and rubbery stir-fry from the buffet just to avoid being home in case Shaniece rang the bell.

She could tell this hurt Shaniece at least a little, because when they did speak, Shaniece seemed nervous in a way that was unlike the new her, her words skipping over themselves sporadically as they had in childhood. Once, Shaniece showed up at the brownstone when Malaya was expecting a delivery from the Jamaican restaurant on Amsterdam, and she answered the door. Shaniece stood with her face bent into a crooked question mark. She said she had gotten off work early and thought she would stop by. Malaya looked at her as flatly as possible and said, "Did you bring any chips?" When Shaniece shook her head no, Malaya replied, "Then why did you come?" and closed the door.

Eventually, ignoring Shaniece's calls got easier—all the talk of diets and men bored Malaya, she decided, and she really didn't miss it. But not thinking about Shaniece was different, and not thinking about the dance at the Fat Cat was impossible.

When she thought of how the dance made her feel, it brought her back to a memory. In the eighth grade, Percy had urged her to enter a painting competition at the Harlem Arts Academy. She had submitted a stipple drawing of Ma-Mère's hair, and had won a $1,000 savings bond, for college, along with a $250 cash prize. When she learned her painting had won, she thought mainly about how far $250 would go for her—it would buy her a year's worth of clandestine meals at least, and perhaps a new acrylic set. But when she climbed to the podium at the awards ceremony and bowed to receive her medal from the event host, Malaya felt something she hadn't felt since running on the playground: she felt both full and light, the entire surface of her buzzing, as though her skin were made of fireflies. It was motion, sparking ravenous through her body. This was how she felt each time the dance with Shaniece came to memory. It was too much to think about, and too much to forget.

She didn't know what the feeling meant for the friendship, or what it meant about her. So she avoided Shaniece altogether—the friend, the idea, the memory. Instead, she made her evening calls to Edgar and plunged herself into whatever hiding place she could find—food, music, and sometimes her canvases, reliable joys that would not betray her.

Dr. Clondon

EACH SATURDAY after her Weight Watchers meeting, Nyela returned to the brownstone with bags of wan produce and lean meats carted in by the skinny boys who bagged groceries at the CTown and carried them to homes in the neighborhood for five dollars. Malaya had stopped going to the Meetings in the seventh grade, and so she watched Nyela return with the groceries and listened as she made grand plans for the meal she would prepare for the weekend. Each week, she dreamed up a traditional Sunday dinner like the ones LaSondra and Percy's other cousins had each week, but with a healthy flare: neat tufts of mashed potatoes made from unbuttered, sugarless yams instead of starchy whites, shimmering collard greens cooked with smoked turkey instead of ham hocks, margarined cubes of butternut squash instead of mac and cheese, all served on Ma-Mère's good dish set. Nyela would bustle in with the bags and detail these plans for Malaya, her eyes glinting like a girl's. Inevitably, there would be a call from the department chair or a set of papers to grade. Saturday would fade away and Sunday would come and go without the stove catching so much as a glow. Eventually Percy would order Chinese food, usually with a tin of pale diet lemon chicken for Malaya as a compromise.

This was part of an all-out war for Nyela, a battle for what the Meeting ladies called "Health-Wealth" for the whole family. As far as Malaya could tell, this was an empty slogan designed to convince middle-aged women that hunger brought on a joy more fulfilling than food, in the same way that self-sacrifice was supposed to produce a magic of abundance for black people. No one ever addressed the fact that, for all their noble sacrifice, all but a few of the Meeting ladies continued to be not only fat, but also strapped for cash.

Even as the Sunday Health-Wealth dinners failed, Nyela tried to make reasonable eating plans for the family each week. Every weekend, she set out dinner ingredients for Monday through Friday, each with a university Post-it note explaining what Malaya was to cook, and how. Malaya, of course, had no interest in this sudden commitment to cooking, and she was sure Nyela knew it. Every afternoon after school, Malaya glanced at the note and left it clinging pitifully to the garden-floor door in the same place where her mother had put it, then waited for Percy to bring home dinner from a restaurant or order in. Eventually, Nyela began to come home with her own dinner from the Gonzales bodega or one of the restaurants near campus. Malaya would hear her climbing to the bedroom, calling hello first to Percy in the family room and then to Malaya upstairs. The three of them would eat dinner that way, each in their own corner, neither together nor alone.

Now, instead of arguing, Percy and Nyela generally stayed away from each other. Percy came home later and later, often after Malaya and Nyela had gone to sleep, leaving fewer opportunities for them to fight. When they did talk, it was in hot tones. Most of their rifts seemed to happen in the hallway between their bedroom, where Nyela retreated after work, and the family room, which Percy had claimed. Once night, Malaya woke up to the sounds of the front door slamming open and Percy's footsteps hard on the floor of the hallway.

"Midnight, Pra?" Nyela said. "Where have you been?"

"Work. You're not the only one who works," he said. His voice was loud, as though it were the middle of the day. He coughed. "Fuck. I don't have to answer to you."

They said nothing, and Malaya wondered what had happened. But then her mother's voice cut into the quiet.

"I need you to tell me. If there's someone else, I need to know." She said it so calmly it frightened Malaya. But there was no response, only the sound of a door slamming closed.

After that, Nyela's Health-Wealth mission went full-force. She subscribed to several magazines, including *Self*, *Fit Family*, and *Woman's Day*, though she rarely had time to read them. Instead, they accumulated in glossy stacks in the bathroom, where she hunted through them after work each night, tearing out low-calorie recipes and food substitution tips, filling the margins with elaborate meal plans for herself and Malaya. Malaya resented her mother's efforts, but she understood them. No one was sure how much Malaya weighed. When she outgrew doctors' scales at twelve, Nyela had decided to update the unused kitchen on the garden floor, which had served as storage space up until then, resolving that it would be worth the expense to move the kitchen far from Malaya's room. The decision came at the suggestion of a string of pediatricians and specialists Malaya had been taken to see as her weight increased. There was Mavis Bigtree, the endocrinologist who had enrolled her in a weight loss medication study for teenagers when she was nine and kicked her out abruptly when the medication turned her stools bright orange. Then there was Carolina Faust, the perky white nutritionist who printed out a diet of Mediterranean yogurts, exotic nuts, and legumes nowhere to be found in Harlem, and Cairo P. Stark, the black man dietician with a narrow face like a letter opener, who frowned as soon as Malaya entered the office and did not stop until he had written up a monthlong food plan of six home-cooked meals a day for Malaya, with no advice as to who should prepare these meals while Percy and Nyela were at work. There were others—more doctors, more nurses, more gurus, poking at Malaya's body and scowling intensely, as though she had done something to them just by showing up in their offices, proof of how unruly the body could be.

All of these people said the same thing: Malaya should eat less and exercise more. As though it were the simplest thing in the world. She left each visit wanting nothing more than to lie down and eat.

When she turned thirteen, Malaya declared a wordless moratorium on these doctors' visits, and on the summers of transformation with Ma-Mère. She missed all the appointments Nyela made, blaming schoolwork or a delayed bus schedule, and assured Nyela that she was trying to lose weight on her own. Although it was a lie, Malaya felt the gesture was meaningful. She had gotten so tired of her body's failure that saying anything about it took more energy than anyone, she was sure, could understand. Even those two words, *I'm trying*, felt like a gift she couldn't really afford, but was required to offer anyway.

While Nyela's Health-Wealth campaign went on, her work life intensified, so that though her income was rising, she was rarely home to oversee the changes she pleaded for. She earned tenure, and even received an award from the Black Psychologists Association for her book, *"One for My Baby, and One More for the Road": A Culturally Competent Family Systems Approach to Addiction*, which she had published earlier that year. The family celebrated with dinner at Copeland's Restaurant and Reliable Cafeteria, which the neighborhood had come to call Reliable for short. However, this honor seemed only to win Nyela more work—later nights on campus reading dissertations, more evenings spent preparing lectures, and a general air of frenzy and overwhelm that began to deaden her eyes.

One night, Malaya crept down to the kitchen for a snack and climbed back up to find Nyela in the bathroom, the door partly open. She stood there in her green nightgown, rattling tablets from a plastic jar. When Malaya asked what the pills were, Nyela said they were for migraines. Malaya looked up the prescription name the next day at Galton's computer lab and found they were sleeping pills. Sleep had always been one of life's best pleasures for Malaya; it was a reliable indulgence, both treat and reward, made all the sweeter precisely because it was effortless. Now she saw her mother differently. She tried to imagine a life in which even sleep was something to work for. *What would that kind of tiredness feel like?* she wondered. *What would it make you do?*

MALAYA HAD NOT spent time with Shaniece since the dance at the Fat Cat, save for brief exchanges in the hallway at Galton and occasional moments of laughter with LaFamille, when Eric said something ridiculous and they caught each other's gaze for a second before Malaya looked away. Sometimes, Malaya went on slow walks around the neighborhood to find foods she had liked as a child—the barbecue ribs from Singleton's on Lenox that shimmered with tangy sauce, and fluffy caramel cake from Wimps Bakery on Fifth. Biggie's voice thick in her ears, she moved through the blocks, imagining the textures and flavors of the foods, how they would feel in her belly. But as much as the promise of Harlem's foods buoyed her, lately the walks felt bittersweet.

Now, with every few blocks it seemed another piece of Harlem had disappeared. Businesses that had been as much a part of the neighborhood as Sugar Hill itself began to close down, leaving a staggered string of empty storefronts along St. Nicholas and Seventh Avenue, like a child's missing front teeth. Harlem's fight had gained gusto, too, and it wasn't uncommon to find groups of Nubian-oiled women gathered in front of Mart 125, the African-inspired indoor market on 125th Street where Nyela had taken Malaya to shop for soaps and hair grease on weekends years ago. Now, networks of dreadlocked and silver-bangled women gathered there over Jamaican health smoothies and Styrofoam plates of Senegalese thieboudienne, devising plans to save the neighborhood.

After these walks, Malaya would return home, past the foyer, where her mother had begun to stack the chairs that had broken under her weight, past her father's coats, which still smelled of smoke and Dentyne gum. She would settle in her room, spread the bags and packages of food beside her easel, and eat. While the house and the neighborhood were morphing past recognition, her room had not changed much at all. The dolls from Ma-Mère were still there, their bushy hair still kissing the ceiling, their beaded dresses now caked even thicker with dust. Malaya had gone through three spring beds, each buckling under her, until Nyela bought her a boxy wooden captain's bed, which Malaya liked, because she could secret her empty food cartons away in the storage shelves underneath. There, too, she kept her pencils and pastels, in a large cardboard box studded with spills of sparkling nail polish and collaged with glossy images of Biggie, Queen Latifah, Method Man, and Mary J. Blige, clipped from the pages of *Word Up!* and other flimsy newsprint rap magazines. The LOVE sign she had affixed to the mirror years ago was still there, though it no longer glowed in the dark, just yelped the same pale yellow whether it was light out or not.

ONE SATURDAY AFTERNOON a few weeks after the Fat Cat, Ma-Mère showed up for a surprise visit. She had just come off a cruise to Bahia with her Senior Sunbirds travel group, and had flown into JFK instead of Philadelphia, planning to stay for a few days. When she appeared at the doorway, her plum-colored Samsonite luggage set stacked neatly by her calves, she said the purpose of her visit was to check on the family, but both Malaya and Nyela were suspicious.

Nyela was flustered by Ma-Mère's sudden appearance, but she rushed immediately to the grocery store to pick up ingredients for what Malaya guessed might be the first of these planned Health-Wealth Feasts to actually reach the table. Nyela called Malaya down to help, and she begrudgingly obliged, thudding downstairs with her sketchbook under her arm. In the kitchen, she found Nyela standing by the sink fiddling with a package of slimy-looking fish. Ma-Mère settled in across the room. She was browner than usual, and she sat with her back straight and her hands folded casually as if sitting for a portrait.

"Well, ain't heard from you in a month of Sundays, Nathallie," Ma-Mère said. "So I thought I'd just come check on you and My Ly-Ly here."

Malaya gave Ma-Mère an air kiss and sat in the chair that had been designated as hers—a wrought-iron garden chair Nyela had had reupholstered in a purple Adinkra print she thought Malaya would like.

"I know. I'm sorry. It's been a busy few weeks." Nyela sighed and wrestled the fish loose from its plastic.

"*Hnh.* Well, I know you're doing a lot. And ain't like I'm not busy, too. Wouldn't hurt you to call a little more often, though." She flipped through one of the home and garden catalogs that sat on the table and looked up at Malaya, then back to Nyela. "What you been fixing for dinner?"

"I haven't had much time to cook," Nyela said, her eyes darting quickly back and forth between Ma-Mère and the fish in her hands.

Malaya pulled out her pad and pencils. "But I've been trying. This week, we had chicken and greens, baked fish, a couple of salads."

This wasn't the first time Malaya had seen her mother lie to Ma-Mère. Each time it happened, she felt closer to her. Nyela raised her eyebrows at Malaya, then looked away quickly before Ma-Mère noticed.

"*Mm-hmm*." Ma-Mère made a sound of either dismissal or disbelief, Malaya wasn't sure which. "Well, I'm glad to hear you're giving them some healthy food. But I see you still working on this kitchen, huh?" She frowned again and surveyed the room. "And seems the yard needs work, too." Percy and Nyela had refinished the brownstone's original brick, and an impressive glossy span of coppery brown covered the large kitchen wall, matching the expensive table Percy had bought to celebrate Nyela's book award. Still, the other walls had not yet been repainted, and the backyard was a small graveyard of broken furniture.

"Yes, I'm working on it," Nyela said, breathing deep. Ma-Mère looked at Malaya again and smiled faintly, holding the fish up in the air in a gesture of mock defeat. Malaya gave a small smile in spite of herself.

"Well, you know, trying's a trap. It's the *doing* makes the donkey drive." She frowned again and looked back at her magazine. "I see you still putting on, aren't you, My Ly-Ly? I'm sure your mother is trying to work on that, too."

Malaya swallowed her spit and looked at Nyela, who raised her head helplessly from behind the stove and tugged a stalk of celery free from its bunch.

As Nyela began to chop, Ma-Mère told a story about the women's health class she was auditing at the community college. She described in detail the instructor's figure—"slim as a second," she said—and the elegant suits the woman wore. There was always a sour note in Ma-Mère's descriptions of other women, no matter how beautiful or even kind she found them. Nyela chimed in, as always, talking about women she knew, how they dressed, whether they were married, whether they'd gained or lost weight since the last time she'd seen them.

Listening to them talk about women was like watching an opera in a foreign language—the emotion was deep and palpable, but the meaning of the words was obscured. A woman they called "sweet" would eventually be revealed as unintelligent; a coworker they identified as "pretty" might turn out to be stunningly beautiful, but also a fool. Nyela's disdain was clearest when she was talking about women she worked with, like her art professor friend, Karen, a pale woman who had the look of a Q-tip, her hair a wispy bulb of white atop her sticklike frame, or Sylvie, her friend from the Black Psychologists Association, who had muscly arms that looked like pea pods and always smelled of Egyptian musk oil. The things Nyela and Ma-Mère seemed to notice about these women were completely different from what stood out to Malaya. Nyela called Karen's figure "delicate," which seemed to her to evoke the exact opposite of the shock of energy Malaya felt when she saw her. Nyela said less about Sylvie, noting only that she really wasn't very pretty, truth be told, but that you'd never know it because she was thin. Nyela smoothed her clothes over her own body as she said this, as though, by being thin, the woman was a living comment on the less-than-seemly about herself. Malaya pulled open the pastel case and flipped the pad to a clean page, deciding to sketch Ma-Mère's hands while she listened.

She was not surprised when the conversation turned to Ethan Windborne. Dr. Windborne was the black woman psychologist who had presented Nyela with the book award, and whenever she talked about her, Nyela's face drew up into a pinch. It was a face that made her look like Ma-Mère.

"Well, you know some women just don't know how to *be*," Ma-Mère said, pulling another magazine from the stack. "Seems like that Windborne's one of them. Wouldn't know a social grace if it ballet-danced on their belly."

Malaya had met Dr. Windborne a few times at Nyela's Black Psychologists Association events, and on each occasion she had been impressed. Dr. Windborne was the kind of woman who, when she entered a room, made other women want to suck in their stomachs and reapply their lipstick. This thrilled and surprised Malaya because, unlike the other objects of her mother's and grandmother's scorn, Ethan Windborne was not even close to thin. She was smaller than Malaya, perhaps about Nyela's size, but her exact weight was hard to tell because, as Nyela had once said, Ethan Windborne took up enough space for five women at least. Nyela had remarked on this bitterly, but the thought excited Malaya. Dr. Windborne had deep skin the color of fired brown clay, and although she must have been in her mid-forties, her hair was an electric bush of silvery gray that would have made her look older than she was if not for all her emerald and cobalt necklaces, the fuchsia lipsticks she wore, and the shine that played perpetually on her face, as though she kept tea lights in her cheeks.

"You should've seen the getup she wore to the awards ceremony," Nyela said, unwrapping a second package of fish. "A big old red dress with gold at the hem, and silver jewelry. Even had the nerve to wear red and gold shoes. She looked like a hot-air balloon about to take off."

Nyela made the Ma-Mère face and gave a quick laugh. Ma-Mère joined in, and their laughter lightened into something tinkling and almost bright that made Malaya want to laugh with them. But quickly, Ma-Mère stiffened.

"Well, you know they're saying we're twice as likely to die from being fat," Ma-Mère said. "Black women, I mean. Did you know that?"

Nyela nodded. She had freed the fish from the plastic and was now running it under water, looking over her shoulder at a Weight Watchers recipe book. "Yes."

"I always told you that, though, didn't I? Ain't have no degree, but all it takes is two eyes and a strip a sense. That's why I'm still tryin' to get these thirty-five pounds off. Some of these women eat like mares at the trough. Plates piled three times high and ready to go back for seconds. Don't see white women eating like that. At least not in public. I've heard stories, though."

Malaya drew a breath and leaned into the paper.

"But you know, they found a solution," Ma-Mère continued. "There's a woman in the class, Cathy. Sweet lady, but big as a houseboat and slow as a barge. She used to wear tacky dresses, her slip always showing and buttons done wrong, just sloppy!" Malaya smudged the crimson pastel along the folds of Ma-Mère's thumb in her drawing, trying not to listen.

"But Cathy don't look like that anymore," Ma-Mère said. She sat up and looked directly at Nyela in a way that suggested this was the true purpose of her visit. "Been dropping weight so quickly you'd think she got in good with Deus or the devil, one or the other. Either way, she looks like half of herself every time she comes to class. So I asked her— politely as I could—what plan she was doing. I thought it was one of those rich people spas you hear about on TV. But she said 'gastric bypass.' You ever heard of that?"

Quiet funneled through the room. Malaya thought she could almost hear Ma-Mère's lipsticked mouth opening, waiting for Nyela's response. Malaya had heard about this surgery on her favorite talk shows, *Jenny Jones* and *Ricki Lake*. There had only been a few operations performed in the US. In Europe, the procedure had helped some people lose a lot of weight quickly, but others had died on the operating table. All of the people in these stories were twice Malaya's age, at least, and smaller than her. She had heard these details in an unhearing way, filing them away with all the other non-options, all the things she didn't want to think of. The procedure was relatively new and controversial, and most insurance companies wouldn't cover it. For this reason, she didn't think it would be an issue. But now, between Nyela's award money and the mounting pressure her weight was causing, Malaya was not so sure. She looked at her mother, who seemed uncertain what to say.

"That's what Malaya needs," Ma-Mère continued. Her voice was relaxed but decisive, as though she were remarking on the time. "Big problems need big solutions. Can't halt a hurricane with a parasol, Nathallie. And whatever you've been doing ain't worked yet."

Nyela looked at Malaya, her face knotted. She raised her eyebrows and opened her mouth, about to say something, but suddenly the fish slipped down into the sink. "W-well . . ." she stammered.

" 'Well' nothing, Nathallie," Ma-Mère said. "She's your daughter and you have to fix this. Shit don't turn to shine by itself." She stood and walked to the sink, reaching down to grab the fish with one hand, ripping off a paper towel and patting it down with the other. "Somebody has to do something."

Neither Malaya nor Nyela said anything after that. Eventually, Percy emerged from the family room and air-kissed Ma-Mère dutifully, and the four of them ate the fish and talked about politics. When dinner was done, they said goodbye to Ma-Mère. Nyela did the dishes, and they retreated to their rooms.

For the rest of the week, Malaya went to class as usual. She avoided Shaniece as usual. She continued to eat dinners up in her room as usual, unremembering. But what she couldn't unremember was the quickness of Ma-Mère's hands coming to the rescue in the kitchen, or the look on her mother's face in that moment. Her forehead was wrinkled with worry, but her eyes looked clear, almost relieved, and more sure than Malaya had seen them, perhaps ever.

Two weeks after Ma-Mère's visit, Malaya sat opposite Nyela on the Metro-North train. She listened to Biggie on her Discman, sketching formless shapes, trying not to think about where the two were headed. Tree-dappled streets rushed toward them outside the window, and the sun glinted on the snowy roofs of the wide homes that lined the streets, their brick frames stretching horizontally like open arms. Malaya noted how different these blocks were, though they were so close to Harlem. She wondered if they could be called "blocks" at all. Blocks were tight configurations of tenement and brownstone wedged together with only enough distance between them for a flirtation, a debate about politics, a spontaneous party on the pavement. These Westchester streets stretched open, the homes separated by wide swaths of space featuring lawn furniture, swing sets, and near-endless green. Malaya pushed herself into the corner of the four-person seat and looked out, leaning against the window to keep her fat from jiggling as the train lurched forward.

"We have to make sure he understands you," Nyela said. She sat across from Malaya, facing her. She stared until Malaya looked back and pulled a single headphone from her ear. "We have to let him know that you're not too young—that you can handle it."

Malaya nodded and moved the headphone back, drawing windows in her sketch pad as Nyela continued.

"And if there's anything you want to say, or if you have any questions, go ahead and ask, okay?"

Malaya nodded again and pressed harder on the page with her favorite graphite pencil—number 7. This pencil produced a perfect heavy line—what her teachers called "high value"—without blurring or smudging on the page. She ran her finger over the weave of the paper.

"Why don't you put your coat on? Aren't you cold?" Nyela reached for her jacket, but Malaya jerked away. Rolling her eyes, she pushed her arms into the tight sleeves, not bothering to try to fasten the zipper.

"I'm fine," she said.

A row of steep hills lay between the train station and the hospital, a compound of large pavilions connected by glass walkways in the sky, through which people scattered and rolled like seeds. Malaya kept her eyes on the tubes as she climbed uphill, heaving breathlessly behind her mother. When they got to the office, the receptionist gave a lipsticky smile and ushered them to a row of plastic seats, where they were to fill out paperwork and wait. Malaya took the last of the chairs, next to a carousel of pamphlets with pastel-colored organs printed on their covers. The chairs were wider than most, but still the arms bore into her hips like fangs. She shifted her weight every few seconds to relieve the pain.

Nyela sat a seat apart as usual and placed her briefcase and coat on the empty chair between them. She unclipped the pen from the clipboard and printed Malaya's name and date of birth neatly on the form's poorly Xeroxed lines. Then she handed it to Malaya.

"It asks you to explain why you're interested in surgery," she said.

Malaya looked at Nyela, then at the paper.

"You know better than I do," she said flatly.

"Malaya," Nyela sighed, "you said you're open to finding out more information. That's all it is. Information about your options."

Malaya took the clipboard and printed INFORMATION ABOUT MY OPTIONS in large letters diagonally across the form, then handed it back to her mother.

Soon, a nurse appeared and asked Malaya in a saccharine voice to follow her down the hallway so she could take her vitals. Nyela gripped her briefcase and pushed herself from her seat, but Malaya said quickly,

"You can stay." She gestured to the form. "I don't know the insurance stuff, so you have to do that part."

Both the nurse and the receptionist looked like something out of a soap opera, their smiles flashing wetly from their heavily rouged faces and their eyebrows arched high like bats' wings. The room the woman led her to, though, was entirely lacking in drama: an examining table, blood pressure cuffs, a familiar artillery of metal tubes and spirals, hanging torture-chamber style from the wall, as always. The only thing that distinguished this room from all the other doctors' offices was a pastel-colored model of a stomach that sat in a large clear case by the hand sink. It was about the size of a fist, with an inch of plastic esophagus sticking up from it like a snorkel and a mess of small intestine pressed around the bottom like a handful of raw ground meat. Each of the model's parts seemed to be removable, and Malaya hoped the nurse would hand it to her so she could take it apart and study its lines. Instead, the nurse took her blood pressure, then asked her to step on the scale.

Though she hadn't been weighed in years, the old feelings bubbled up quick and hot immediately. She regretted not having fought harder to get out of the appointment. When Nyela first mentioned the surgery, Percy had wailed that he would not agree to have his daughter's stomach cut in two, to which Nyela had demanded, over and over, that he come up with a better option. Malaya agreed to the consultation partly in an effort to end the fight. But this conciliatory gesture seemed meaningless now as she stood at the scale alone. She took off her Timberlands, emptied the pager and pencils from her pockets, and stepped on the wobbly metal box, which was marked DETECTO in black lettering. It had a wider platform than most, but its design was otherwise familiar. The nurse reached up behind her and pressed the metal measuring strip against her head, then fiddled with the buttons and frowned. She looked at Malaya, then back at the scale, and fiddled some more. Finally, she scribbled something on her chart and told Malaya to step down. Malaya waited for the familiar moment when the nurse would announce her weight, her voice sodden with remorse, as though it pained her to be the bearer of news so sad as this. But the nurse said nothing, and Malaya didn't ask.

She followed the woman back into the waiting room and sank down into her seat. Just as her hips began to numb once more, a pink-skinned doctor appeared, rushing toward her with his hand extended. Malaya struggled out of the chair and reached up to shake his hand. His eyes on her belly, he introduced himself as Dr. Daniel Sawyer. He ushered her and Nyela toward a long hallway, his eyes still on Malaya, beaming at her as though she were the guest of honor at a fancy ball.

"We're quite excited to work with Muh-lee-yuh here, Mrs. Clondon," he said over his shoulder as he sailed down the hallway. The back of his neck was covered with red and white splotches, and his half-halo of hair tapered into a scruff of calico gray. He moved quickly and Malaya struggled to keep up, as always. Eventually he noticed and slowed down.

He ushered them into a large square room at the end of the hallway. The space looked more like a boardroom than a surgeon's office. It was completely vacant of any recognizable medical apparatus. Instead, a long mahogany desk sat at its center, and a single pane of glass spanned the length of the far wall. A half dozen awards and degrees hung behind the desk. There was little other decoration beyond that. The room's single ornament was a spindly wooden easel that sat awkwardly beside the desk, displaying the now-familiar image of the gastrointestinal tract that she'd seen on the pamphlets and the plastic model. The chairs in this room were wide and plush. She let her hips sink deep into the soft leather.

"We have an excellent track record with the Roux-en-Y procedure, May-lay-yuh," he said, resting on his elbows and leaning in toward her. His eyes were an unusual grayish-green color, flecked with bits of gold. "We've got a dozen or so patients who'd love to talk with you about their success." His mustache spread like wings above his lips, revealing a gummy smile. Malaya wasn't sure what she was supposed to say, so she smiled politely at the man and looked at Nyela, who only nodded.

"Right," she said in her business voice. "Well, we're eager to learn more about your practice."

"Alright," he said, running a hand over his half-nude head. "Well, let's get started." He clicked his pen and laid it down on the desk blotter.

"Obesity is a disease," he announced, looking at Malaya. Nyela shifted in her chair. All the doctors since childhood began their speeches this way, and on the way home from each visit Nyela would clarify: "It is a disease, but it has no cure but you."

"Evidence suggests," the man continued, "that among its many causes may be a genetic predisposition, and behaviors learned in the home."

With his eyes trained on Malaya, he went on to describe how his patients had come to weigh hundreds and hundreds of pounds, and how, thanks to this procedure, they had stepped into sleek new bodies and full new lives. He pulled his chair to the corner of the desk and pointed at the easel. Flipping through pages, he explained what Malaya had gathered from studying the model in the exam room—how packing the stomach with food for years would stretch it gradually until people could perceive little or no physical indication of hunger or fullness, how it could create hernias that were just one of the many hazards of obesity. Like all doctors, he made sure to go through the list point by point, as though she'd never heard it before: *high blood pressure, cardiovascular disease, gallstones, high cholesterol, sleep apnea, stroke, death, death, death.*

He directed his presentation to Malaya, but as he talked Nyela nodded and cleared her throat, saying "Yes, that's right" and "I see" loud and sharp every few seconds. Each time she spoke, it seemed to startle the man, as though he'd forgotten she was there. Finally he flipped to the last page on the easel. In this image, the stomach was divided a few inches past the throat by a thick black dotted line. The caption that crested at the top of the page read "Roux-en-Y Stomach."

"This procedure has a double benefit." He gave Malaya what Ma-Mère would call a Cheshire Cat grin, his lips stretching like a clothesline between his ears. "The small pouch will keep you from eating more food than you can cup in your palm. It will be about the size of an egg, and you will be able to eat that amount about six times per day. But by decreasing the length of the intestine, the procedure will also limit your ability to tolerate certain foods, usually the foods that you"—he paused—"that some of our patients have trouble limiting on their own. Fatty, sugary foods, for example, take longer to digest. With a shorter intestine, your body won't be able to tolerate them. Eating those kinds of foods will induce vomiting, and patients report that they quickly learn to avoid problem foods this way."

Malaya thought of the model stomach, its pale pinks and greens squeezed to the size of an egg inside her. She looked at Nyela, who seemed to wince, though Malaya couldn't be sure.

"Now, for most patients, surgery is a last resort," he said. He looked at Malaya, then at the clipboard, where her mother's handwriting swirled over the page. "And it seems that's the case for you, too, Muh-lee-yah. Like you, our patients tried pretty much everything before coming to us. And across the board, their only regret is that they did not pursue surgery sooner."

Not knowing what to say, Malaya nodded again. She clasped her hands together and flexed her wrists back and forth. She wanted to be out of the room, back on the train with Biggie and her pencils, imagining the luxurious lives on the other side of the glass.

"What are the risks?" Nyela asked.

The man turned his body fully toward Nyela for the first time. "The risks of morbid obesity, Mrs. Clondon, far outweigh the risks of surgery," he said. "In addition to the physical dangers we've just gone over, studies have shown that childhood obesity leads directly to morbid obesity and depression in early adulthood, which can become lifelong. It can interfere with the achievement of major life goals as well as overall development, and can make it extremely difficult to find marriage and employment prospects." He glanced at Malaya, then looked back at Nyela.

"As I mentioned, in addition to the possible genetic connection, obesity often results from compulsive behaviors learned at home, Mrs. Clondon. What I mean by that is—"

"Dr. Clondon," her mother said. "Right, I'm aware of that."

The man's brow stiffened. "Well, those behaviors are extremely difficult to unlearn, especially when patients have been exposed to them since birth. They often repeat over generations, unless there's some intervention. In cases as extreme as Muh-lee-yuh's here, the intervention needs to be drastic. Now, at her weight . . ." The man flipped through the pages of his clipboard. "How much does she weigh, exactly, Mrs. Clondon?"

"*Dr.* Clondon," she said again. Then she turned to Malaya.

"I don't know," Malaya said, looking at her hands. She took a breath.

Nyela straightened her back and looked at the man. "Didn't your nurse take her weight?"

"Well . . ." He propped an elbow awkwardly on the desk. "We're working on getting an extended high-capacity scale in now. Unfortunately, we don't have one at this office yet. Our current high-capacity scale reads up to four hundred pounds, so that pretty much tells us what we need to know." He gave a small chuckle. Nyela's face remained unchanged.

"But the good news is that at her age—sixteen, right?" He spoke quickly, turning back to Malaya. "At sixteen, you've still got a good chance of avoiding the worst risks of obesity. And because of your age, the risks of surgery will be minimal."

Malaya nodded, trying to look like she was hearing, trying to hide the mix of relief and fear she felt as the man rushed forward with his spiel, past the question of her weight. She thought of the model stomach and clasped her hands tightly, holding her wrists against her belly.

"What are the risks?" Nyela asked again.

"Right," he said, flipping the easel back to the cover page. "Well, every patient is different." He looked at Nyela, then back at Malaya. "There's usually nausea and vomiting, which happen when patients try to eat the bad foods we talked about. Some patients also try to eat the quantities of food they're used to, which can cause the staples to come undone. And with every major surgery, of course," he said, giving a shallow shrug, "there is a risk of death. It's rare, and it's extremely unlikely that anything like that would occur with a patient as young as May-lee-yuh here."

"*Ma-LIE-ya*," Nyela said to him. "And how many patients Malaya's age have you treated?"

"Actually," he said, leaning in on the desk as though getting to the good part, "that's why we're so excited to work with Muh-lae-yuh. She'll be the youngest gastric bypass patient in the city. One of the youngest nationwide." His smile broadened, and his eyes grew hot as cider. "This is a great opportunity not only for you," he said, "but for the medical community. And for people all over the country who have this problem. You're the first adolescent patient we've come across in our practice with a body mass index high enough to qualify for surgery without any comorbidities." He gave Malaya his widest smile yet, then perched on the near side of the desk. "In fact, we're so eager to work with Muh-lee-yuh that we've been able to move some things around to get her on the table before the end of the month." He patted Malaya on the shoulder. She gave another polite smile, but the sting of his hand lingered even after he moved it away.

"Now, Mrs. Clondon," he said, frowning, "I know this is all very complicated. I'd be happy to go over the procedure again if you need—"

"Dr. Clondon," Nyela said. "I believe I understand."

"Right." He leaned back. "Well, any other questions, then?"

Nyela paused. Malaya watched, wondering what she might say, grateful that she wasn't being asked to speak for herself. She felt close to her mother, though their seats were a yard apart. There was no touching—Malaya's hands stayed folded in her lap, her fingers laced together, an echo of her mother's—but still, a connection was there.

"Do you have any children, Dr. Sawyer?"

He rested his arms on the desk, the pen still in hand. "No," he said slowly. Then he drew a breath. "But if I did have a child with a condition as serious as Muh-lae-yuh's"—he looked into Nyela's face, the gold flecks in his eyes sparking beneath his eyebrows—"if my child had somehow developed a life-threatening problem like this one, Dr. Clondon, I would not waste any time in correcting it."

Nyela sat for a second, her lips parted. Then Malaya watched her mother stand, fierce and angry and beautiful. Malaya wondered what a woman might say in a moment like this. Nyela waited for Malaya to stand, then she turned toward the office door.

"Thank you, Mr. Sawyer. We'll see ourselves out."

Outside the office, Nyela stood at the desk calmly as the receptionist pulled up the post-visit paperwork. Malaya excused herself to the bathroom. She retraced her steps down the long hallway to the examining room, looking around the corner before opening the door just wide enough to slide in. She looked at the scale. The number 400 was etched, thinning and faded, into the bulky metal ridge. She pulled her number 7 pencil from her jacket pocket and ran the tip along the silver digits, blacking them out until all that could be seen of the numbers were specks of graphite dust floating down to the floor. She stood for a moment, looking at the scale, its impossible math.

She slid the pencil back into her pocket and moved toward the door, stopping with her grip on the handle. She wanted something to take with her. She didn't want to think about the missing number on her intake chart, or about the man's slippery smile as he appraised her. She didn't want to think about her mother's face. She didn't want to think at all, and there was no one to think with anyway, now that Shaniece was gone. And yet, standing in front of the numberless scale, not-thinking suddenly seemed dangerous. She turned back into the room, lifted the model stomach from its case, and slipped it slowly into her pocket, doing her best to keep its little plastic parts intact.

They rode the train back in silence, Nyela grading papers on one side of the train and Malaya listening to Jay-Z's *Reasonable Doubt* in a two-seater across the aisle. But when they said goodbye at the exit of the 125th Street Metro-North station, Nyela's air kiss lingered a second longer than usual as the trains whirred by on the elevated tracks overhead. Malaya said she would take the 6 train downtown to Galton. When her mother was gone, she left the station and took the M101 bus back home.

That night, Nyela paged Malaya from work three times in a row. Each time, Malaya looked at the Drummond University number and didn't call back. After the fourth succession of chirpy beeps, she checked her messages, worried that something might be wrong. In a nervous voice, Nyela invited her to dinner at Copeland's Restaurant and Reliable Cafeteria. Reliable was still Malaya's favorite, and she resolved that whatever news Nyela wanted to tell her, at least there would be a good meal to soften the blow: cornbread as sweet and fluffy as birthday cake and collard greens so good they could hardly be counted as vegetables at all.

"I really need to talk with you," Nyela said. Malaya took a breath and agreed. She hadn't eaten with her mother since Ma-Mère's visit, but the sound of Nyela's voice worried her.

When they got to the restaurant, Malaya slid into the too-tight booth, sucking in her breath and folding her arms to cover her belly, which spilled onto the table. Nyela ordered a basket of cornbread to start, along with a glass of chardonnay, both of which surprised Malaya. Taking this choice as permission, she ordered baked chicken for herself, with a side of fries. As they waited for their entrées, Nyela nibbled on the cornbread and asked about the rest of Malaya's day. Malaya made up a lie, but Nyela didn't listen, which worried Malaya more. She wondered if there was bad news about Ma-Mère's health, or if she and Percy had finally decided to divorce. Once the basket of cornbread had crumbled down to pale gold dust, Nyela looked at her.

"I want to talk to you about something," Nyela said. She looked down and swirled the wine slowly in the glass as their entrées arrived. "The women at the Meeting ask about you every week, you know. Do you think you'll start coming back soon?"

Malaya filled her mouth and chewed. She shook her head. "I need to focus on school." She kept eating, waiting for the topic to fizzle out and the real conversation to begin.

Nyela pushed string beans around on her plate as music began to play from behind the bar. It was Miles Davis's "All Blues," one of Percy's favorites. As a child, Malaya had loved how the song's piano and saxophone notes trickled down over the bass like water in a fountain. Her mother liked the song as well. Malaya remembered the three of them listening to the album, *Kind of Blue*, in the tiny apartment downtown some evenings while Nyela worked on her dissertation and Percy cooked dinner. The album reminded Malaya of closeness, of the smell of onions frying and nights spent together, the three of them, evenings that stretched on endlessly, as long and clear as the pages of a blank sketchbook.

But now, as Nyela sifted through the empty bread basket, gathering loose crumbs of cornbread and running them along the buttered edge of her knife, the saxophone struck Malaya as sad, and the bass seemed heavy with longing. Fleetingly, Malaya hoped her mother would order pie à la mode for them to share as she had when Malaya was young, but she didn't. The conversation she came for was not coming, she realized. There was only this.

After a few chords spent chewing in silence, Malaya felt her mother's gaze again.

"Have you given up?"

Malaya began to tackle the fries, lifting the glistening yellow strips one at a time with her fingers and folding them into her mouth. She tried to find the feeling she'd felt at the doctor's office, fear suited up in anger. But all she felt was weight. She showered the fries with salt and picked at them, praying that if she just kept chewing, Nyela would swallow the question on a smear of butter, and turn the conversation to better things. But she would not stop, and the question lingered, floating through the restaurant on the notes of the album's last track.

"Have you?"

Malaya did not answer. When the food was almost done and there was nowhere else to look but at each other, Nyela raised her head and sighed. She reached into her bag and produced a stack of computer printouts showing "before" and "after" photos of weight loss patients, with testimonials from each framing the page in a cartoonish dialogue box.

"Have you thought about the surgery?" Her face was desperate. "Just look," she said, pushing the papers toward Malaya.

She took them and said nothing. There was a photo of a middle-aged Belgian woman in a cheap-looking red dress who had lost 130 pounds with this surgery, going from a size 28 to a size 14. She had also rid herself of diabetes, she said, and fallen back in love with her husband in the process. "This is the best life I ever had!" shouted the caption beneath her "after" photo. Below that was an older man from Sweden whose "before" photo showed him in a motorized chair, his body floating over its sides and his ankles thick as wall beams. In his "after" photo he stood upright, down 178 pounds and, as he put it in his testimonial, "at least three chins."

The photo that seemed to excite Nyela most was of a twenty-five-year-old black man from Leeds with a muscular chest that curved like a potbelly stove, posed on a soccer field with a broad smile and a back-turned baseball cap. "I have no 'before' photo," his caption said. "There are no pictures from that time in my life, because I wasn't a person anybody wanted to see. Now I want people to see my story."

The photos were not so dazzling to Malaya. She was suspicious of them, of the simple stories they told. But watching her mother talk through these narratives, she saw how all of it—the images, the quotes, the way these people talked about their bodies and how they'd changed— it made Nyela look alive.

"I know it's scary," Nyela said, "but we think it's the best thing. Your father and I. You have to think about it. Please promise me."

Malaya looked down at the fries again. She smacked the side of the ketchup bottle with her palm, watching red splatter on the plate in thick globs like acrylic paint. She slid the fries through the pool one by one, working her way first through the crispest strips, moving on to the pale ones that curled limply on the plate. Still, she felt her mother's eyes on her. It felt like a betrayal, though Malaya could not say why. She felt she and her mother had been in something together all these years, and now she was being dropped off, nudged forward, alone.

"I wish you would tell us what you need," Nyela said finally. "We don't know what to do. We can't just watch you die."

Her face seemed to go gray with these words, and Malaya could say nothing. She could only lower her head, close her eyes, and drag the last French fry across the plate.

The Outside Weight

THE NEXT MORNING, Malaya couldn't get up. It wasn't just the usual longing not to go to school. This feeling was different. It was as though along with the weight of her body, there was another weight on top of her, a larger weight from the outside, pinning her to the bed, pressing on her from the hallway skylight, pulling at her from the floorboards. Her skin felt heavy, her shoulders felt heavy, all the pulp of stuff from her head to her muscle to her bone and nails felt anchored, impossible to lift. It was like nothing she had ever felt before, and yet it was familiar, a deeper shade of a feeling she had known forever.

It was warm for February, but the brownstone's old, failing pipes couldn't keep up with the winter, which made it seem colder in the house than outside. Malaya lay in bed under stacks of blankets, waiting to hear her parents leave: first Nyela, then Percy. She tried to plan the lie she would tell later if they noticed she wasn't getting ready at her usual time, but even that exhausted her. Percy seemed to linger longer than usual, but eventually, hours after the clock radio buzzed its alarm downstairs, both were gone. Still, Malaya couldn't move. It took three more hours of lying there before she could push herself from the covers and out to the bodega for dollar pies and plátano chips.

Outside, the sun was too bright and the music too loud. Someone was playing bachata from a car near Broadway, and it grated on her. The sounds of men joking on the corners scratched at her ears, and for a reason she could not explain, the children popping gum and the smell of roti from the Jamaican spot—things she usually enjoyed—now made her want to cry. It must have showed, because when she walked into the bodega, Mr. Gonzales said, "Mija, you okay?" The question surprised her in a vague, distant way. She nodded and said, "I'm fine," smiling faintly. By the time she rounded the corner with her bag of food, her small store of energy was gone, and all she could do was drag herself back up to her bedroom.

The next morning was the same, and so was the next, and the rest of the week after that. By the following Monday, Malaya called the school to explain that she had been ill and would be bringing a doctor's note. Galton High prided itself on its progressiveness, and it treated students like young adults. If you said you were sick, the administration was inclined to believe you with little drama, provided that you kept up with major assignments and didn't miss tests. Even in those cases, an absence note signed by a parent was sufficient, and no one seemed to inspect the signatures too hard. The goth girls and the Mandys forged absence notes often, and so, Malaya figured, she should be able to do it, too. She didn't have a choice. The outside weight enclosed her, folded her into stillness, leaving her with only enough energy to find food, watch television, listen to music, and occasionally draw. If her parents asked why she was late leaving for school, she resolved, she would say she'd been switched out of her morning class. But they never asked.

ONE MORNING two weeks after the doctor's appointment, she woke to hear her parents talking downstairs as they dressed for work. Their voices were brusque, but they weren't yelling. At first it didn't seem like anything out of the ordinary—Percy talked about a client he had to meet for brunch, explaining why he wouldn't be going into the office today. He was having a tough time at work, and Malaya had heard him complain on the phone to Uncle Book about feeling pushed out by a new generation of programmers—"the gunners," he called them—who showed up fresh out of business school with boyish faces, ready to snatch clients right out his hands. Normally, he talked about these men as mild annoyances. But today, his voice was loud and quick, and his words seemed to rush nervously over themselves as he spoke, as though with each sentence, he wasn't quite sure what he would say next.

"This guy wants the grand old tour from a native perspective," he said. He coughed, and his footsteps creaked toward the hallway. "He wants the Harlem sampler. Sylvia's, the Schomburg. Then a stop at that fancy new coffee chain on Lenox. He'll probably expect me to show up in a zoot suit and serve him some chitlins and hush puppies while we Lindy-hop down 125th." He chuckled quickly and coughed again. Nyela didn't respond.

Malaya lay in bed, waiting for them to leave. She heard the sink run and stop, the buzz of her father's electric razor, then more coughing. After a few minutes, Nyela said sharply: "Did you talk to Malaya?"

Malaya didn't hear his response, but it must have been the wrong one. Nyela's tone grew exasperated: "You have to talk to her. You said you would, not that that means anything. She won't talk to me about this, so you have to do it."

"Fuck, Ny!" She could tell he was shouting, though his voice sounded far away. "I can't even get out the house without you giving me shit, can I? I can't deal with this!"

There was more cursing, more coughing. There was the squeal of the bedroom door closing, and the voices fell away.

Lying under the outside weight, Malaya waited to breathe. She remembered a conversation she'd had with Ma-Mère when she was ten. Ma-Mère had asked her how things were going at home, and Malaya told her about a recent argument between her parents. It must have sounded worse than she thought, because Ma-Mère asked her a question she hadn't expected: *Does he hate her?* At that age, Malaya had never considered that two married people could hate each other. And yet, when Ma-Mère said it, it seemed to make sense. She thought for a moment and answered honestly: "I don't know." Ma-Mère made a face Malaya couldn't understand at the time, and then said, "Well, he never seemed like the fighting type. But with some men you can never tell what's cooking till the pot boils over." Malaya had listened, confused, until she realized that she'd misheard the question—Ma-Mère had asked,

"Does he *hit* her?" not "Does he *hate* her?" At first, she worried that her response would get her father in trouble—that Ma-Mère might think he had gotten violent with her mother. But the question stayed with her. Did he hate her? And if he truly did, wasn't that almost as bad?

Now, there were moments when it seemed that he did hate her. In some ways, Malaya could understand why. It was her relentlessness—the way she seized on an idea, a word, a vision, and fed it like it was the only thing that could give her peace. Usually, the topic was weight: either Malaya's or her own. Malaya had once heard Percy tell her mother that if she fed her relationships the way she fed her anger, the whole family would be happier. Hearing it made Malaya wince then, and it stung her to remember it now. It seemed obvious that both the feeding *and* the anger were inescapable. This, too, brought back that conversation with Ma-Mère—not only because of the misunderstanding, but because, when she had had the chance to explain her mishearing and clear her father's name, she said nothing.

DURING THE TIME of the outside weight, Malaya ignored Shaniece's beeps and calls until they stopped completely. RayShawn still called occasionally in the evenings, and he and Malaya would talk on the phone late into the night about books and music and what it was like to be a young black man. While he talked about his life, Malaya would listen and murmur her understanding as always. It was a curious discovery for Malaya—how if she focused her energy intensely, she could break through the outside weight and beam out another version of herself, a vibrant, smiling hologram of the girl she couldn't be. It was also curious to discover that no one could tell she wasn't really Malaya—at least now that Shaniece was gone.

At the end of their call one evening, RayShawn announced that he was coming over the following day. Malaya hadn't really gotten dressed in weeks; each afternoon she showered and brushed her teeth, then put on the same worn jeans and T-shirt to go out and buy food. When she returned to her room, she peeled the clothes off and slid into her sweatpants again. But today she put on her best EMCEE shirt—pale pink with gray lettering—and braided purple into her hair. Still slow, but finally

moving, she dabbed a glittery lavender shadow over her eyelids like Lil'
Kim and filled her lips with Avalon "Darkest Desire" lipstick from the
99¢ store on Amsterdam. She didn't eat. Instead, she put on her Junior
M.A.F.I.A. CD and stood in the mirror bringing her face to life. She
pouted and grinned, perfecting the look she would give RayShawn that
might inspire him to kiss her, finally, after whatever it was he wanted.

When he rang the bell at around three that afternoon, he gave his
usual broad smile and glided confidently into the foyer as though it were
his own. For Christmas, Malaya had given him a small bottle of Cool
Water cologne—the real kind, not the knockoff oil he usually bought
from the incense man on Jamaica Ave. She didn't particularly like how
it smelled, but he loved it, and when he saw it at the bottom of the gift
bag, he looked her in the eyes and said "thank you" in a deep, lingering
voice that struck Malaya as obnoxious, but still meaningful. Now the
prickly scent trailed thickly in her face as he took the stairs two at a time
toward the family room.

"I brought you something," he said. He dug into his backpack and
produced a thin stack of crumpled papers. Malaya could not help but
hope it was something he'd written her, a story, a set of poems. Instead,
he produced his AP literature final, a paper draft on depictions of mas-
culinity in James Baldwin's plays.

"I want you to read it for me," he said, dropping down on the sofa with
his legs spread wide. "I can trust your judgment."

She imagined herself snatching the pages from him, ripping them
into slivers, climbing onto the sofa, and waiting in a sexy lounge-like
pose for him to ravage her atop the shreds. Instead, she gave the smile
she'd been practicing, a slight parting of the lips and a flash of eye contact. "Thanks," she said, and pretended to read.

On the television, BET was playing "4 Page Letter," the new video
by Aaliyah, her alter ego's muse. The singer stood, thin and angular,
her skin the color of sand, a torrent of straight black hair licking at her
waistline. RayShawn watched, captivated, as she slinked across the
screen like a falling scarf, her narrow body rippling at perfect pace with
the music. Malaya thumbed through pages, murmuring her agreement
as he commented. *Yes, she was the most beautiful artist out. Yes, the way*

she moved her body was amazing. Yes, it reminded her of a waterfall. No, she couldn't look away.

Malaya tried to catch his eye so she could give the other look she'd been practicing—a blank-faced, soft-lipped stare that she hoped said, *I will do what you want.*

RayShawn didn't look at her. So, while Aaliyah sang, she pushed herself closer to him on the couch, the springs groaning beneath her, and unbuckled his jeans. She lowered herself to the floor and kneeled in front of him, lifting her T-shirt over her head, its fabric gathered at her armpits so that her bra was exposed and her back fat covered. The shirt smudged her lipstick, but she tried to ignore it. Instead she unfastened her bra. It wasn't touch that she wanted. It was acknowledgment— evidence that she was there, eligible for touch, for desire. She rubbed and pulled beneath the denim, looking up occasionally to see if he was looking at her, but he never did.

Suddenly the door slammed open downstairs. Malaya moved as quickly as she could, but still the scene unfolded in slow motion, as though through water: RayShawn jerking into action like a marionette, his knee clipping her mouth. More smudged lipstick, more looking away. RayShawn lunging for his shoes. Footsteps on the stairs, slower than ever and impossibly fast as she tried to rope her bra around her middle and tug her shirt back on. Coughing in the hall, the smell of smoke, Percy in the doorway, his face a cracked plate, flat and broken.

"Malaya," he said. His voice was almost warm, almost soft, as though he were about to walk over and put his hand on her back. She pulled herself up on the couch and looked at him, then at RayShawn, who bent down to tie his shoes.

"RayShawn came over for help with a paper," she said.

Percy stood, saying nothing, taking her in. Then he looked at RayShawn. Malaya felt a fleeting wish that RayShawn would puff up in his usual way and say, "Hello, Mr. Clondon," shake his hand as a boyfriend might. But he only glanced up at Percy as though to verify he was really there, then went back to fiddling with his laces.

Moments like this happened often on television, and always—comedy or drama, good father or bad—the father would move on a moment like this. He would grab the boy up by the back scruff and scream rage into his skull, then push him onto the street, out of his house. The boy would simper and grovel, look longingly at the girl on his way out, but the father would refuse all sympathy. Malaya wondered if Percy saw himself in RayShawn, a black boy discovered messing with some girl, caught in her father's glare. Maybe it was sympathy that kept him silent. But then a worse fear rose in Malaya: maybe he was relieved. As bad as this moment was, maybe he had quietly worried it might never come.

Finally, Percy turned toward the computer desk and picked up a stack of books.

"Had to get some files for work," he said. He coughed again, then took a breath and added: "I don't know when your mom's coming home, but you might want to start straightening up soon."

He left without looking back at Malaya. As soon as he was gone, RayShawn smoothed his clothes down as if to sweep the moment off him. He smirked at Malaya on the way out the door, a conspiratorial gloating over a narrow escape.

Alone in the house, she felt her body slow again. The outside weight crept back over her as she struggled to shake the nervous press of the day. It wasn't the shock of what had happened that stayed with Malaya, or even RayShawn's smirk. What she couldn't forget was the sight of her father. He was wearing jeans and an old gray sweater. His hair was overgrown and smelled like smoke. It was an odd thought to have in the moment, but there it was. It felt as strange to her as anything—her father home in casual clothes on a workday, his voice lax in a moment of panic, his breath the only evidence that something might be wrong.

THAT EVENING, Percy knocked on her bedroom door.

"I got some Chinese food," he said. His voice was gravelly now, and his face slightly ashen. "Egg foo young for you, just in case you're hungry. It's downstairs. I can bring it up here if you want. Your mom's working late."

"No," Malaya said. "I mean, thanks. I'll come down."

The family room had become a world in transition. Its structure was more or less the same, but aged. The photos of Ma-Mère and Uncle Book and her father's twin cousins Ro and Augustine still hung on the walls, but now the frames were connected by great cracks in the paint and jagged buckles in the plaster. The picture frames' glass plates were grayed over with a thick fuzz of dust. Though they still called it the "family room," the family hadn't actually spent time there together in years. Now it was Percy's space, where he sat at his computer desk and did whoknew-what. It was a place her mother never touched.

Percy pulled a tin of food from a greasy bag on the computer table when Malaya entered.

"My Laya, can I talk to you?" He handed her the tin. She took it and sat on the sofa, squirting duck sauce into the ravine of gravy, the smell warm and sweet in her face.

"How are things with your boyfriend?" he asked. His voice was soft again, but tired. "I don't think I've met him before."

"He's not my boyfriend," Malaya said.

Percy unwrapped an egg roll and bit. "Huh?"

Malaya hadn't eaten in front of Percy since Ma-Mère's visit, and though the food smelled good, the moment embarrassed her. She sloshed the rice and sauce around with her fork. She could hear in his voice that he wanted to talk to her, really *talk* to her.

"Nothing," she said.

"So, what's his name again?"

"RayShawn." She ventured a small bite of rice.

"Okay," he said. "So do you like him? I mean, does he make you happy? Does he make you feel beautiful?"

Malaya took a breath. She remembered the Friday nights they spent together in childhood—sitting here in this room with a spread of food in front of them and nobody to tell them what to eat, what to do. But now there was no laughter, no family sitcom playing. Now the secret sharing was heavy. The outside weight pressed on her. She took a bigger bite.

"No one thinks that but you," she murmured, her mouth full of rice.

"Hmm?" he said.

The tin was hot in her hands. Perfect cubes of ham poked up from a moat of gravy, greasy and glistening in the room's pale light. She dug the fork deep into the tin and lifted a heaping mound to her mouth, the sweet peas and salty sauce bursting like music.

"Laya, what did you say?"

She swallowed and pushed herself further into the corner of the sofa, trying to make herself small.

"I said he's not my boyfriend."

This was what teenagers did, Malaya knew. Quick, short statements designed to shut down conversation, shore up the borders, like wrapping herself in barbed wire. It was a move she made often, but now she felt the guilt swell in her chest. RayShawn had given her nothing, had asked no questions of her. But her father had. Still, she closed to him.

Percy sighed. He walked to the window, pushed it open, and pulled a pack of cigarettes from his back pocket. Malaya had not seen him smoke since before the move to Harlem. It brought a jolt to see it now—a mix of terror and relief.

"Can I tell you something?" he said, blowing smoke out the window. The air from outside cut quickly into the brownstone's thin steam heat. Malaya nodded.

"I quit. A couple months ago. I had to." He muffled a cough. "That job was trying to kill me."

He looked back at Malaya, then out the window again. There was nothing behind the brownstone except for the broken chairs, an abandoned lot, and the empty backyards of the neighboring brownstones, one of which was a crack house and the rest of which had recently been put up for sale. Still, Percy stared out the window as though he saw a story there.

"Well, maybe they weren't trying. But good intentions don't always get the job done, do they?"

He didn't look for her response, but she nodded anyway.

"Your mom doesn't know," he continued. "I'm not going to ask you not to tell her, 'cause that would be wrong. But I wanted to tell you. You understand. I want you to know that life isn't neat. Sometimes you have to pull a thread, make a choice for you. Once in a while, you have to make the choice that has your name on it, even if it makes no sense to anyone else. That's what I want for you."

He took another drag of the cigarette, then lifted the screen and put it out on the ledge of the windowsill.

"I'm going to write a book," he said. He closed the window and leaned over it the way he did when gunshots rang outside, looking out over the trash-filled lots.

"It's gonna be about the neighborhood, and how it's changing. This place has meant a lot to me, and I know it in a way that these folks don't. I was out today, just walking, and a white woman with a little dog walked right into me, talking about 'Look where you're going! Use your eyes!' She couldn't have been more than twenty years old. A young white girl, walking around Harlem, yelling at *me*, telling *me* to look around. And I did. And what I saw, I'm telling you, was nothing but memory. Things I thought would always be here, now just gone. And I thought—someone needs to write this down."

Malaya let her body spread a little on the couch as she listened. He talked about how the five-and-dime where he had his first job was now the fourth or fifth HMV record store in the city, and how the new Old Navy stood where the Top Flight Ladder Company had been. And so, he said, memory was all there was. And that was why he was writing.

Malaya lifted forkfuls of oily meat and rice into her mouth while he told her how he'd been spending his days for the last two months, retracing the streets he'd climbed over as a bright-faced brown child, taking notes on which church had disappeared, which project had been razed, which numbers spot had become a health food store, and which mom-and-pop shop had been replaced by a sporting goods chain. He talked about spending long mornings on Edgecombe Avenue, where he and Book had once roamed with a gaggle of pea-headed boys and played bottle caps and commando, and the street corner where he had pushed Uncle Book out of the line of fire in the first of many gunfights to interrupt their play. He told about the first time a cop pulled a gun on them, when he was twelve and Book just nine. He told her about the abandoned lot on Seventh Avenue, which was once an exhausted tenement where he had shared a room with Book, his mother, and his father, before his father left. Again, he told the story of the Top Flight Ladder Company, where he got the disease that gave him life and took it from him. Again, he told about the United House of Worship on 125th, where his father put down the bottle, learned to read, and became a preacher, finding Jesus and the comforts of holy women just in time to leave his wife and children behind. He told her how it hurt then, how it hurt still, but how, in some ways, he now understood.

Finally, he told her how easy it was to quit his job—two short syllables, and he was free as wind.

"That kind of freedom is a rush," he said, still propped at the window. "But once that rush is gone, all you want is more of it. One wild choice can lead to another. That's the thing with freedom. Freedom can get you hooked.

"What your mom and I have is memory," he said, finally. "Plenty of it. And memory's not bad. But it isn't freedom. I always knew what I wanted, but I never knew how much until now. More than I want to be happy, healthy, even whole, I want to be free. I want that for you, too."

He turned away from the window and coughed again.

"Sorry," he said, not to Malaya, but to nothing. "It's just, sometimes thinking about the past, you can almost grab a feel of the future. Like maybe you can change it. You know what I mean?"

Malaya felt she did.

"Your mom will be home soon," he said, looking at her. His face was weathered but calm. He pulled a can of air freshener from a corner behind the computer desk and sprayed, then bent to gather the empty Chinese food tins. He coughed again.

"Thanks," Malaya said. "For dinner, I mean." She pushed herself up from the couch, holding the empty tin in her hand. "I can clean up," she said, but he was already busy hiding away the mess.

AFTER THAT DAY, Malaya and Percy shared a secret once again. Now, he left the house later and later each morning, never mentioning that Malaya had not yet gotten up for school. Sometimes he came back unexpectedly in the middle of the afternoon, and she would hear the family room window screech open as he lifted it up to smoke. Once in a while, she noticed a faint smoke smell behind the closed door, even when Percy wasn't home. Malaya worried Nyela might smell it, but if she ever did, she said nothing. Most days, Percy played music, too—old Stevie Wonder and Earth, Wind & Fire songs that reminded Malaya of the lazy Saturdays downtown.

Now that she knew how Percy spent his days and he knew how she spent hers, they protected each other. Occasionally, Malaya would drift downstairs to find he'd left her a bodega pie or a two-piece from the chicken spot on the foyer table, the crinkly arms of its plastic bag tied in a bow.

One afternoon in the middle of February, Percy left her a twenty-dollar bill, with instructions to treat herself to a movie and popcorn. He'd seen the new John Singleton flick, he said, and he thought she would like it. Malaya appreciated the gesture, but with the outside weight still on her, the thought of taking the bus downtown, sitting and eating in public in the tight theater seats, even in the dark, was daunting. Instead, she went to the corner bodega for a plate of pernil and arroz con gandules, standing in the entryway of the crowded storefront for fifteen minutes under Mr. Gonzales's appraising eye while his wife, Aracelis, prepared the food. When Malaya finally climbed the brownstone stairs with the bag, she found Percy bent over in the doorway of the master bedroom. Her chest panged as she neared the doorway. A few steps in, she saw he was staring into the open flaps of a cardboard box. He heaved loudly, hoisted the box to his chest, and turned toward her, surprised.

"Laya," he said. "How long have you been home?"

Malaya paused. She hadn't had to explain herself in so long, and now she had no lie ready.

"I mean," he said quickly, "I just didn't know you were back already. How are you?"

"Fine," she said. Then, in a quick reflex of self-protection, she added: "Is everything okay?"

"Yeah." He heaved slightly as he put the box down. "I'm just moving some things. Make some space for myself in the family room, I think.

Figured I'd take care of it today while your mom's at work." He brushed his palms together and stretched.

"Some unsolicited advice," he said. "When you buy your first house, unpack everything right away. You'd be surprised how much you can learn to live without. Even things you think you need like air—you wake up one day and can't even remember what they looked like. If you want to keep things important, you gotta use them. Otherwise you spend your whole life just making do."

He fished an old computer joystick from the box and held it up.

"Like this," he said. "Remember?"

Malaya did remember. This was the joystick whose Skittle-sized trigger button she had pounded eagerly as a child playing games like Dream Home and Air Force Attack. The joystick, and the old Commodore computer it came with, reminded Malaya of the easy weekend mornings and summer vacations, light pouring thick as orange juice through the old apartment's walls.

"Yeah," she said, "I remember."

"Remember Pac-Man?" He gave a shallow chuckle. "Remember how hard I tried to get you to play Ms. Pac-Man? You didn't like it. Said her hair bow looked fake, and the marshmallows, too."

"Yeah," she said. "They looked like plastic. Not very appetizing."

He smiled and leaned against the doorway.

"So your mom wants me to talk to you. About that surgery."

Malaya held the bag behind her. She stared over his back into the bedroom. The books and papers that once sat in tall piles on Nyela's side had been knocked like a set of bowling pins over the bed, desk, and floor. Stacks of Percy's suits lay limply across his side of the bed, the hems of the pants trailing into the open mouth of a suitcase.

Malaya parted her lips to say something, but before she could get a sound out, the front door slammed open downstairs. Their eyes met. It was 3 p.m., several hours before Nyela should be home.

They listened to the rustling of bags and the clanging of bangles downstairs. Soon, Nyela appeared, her eyes bright and confused. They hung together in quiet, three pairs of lips parted on the verge of sound. Finally, Nyela gave a cautious smile.

"Hi," she said. She was holding her briefcase, a broom, and several black garbage bags. Her voice was pleasant, but unsure. "What are y'all doing home?"

"I wasn't feeling well," Malaya said. "I left school early."

"Oh," Nyela frowned. "Why didn't you call me?"

"I was here," Percy interjected. "Working from home. I told her she should take it easy today."

Nyela pressed her lips together and looked at Malaya. Malaya thought about the food in the bag, the juicy pork shoulder and the tufts of rice peeking through mounds of plump, tender beans. She shoved the bag behind her, hoping her mother wouldn't smell it.

"So you're feeling better?"

"Yeah," Malaya said. "I think I just needed to rest."

"Okay," Nyela said. "Well, I was just going to clean up in here, finally. I was going to surprise you." She turned to Percy, then back to Malaya. "But let me just put all this down and I'll see what we have downstairs. Maybe I can make you something. Some soup. I'm glad I'm here."

Nyela moved past Malaya toward the bedroom. She stopped in the doorway and lingered for a moment, then turned around. The broom smacked to the floor.

"Are you going somewhere?" She looked at Percy.

"What?" he sputtered. "Oh. No."

"Pra," she said, letting the garbage bags fall to the bed. "God, are you serious? You're gonna do it like this?"

His mouth hung open.

"No conversation? No apology? I just come home one day and your things are gone? I never thought you'd do it this way."

"Ny," he said, his voice a plea, "I'm not going anywhere. I'm just moving some of my things into the family room."

Nyela dropped her briefcase. Malaya sucked in air.

"I'm not leaving," he said. "I'm moving my things into the family room. It's not like there's any room for me in here." He pointed his chin toward the bedroom.

"What is that supposed to mean?" she said, her eyes wide.

Percy looked at Malaya, who looked at her mother, then at the ceiling, then at the floor.

"My weight?" Nyela's voice was stark and sudden. "Are you talking about my weight?" The room tensed. The kitchen was so far away.

"No," he said. "No. That's not . . ."

Nyela's eyes grew moist.

"Right. It's never that, is it?" she said. "So what? What are you not telling me?"

In all the years of their fighting, Malaya had never heard her mother beg.

"I'm not working," he said. "I quit."

Nyela's face twisted into an expression Malaya had not seen before— a helpless grief as thick as anger, like the face of a child watching her favorite doll break in her hands.

"Did you think you didn't need to tell me that?" Her voice was electric, a frantic song. "Why wouldn't you tell me that? How . . . Don't you think that's something I need to know?"

"I'm telling you now," he said, looking down.

Malaya shifted her weight. Her back felt like cement against the banister.

"Telling me now," Nyela repeated. "I came home early to take care of things in this house. Clean up. Make dinner. I thought it would be a nice surprise. For you. I'm trying for you. To be . . . to do things for you."

"Look, I should have told you," he said. "But it's not a bad thing. I mean, it doesn't have to be. I'm writing a book."

"A book," she said to the window.

"You know I've always wanted to write a book about the neighborhood," he said. "About how it used to be. It's important. People will care about this."

Nyela sat on the edge of the bed, her back toward them. She shook her head.

"'People will care . . .'" she said over her shoulder. "Percy. All those things you can say to *people*, because people will care. And you can't say a damn thing to me. Not a damn thing."

Malaya's chest was tight. She couldn't remember the last time she heard her call him Percy.

"I'll get something else soon," he said. "I will. Don't worry, Ny." He was begging now. "It'll be fine."

Nyela turned around and steadied herself on the bedpost. She looked up, reading his face. She began first to shake, then to cry. This was the couple Ma-Mère talked about, stumbling through arguments like a game of tag, chasing and being chased, finding solace in each other for a few seconds' breaths, then running frantically apart again.

"I don't know what these tears are," Nyela said, wiping at her face. "Anger, I guess. And something else." They looked at each other with an intensity that told Malaya they had both forgotten she was watching. "I thought it was a woman. All these years. I thought you found someone else you wanted to be with. Now I know you just don't want to be with me."

Percy stepped toward Nyela slowly, his hand reaching for her back.

"Don't touch me," she said, turning toward the window. "Keep going. Pack your things. Pretend I'm not here."

Notorious

PERCY HAD NOT moved out of the house, only across it, but still he left an absence. The brownstone carried a constant air of his waning, even when he was around. He slept on the family room sofa, amid piles of computer equipment, stacks of file boxes, and the suitcases he'd dragged from across the hall. He lined his slippers along the TV console and hung his bathrobe from the record stand, so that when Malaya entered the room, she felt she was intruding on a man's private space. This meant that the family room, too, was gone.

Outside, storefronts and restaurants disappeared more quickly than ever. Now several of them became construction sites, their doors splayed open to the street as workers carried old plumbing and electrical fixtures out. By the end of February, the tiny Garrison & Sons Harlem Hardware on St. Nicholas was gone, as was the Jamaican weed spot on Broadway. Excavator trucks descended on several of the empty lots, raking them of gravel, trash, and limestone, and there was a rumor that Mr. Gonzales's bodega was at risk. Each time Malaya pushed through the slim store doors for a fistful of dollar pies, Mr. Gonzales gave the same distant smile as always, but now a mix of fatigue and worry played at the corners of his eyes.

February's flash of springtime ended, and March came in cold and cruel. Malaya fell asleep every night under a pile of old blankets, full

172 MECCA JAMILAH SULLIVAN

of food, listening to wind rush in through a crack in her bedroom window. Each morning, she woke to the desperate clang of the brownstone's aging pipes. Sometimes, she could catch a beat in the pipes' rhythm, and she found herself making up rhymes in her head as she waited for her clock radio to sound. Other times, on the coldest days, the clanging was more like a barrage, and it ended with a loud sputter as a spray of boiling hot water shot clear across the room.

One morning, Malaya woke to the sound of a woman's voice, a half-scream, half-moan outside. Most of Harlem's screams were loud and deliberate—a grandmother calling a boy from a window, a girl squealing giddily as she ran toward her boyfriend. This sound was vague and directionless, a wordless wail. Soon, a car radio came on, and then another, and a third.

Malaya lay in bed and listened as they blasted the news that Biggie had been killed. They said it was in connection with the killing of Tupac Shakur months earlier, but Malaya didn't believe it. As much as he had rapped about death, his cheeks always shone with possibility. His voice was thick with it—this was why she liked him. But now, his sad-and-sparkling collage of full-throated blackness seemed to flatten into a simple grief, oozing thick and hard from the radio into the streets. Malaya felt the news in her stomach. It was a shock made all the more painful because it wasn't a surprise.

She wanted to talk to Shaniece, but Shaniece was gone. Instead, she spent the morning in bed listening to the radio station's tribute, which seemed to echo through the neighborhood from stoops and apartments and car radios speeding down the block:

> *Biggie there e'ry night!*
> *Poppa been smooth since days of Underoos . . .*

The songs played one after another, from the upbeat new single, "Hypnotize," to the heavier tracks—"You're Nobody Til Somebody Kills You," "Everyday Struggle," "Ready to Die."

Malaya lay in bed listening numbly until Edgar's number appeared on her pager. There was no one to lie to today, no one for whom to spin a story about her fantasy man Clarence. But still she was grateful for the call. When Edgar asked, yet again, if he could come pick her up, this time she agreed.

"Big Woman," Edgar said, craning his neck toward her from the driver's seat as he pulled up to the tenement beside the brownstone, where she'd told him to pick her up, "I asked you to meet me so many times. Finally you say yes. Today is my good day."

It had been two months since the Big and Tall, and though they had had several phone conversations, Malaya knew little about the man. Still, she had come to feel a sort of tenderness toward him. She couldn't be sure how old he was, but whatever his age, he still had a youthful buoyancy that made her want to trust him. It was evident in his eager smile and the unwieldiness of his voice, which sometimes lurched up in volume unexpectedly, a gruff sound like the revving of an engine. Sometimes she asked him to teach her words in Gola, and when she repeated them, he complimented her on her accent, which she liked. He was a lonely man who lived on Long Island and worked the bag check counter of Harlem Jeans on weekday afternoons for the extra money; he made his real living as a driver for one of the private car services that filled the streets of Harlem and Washington Heights, where yellow taxis refused to go. The companies all had names that advertised luxury—names like *Hi-Class* and *Presidential*. The car he drove was *First Rate*.

Malaya moved toward the backseat door, but he called to her again.

"Big, Pretty Woman!" His voice was eager. "Why would you sit back there? You are a very special passenger. Come to the front so we can talk like friends."

He reached over to the window and fumbled with the door. Malaya had almost forgotten what he looked like. He had a smooth, broad nose, and high, round cheekbones that sat just below his eyes like two plums. She remembered his scar as deep and garish, but now she saw it curved along his jawline in a way that was almost pretty. He was a little chubbier and taller than she remembered, and his smell was earthy, like scorched wood.

The car sprang beneath her as she sat. She counted the loose change in her pocket as he drove over Macombs Dam Bridge, toward the Bronx.

One dollar and thirty-two cents—enough for several phone calls, but not enough to get her home if anything went wrong. Years ago, Percy would pin emergency money to the insides of her backpack, a new five-dollar bill each September; she spent the money on cookies or Starbursts at the ice cream truck before the first Jewish holiday. As a child, she could not imagine any emergency greater than a bus ride home without some sweet thing to fill her mouth. Now she appreciated her father's concern.

"Are you comfortable?" he asked. He reached down beside him and Malaya felt her seat sliding backward, giving her thighs room to spread. She nodded gratefully.

She did not know the man or where he was taking her, and she now realized how much he knew about her: her pager number, her phone number, what block she lived on and where. The most meaningful thing she had withheld from him was her name, which suddenly did not seem like much. But the outside weight pressed on her, and even her worst fears were flat and vague, as though she were looking at them through a glass.

As he drove, he talked about the Hempstead apartment he shared with two strangers and one childhood friend. He told her about his children's young mother, whom he'd left behind in Monrovia. "Better for them to be together at home now," he said. "But they'll have to leave soon." Malaya wanted to ask more questions, but his gaze was fixed far ahead on the highway, and she knew he did not want to talk about who the real Clarence had been.

While he told his stories, Malaya tried to turn herself on for him, to spark herself to life as she had for RayShawn. Prettiness was the price of attention, and for fat girls, prettiness alone was not enough—one had to shine with a confidence so complete it looked like desire. Malaya examined the reflection of her eyebrows in the windshield and arched them as he spoke, cocking her head to the side and pursing her lips into a plump pout.

"I thought I would never get you," he said. "I'm so glad you are here."

Malaya thought about what Alya would say. She hefted her weight onto one hip and turned her face toward him, pushing her breasts out and giving a sigh. "Like you said, today is your good day."

It sounded like the kind of thing a man would want to hear, the kind of thing a woman would say.

Edgar placed his hand on her knee. She thought about pulling away, but she didn't. Instead, she nodded and pretended not to notice as he pushed his fingers against the seams of her jeans, his eyes fixed on the road.

"I like you, Al-yuh," he said, lifting her hand and pressing it between his legs. "Do you see how much?"

AFTER TWENTY MINUTES of driving, he pulled into the parking lot of a low, flat building off the Bronx River Drive.

"Stay here, Big Woman," he said. "Let me take care of some business."

He walked toward an awning that revealed in weathered grayish paint THE DAYLIGHT IN, the final N of which had either faded off completely or had never been there in the first place. He disappeared under a door marked "Office."

The streets were playing Biggie here, too. Sitting in the parking lot, Malaya could hear two different songs—"10 Crack Commandments" and "Brooklyn's Finest"—their beats thumping toward her from different directions.

Edgar appeared a few minutes later, his face spread into a wide, toothy smile. He extended an arm to help her out of the car and led her down a long walkway, past a row of old, dented burgundy doors and windows covered in peeling gray blinds. He ushered her into room 209, a bare room at the end of the hall whose walls were covered in dusty, glittered stucco that strained to shine under the buzzing light. In the center of the room was a queen-size bed covered with a faded bedspread the color of oatmeal. The only other furniture in the room was a wooden folding chair and a desk on which an ashtray sat, stuck to a plastic place mat. Malaya had to look up to notice the room's one interesting feature—the whole ceiling was covered with mirrors.

"It's nice, Big Woman?" He unzipped his jacket and laid it on the folding chair. Malaya dropped her backpack on the floor and took her jacket off.

"Yeah," she said.

He turned on the TV set at the foot of the bed and Malaya watched as five or six naked blond white women sprang up on the screen, pressing together and licking each other like a group of kittens. She had seen pornography only a few times before, with Shaniece at Eric Martinez's house after school when his mother wasn't home. But seeing it here with this man was different. Before, she had watched excitedly, wondering what it might be like to be one of the women—or to be the man with them—sweating and writhing on the screen. Now, she watched it like a round of checkers, observing each move numbly, wondering when the game would end.

Soon, Edgar took his shirt off. His belly was round but his arms were spindly, and his skin was smooth and even, the color of root beer. He turned the volume up on the TV and moved toward her on the bed, sinking his fingers into her braids and pressing her face into his brittle chest hair. With his clothes off, he still smelled like firewood, but also like sweat and cumin and some kind of soup. He put her hand on his crotch.

"See how much I like you?" he said again.

She pulled her hand away, then tried to cover her awkwardness with a smile. She tried again to imagine herself as Alya—the arched eyebrows, the sandy brown skin. She felt her stomach jump as he kissed her, his tongue darting into her mouth like a mouse into a dark corner.

"So tell me," he said, "what do you like, pretty girl?"

Malaya tried to give an inviting look she hoped could pass for an answer, but it didn't come off right. When he moved to unfasten her jeans, she pushed his hands away. Instead, she eased the button slowly from its hole on her own, holding the denim carefully away from her skin, taking care not to touch the raw strip of flesh around her middle. She took her shirt off, sat on the edge of the bed, and looked up at the mirror: her pink cotton panties hidden in her folds, her face straining to look like it knew what to do.

"Stand up, big, pretty girl."

He tried to turn her around with his hands, but he couldn't move her. When she realized what he wanted, she said "okay" and climbed onto the mattress. The fan whirred dizzily above her, and her shoulder ached.

She tried not to think of how strange it felt, the small squish of a for-eign thing, nudging her from the inside. She tried not to notice how quickly he moved, how much she felt in that one place in her body and how little she felt everywhere else. She tried not to think of the dull pain it caused her, as though pain were just a part of breathing. She tried to imagine Alya here instead of her, or her own self someplace better, with clean floors and no dusty television, with the touch of someone she truly wanted moving through her. She tried to imagine feeling good, the tightness between her legs igniting, erupting into fireflies. She tried not to look around her. She tried not to think of anything. She tried not to think of Shaniece.

After a while, Edgar grabbed the meat of her sides and grunted, his sweat slick on the backs of her thighs. "Big girl," he said. "So big."

Finally, he gave a deep sigh and lay down on the bed.

Malaya lay frozen, juice leaking slowly from her as the blond women whirled on the screen. For a second, the outside weight was gone, along with everything else—the bed, the room, gravity. She tried to still her-self, to time the heaving of her chest with the rhythm of the fan, but she couldn't. In an instant, the weight came back, heavier than before. She held her stomach, willing herself to inhale, exhale, to keep herself from crying.

"Do you want food, pretty girl?" Edgar said, looking up at the ceiling. "We have twenty minutes. Not too long." He paused, tracing a circle in the air with his finger and studying his reflection.

Malaya looked up at the mirrored ceiling again, at her body spilling in waves over the cream-colored sheets.

"No," she said, lifting herself up as best she could, "I'm not hungry. Please just take me home."

THAT NIGHT, Malaya ate a mixing bowl full of instant oatmeal in bed and waited to feel different. She thought she should feel something—if not womanhood or change, then an ending, at least, a loss she could grip. She wasn't sure what had happened with Edgar. She had wanted it, had wanted something, though perhaps not in a bodily way. And yet, this bodily want now seemed tiny in her larger universe of need. She had needed touch, an escape from the outside weight. She had needed to leave home. And she had gotten those things, at least in some way.

Running her hands over herself, between her legs, she noticed her body did feel a little odd—rawer, spongier to the touch. But the other sense of feeling, the feeling from the inside, was still the same. Still nothing.

It struck her that she had no language for this absence. And there was no one she could tell about it, even if the words had been there.

In that moment, her pager buzzed loudly. The old code appeared: 8008135. Malaya moved quickly to the phone.

"Hey, girl." The familiar voice, the wavering tone.

"Hey," Malaya said.

"I didn't want anything. I just thought I would say wassup."

"Word?" Malaya said. Feeling rushed to her skin.

"Yeah," Shaniece said. "Word."

They sat in silence for several breaths.

"It's been a minute." Shaniece's voice was clear now, but gentle, still skimming whisper tones. "You okay?"

The receiver felt heavy in Malaya's hand. She wanted to say yes, and no. She wanted to tell Shaniece about Edgar and the outside weight. She wanted to say the real, true things she had not named. Quiet hung between them, and her mouth went salty and dry. There was something else she wanted to say most of all, something full and urgent that clattered against the hollow of her throat. But she had no words for that, either.

"I don't know," she said into the quiet.

"I feel you," Shaniece said after a while. "That's all I can say, I guess. But I mean it, Malaya. I really do."

Malaya sat for a second, soaking in Shaniece's voice, the sound of her breath. By the time she opened her mouth to ask, "Are *you* okay?" Shaniece had said goodbye.

LATE INTO THE NIGHT, Biggie was still playing. What had started as a funerary tribute had become an outright celebration. People sat on parked cars holding bottles in the air and spouting the lyrics to "Big Poppa." Clusters of men and women sat on the tenement stoops, bounc-

ing children on their laps in time with the rhythm of "Hypnotize."
Malaya even thought she heard the "Juicy" beat play from her father's
room downstairs. It was a small thing, but it comforted her. The artist
was gone, but his voice was everywhere.

When the oatmeal was done, she pulled her largest sketch pad from
the bed and dug out her color pastels. Listening to the music, she
swept her arms across the salt-white paper as quickly as she could to
the rhythm. Soon something caught, and she let her hands go faster,
wider, with no beat or plan at all. Almost wild. Orange palms cupped red
cheeks and purple eyes closed or slung low on the paper. Side-cocked
heads rested against the edges of the pages, their necks and bodies falling out of the scene, their chins and cheeks round as gumballs with
peach and magenta and Day-Glo green. She moved quicker, pressed
harder, as though she were outrunning the outside weight, outweighing
it. She pushed shade over shade, pressing and moving until the paper
was thick and shiny with color.

The block moved from Biggie to other songs, going from eighties hip-
hop albums to classic soul anthems to funk songs she recognized from
her parents' collection and B-sides from the school bus days. After several sketches and what might have been hours, she wiped her smudged
fingers on her belly and looked at the drawings. They were interesting.
Pleasing, in a messy, asymmetrical way. She liked them—they reminded
her of quickness, of space and good feeling. Of dancing.

When her arms were finally tired, she moved to the window, her
thighs and behind piling in the narrow bay of the windowsill. She
propped herself there and looked out. Men leaned against car hoods
swigging drinks out of brown paper bags, and teenage boys popped
wheelies on their bikes in T-shirts, as though there was no ice on the
ground, no cold in the air, no such thing as winter at all.

Two girls about her age huddled together, whispering to each other on
a brownstone stoop across the street, and Malaya thought of Shaniece.

She propped herself up on the windowsill and stayed there until the
sun spilled its pale pinks and creams onto the avenue. She stared over
Harlem as it danced beyond the glass, wondering how it might feel to
join in.

Fakeout Summer

OVER THE NEXT FEW MORNINGS, Malaya felt the outside weight begin to lift. It was as though a heavy thing inside her had pulled loose as she watched the neighborhood celebrate that night, an old pain uprooting just enough to reveal the tender space it left behind. Her body still felt slow in a way she couldn't name, but now the slowness was uncomfortable, and her skin yearned to be free of it. She continued to skip school, but sometimes a whole day passed without her needing to burrow into bed. Instead, she sat at the easel listening to "Juicy" and drawing wide pastel skyscapes between bites of her egg foo young. Sometimes she stood at the window remembering the perfect music of that night, how Shaniece's call and the block's spontaneous party had struck through her numbness, made her feel that hip-hop's dazzling futures might be possible after all.

She still kept her distance from Shaniece—she wasn't sure what the phone call had meant and hadn't found the words to ask. She didn't reach out to LaFamille either, but she began to beep Mei-Lin, the goth girl in her social studies class, to see what was going on at Galton, just in case. When Mei-Lin called her back, she joked about the white students in a calm, breathy deadpan. "The Mandys are losing their minds," she said, her voice rasping. "They've discovered rap music. They're holding so-called 'rap battles' now. They follow each other around all day going,

'My name is Mandy and I'm here to say!' One after the other. Send help."
Each time they talked, Malaya laughed gratefully.

In the middle of March, she woke to find that the banks of dirty
snow that had lined the block for weeks now gleamed, slick and melting under the sun, and rivulets of slushy water carried candy wrappers and bottle caps toward Broadway. In the fall, the weather people
called these miracles "Indian summer," though even then, the term
seemed absurd and inaccurate—one of those historical inversions
that seemed to slip into people's heads unchecked, like Independence
Day, which should have been called Colonial Codification of Black and
Brown Unfreedom Day, as far as Malaya was concerned. She had said
this once in the ninth grade, and all of LaFamille had agreed, making
it part of their unofficial creed, which Eric etched along the underside
of one of the loose backstage floorboards with an X-Acto knife. Malaya
had been glad for the affirmation then, and now the memory made her
miss LaFamille. She was sure they would have welcomed her critique
of Indian summer with gusto. What did Indigenous people have to do
with a weatherman's lies? Call a fakeout a fakeout, was her feeling. And
so, quietly, to herself, she thought of it as a Fakeout Summer, smack at
the height of the snow-falling months.

A few days into the Fakeout Summer, Percy and Nyela sent her to
Philadelphia to stay with Ma-Mère for a long weekend. It didn't seem
to be a punishment—she had succeeded in intercepting mail from the
school, erasing her teachers' messages on the answering machine, and
lying about her new late-morning schedule. Nyela had no reason to suspect she was missing school, and she knew Percy would not expose her.
She wasn't sure what their reasons were for the trip, though she imagined it had to do with the surgery and her weight. She had continued to
get bigger since the surgical consult, but no one had mentioned it since
Percy's move to the family room.

Malaya hadn't been to Ma-Mère's since she ended her summer visits
years ago. Yet now, at sixteen, she was being remanded to three days in
the Philadelphia townhouse, where all the furniture was still covered
in plastic and every room had the forbidding air of an old museum.

Over the years, Ma-Mère had intensified, like oil paint on a canvas, deepening coat by coat. Now well into her sixties, she continued to be unrelenting in her critiques of fat, and the elaborate acerbity of her comments had only taken on extra flourish as she aged.

On the day Malaya arrived, Ma-Mère spread her arms as wide as she could and said, "Guess I'll have to take the doors off the hinges next time I see you, big as you're getting," and leaned in for an air kiss.

When lunchtime came that afternoon, they sat at the Formica kitchen table before a spread of crudités and finger sandwiches she had bought at her favorite delicatessen in Center City. Hungry from the trip, Malaya finished a petite wedge of turkey and cheese and reached for another, but Ma-Mère sat up at the table and cleared her throat. "You sure you need to eat that, My Ly-Ly? One more bite of that sandwich and you're liable to blow like Willy the Whale." Malaya put the sandwich down and leaned back in the hard wrought-iron chair.

The worst was the way Ma-Mère now talked about Nyela. This had always bothered Malaya, but now Ma-Mère's every sentence seemed to begin with some version of "Your mother doesn't understand this but . . ." and continued on from there, usually with a criticism of Nyela's weight, or Malaya's, or, most often, both. "She just doesn't believe fat meat is greasy," Ma-Mère would say, sucking her teeth and fastening the buckle on a stylish belt or purse. "If you two sit around getting big as a pair of jack shacks, won't be 'cause I didn't try to tell her." Malaya had no idea what a jack shack was, but she knew whatever Ma-Mère said to her was just a thin slice of her criticism of her mother. She had heard Nyela complaining to Percy about Ma-Mère's cruelty over the years, sometimes crying. Years ago, it was one of the few conversations that usually ended sweetly between them, with his arm around her and her looking at him with wet eyes, saying "Thanks, Pra."

On the first morning of the visit, Malaya came down to the kitchen to find Ma-Mère drinking her coffee in a pale pink blouse and a tan pencil skirt, half a grapefruit sitting on the table before her on a white saucer. She held a neatly folded newspaper in her hand. "Well, you seem to think you're a boy now, My Ly-Ly," she observed, peering over the day's crossword puzzle at Malaya's Timberlands and the old EMCEE jeans that still cut at the waist. She put the paper down and spooned a perfect chunk of bright pink flesh from the grapefruit, lifted it to her mouth, and swallowed. "I do wish your mother woulda taught you to be at least some kind of lady," she said, taking a sip of her coffee. "Not sure how she let you get even *that* confused. But I suppose you can't stuff a porker into a pinafore no-how. Guess those dungarees and hoodlum boots will have to do." She returned to the paper with a sigh, as though this was one battle too many for her to fight alone.

It was hard to admit, but the woman could still turn a phrase like nobody's business. Even when she was insulting her, Malaya often felt herself wanting to pause, just for a second, and sip on the language. *Jack shack. Porker in a pinafore. Willy the Whale.* She was never sure which of these sayings were passed down and which Ma-Mère had made up herself on the spot, but they all sparkled with a sheen of history. *Don't buy a man shoes or he'll walk right out on you. Ladies don't pass gas, they break wind. A tiger don't change his stripes—until white folks skin 'im.* Sometimes, the things Ma-Mère said were so strange that even when they stung, Malaya had to stiffen her face to keep from smiling.

After breakfast, Ma-Mère began her morning exercises, though she could no longer force Malaya to join in. Then there were flavorless meals and afternoon soap operas, with, it seemed to Malaya, the same story lines from a decade ago continuing to unfurl at a glacial pace. The Bored Bag had disappeared, and Malaya missed the Crypt-o-Quote, though of course she couldn't say it. But still, there were Ma-Mère's stories, which were distraction enough.

AT FIRST, the visit to Ma-Mère's was typical. On the second afternoon, Malaya sat in the living room with her sketch pad as she had in childhood, while Ma-Mère fumbled with the plastic covering on the aging chaise longue, waiting for their Jell-O to set so they could eat dessert. They had just finished a dry dinner of cabbage and halibut, and Ma-Mère had complained all the way through, saying she would rather have at least had a little rice with the meal, but that she'd had to forgo the side dishes because of Malaya's "problem." Malaya had begun a pastel sketch inspired by the word—*problem*—a thickly layered whirl of blues and grays circling tornado-like toward the center of the page in a way she hoped evoked van Gogh's impastos.

"What your mother needs to do is give up the ghost and take you back to that surgeon," Ma-Mère said, tugging at the edge of the sofa's plastic covering. "Course, she would probably want to run it by your father. And I know he thinks the sun'll turn to salamander spit the minute his daughter hears the word 'no.'"

Malaya looked at Ma-Mère, the stiffness of her skirt, the precise trim of her hair, how she held her belly in so casually, as though sucking in was more natural than breathing. She imagined what Ma-Mère must have looked like at her own age, a thick 1930s girl with deep brown skin, smoking a cigarette, an earnest teenage attempt at elegance.

"Of course, nobody listens to me," Ma Mere said, folding the crochet blanket and laying it on the chaise longue just so. "I just talk and talk, might as well be nothing but wind."

That's not true, Malaya wanted to say. Nyela always listened, more intently than she should have. This meant Malaya, too, had been listening all her life. She glanced toward the kitchen, where the Jell-O was taking shape in its goblets.

"But that's alright, My Ly-Ly," Ma-Mère said. "We don't need nobody to listen, at the end of the day. Even wind gets heard when it needs to."

Ma-Mère bent over to tug at the plastic on the chaise longue, and it made a loud ripping sound. Immediately she whipped her head around at Malaya to see if she had heard.

Malaya couldn't help but remember the words: *Ladies don't pass gas, they break wind.* A smile surged up from her belly and took over her face. She couldn't help herself. She let the smile spread into a laugh. Ma-Mère looked indignant at first, but her face cracked open into a small smile, too.

"What you laughing at, little girl?" she said, straightening herself by the sofa. But her smile was growing, and so was Malaya's. The sound had come from the sofa, but the humor had not escaped Ma-Mère. "I know you not laughing at me! That was this old plastic. And even if it was me, it'd be your fault, anyway. Got us eating all these legumes and whatnot, trying to help you out, with your big self."

It stung, but Malaya couldn't feel too hurt watching her grandmother fight for her composure, her body betraying her, her face helpless against laughter. *Little girl.*

Ma-Mère leaned on the arm of the sofa, struggling to keep herself straight.

"I don't know what you're even smirking about over there," she said, her belly shaking chuckles out into the room. "That was the chase lounge cover, you know. This old plastic went and ripped, is all." She laughed again.

"I know it was." Malaya felt daring. "'Cause ladies don't pass gas."

"That's right," Ma-Mère said. Her laughter elongated. She sat on the arm of the sofa. "They break wind."

They both laughed, deep and from the belly. It felt good, and new— an intimacy of uncontrollable bodies, forgiven. They laughed until Ma-Mère was crumpled like a handkerchief on the sofa, almost completely at rest.

"Well," Malaya said, "at least we know we're both ladies now. We have scientific proof."

Ma-Mère let out a loud squawk and the two laughed so hard they had to hold their bellies. Malaya felt more grown than she ever had. It was a simple joke, and in poor taste. Yet it had brought a deep body laughter she had never had with a woman in her family—with anyone but Shaniece. It was strange and thrilling, and it made her wonder whether other possibilities were hiding in her silence, what else could happen if she let herself speak.

"Enough of all this," Ma-Mère said finally, straightening her back. "I'm taking myself to bed. But first, I'm making a stop by the washroom. Don't stay up all night eating. We don't need no wind symphony chiming into the wee hours, do we?"

As Ma-Mère went upstairs, Malaya picked up the sketch pad again and opened to a new page. She let herself wander over the paper as the sounds upstairs settled, the feel of the laughter echoing in her belly. When it was clear Ma-Mère was in bed, she walked quietly to the kitchen, where the Jell-O was waiting in its goblets, still plain and soupy, but a little sweeter than she remembered.

———

WHEN MALAYA RETURNED to Harlem, Fakeout Summer was still going strong: the sun appeared outside her window, round and full as a lollipop each morning, and streams of garbage-ridden water flowed down the slopes of Sugar Hill as the snow mounds melted. Percy and Nyela still argued, but it didn't matter as much. Malaya wasn't sure if it was the trip to Philadelphia or something else, but she felt as though she could see a glimmer of a different version of herself. Someone who could laugh freely and easily, and who could make other people laugh, too. It seemed like a superpower. She could open her mouth and let the weird, wandering chunks of her thoughts out, and those thoughts could *do* things in the world—make her grandmother laugh, make her body a rush of bubbles. Who knew what else might happen?

As the outside weight lifted, Malaya took the Fakeout Summer's persistence as a sign. It was as though the weather had synced with her own internal climate, and she had to take advantage. One morning, she lay in bed, her muscles buzzing, restless, and rather than turn on her side and swat the day away, she got up. She put on a crisp new EMCEE sweater, lifted herself onto the bus, and went to school. On the bus, she wrote absence notes for each of her classes, signing them as steadily as she could in her mother's looping hand. Armed with the stack of forged notes, she climbed the stairs. She pushed herself to take them quickly, trying hard to keep her breath.

"*Kaboom!* Guess who stepped in the room!" Eric called when she rounded the corner to the auditorium. He swung around the back-stage railing to greet her. "The homie Malaya in the building!" They exchanged pounds, and he folded her into a tight hug that made her feel both large and small at once. "What up, son! We missed you." He tapped a beat on the railing with his pen.

"Hey, Malaya." Shanté smiled and hugged her, the sheet music she held in her hand pressing against Malaya's back. She offered to catch her up on the Mandys' latest doings. "You know they're always on some mess," she said, wrinkling her nose and smoothing her bangs.

RayShawn wasn't there, and Malaya was glad.

When Shaniece appeared, she looked at Malaya, her thin eyebrows arched in surprise. She was wearing a pale yellow sweater, and her braids were swept up into a bun that made her look old and young at the same time.

"Hey," Malaya said, trying to sound casual.

"Hey, girl," Shaniece said. She gave Malaya a loose hug, the scent of her braid spray sweet and nutty in Malaya's face. "Where you been at?" But Malaya did not answer.

She went back to Galton daily after that. She braided her hair blue and green and purple to match her tops as always, but now with pricier lip liner from the beauty supply, more eye shadow, crisp, colored socks, and new Timberland boots she bought at the sleek sporting goods chain that had opened on 125th. She laughed as loud as she could in the hallways with LaFamille and made small talk with Rachel Greenstein and Mei-Lin before art history, singing made-up songs from the Z *Morning Zoo* radio show and recounting with hearty enthusiasm Phoebe Buffay's best one-liners on *Friends*.

Still unsure what to say to Shaniece, Malaya began walking after school to avoid time alone with her. For a few days, she walked an extra two blocks out of the way to the Lexington Avenue bus down the hill, which she knew did not stop near the CTown. Then, eventually, she began to walk all the way across Central Park to catch the bus on Broadway. At first, she felt strange and mountainous walking across the park, past the soccer fields and the statues and the Caribbean nannies shuttling their charges. It was still unusually warm outside, and sweat slicked up beneath her chin, under her arms, between the bulges of her back and the folds on her belly as she walked. It was uncomfortable, even painful. It made her feet ache and her thighs throb. Sometimes she worried she might forget to breathe and pass out at the mouth of the Central Park Reservoir. But walking also stirred up a pleasure she had forgotten. She remembered the lightness and speed of playing freeze tag as a child, and the one time she tried to jump double Dutch on the block. Those moments were fleeting— each time there was someone pointing and laughing, reminding her how silly she looked, a fat girl trying to get free. It had always ended in hurt; but still, the moments of moving had happened.

When a cluster of gray-uniformed Catholic school boys followed her the whole way across the park one afternoon, shouting "THUN-DER DOME!!!" and making farting noises with each step she took, Malaya put her headphones on and flipped both middle fingers behind her as she passed them. Rhyming along with Biggie, she kept it moving, timing her steps to the beat. Later, when an elderly woman sitting on a bench in a scruffy wig chucked a handful of bread crumbs at her stomach and shouted, "Fat and ugly! Fat and ugly! Fat!" it stung and confused Malaya, but she turned the volume up, brushed off the crumbs, and called out, "Fix your fucking hair, lady!" Then she walked faster. Her eyes were moist, but she opened her mouth and let the breeze rush against her tongue, swallowing the air like juice.

At home in Harlem, she began to walk past the Happy Family Chinese restaurant and Mr. Gonzales's bodega every day without entering. Instead, she saved her money for new packs of teal and indigo to braid into her hair. Within two weeks, she noticed her jeans had loosened a little, and the strip of flesh around her middle began to heal.

One night, Nyela passed her in the second-floor hallway as Malaya was climbing up to her room. "You look beautiful, Malaya!" she said. Her eyes were bright, but also quizzical. "Your face looks so slim."

The compliments felt nice, but Malaya could not trust them. They felt like part of another scheme to make her change, instantly and for good. What would happen if she couldn't keep it up? If the weight loss stopped, what would she lose then? She responded to these comments with a vague "thanks" and shuffled out of sight quickly, before her mother could see her smile.

She hadn't aimed to lose weight at first, but now, seeing how it changed things, she felt the cool rush of intention. For the better part of a month, Malaya ate less, moved more, and worked harder than she'd ever worked at anything. She walked to the Rite Aid on 145th and spent thirty-five dollars on supplies—Diurex water pills, SlimFast shakes, and a calorie-counting manual as thick as a dictionary that she found in the discount bin. When Galton's annual magazine drive fund-raiser began, she bought subscriptions to *Elle* and *Cosmopolitan* for inspiration. Embarrassed to be seen with such white girl propaganda, she stuffed the magazines into her art history and social studies textbooks and pored over them on the bus up to Harlem, looking at the models' long, bare torsos, admiring all the ways they could twist and pose. She got off the bus a few stops early each day, walking past Copeland's Reliable Cafeteria, past the CTown, the chicken spot, with its sweet smell of spicy meat and grease, past the new Italian trattoria that had opened up where the Woolworth's had once been. She walked as fast as she could until she was sweating in the chilly air, and then she walked faster.

Before, hunger had been a sixth sense, a whisper on her skin, telling her that something was urgently needed, and that food would make it better. She knew hunger's voice so well she didn't really need to listen to it; she heard the signal, and she responded with fries or chips or a four-piece chicken dinner, and she felt better until hunger sighed her way again. But now her stomach clenched fist-tight throughout the day, groaning and banging like the brownstone's pipes until she fed it with a rice cake or a light yogurt. Often it clanged so long and so deep it left her feeling weak. Once, during a Spanish literature dictation, she had to steady herself against the desk of the teacher, Mr. Vallejo, to keep from losing her balance and sinking to the floor right there in the middle of class.

The idea of being a frail, fainty thing was brand-new to Malaya, and it held a surprising lure she could not describe. This new hunger felt glamorous. Eating disorders, like fashion magazines, were the province of skinny white girls, so no one would suspect her. Sometimes, she would pass store windows near Galton and try to imagine herself slim as a mannequin, draped in the latest Hugo Boss or Ralph Lauren dress, but she could never make the vision stick. She saw herself walking faster, farther than this current body could take her. She imagined herself running, a ponytail of braids whipping behind her like a white girl in a sneaker commercial, her breath and heart pounding a steady rhythm against the pavement. For the first time since childhood, she did not cut off these fantasies when they came to her. This was the reward for enduring the punishments of hunger. She let herself truly imagine being thin.

There had been no discussion of Dr. Sawyer and the surgery in weeks, but now Nyela began to slip brochures into Malaya's stack of mail. "You're getting such a nice jump start," she'd write on Post-it notes stuck to the paper. "We're so proud of you! Just let me know if you'd like me to call!"

The thought of sitting in spooky Dr. Sawyer's office again, staring at diagrams of bisected stomachs, made Malaya nauseous. Still, it was hard not to be swayed by the notes' bright tone, her mother's voice chirping in blue ink from the milky yellow paper.

She didn't paint during this time. She pushed the easel into the corner of the room and used it to hang the clothes she'd outgrown, its planks and levers draped in great swaths of denim. But late one night, she sat staring at the stomach model she'd stolen from the office and pulled out her sketch pad. Perched on the bed, she drew out her questions in brownish-pink pastel: What would her insides look like, forever rearranged? She drew a pink pouch of stomach, smeared the color smooth with her fingers, then raked black dashes across the middle with her Sharpie, pressing deep into the paper so that the lines emerged against the oil. She tried to imagine her intestines snipped, bisected, and resutured inside of her, hoping that if she could only *see* it, really imagine it, it would scare her less.

Slowly, she began to consider that this could be the start of something new and permanent: Malaya but better, minus her "problem" and plus the safety of a world in which she could finally fit. She imagined things around her changing, too. Family photos frozen in deep belly laughter, firm, fleshy hugs, and smiles as wide as honeydew rinds. She ran her fingers over the plastic stomach, then over the drawings. For her, "stomach" had always meant the wide, heavy pillows of fat that puffed from her abdomen and sandwiched together under her jeans. Now, she tried to imagine her own stomach as a muscly, fist-sized organ deep inside her, joined weblike to her lungs and heart. She thought and she drew. She remembered Dr. Sawyer saying that she would have to lose twenty pounds before they could operate. She tried not to remember the sound of his voice, the gold flecks sparking like firecrackers in his eyes.

By the end of March, Malaya's jeans drooped from her hips, and the clang of hunger began to comfort her. Sometimes, if she pressed hard, she could feel her collarbone emerging, a fleshy cliff below her neck. The Fakeout Summer was long gone and now gray Manhattan snow lay stiff on the ground. The cold and ice made walking hard, but she had two choices: go backward, lose ground, and revert to the girl she had been, or walk more often, for longer distances, no matter how it felt. Each day, she got off the bus on Amsterdam, across from the gargantuan tenement where Shaniece lived, and made a game of sailing as quickly as she could up the blocks to the brownstone, her braids smacking behind her on the air. Sometimes, it was all she could do to beat the senior citizens from the Mount Calgary Senior Center across the crosswalk. Other times, she moved so fast she felt the ground vanish beneath her.

SHE WAS STANDING at the crosswalk on Amsterdam one day, waiting for the light to change, when she saw Shaniece appear in her building's courtyard and walk toward the curb, RayShawn a few steps behind. He hadn't spent time with LaFamille lately, at least not when Malaya was around, and her efforts to avoid Shaniece had succeeded. She hadn't said more than a few words to either of them, and hadn't seen them together since returning to school. She slid into the doorway of the Twin Donut on the corner and watched: Shaniece zipping up her bright yellow bubble jacket, her peach paisley scarf catching in the zipper, shaking her head as RayShawn held the zipper still. The two standing together, Shaniece slim as a pencil stroke as he held her face and kissed her, right there on Amsterdam Avenue, for all the neighborhood to see.

When they passed the doughnut shop window, Malaya drifted behind them. For a reason she couldn't explain, she watched. RayShawn put his arms around Shaniece's waist, his hand sinking into the yellow fluff of her jacket. For the first time in weeks, Malaya slowed herself, lagging behind them as they walked up the avenue holding hands, their bodies slight and straight. At the entrance to Copeland's Reliable Cafeteria, RayShawn swung the door open in a gallant swoop, and Shaniece half smiled behind her scarf as they walked in.

Malaya stood at the restaurant's entrance, her face and body numb under the shadows of the silk trees and plants that crowded the door-way. She watched as they ordered their food, carried it to a booth in the back of the room, and sat, eating boldly, playfully, in the cafeteria's stark light. She thought of Giselle's lesson from childhood: *hurt the pain back.* She rounded the doorway and slunk toward the corner booth, preparing herself to watch. Gripping the edge of the table, she tried to slide her body down into the booth, but the tabletop pressed hard into her belly, shoving her middle up toward her breasts, packing her breasts so tight against her neck that it was hard to swallow. She tried to hold herself up in the seat, but her bones turned to water. There was a loud *pop!* and a dull metallic crash, like the mouth of a garbage truck opening. She felt the bench and the booth buckle beneath her, felt herself tumble, back-first, in a slow, sprawling heap onto the cafeteria floor.

"Oh shit!" someone yelled behind her.

"Whoa!" Someone else stifled a laugh.

"Ma'am, are you alright?"

Malaya felt the familiar force field of eyes on her. Her hand was wedged beneath a piece of the bench, and her left leg was numb. A man in a suit reached down to help her up. She grabbed his hand and pulled, but her body would not move. He staggered against her weight and looked around wildly for help. Another man in an apron appeared and began to tug uselessly at her shoulders. The suited man shoved his arm under her armpit and heaved, but still she could not stand. After endless minutes of tugging, she could not see or hear either, the whole scene blurring over with breath and tears.

She sucked in, closed her eyes, and pushed herself across the floor, through a bramble of legs and feet, leaning her weight on the wall and praying for the strength to hoist herself up. She did not look at the broken bench behind her. She did not listen to the woman who said, "Somebody gone have to clean this mess up," from somewhere in the crowd. She did not see RayShawn's face. She did not look for Shaniece's. She moved out the door as quickly as her body would take her, not nearly fast enough.

Not Nothing

WHEN MALAYA FELL, she fell totally. Afterward, when she recalled her weeks of walking, shame clawed at her chest. Nothing would hold her, she felt. If she knew anything at all, it should have been that. So she retreated to her room, where she studied the paint-thick molding arched above the windows and practiced not-wanting, Biggie playing from the stereo once again. She tried not to want anything but the bed and the music and the four walls around her. She tried not to want someone to call—especially not Shaniece.

Eventually, after two days of nibbling at the vegetables and frozen Lean Cuisine dinners that had accumulated in the freezer, Malaya walked out of her room, past the closed door of the family room, toward the Happy Family Chinese restaurant on Broadway, where she ordered a heaping mass of egg foo young with fried rice, fried wontons, four chicken wings, a large order of fries, a bag of sugary apple bites, two egg rolls, and extra duck sauce. She did the same thing the next day, and the next. She tried purging the food in her bathroom, but that became too loud and too exhausting. And ultimately, it seemed pointless. Nobody her size ever purged their way to thinness; that was a skinny white girl thing.

And so she ate—all the fried and sauced and caramel-dipped foods she had ignored during her walking weeks. She returned to food gratefully, like a remorseful lover, secreting plastic cake packages and dollar boxes of ice cream in her backpack, swallowing them with attentive care in the quiet of her room. She watched herself puff up again, her breasts rounding out, her face swelling quickly, as though bitten. It was like hugging a friend whose smell she'd forgotten.

Sometimes in the morning, she would wake up early and creep downstairs while Percy and Nyela got dressed. She would swipe a few loose bills from Nyela's coat pocket for lunch as she had in childhood. Sometimes, Malaya checked her father's pocket out of curiosity, but she never took from him. He was out of work, she reasoned, and he had never been good at saving, which meant all his pocket money came from Nyela anyway. Still, she liked to thumb through the bits of paper, the scribbled notes and matches that sat tangled with crumpled bills in his pockets, all clues to the details of his days. A few times each week, Percy brought Malaya something—a slice of pizza, a can of soda, a bean pie— from his walks across 125th. It was never enough to fill her, but it was a kindness, and each time she remembered what Ma-Mère had often said about him: *Men who grow up with nothing go one of two ways: they either can't stop taking or they can't stop giving. Both are dangerous.*

One morning, on her way downstairs, Malaya noticed a long smear of brownish red in her parents' bathroom sink. Walking in, she stopped stiff. A thick worm of blood curled down from the side of the sink and looped around the drain. It was the length of her forearm and the thickness of her ring finger. It looked like something that belonged on a sanitary pad or in a toilet. She called to her mother and gestured mutely at the sink, panicked.

"Pra?" Nyela said, first a question. Then, louder, "Pra."

He came quickly from the family room, coughing at the bathroom door.

"What happened?" Nyela said, pointing at the sink with her chin. Her eyes were wide. It was a look Malaya recognized, an anger useful only because it was easier to find than fear.

Percy put his hand on his hair and then brought it to his face.

"Nothing," he said, stroking the rug of stubble on his cheeks. "Look, just. It's nothing." He turned to her, still looking down. "This is nothing, My Laya. Go ahead. Don't be late for school."

Malaya looked at him—the ash of him, his fallen face and tired eyes. He coughed again. The scene started to piece itself together, imperfect shapes connecting like a scrap collage: his accordion breath, the smoke curls drifting out the window, all their shared secrets. She wondered how much of life would feel this way—shock without the grace of surprise. She should have known, and she *did* know. And yet, the knowing did not help her understand. How sick was he? For how long? And how had no one intervened? She walked to the steps and sat on her familiar perch, craning her neck to watch from the banister as she had in childhood.

" 'Nothing,' " Nyela repeated. "Nothing?" She looked at him as though she had never seen him before. Then her eyes expanded like pools of milk. "This much blood in the sink is not nothing! You don't have to care about yourself, but you do have to care about your family. That is your only job. I'm tired of doing your job for you."

Malaya gripped the banister and tried to will herself calm.

Percy shifted his weight in the doorway. "Is this about Malaya?"

"No!" Nyela said. Malaya's body felt like a struck match. "God, Pra. This is about you. Do you see what you are doing to yourself? And of course it's about Malaya." Nyela sounded confused. "What is it going to take for you to pay attention? How is she going to care about her body when you don't give a shit about yours? This much blood. This much blood and you don't even see!"

She screamed, a sound that was almost a word—"Pra," perhaps—but it ended up a mash of garbled syllables. Nyela had made an art of stiffening, tucking, sucking herself in to fit. Now here she was, unlatched, a whirl of feeling let loose through the brownstone halls.

Percy tried to touch Nyela's arm, but she jerked away. They moved deeper into the bathroom and Malaya couldn't see what was happening, only her mother's back bending down by the sink. Then she made a sound, a long, deep draw of breath like an organ chord. She was crying.

"How can you not be scared?"

Malaya saw him move toward her, saw her pull away.

"You have to be a grown-up with me," she said after a few seconds. "I can't be the only one."

She turned on the faucet, pulled the can of cleaning spray from the cabinet, and scrubbed. Malaya watched as Nyela leaned against the sink and looked at her own face in the mirror. She ran a hand over her cheek and poked at it curiously. Then she sighed and turned around.

"Take yourself to the doctor, Percy. If you actually care about your daughter, that's what you'll do."

"Okay," he said, "I will. I'll call today."

"I hope so," Nyela said. But she didn't look at him. She turned back to the mirror and stared, unblinking, and Malaya knew she didn't believe him.

LATE THAT EVENING, the mattress springs squealed under Malaya as she perched on the bed. She played "Juicy" and pulled a family-size bag of sour cream and onion chips from the bed's bottom shelf, chomping to the rhythm. She had spent the day on Riverside Drive, eating bodega pies furtively and drawing the boats and pigeons along the Hudson. Now, she tucked herself into the sheets gratefully, as though into a wave. But something kept her up.

For no reason she could name, she pulled out the old easel, which she hadn't touched in weeks, and set it up in the corner by the window. She unwrapped a large canvas board from its plastic, put it on the frame, and looked at it, but no image came. She lay down again, ate more, turned on her side, tried again, but every time she closed her eyes, something said *open them.*

Eventually, something told her to get her pastels and her pad. So she drew—long crisscrossing red and purple lines that looked first like blood, then like windows, then like the bass line of "All Blues." She had read once that Miles Davis wrote *Kind of Blue* somewhere in Paris during what he called "a blue period," strung out on heroin and unable to work, pay rent, or, really, to live. When she read this, she had felt sad but also grateful, glad to have some language for the nameless feeling she had had for so long: *a blue period.* She had braided blue into her hair when she heard it, and each time she looked at the braids, they made her feel better. Now she pulled out the deepest blue pastel—a color called "indigo smoke," which she thought of privately as *sincere blue*. She pressed it hard into the page, smearing it over the tracks with her fingers.

She needed words, but it was a strange thing—she didn't need music. Something told her to listen. She needed quiet, something told her. She needed to look, to see: the red, the purple, the sincere blue smeared on the paper, smudging the skin on her wrists. Something told her. Something said to smell the air: old pipes and the breaking spring, salt and grease, the mild alcohol smell of the pastels, the light funk of old paper. Something told her to feel her fingers, the muddy ink of the pastels stuck on her finger pads. Something said *be still*. Something said *be quiet*. Something told her to listen so she could save the sound and remember it: her mother's voice downstairs, a wounded howl . . . the look of the walls scrolling by her . . . the dizzy unbalance of the steps. The motion down, down, down to the bathroom, to feel the thickness of the air, to smell her father's smoke and hear her mother's wordless wail and see her face falling, falling into the still of her father's soundless chest.

Please Go

THERE WERE NO COLORS in Malaya's hair the morning of the funeral. She undid her purple braids the night Percy lost his breath and let the hair fall to the floor of her bedroom, where it sat in a tangle all week. She left her bed only a few times each day, to eat from the pans of chicken, candied yams, and pasta salad family members dropped off, and, occasionally, to stare at the blank canvas in the corner of her room.

Nyela said nothing about this. She did not force Malaya to come downstairs to sit with the visitors, to wade through Percy's papers, to help her pick the casket at the funeral home. Instead, Ma-Mère flurried in from Philadelphia, smelling of Fashion Fair makeup and Gold Medal pomade, her face set in a taking-care-of-business expression. Since then, Malaya was required only to try on the dress Ma-Mère had ordered from Ulla Popken, the German company that made women's clothes in her size, and to keep the crazy colors out of her hair. She imagined herself as a ghost—the wide, capacious, slow-drifting kind, the kind that might gobble someone into its vaporous body—floating around the brownstone's top floor, three wisps of unbraided hair reaching up from her scalp like weather vanes.

It wasn't until the morning of the funeral that she replaced the purple with black at Ma-Mère's request. She let the braids swing wild over her face in defiance. On an impulse, she smeared a sparkly purple shadow over her left eye and a matte blue over her right, but as soon as Ma-Mère saw her she said, "What you *not* gonna do is shock your father out his casket and shame your mother into hers with that nonsense. Go up and try your face again."

Malaya went upstairs silently and wiped the color from her eyes. She dug into her pastel case for a pale, watery teal—a color that had always reminded her of her father. She smeared it thick onto each of her pinkie nails, sprayed each finger with hairspray to set the color, and went downstairs, her fingers twisted in the hems of her dress sleeves.

The R. J. Sutphin Homegoing Chapel was thick with perfume and stale breath, and the pale yellow lights from the plastic candelabras along the walls seemed to ooze down the thin wood paneling, giving the whole place a Halloweenish glow. Nyela had wanted to give Percy a Catholic burial, but his side of the family protested, and, against Ma-Mère's advice, she had acquiesced in an effort to keep the peace. The room was small, with seating for about forty people, but at least seventy had shown up. The back of the chapel was a grumble of activity, with people stepping over one another and shuffling in spare chairs from the undertaker's office. Nyela had predicted this, and Malaya remembered Ma-Mère's comment: *If they want it at the family chapel, give 'em their way and let 'em grieve on folding chairs. Tradition costs.*

Most of the people there were aunts, uncles, cousins, and old family friends Malaya had known as a child but hadn't seen in years. Nyela's friend Karen was there, along with Ms. Claire, the kind-eyed department secretary at Drummond, and Sylvie Watkins and others from the Black Psychologists group. Malaya even saw LaTisha, the black girl student whose doorknocker earrings she had admired as a child, now grown and wearing a slick navy blazer and slacks. A handful of white men from Percy's old firm were there, too, sitting together in their black and gray suits with black all-weather jackets draped over their laps. There were men Percy's age whom Malaya had never seen before, some in slacks and jackets, others in sweatshirts and dark-colored jeans. They gathered in the doorway of the chapel, exchanging fist bumps and hugging as though they hadn't in a while. At the back of the room, Malaya thought she saw Shaniece, but she couldn't be sure.

She floated behind her mother and grandmother during the procession, Uncle Book's arm wrapped awkwardly around hers, his cologne-and-liquor smell stuffing up her throat. When Nyela reached the casket, she lowered her head, her body shaking in place like a dress hung against a breeze. Malaya wanted to turn away, but she felt a strange responsibility to look.

Eventually, Ma-Mère squeezed Nyela's arm and walked her toward the pew, leaving Malaya and Uncle Book standing square in front of the wooden box. Malaya hunched forward and studied the curve of the casket through her curtain of hair. Her feet were tired and she wanted to sit down, but she knew it wouldn't look right. She stood, not knowing what to feel. It wasn't hard to look—he didn't look like himself. And yet, seeing him, still and painted like terra cotta, something in her dislodged, as though she'd been holding a breath for days without noticing. Suddenly she was aware of something she'd been feeling deeply, when she thought she was feeling nothing. A pit coiled tight inside her, then unraveled into a faint black question mark. The tears came. She caught them before they made too much fuss, but she couldn't stop the feeling. Here it was: a hot, hollowing grief, and it rushed through her, thick and limitless, like steam.

The organist played "How Great Thou Art," and people passed along the front of the chapel, stooping to greet the family. Malaya had never seen her mother touch or be touched so much. White coworkers gave deep, solemn gazes and moist handshakes. Others, like the Black Psychologists group, bent low and put their arms around Malaya and Nyela, their dreadlocks flapping against their shoulders, their perfume oils falling across Malaya's face. A few family members whispered raspily in their ears, things like "Joy comes in the morning," or "Keep looking up. He's watching." One woman bent down in front of Malaya and whispered, "You have to take care of your mother, now," and she didn't know why, but it snatched her breath.

As she sat in the pew, Malaya's legs felt like meat stuffed into her pantyhose. Her thighs were hot with the friction of ripping nylon and the press of her mother's hips on her right and her grandmother's on her left. The black dress Ma-Mère had chosen for her was long and tarp-ish, and each time she leaned in for a hug she felt the zipper—its single feature—strain against the breadth of her back.

The service was nice enough, though Malaya couldn't say it was "what Percy would have wanted"—a phrase she'd heard several times since the day of his death. People seemed to offer this phrase as a comfort—*Percy would've wanted the service at Benta's. Percy would've wanted Cousin Charisse to sing.* To Malaya, the phrase was ridiculous. In her mind, what her father would have wanted was a small goodbye in which people relaxed and listened to good music until they were ready to go home. Or perhaps he would have wanted not to die at all.

One by one, people came to the pulpit—to read scripture, to share condolence cards, to improvise a eulogy on the spot. All ended up sharing a version of Percy Clondon's life that was ultimately about the teller, rather than her father. This made sense to Malaya, but still it struck her that despite all the funerary business and etiquette, the needs of the living mattered much more than the wants of the dead.

After a while, Uncle Book swayed slowly toward the front of the chapel, hanging his head dramatically before lifting it into the light, a single tear flickering in his eye.

"Y'all think you know my big brother Percy," he said, "but you don't know him like I do. Percy wasn't a street dude. Y'all know that. He was a family man. He knew the streets well enough to stay off them. Kept me off them too. Ever since we was young. He was like a father, if a brother could be a father." A tear mixed with sweat and fell from his nose onto the pulpit. He steadied himself.

"Take your time!" someone called from the back of the room. Uncle Book looked up and nodded.

"Percy made me the man I am now," he continued. "And I know he's still here. And he is telling me to go back to school, to get my education and do better. And I want to say I hear you, big brother. And that is what I am going to do. Y'all mark my words. Next time you see me, I'ma be a better man. Like Percy." The room murmured *alright*'s and *that's okay*'s as Book hung his head again, sniffling into the microphone before reading from the Book of Psalms.

Next was Cousin LaSondra, who announced to the mourners that in two weeks she would marry the father of her child. "So I just want y'all to know," she said, shifting her weight to her left hip and smiling nervously, "that I been blessed. 'Cause God has given me a man as good as my cousin Percy. JaQuan is the love of my life, and I just hope I can be as happy as Cousin Nathallie and Cousin Percy been. I'm gonna marry this man at Mount Bethel Baptist Church. We having a shower at the house. The registry's at JCPenney's."

As LaSondra moved away from the pulpit, Ma-Mère muttered, "No time like a funeral for nigga mess and grandstanding." She darted her eyes at Malaya conspiratorially from under her low-slung tam cap, but Malaya pretended not to hear. Instead, she looked around the chapel, wondering what Percy might say to all of this if he were here. There was a small stained-glass window the size of a marble notebook in the back of the room. The design featured a cluster of leaves and fruit in the center of a milky blue sky, lit with real light from outside. It looked like candy, as though it had been made of gumdrops, and the light shot through, illuminating the swirling dust like curls of smoke. The organist hit a moaning high note, and the sound and the image together felt, to Malaya, like her father: like longing close as air, a tremble of mist, slow, labored, but moving still. She watched the window for the rest of the service, witnessing the light as it breathed through the colored glass.

"WERE YOU PLEASED with the service?" Nyela asked above the chatter of voices in the brownstone. She gripped a serving spoon Malaya had never seen before and plunged it into one of several tins and trays that covered the dining room table. This tin held a baked macaroni and cheese, a swirl of bright yellows and oranges that reminded Malaya of melted crayons. She wondered what the protocol was for this—would they be overrun with dishes and flatware when it was all over, a mountain of ladles and empty casseroles taking the space her father left behind?

The rituals of the day had felt empty to Malaya. The gathering in the funeral home foyer, the frail smiles and lipsticked teeth of family members, the ride from the funeral home to the cemetery on Broadway—none of it reached her. She felt like she was in a movie and watching it at the same time. The tasks and conversations passed before her as though on a reel, and each time someone appeared in front of her, saying "I'm so sorry," it took her several seconds to truly realize that they were talking to her.

Now, the first floor of the brownstone was choked with people she had not seen in years, if ever. The din of warm voices and the clinking of forks and glasses that filled the house seemed more suggestive of a party than a death. Baby cousins ran in and out of the front door and up and down the stairs, aunts and uncles swarmed not far behind them, hugging, chatting, occasionally scolding a child. Uncle Book sat with a woman Malaya didn't know in the corner of the dining room, clutching a bottle the size of his hand, still in its paper bag. Giselle sat in the parlor with her two toddlers, knees pressed together, her eyes flitting around the room and landing, every few seconds, on Malaya's belly. Nyela's friend Karen was there, too, on a folding chair not far from Giselle. She gave Malaya a reassuring smile every time they exchanged a glance, her eyes round and sparkling like thimbles of blue glitter. Malaya was glad for the noise. She could almost forget, for seconds at a time, what the brownstone had been, what it felt like, who had lived there.

Out of the corner of her eye, Malaya thought she saw Shaniece again, this time on a folding chair in the foyer, but each time she tried to get closer, an aunt or a cousin stopped her to express condolences and comment on her weight, and by the time she was free the figure was gone.

Nyela cut a narrow rectangle of macaroni and cheese from the pan and slid it onto her plate. She handed the spoon to Malaya. Malaya looked at the pan, wishing she could section off a hunk the size of her face, or, better yet, dive in headfirst and submerge herself in pasta and cheese. Instead she took a piece slightly smaller than her mother's, watching the grease gleam in the room's dull light.

"I thought it went well, right?" Nyela said.

"Yeah," Malaya replied, "it was nice. I'm sorry I didn't help more."

They moved down the line of meats, potatoes, pastas, and salads, Malaya checking Nyela's plate, Nyela glancing occasionally back at hers. When they reached the end of the line, Malaya followed her mother through the foyer and watched her get swallowed into the marsh of arms in the front parlor.

Malaya stood there looking for a corner where she could hide and eat. She thought she saw an unoccupied folding chair in the vestibule, and she was deciding whether it looked strong enough to hold her when LaSondra came whirling up, her gold-tipped nails wrapped around the arm of a bald man the color of peanut butter.

"Hey, Malaya," she said, her voice breathy and sweet. "How you holdin' up, baby?"

LaSondra untangled her hand from the man and leaned in to give Malaya a hug. It was real and tight, and Malaya felt her body sigh into her cousin's.

"I'm alright," Malaya said.

"I'm gonna miss your daddy," LaSondra continued, perching her hand on her hip. "You know he was the most generous man in the family. I mean it when I say it. Hey, you know what your mama's gonna do with the in-surance? Percy been paying on his policy since he turned twenty-one. 'Cause, you know, of his condition. I remember 'cause my mother told me. She was always talkin' 'bout, 'See? Tha's the kind of man you need. Responsible.'" She laughed and flashed the bald man a smile.

"No," Malaya said, "I'm not sure." In all of the week's slow pain, she hadn't thought about money at all, though now it seemed a reasonable question to ask, and not having to ask it felt like a luxury.

"Well, I just thought I'd mention it," LaSondra said. "'Cause I don't know if there was a will or anything, but you know me and Percy was real close back in the day. He was like a big brother to me. I was even gonna ask him to give me away. And girl, weddings are *expensive*! Wait till you find out."

Malaya nodded.

"If your mama talks to you about it, you just tell her, okay baby? You don't have to mention I said anything." She gave Malaya another kiss, her earrings clanging behind her as she sailed away. Malaya turned to push through the crowd toward the chair, but Ma-Mère swooped in beside her.

"How you holdin' up, My Ly-Ly?" she said, her hand stiff on Malaya's shoulder. "That your first plate today?"

Ma-Mère had taken off her suit jacket, and her cream-colored blouse was snug against her breasts and middle. She pulled at her small tam cap, which she still wore, even in the house. She had her hair in a short brown Afro, and now, up close, Malaya noticed that it had thinned in places along the sides, leaving tiny clearings of scalp visible. Malaya liked these spaces. She liked the idea of carrying spans of free skin around on one's head. But Ma-Mère pulled the ends of the cap tightly over her hairline so that her head looked like the tip of a bullet. Every few seconds, she reached out and smoothed her blouse down with a long, French-manicured hand, a gesture that reminded Malaya immediately of her mother.

"Yeah, I'm okay," Malaya said, looking down at the plate. It wasn't her first. Or her second. The first had been a bowl of oxtail and a heaping plate of the peas and rice Sylvie had brought over during the week, which she'd snuck into her room around 5 a.m. She'd gone back for a couple of turkey wings before people gathered at the house that morning, and ate three beef ribs straight from the refrigerator just before the limousine picked them up to take them to the funeral home. "I'm really hungry," she said. "I haven't eaten all day."

"Hnh." Ma-Mère pursed her lips and looked around the room. Malaya wasn't sure how to read Ma-Mère now. Since she'd arrived, she seemed to be her usual cutting self, but occasionally she showed glints of tenderness that surprised Malaya.

"Where's that friend your mother's been telling me about?" she asked, reapplying her lipstick in her monogrammed compact mirror. "The one from school you always on the phone with."

"Shaniece?" Malaya asked, trying to sound neutral.

"No," Ma-Mère said. "The fine one. The boy. What's his name?"

Malaya looked into the plate and said nothing.

"Mm-hmm." Ma-Mère smoothed down her blouse. "Come on in here and talk." She ushered Malaya into the dining room, where she put herself to arranging dishes and adjusting serving trays, lifting pans of ham-hocked greens onto hot plates and covering baskets of rolls and cornbread with cloth napkins. Her arms moved like subway cars, thick and heavy, but quick as darts. "Lord," she muttered, "all this food.

These people better eat it up so you and your mother don't sit around getting big as this brownstone."

Ma-Mère pulled the lid off a pitcher sitting on the table and tapped her finger lightly on the liquid's surface, then brought the finger to her tongue. "Don't they think we can do better than some powder-mix tea in a plastic pitcher?" She lifted the crystal punch bowl she'd given Nyela onto the table and filled it with the tea. Malaya watched solid patches of the sugary mix float across the bowl, its crystals coppery in the light.

"Anyway," Ma-Mère said, "there's some things you need to hear, My Ly-Ly. Your mother learned these things the hard way, and I see you might want to do that too. But I'm just gonna tell you straight out so nobody can say I didn't try." She pulled a spoon from the server and began to make a whirlpool in the tea. "Your mother doesn't believe fat meat is greasy. She thinks she can just smile real big for everyone and everything will be okay. She wants to go on and pretend that if she looks out the window and say she see winter, that means it's gonna snow. But that ain't real." She dipped a plastic spoon into the tea and tasted it, then started stirring again. "Now it looks like she learned a little too late that some things just don't end up alright. Some things aren't alright no matter how pretty you truss them up, or how tight you squint to keep from seein' them in full." She stirred again, and Malaya watched the copper islands grow muddy and sink into the tea.

"I tried to tell her to go a little harder on you," Ma-Mère said, wiping a smudge off the metal serving tray under the punch bowl. "Just a little harder. Stop letting you wear those sweatpants all the time, make you stick to the Weight Watchers." She tapped her finger in the tea again and tasted it, her lips making a sour kissing noise against her fingers. She pulled a lemon from the fruit bowl at the center of the table and began to slice. "Sometimes she'd slip up and I'd tell her to watch out. She didn't know it then, but I did. Young people think love is mathematics. They think if you add it up and add it up and keep adding, you can save it until you're ready to cash it in. But it doesn't work that way. You might be making the deposits, but your whole life cashes the checks. Work, children, bills—it all takes its cut. Then you go back to love, thinking it'll be there, and sometimes it's not." She straightened her back, wiped her fingers on a napkin, and kept cutting. "It's hard enough to do all the things we have to do: find a job, live a life, get a husband—a good one—and keep him. You'll see. No sense in burying yourself in a vat of Crisco on top of all that. No woman's ever learned that lesson harder than I did. I thought she'd catch a clue by looking at me. But she's like you—coulda spit you out herself. She wanted to learn on her own. And now look at her," she paused, dropping the lemon slices into the bowl, each hitting the tea with a plopping sound that reminded Malaya of the toilet. "And look at you."

Ma-Mère passed her eyes over Malaya's body as she often did, moving from her chin to her shoulders, to her breasts and her stomach, over the bulge of her gut and down to the pucker of her thighs.

"I'm just telling you now, so you know," Ma-Mère said. "Right, My Ly-Ly?" She smoothed her skirt and gave a resigned smile.

Malaya opened her mouth to respond, but her grandmother waved her hand in front of Malaya's face as though swatting the moment away.

"He'll be here soon, I'm sure," she said. "Your friend, the boy." She pulled a package of plastic cups open and stacked them near the bowl. "Well, I hope so anyway. Be nice for you to have someone here just for you, you know?"

Malaya nodded, her face beginning to sting.

"Now, go ahead and talk to folks. But make sure you watch what you eat," she said. "We have to be careful. We can't just go around stuffing our mouths with everything from jump to Gibraltar." She pulled at the bottom of her blouse and ran her palm over the curve of her stomach, sucking her body in as though she'd just ironed herself flat.

"I don't know if that's your first plate today or not, but no reason why it can't be the last." The plasticky smell of her lipstick floated in the air behind her as she stacked the last of the cups and walked away.

Malaya glanced at the clock. It was one in the afternoon. She looked down at the plate, but by now the chicken skin had gone limp and the macaroni had faded to a dull brownish mush. Planning to head to her room, she covered the plate with foil and held it behind her. She turned in and out, making her way through the crowd with a few small 'scuse me's, trying her best to be invisible.

Finally, only one person stood between her and the stairs—a tall, thick woman with gold jewelry and a doughy face the color of pumpernickel bread. She was smaller than Malaya, but larger than her mother, and she wore a snug-fitting indigo suit with shiny black lines that followed the curves of her bust and hips like lane lines along a freeway. She had a shiny black leather hat to match, and its brim was cocked up on one side in a way that framed her face and made her cheekbones look like well-polished apples. It was a look that Malaya was sure her mother and grandmother would find inappropriate for a funeral, and so Malaya loved it.

The woman looked at her. Caught staring, Malaya tried to give a bereaved daughter smile and glance away. But the woman held her gaze.

"Malaya," she said, as though surprised. Malaya felt herself stiffen immediately, ready for what would come next: *Malaya . . . is that you? Wow, still putting on weight, huh? Malaya! Well, lord, you've gotten so big! Malaya! Look how time has flown!*

But the woman only let a slow smile break over her face, and moved aside to make room for her. Then she said: "I love your nails."

Malaya looked down nervously at her pastel-smudged fingers, and the plate thudded to the floor. Her face hot, she tried to bend at the knees, straining to pick up the plate without careening into the woman or the pile of coats on the banister, but she stopped mid-bend, worried her pantyhose would rip. She felt like she was back on the playground, at the Meeting, in the dressing room stall, on the floor at Copeland's Reliable Cafeteria, stuck in a thicket of eyes.

"Here," the woman said. She dipped to the floor more quickly than Malaya had ever seen a big body move, folding her back neatly and gliding down, her hand sweeping nimbly against the carpet. She popped back up like a piece of toast and handed Malaya the plate, its foil intact. "Here you go," she said, still smiling.

"Thanks," Malaya said. "I'm sorry."

"For what?" The woman smiled again and handed over the fork, still wrapped in its napkin. "Smells good . . . What is it?"

"Macaroni and cheese," she said. "And a few other things. I think Aunt Ro made it." She held the plate awkwardly in front of her now, her contraband revealed. "Um, I'm sorry. I don't remember your name."

The woman extended her arm and gave Malaya a tight, muscly handshake.

"Ethan Windborne," she said. She brushed a puff of silver hair from her face, revealing a thick gold bracelet. "I'm a colleague of your mother's. And I'm about to get myself a plate!"

She gave a broad, loud laugh that sprinkled over the busy foyer like confetti.

"Thanks," Malaya said. "The food is really good." And then she repeated: "Ethan Windborne," just because she liked the name.

IN THE BROAD VIEW, the days just after the funeral were not very different from the days before. But to Malaya, the world was unrecognizable. After all the cousins packed their plates and went home, an uneven stillness settled over the brownstone. The quiet coming from the family room was total, and it seemed to spread over the house in waves, charging the air in an unsteady rhythm Malaya could not catch. Sometimes the stillness was thin enough she barely noticed it, and she felt she could brush her teeth and live her day almost as usual. But other times, the stillness was so thick she felt it could choke her.

Now, the days felt fake, like a strange game of house that Malaya, Nyela, and Ma-Mère were playing together, only no one could say who was playing what role, or what the rules were. Ma-Mère installed herself in the brownstone, sleeping in the spare room on the garden floor, which now stored Malaya's childhood bed, the old exercise bike brought down from the family room, and several boxes of papers and books. The room was crowded with junk, but Ma-Mère surprised Malaya by not complaining. For the first few mornings after the funeral, she woke up early and made coffee, and she and Nyela left the house. "We have to take care of your father's affairs, since he never bothered to," Ma-Mère said when Nyela wasn't around. They spent the day out in the world—at the safe deposit box, the accountant's office, the lawyer's, and the insurance company—cleaning up the messes of Percy's life. Sometimes they were

just in the family room, which might as well have been another country. Malaya spent her days in her room, eating, sometimes sketching,
never calling Shaniece. Around six in the evening, Nyela and Ma-Mère
would return from wherever they'd been and descend to the kitchen,
where they would sit for hours, going over the business of the day. When
dinner was ready, they would call Malaya down and the three would eat
together, each woman watching the others' plates. They would dawdle
over cleaning and small talk before making the trek back upstairs. Neither woman talked about Percy, at least not while Malaya was around.
She hadn't seen her mother cry since the day of the funeral, but there
was nothing she could say about this because no one had seen her cry
either. In the day and the evening, everything looked to Malaya almost
like it had when Percy was alive, except that he had been erased and
Ma-Mère had been pasted in his place. But late at night, she sometimes
heard her parents' bedroom door creak open, then heard her mother's
slow feet on the stairs going down, how far down she didn't know.

One evening after returning from the bank, Ma-Mère called Malaya
to the kitchen early. "Won't hurt you to sit with us women, will it, My Ly-
Ly?" she said. Malaya wanted to answer that *yes*, it might hurt. But that
would be against the rules. And so she joined them for more of what Ma-
Mère called "waistline-friendly fare," which meant waterlogged string
beans, gray, skinless chicken, and sugar-free instant pudding. The
pudding was always lumped and runny because, after the unsatisfying
entrée, none of them had the patience to let the pudding set properly in
the fridge before eating it.

"I did like Sylvie's suit, though I didn't care for the way she wore it," Ma-
Mère said, snapping the ends off a heap of string beans in a bowl. "The
blouse was too tight. I thought her bosom was ready to bust out and run."
Nyela nodded and sprayed a cast-iron skillet with light cooking spray.

They debriefed about the funeral for the third or fourth time, going
over details they'd forgotten to mention just after the wake and obser-
vations that had dawned on them after a few days of reflection. They
talked about who had slimmed down, whose dress was gaudy, who was
still battling her pregnancy weight even now that her youngest was in
his terrible twos. They talked about what they thought of each woman's

hair, who had eaten too much at the repast and still had the nerve to take home a plate. They talked about who didn't come and gave their guesses as to why. They talked about LaSondra's speech and her nails, both of which, they agreed between mouthfuls, were better suited for a day-time talk show than for a funeral. And they talked about the food—who brought what and who didn't bring anything, how good the greens and the pasta salad and the peach cobbler were, whose dish was overloaded with butter and whose lacked salt.

During this part of the conversation, each woman made a point of shaking her head at the mention of at least one food. "Oh no," Nyela and Ma-Mère took turns saying, "I didn't have any of *that*. Did you?"

It was impossible for Malaya not to feel implicated in these discussions. She pulled her favorite pencil, the number 7, from her pocket and drew on a napkin. She felt trapped, a fish stuck in a bowl on the table, angry both at the glass and at the world that lay beyond it. She drew circles, dark and tight, on the ridged cottony paper.

"And then there's Tweedledee and Tweedledum," Ma-Mère said, pulling a bowl of carrots toward her and beginning to slice. These were her names for Aunt Ro and Aunt Augustine, Percy's twin cousins, who Ma-Mère always said talked loud and dressed louder. "Someone needs to tell them that just 'cause leather is legal don't mean they can kill all the world's cows to make their big selves some pants." She slid an orange disc into her mouth and gave a conclusive chew.

"Yeah," Nyela said, her voice tilted up to question-mark tones, "I'd hate for people to see me looking like that." She brought a shard of stiff chicken to her face.

As Malaya watched, she noticed how Ma-Mère and Nyela became echoes of each other, their dinnertime talk a well-rehearsed tradition of call-and-response in which the rhythm was always the same. One called out the fat in a searing declaration and, with metronomic certainty, the other offered up a derisive judgment of her own. "She should be ashamed," one would say. "Nice necklace," the other would respond. "Though I can't see how she finds her neck, with all them chins she got." "Course more than anything I just feel bad for her." "That's a sad, sad life."

There was no place for Malaya in this rhythm. She could only sit there, quiet as an elephant at the zoo. Whatever was being said about the woman in question, much worse could be said about her. She wondered if Ma-Mère and Nyela were thinking of her as they talked. Then she wondered if they were all three sharing a version of the same thought: *I wonder if she's really talking about me.*

BY MID-MAY, spring broke rash-like into an early summer. The air in the brownstone thickened suddenly with heat as the city streets blazed to life. Screeching cranes and jackhammers rang through the air, mingling with Harlem's regular summer sounds: laughter and car horns, the blare of merengue, lilting R&B. There were a few weeks left in the school year at Galton, but no one had bothered Malaya about going to school since Percy's passing. Nyela had made a call to the office promising that Malaya would complete her outstanding schoolwork. She was grateful that she'd gone back to school during her walking weeks. Between those weeks of attendance, her made-up assignments, and her stack of absence notes, she had enough to avoid a leave of absence, and though she knew her grades would be horrific, it was nice to trust that Nyela would show compassion now.

Drummond University had let out for summer, and there was still no indication that Ma-Mère would return to Philadelphia anytime soon. This left more time for Nyela and Ma-Mère to spend out in the world, tying up the last of Percy's loose ends, and more time for Malaya to sit with his absence, feeling the itch of summer alone.

Left to herself in the hot house, Malaya found herself sitting at the window filled with urges. Some days, the urge was to raise the glass and see how much of her body she could fit through the frame. On bad days she thought of leaving her body. But on other days, she imagined doing strange things that seemed unlike her, leaving herself in other ways. She envisioned herself leaning over the windowsill like the old women on the block, hollering down at strangers on the corner: *How you been?* she might say, craning her neck and giving a purse-lipped smile as though she knew the people below. *You know Percy Clondon passed? Yep. Pneumonia, they say, but I don't know. You wanna come in and fix yourself a plate?* No one she knew was there, of course, and all the food had been gone for weeks. Still, the simple fantasy of shouting tickled her.

When Edgar left a message after weeks of paging and asked where Alya had been, Malaya called him back and gave him the only voice she had, a croak like the closing of a door, and said the man of the house had died and the family had moved away.

"There is no one named Al-ee-yah here," she said. "Stop calling. Leave me alone." She hung up just as he murmured, again, "Al-yuh, I am not one to hurt you."

Malaya drifted by the easel more regularly now, sometimes scratching at the canvas board with whatever was handy—a pencil, a tube of lip gloss, a rusted nail—wondering with a detached curiosity whether anything meaningful would materialize on the surface. Occasionally a family member called to offer condolences, and Malaya tried to act as her mother's representative: "Thank you," she would say, assured and businesslike. "Yes, we're holding up as best as can be expected. Yes, we got the card. Thank you—we love you, too." It was a strange exercise, this taking on of voices. It was exhausting, and part of her resented it, but it also gave her a quiet thrill to come out of herself, to be something different, something that surprised her. Each time she opened her mouth, she wondered what more was there.

One Friday, Malaya was looking out the parlor window when Shaniece appeared on the stoop. She paused before the doorbell, fidgeting with a stack of books in her arms. She wore faded jeans and a worn green hoodie. She had taken her braids out, and her hair jutted down at her neck without fanfare as it had in the elementary days. She looked even narrower than the last time Malaya seen her. But whereas lately her expression had bent into a fierce aloofness, now she looked tentative, almost nervous. Her small eyes darted left and right as she rang the bell, and her tongue peeked out to moisten her lips. Standing there alone, bulky with old cotton, her arms piled with books, she could almost have been the old Shaniece.

Malaya felt her skin rush to life. She opened the door.

"Hey," she said, her hand on the doorknob.

"Hey, girl," Shaniece said. "You busy?" She raised her eyes directly to Malaya's and let them rest there. She felt Shaniece take her in, slowly, curiously, but through her eyes, not her body.

Malaya stepped back from the doorway, making room for Shaniece to come in. "I didn't see you at the funeral," she said, though she wasn't sure if it was true.

"I was there," Shaniece said. She followed Malaya into the humid foyer. Her voice was earnest and surprised, almost frail. She held the books out and hovered by the banister. She had borrowed them from the family room library for a term paper, months ago, back in their days of fullness. Now the books looked strange and uncomfortable in her hands. "I know I've had these a long time. I didn't want to bother y'all, so."

"They go in the family room," Malaya said. She looked at Shaniece's soft face, her quick eyes. For the billionth time, she tried not to think of the dance at the Fat Cat, and for the billionth time she failed. "You can bring them."

When they reached the second floor, they both stood still before the closed family room door. Malaya had passed it many times, but she had never lingered there. Now, catching her breath with Shaniece, she noticed it still smelled like smoke. "I'll keep the books upstairs," she said.

Her bedroom smelled different with Shaniece in it—less dusty, warmer, sweeter even, though not quite comfortable. The last time someone had sat with her there it was her father, when he'd come to invite her to lunch on one of their secret hooky days. Now she perched on the edge of the bed and placed the books on the floor. Shaniece sat at the foot of the bed, a few hip-widths away. They looked out at the old dolls that topped the mantel.

"Is your mom okay?" Shaniece asked, her hands in the front pocket of the hoodie. "I mean, I know she's not *okay*, but, you know."

Malaya nodded. "I guess. My grandmother's here, so that's good. They're out dealing with stuff. Loose-end patrol. My grandmother keeps her busy fixing things, so that helps. I mean, it helps my mother at least."

"Not the most fun for you, though, huh, My Ly-Ly?" Shaniece smiled mischievously and looked down at her feet. Malaya felt laughter bloom in her belly.

"Is she letting you eat?" Shaniece looked at her.

"Barely," Malaya said. "The dinners are brutal."

Shaniece reached into the pocket of the hoodie and pulled out a brown paper bag stained with grease. "I have something for you."

Malaya opened the bag. It was a pack of dulce de coco candies, wrapped in wax paper. She bit into a candy and handed another to Shaniece. She rolled the flavors over her tongue, letting the sticky juice fill the wells of her cheeks. She hadn't had one of these since the night on the stoop a year ago, but the taste was familiar as breath.

"From your mother?" Malaya said. "Pat-*ri*-cia Guzmán?" She pushed the name out of her mouth dramatically, poking at the mystery of the woman, still untold after all these years. It was a jab, and as soon as it came out, she regretted it.

"No," Shaniece said. "From me."

Malaya thought about all the fantasies between them, about Clarence and Patricia Guzmán. About who they themselves had both been, not so long ago. She had imagined Shaniece would say she was sorry—for the dance and the bus ride, for leaving, for becoming someone other than who she'd been. But she didn't apologize, and Malaya didn't either. There was nothing about RayShawn or the man at the Fat Cat. Nothing about Malaya's fall on the cafeteria floor. Instead, Shaniece hunched forward on the bed and fumbled with the books, and the two sat there watching the dust curl in the hair of the smiling dolls, listening to each other chew.

"It won't stay so terrible," Shaniece said after a while, still looking out at the mantel. "The pain never goes away, but it stops being pain at a certain point. It becomes something else. Something that just walks around with you. You remember what you can about the person, and you keep the pain, in whatever way you can handle. Maybe that's making up stories, pretending things are what you wish they were."

Malaya nodded. She pulled another dulce from the package and listened.

"All I can tell you is how it is for me," Shaniece said. She looked at Malaya, then at the mound of coconut in her hands. "Me and *Pat-ri-cia* Guzmán, as you say." She gave a half-chuckle and bit into the candy. "The truth is, she's nothing but a stack of birthday cards and a last name," she said, straightening her back and looking again toward the dolls on the mantel. "And most of the cards came late. She left the country before I could say my first word. I never really even met her." Malaya looked at her friend, Shaniece's palms sure and firm on her own thighs as she continued.

"My dad used to tell me stories about her, and that, plus the cards, was almost enough. But the cards stopped coming years ago," Shaniece said plainly. "Just stopped. The last time I heard from her was the seventh grade." She turned to look at Malaya, her eyes soft but clear. "I don't know what happened after that. But I don't know what happened before that, either. I just know she did what she wanted. Went where she wanted to go. And she didn't want to stay here, so she left. That's the kind of woman she is," Shaniece said, leaning back on the mattress, her face tilted to the window. "She's a choice made."

As Shaniece spoke, Malaya watched the curved cheek of her, the tight, round eyes slung low. It wasn't the new slope of her waist or the familiar yellow of her skin or her stick-straight hair, which she had pushed simply behind her ears. The lair of Shaniece's beauty, Malaya now saw, was in the fierce quiet she had had since always. A look that said, *I may not know what I need to do, but if I have to, I'll learn.* A look that said, *I'm here.* She had grown into it now. Shaniece looked like a woman. Malaya realized she herself was only just starting to understand what that meant.

"Eventually it feels better," Shaniece continued. "That feeling of losing. It gets to be something you can kind of cozy up to. And it feels better. The trick is to just keep moving. However you can. If you're moving, you're still alive."

Malaya sighed and let her body fall closer to Shaniece on the bed. Shaniece tilted toward her on the dipping mattress, and their arms pressed together. Malaya wasn't sure if Shaniece was turning toward her or if it was just an effect of gravity, the force of her weight on the springs, but her skin felt like fire. She breathed out and let herself expand, her belly relaxing along Shaniece's waist, her breasts resting full at her side. She breathed with Shaniece for who knew how long, feeling her skin light up like coal, the old flurry of ants making a map of her limbs.

When she raised her head, Shaniece kissed her—first her cheek, then her lips, only lightly, as though dropping off gifts on the run. Malaya sat up and kissed her back, first to thank her, then to apologize, though she wasn't sure for what. When she looked up, Shaniece's face was calm and questionless. She reached into the wax paper, took a candy, put it in her mouth, and they kissed again.

Tangled together, they sat, sipping on each other, lapping the dulce's buttery juice. When the candies were gone, they kept kissing. When they got so deep into it that they clinked teeth and the wax paper fell to the floor, they laughed. And the afternoon went on, the two talking just like always, just like never, until the sun sagged low outside the window. Then Shaniece said, "Shit, girl, it's late. I have to go home and cook."

They said goodbye and hugged only quickly, but after Shaniece left, Malaya thought of the skin. She thought of how nervous it made her at first, the breathless feel of this soft body against hers. She recalled the relief she felt when she let herself be full of Shaniece, how her whole weight seemed to double and disappear at once, how she became an ocean, her body formless and invulnerable, a tiny part of a gorgeous moment. She recalled Shaniece's bottom lip against hers. She imagined sealing it in her mouth, holding it there between her tongue and her teeth like a candy, or a good meal, or a sentence too true to say.

When she lifted the stack of books to bring them down to the family room that night, something glossy sailed to the floor. She picked it up and studied it. It was a booklet written half in Spanish, half in English. The cover was spattered with photos of smiling models swimming under palm trees, hang gliding, hunched over desks writing, standing with muddy hands before a pottery wheel. In one photo, a round brown woman about Malaya's age sat with a sketch pad at the foot of a huge mountain, staring up at its miles of trees, her body a small brown dot before a sky full of color. It was a brochure for a summer arts exchange program in Sosúa, in the Dominican Republic, a place Malaya had heard of and imagined for years, but that had never felt real. When she flipped the booklet over to the back, she found a Home and Office Post-it note and Shaniece's bubble-gum handwriting saying: *MALAYA, PLEASE GO.*

Ethan Windborne

By the first week of June, it seemed everyone was telling Malaya to go somewhere. Visiting cousins swiveled on their hips, neighborhood women leaned over the stoop, concerned aunties breathed hotly on the phone: *Go get some fresh air—it'll heal you. Go get your mother a glass of wine, you know she's had a hard day. Go to the store. Go see who's at the door this time. Go put your father's coat where your mother can't see it. Why don't you go back to church? Nuthin' the Word can't conquer. Why don't you go to the movies with one of your girlfriends, take your mind off things? Go on and take a walk; summer came early this year—you know it's your father did that, don't you?*

The commands came from all corners—first from Shaniece, then from Ma-Mère, then in phone calls from family friends and relatives whose faces Malaya could not remember, but whose voices evoked the smells of mothballs, wood, and mint in her memory. Once directed, Malaya would hang up the phone or leave the room baffled. She understood the *why* of going, but she was lost on the *how*—how, exactly, was she supposed to just leap up and move? So much weight and history was against it. Immediately after Percy's death, she'd felt like she was a ghost. Now, with every motion she made, she felt like she was pushing through a ghost, its residue always on her. She couldn't understand how anyone could be expected to just jump up like a kernel of popped corn after a certain number of weeks of bereavement and get on with the going of life. This seemed even less feasible for someone like her. It was as though all these people had forgotten who they were talking to, forgotten the bulk of her and replaced it in their minds with a handy template of a grieving girl, someone frail but steely enough to get things done. That was not Malaya. It was all she could do, she felt, to go through the motions of her same-old, same-old day, eating in her room, painting halfheartedly, making up stories. As soon as she felt she'd mastered the art of cosmic rewind, spinning herself slowly like a spool of tape from a broken cassette, back to a place where she could just watch TV, eat, and pretend everything was normal, now all anyone had to say to her was, *Change. Move forward. Go.*

The whole of Harlem seemed to heed these demands, changing quickly and dramatically like a teacher's pet, eager to set an example: *This is how you change.* On the day of the funeral, the Quisqueya Grocery and Envios on Amsterdam closed quietly and without fanfare. It stayed boarded up for five weeks, and then suddenly, on a single day in the first week of June, a Modell's Sporting Goods sprang up in its place with slick, shiny windows that sliced the top of Sugar Hill with light. That same week, the sprawling discount store on 145th closed, and a small sticker reading NEW YORK FITNESS COMING SOON was perched on the door like a price tag on an orange. Now, when Malaya went to 125th looking for a new pair of sneakers and a few EMCEE T-shirts for the summer, she found that Uncle Bruh-Bruh's Apollo Sneaker and Leather Shop had vanished behind a padlocked metal gate and Harlem Jeans had turned into a Disney store. A few days later she heard someone on the block say that the Harlem Arts Academy was about to close. "Budget problems," the man muttered. "I hear they got a GNC coming, and a CVS too. You know what *that* mean—GNC, CVS. All that spells is R-E-N-T. They keep this up, I'ma have to go down south with my cousin. *Shoo.*"

ONE OF THE more reasonable directives Malaya was given during that time was to collect the condolence cards that continued to straggle in, and to keep them somewhere safe and invisible until Nyela was ready to read them. Malaya protested at first; she had had enough condolences. The phrases "sincerest sympathy," "time of sorrow," and "joy comes in the morning" had begun to play on repeat in her mind as she tried to fall asleep, and sometimes she thought she heard them crop up awkward and out of place as she watched family sitcom reruns on television. *Heathcliff Huxtable! What in sincerest sympathies are you doing with that sandwich in your hand? Aw, nothing, Claire, nothing! Cross my heartfelt condolences, I was just holding onto this for a friend!*

But Malaya saw that her mother was in an even worse position to collect the cards than she was. At first, when the most urgent ghost-boxing business had been done—the credit cards canceled, the funeral bills settled—Nyela seemed to return to normal; each morning, she called goodbye to Malaya and Ma-Mère (who still had made no signs of going back to Philadelphia) and pushed through the thickening summer to her campus office on the Upper West Side to do research for her next book, the precise focus of which, she said exasperatedly, she hadn't discovered yet. Sometimes, Nyela would give a strange look at dinner, lower her voice, and say what she thought the old Percy would have said to comfort her, back in the Pra Clondon days: "Too many ideas. You're a thick thinker, Ny. That's a great problem to have!" But most days, she came home frayed and put herself to washing dishes absently, stacking and restacking the coffee mugs in the overcrowded cupboard, playing at unpacking the cardboard boxes of Percy's papers that sat limp and weary on the kitchen floor. On those days, she said very little, and when Malaya or Ma-Mère tried to talk to her, Nyela shivered and gave tiny answers—*Thank you. Thursday. Roast corn*—her voice knotting up like a necktie whenever someone mentioned Percy's name.

So Malaya agreed to collect the cards. The task involved a kind of attention-paying that challenged her. Which card would be best to show Nyela today? Which should she save for later? The cards from the people she knew best had all come weeks ago, and the most important ones had been read at the funeral. The ones that came in now were from the last people to get the news—Percy's old classmates; Nyela's first college roommate; the North Philadelphia neighbor, Miss Agnes, who had let little Nathallie Smith stay with her from time to time when her father came home drunk and ready to fight.

There were also cards for Malaya. They started to trickle in after the funeral, but she hadn't been able to look at them. Reading the cards now reminded her of the "This Is Your Life" segment on Sesame Street, which had been her favorite as a child. Strange, puppetish versions of people she had known popped up out of nowhere, each struggling to say something poignant but triumphally brief. There was a card from Rachel Greenstein and her family: heavy, expensive cardboard, printed with a simple message and signed "sending you love" in Rachel's leafy handwriting. There was a plain forest-green note card from RayShawn reading: "Your father was a wonderful man, and while words cannot comfort you right now, please know that you have all my caring."

Truth be told, only one of these seemed to Malaya to express true sympathy. It was from Eric Martinez, who'd sent a dollar-store card with a picture of a sunset on the front and a long note inside, written in pencil. The note closed with: "Much love to you and your family, Malaya. LaFamille loves you and we will always have your back. If you ever need anything, just holla at us, for real. That's word." On the same day, another card arrived for her in a stampless pink envelope with no name, no address, nothing written on it but "Family Condolences." It was an inexpensive card with the image of a tired lilac on the front and a Bible verse inside. The note beneath the verse read: "Sorry for your lost. My heart is with your family's. —Sincerely, C. Edgar Kollie." Malaya placed the card from Eric between the dolls on her mantel. She ripped the other one with a force that surprised her and left the pieces in the trash.

On one of Nyela's better days, Ma-Mère determined that she would go out for air after dinner, and that Malaya should join her. "You know, My Ly-Ly," she said, "won't hurt us to walk around the block once or twice after eating like that," though all they'd eaten was one helping of water-logged tuna and a half cup of cabbage each. The thought of Ma-Mère suited up in a two-piece windbreaker outfit and silver jewelry, speed-walking around Harlem on the lip of dusk, seemed strange and impossible to Malaya, and it jogged something in her.

"No, thank you," she said. Then, bolder: "I don't feel like I ate too much. I feel fine." She shifted her weight and tried to settle into the quiet thrill.

Ma-Mère gave her a look and zipped up her windbreaker, leaving

Malaya and Nyela alone to clean the kitchen. Once she was gone, Malaya went to her stash and selected three cards: a simple note from one of Nyela's graduate school classmates; a plain floral envelope from one of her Black Psychologists friends; and a card from the colleague with the flashy suit, Ethan Windborne. Dr. Windborne's card looked like the woman who'd sent it—an overload of color and shine. Both the envelope and the card were a deep fuchsia, and the card itself seemed over-dressed, studded with soft, copper-colored glitter around its edges, a neatly frayed gold braid looped around its spine.

"Lord, that woman," Nyela said when she opened the card. "She has no shame."

Malaya nodded dutifully, but she wasn't sure why. She'd seen the call-and-response of woman critique as a rite of passage, an invitation to a special matrilineal tradition passed down over generations like an heirloom brooch. But now, it made her squirm. She wanted to say, *What good has shame done you?* but she didn't know how to say it without sounding cruel. Instead, she fixed herself a second helping of Ma-Mère's bland tuna bake and ate it silently.

When she was done, she put her plate in the sink and said, "I'm going upstairs. You can leave the food on the stove. I'll put it away later." She pulled two dinner rolls from their packaging and put them in the pocket of her jeans.

"Malaya," Nyela said. She pursed her lips and took a breath. She looked at the bulges in Malaya's pockets, then looked up at her. "I think you should go talk to someone. A professional, I mean. This is a hard time for a teenager—for anyone, but for a teenager especially. And your eating . . . The way you're handling it, I think it would be helpful for you to have someone to talk to."

Nyela pushed her plate away from her stomach. "There's no stigma in it, Malaya. I just think it could be good for you." She paused as though waiting for Malaya to say something, but Malaya did not know what to say. It struck her now that despite all the directives from everyone else, her mother hadn't actually told her to do anything in a long time.

"I'll try to find someone you'll like," Nyela continued, crumpling her napkin and placing it on the plate. She gave a worried look. "But I want to be clear—this isn't a suggestion. It's something you need to do. You have to go."

Malaya looked at her mother, perched stiffly on the chair like a statue of herself. She looked uncomfortable, and again Malaya felt a surprising surge. She wanted to put a blanket around her, to tell her it was okay to go to bed. It was an unfamiliar shot of feeling, of wanting to help her mother feel better, feel okay.

"I'll find someone," Malaya said. "I mean, if I have to do this, I'd rather find whoever myself."

"Okay," Nyela replied. It sounded like a question, but Malaya said nothing after that. She cleared the table, washed the dishes, and drifted out of the kitchen, climbing up through the ghost's weight, back to her room, thinking about the bold raspberry of that one envelope, the shameless gold of the braid.

It didn't require much trying at all, really. The key was to do the wildest thing she could think of. In those weeks of constant surveillance, directives, and the ghost, the only thing that could console Malaya was her will to luxuriate in the unexpected. She could never be right, or do right, but in this suspended moment of directionless grief, *right* did not exist. And so, why not just let herself unhinge? In the seventh grade, the white kids at Galton had taken up the habit of developing personal philosophies, like "Never Run for the Bus If You're Already Late for Class," or "Only Make Mixtapes for Your Friends; Boyfriends and Hookups Come and Go." The trend had seemed silly to LaFamille, with their loftier sociopolitical pronouncements. But after Nyela's decree, Malaya found herself revisiting the idea. In a moment like this, when nothing made much sense, and every conversation sought to push her from place to place against her will like a pet in a carrier, a personal philosophy could be useful. Hers came to her now: *If you have to go someplace you don't want to be, your only concern when you get there should be your own entertainment.* Malaya could think of no better place to practice this philosophy than in the office of Dr. Ethan Windborne.

When she called to arrange the first appointment, Malaya let herself be as surprising as possible.

"My name is Malaya Clondon," she said to the answering machine. She tried a dull, flat voice like the kind Percy's favorite comedians used in their stand-up routines—Whoopi Goldberg and George Carlin in one. "We met at my father's funeral. My mother is making me call you." She thought about adding, in a thick, TV announcer voice: *Why is my mother making me call you? Why did my father die? Find out on the next Phil Dona-hue!* But instead she said, "My father is dead and my mother is making me call *you* to talk about it. I suppose that gives us something to start with right there."

ETHAN WINDBORNE PRACTICED in her duplex Upper West Side condo, in the kind of building with both a doorman and a set of huge, hulk-ing gargoyles watching over the outer door—*just in case*, Malaya thought, looking up at the gnarled stone faces. Even the trip to her office offered Malaya several opportunities for wildness. As a visitor to the building, she was forced into interactions with people who seemed never to have beheld a body like hers before, at least not there in the glitzy halls of West End Avenue. First, there was the doorman, a tall, mustached man who smelled like aftershave and peppermint, who was reading a book behind his post the first time she entered the building. He greeted Malaya with a rehearsed "hello," then eyed her belly over the receiver while he pressed the intercom. Once he'd given her permission to enter, she thanked him. Then, as though the thought had just snuck up on her, she said: "Oh, be careful! Side-eyes give you migraines." Then she added: "Possibly cancer too," and walked toward the elevator.

A narrow pink woman with skin like tissue paper gave a small gasp and said, "Watch out," when she stepped on the elevator, waiting for Malaya to suck herself in so she could pass.

"*Watch out*'?" Malaya said. "For what?" She looked in the air as though checking for lightning or a coming flood. "*Oh*, you mean *excuse me*. Is that what you mean?" She stepped off the elevator just as the woman gave a waxy, bewildered smile.

Malaya had always thought of herself as a medical patient extraor-dinaire. She couldn't imagine anyone her age having logged as many paper-gown hours as she had, save for leukemia patients. She thought she knew the spectrum of doctors' offices well—the dizzyingly sterile ones, the falsely warm ones, the ones that seemed soaked in disappointment, with self-important doctors and tired, fidgety staff. But Dr. Windborne's office felt like a portal to a different realm entirely. While most of the offices she had visited featured pale wall art that could have been mass-printed in an Easter egg factory, Dr. Windborne's office was filled with wood-carved and silver-plated curios from around the world. An expensive-looking replica of an Australian Indigenous carving sat on an end table; a piece of rubble from the Great Wall of China hovered in a glass box on the bookshelf; small statues of Shiva and Ganesh sat on either side of the desk, which was covered in a run of Adinkra cloth. There was a small portrait of the Hindu Divine Mother, which she recognized from her Eastern art class, perched over the doorway.

"Hello, Malaya," Dr. Windborne announced as she opened the door for their first session. Her voice was thick but piquant, like something spicy stewed for hours. She offered Malaya a glass of orange juice, but Malaya declined.

The office was in the loft space of the duplex apartment, and the wall leading upstairs was covered with black-and-white family photos gone honey-colored with age. Instead of the standard oak desk and tight chair setup, Dr. Windborne's office had the feel of a world traveler's living room. There was a low coffee table in the middle of the space, and Dr. Windborne sat behind it in a huge purple and cream-colored easy chair that reminded Malaya of a blueberry muffin. For the patient, there was a plush green love seat, which sighed only slightly under Malaya's weight when she sat. She imagined the two-person seat meant that Dr. Windborne saw couples sometimes, too. She pushed herself into the corner, trying to keep her body to one cushion and leave a lover's-worth of space beside her.

Dr. Windborne handed her a purple clipboard and a printed questionnaire. She went to get herself some juice, leaving Malaya to fill out the form alone. It was a bubble-sheet exam like the state Department of Education tests she had to take at the end of every school year, the kind that seemed perpetually smeared with gray pencil dust so that they looked useless and dejected, even when all the answers were right. This one read "Diagnostic Mood Assessment," a phrase that seemed redundant to Malaya. What was a diagnosis if not an assessment? The exam asked questions like: *On a scale of one to five, how hopeful have you felt over the past three months? (a) 1—very hopeful; (b) 2—hopeful; (c) 3—somewhat hopeful; (d) 4—less than hopeful; (e) 5—much less than hopeful,* and *Which of the following best describes your current mood? (a) very content; (b) content; (c) somewhat content; (d) less than content; (e) much less than content.*

After reading the first few questions, Malaya marked the bubble sheet with a long column of messy *c*'s. Then, with extra time to kill, she went back and varied the answers so they made a winding pattern, a yellow brick road of unfeeling, with mostly *b*'s, a few scattered *c*'s, several *a*'s, and one *d*, just for color. She imagined Alya on the couch, in her body, speaking through her lips. *I'm fine,* she imagined her saying. *I don't have time for this. Pshht.*

When Dr. Windborne came to retrieve the test, Malaya handed her the bubble sheet and said plainly: "These things don't make sense. If you want to know if someone is depressed, why not just ask them?"

Not missing a beat, Dr. Windborne leaned back in her muffin and said: "Okay. Are you depressed?"

Malaya tried not to smile.

"I don't know," she said. "It depends on what you mean by *depressed*. But if I am, it's not because of my weight, just so you know. I wanted to write that down, but there's no space between the bubbles."

Dr. Windborne slid the test into a folder beside her chair and put down her pen.

"So what can I do for you today?" she asked. There was no oozy tone, no curved lips seeping across her face into a fake smile. She simply looked at Malaya: one person in a conversation, waiting for another to speak.

"Well," Malaya said, "I guess you could tell my mother we fixed the problem and just let me leave."

"Do you think she would believe us?" Now a conspiratorial warmth broke over Dr. Windborne's face.

"You'd have to really lay it on," Malaya said. "Tell her it's the most miraculous transformation you've ever seen. One for the record books.

What is it—the *New England Journal of Medicine*, right? Tell her it's really a credit to her stupendous mothering skills. Then we'd have a shot."

Dr. Windborne laughed, her loud, deep chuckles pouring out into the office. Malaya felt her thighs ease up a little on the springs of the love seat, and she let herself laugh, too.

FOR THE NEXT SEVERAL WEEKS, Malaya made up stories about her life that she could trot out, both for the bougie building people and for Dr. Windborne. In the hallway, she pretended to be the best friend of one of the television starlets who lived there, coming to bring her weed and fancy bakery cookies—petits fours—while her parents were at work. Other times, she was the secret black daughter of the couple who owned the penthouse apartment. On those days, she tried to move quicker, with a sharp, defiant stride. "Hello," she would say with a tight smile. Then she'd add, "I'm fine, thank you," whether she'd been asked or not. Mostly the residents glanced over her middle, then ignored her. Occasionally, they made small talk, and the strangeness of their lives put Malaya's own wildness to shame. Once, in the elevator, she found herself chatting with a wealthy-looking woman soaked through to the bone. "I didn't know it was raining outside," the woman said, scraping a string of wet hair off her forehead. "I went out with no umbrella, no jacket, nothing! I had to just run all the way to D'Agostino's." Then she shrugged and smiled as if to say, "Oh well! Life!" and popped through the open doors into the comfort of the hallway, leaving Malaya no time to say anything at all. She wondered what it would feel like to be so carefree.

"So, Malaya, how was your week?" Dr. Windborne would say at the beginning of each session, her thick legs crossed like two stacked hams, her back tall and without apology.

Dr. Windborne seemed to treat her body like a juicy secret she couldn't wait to tell. Her wardrobe was a splash of iridescent blues, greens, and pinks, and her clothes covered her up only reluctantly, revealing spans of nut-brown chest and smooth, hoseless calf without a second thought. The way she lived her life fascinated Malaya, too. Where her mother and most of the women she knew seemed to rush constantly between appointments and tasks in an endless stream of work, Dr. Windborne spent exactly six hours a day, four days a week, sitting in a recliner the shape and color of pastry dough, talking to people about their lives.

Malaya pulled equal scraps from memory and fantasy to put together what she thought was an entertaining version of her life for Dr. Windborne. She gave herself license to say what she wanted—to surprise and entertain herself with whatever came to her mind, jokes and lies and slivers of the truth flying out of her like doves out of a magician's hat. She talked about her mother's job and her father's book idea, both of which she said were "absolutely titillating, believe you me." She told a few stories about their relationship—she said they'd met at the first-ever space camp in Florida as high school students, but that they'd been estranged until a chance reunion in the grocery store nine months before she was born. She tried to remember the last time she had seen them kiss or touch, but she couldn't. She talked about her Uncle Book, how he was secretly gay and covered up his hunger for men by sleeping with too many women—which, she decided after careful consideration, may have been true—and how it made her sad to think that he might never stop smelling like a bottle of gin. She mentioned RayShawn, laying on her immense concern for him. He was a ruthless player with no regard for women, stemming from his troubled childhood. "I love him, of course. Him and Eric and Lavar Hillings are all great." She said it in a sweeping, yawning voice she hoped would evoke a rich and dour white lady, like Liza Minnelli or Zsa Zsa Gabor. *I love them all, DAH-ling!* She tilted her head back and lifted her arm to rest it on the back of the love seat. She imagined an opera-length cigarette holder in her hand, a veil of smoke curling over her eyelashes.

It was exhilarating, this wildness of mind. It felt like painting and lying and eating Marshmallow Fluff all in one. For an hour each week, she let herself flap around in whatever direction like a paper doll cut loose from its chain, saying and being whatever came to mind.

While Malaya told her stories, Dr. Windborne wrote in looping blue ink on the small pad that sat in her lap. At first, it made Malaya nervous, but Dr. Windborne reassured her: "Writing helps me really think about what you're saying. If it distracts you, I can stop." Malaya liked the idea of someone going out of their way to really think about whatever strange things she had to say.

Soon, she began to accept Dr. Windborne's orange juice, and to enjoy it. She pulled her shoulders back between her stories and let the sweet cool slide down her throat. Sometimes she asked for a second glass and drank it with abandon in the bald-faced arc of the afternoon, right across from this woman so like and unlike her mother.

She never mentioned Edgar, but sometimes she talked about Clarence, about his hair and his poetry. She indicated vaguely that he tended to be possessive, but she didn't feel a need to say more than that. A few times, she thought of telling Dr. Windborne about Shaniece, but she stopped herself. Then she looked out the window at the gargoyles on the building across the street. They were huge, with cartoonish eyes and greedy mouths that were sometimes stained with bird feces. Still, she liked them. What would they say if they came alive?

At the end of their third session, Malaya told a made-up story about going jet skiing in Miami with Eric Martinez, which led her to mention the Harlem Arts Academy competition she had won back in the eighth grade. She talked about how it felt to bow under the blinking lights as the host placed the medal over her shoulders, how her core rushed inside her, as if she were moving at rocket speed while standing still. How good it felt to win, like running in the playground with nothing to stop her. When Dr. Windborne asked, "Have you felt anything like that since then?" Malaya thought about Shaniece again, about the dance and the dulce. "Nope," she said. "The program ended. The arts center closed down in February. They're putting up a Hallmark store." It was an answer, incomplete but true. Dr. Windborne seemed to want to hear more, but Malaya wasn't sure what should come next in the story. She sipped her juice and looked out the window. *What would the gargoyles say?*

BY THE FOURTH OF JULY, Harlem had put on its party dress. A run of slick, colorful awnings sprang up along St. Nicholas, and the sheen of new glass covered over the old brick-faced storefronts where Wilson's Soul Food Restaurant and the 99¢ & Plus Beauty Supply on Amsterdam had been. The next week, the once run-down Rite Aid on 145th Street got a face-lift, and a French fusion restaurant sprouted up in the empty lot next to where the Harlem Arts Academy had been. On one of her walks, Malaya discovered gratefully that the delicious hole-in-the-wall seafood takeout on St. Nicholas whose awning had never said anything more than FISH was still standing, though Malaya heard a woman in Mr. Gonzales's bodega say it would be closing next month. At first, only scattered handfuls of white twenty-somethings had appeared in the neighborhood, like the woman who had yelled at Percy months ago. But now, whole families of white people could be seen idling up and down Convent Avenue like tourists, walking their dogs and pushing their children in expensive strollers, carrying grocery bags from the shiny new Pathmark that had opened on Eighth Avenue, where Shaniece now worked. Even the AME Mount Canaan Community Center, where Malaya had spent so many Saturday mornings at the Meeting as a child, had closed. Now the Meeting had a fancy new name—the Northern Harlem Chapter of Weight Watchers, Inc.—and a bright new storefront on 148th and St. Nicholas, where Uncle Butter's Rib and Soul Shack used to be.

Malaya didn't hear anything from Shaniece, but she did find a flyer in the mail slot for a series of cooking classes being offered at the Pathmark. Stuck to the flyer was a Home and Office Post-it that said, "Use my name if you want the employee discount. Part-time Assistant Floor Manager S. Guzmán. Movin' on up, Weezie!" Then, at the bottom: "Of course, the food in Sosúa is better than the shit we get around here."

Malaya described the flyer to Dr. Windborne, telling her about the bright, plump tomatoes in the photos, the gleaming aisles, the plums dense with purple, the spinach greener than anything the dingy neighborhood CTown had ever seen.

When Dr. Windborne asked her the name of the friend who gave her the flyer, her pen poised on her notepad, Malaya pursed her lips. "Oh, Shaniece?" she said in her Zsa Zsa voice. "Have I not mentioned her before? She's nice. A good friend."

Dr. Windborne nodded. "Sounds like it. So what do you think about the cooking classes?" she asked from her muffin perch. "Do you think you might want to go?"

Malaya sat for a while, looking from the window to the glass in front of her. "I can't," she said. Her voice felt foreign to her—she wasn't sure who she was being just then. She looked up at Dr. Windborne. "I'm still grieving," she said finally, and took a sip of juice. Then, letting the sweet cool fill her mouth, she picked the glass up again, thought about it, and took a bigger gulp.

Room

MA-MÈRE STILL HAD made no sign of returning to Philadelphia, though it was almost June. When Malaya asked who was holding her seat on the community garden council or filling her place in the Silver Sparrows Bowling League, Ma-Mère simply said, "I go where I'm most needed, and when I'm not needed I'll know. Till then, let 'em miss me. Might do them dusty old doilies some good."

One evening, Nyela came home from campus in a gust of flustered energy, her eyes wide. Malaya was sitting propped at the kitchen table while Ma-Mère prepared the vegetables for another dreary dinner, and both looked up to find Nyela standing in the doorway of the kitchen, holding onto the chest strap of her briefcase as though it were the only thing keeping her from flying away. Malaya watched as Ma-Mère looked Nyela up and down, her eyes catching on every bump and bulge like a rake. Finally, she said: "Well, damn, Nathallie. What happened to you?"

"Reliable is closing," Nyela said. "I heard someone talking about it on the train this morning. I just stopped by there tonight and they said it was true. It's the last place we went," she said, pulling the strap from her chest and letting it fall again. "The three of us, I mean." She turned to Malaya, her face splashed with loss. "Do you remember?"

"Yes," Malaya said. She watched her mother sway there. The bewilderment of grief hit her. She did remember. It was last year, before she had stopped going to school, before Percy had stopped going to work and the family room vanished. He had come home earlier than usual, happy about a new contract he'd won, and they had all gone to dinner to celebrate. "You had the grilled salmon and vegetables," Malaya said. "And Dad had macaroni and cheese, like always. He kept telling jokes about the waiter's hair. He said he looked like Alfalfa, and he did an impression."

Malaya didn't know why she had said the last part, about the joke. She wasn't entirely sure if it was true, but something came to her—the outrageous urge. She raised her hand to her head, pulling up a cluster of braids, holding them three inches in the air, and curling her upper lip against her teeth like a gopher. It was a strange stab in the dark—she didn't know what Alfalfa looked like. But she smiled, and then Ma-Mère smiled, and then Nyela did too. The three women laughed.

"Did he do that?" Nyela said. She held her stomach, her eyes moist. "You're right. He did." She leaned back and wiped her eyes, still smiling. Malaya lingered in the feeling of the laughter, in the knowing that she had caused it, just by doing the unexpected thing.

"They're having a closing dinner in a couple of days," Nyela said finally. "By invitation only. For regulars. I'd go, but I've got a ton of work to do."

"Nathallie Yvonne Smith," Ma-Mère said, holding an unsnapped string bean in the air. "There's no work more important than memory. If I thought you didn't know that, I'd swear I raised a fool." Then she snapped the string bean in two and threw it in the bowl. "In other words," she said, "we're going."

ON THE DAY OF the closing, the three women shuffled through the doors of the restaurant behind a line of old-school Harlemites. Malaya had not been to Reliable since her fall, and she had dreaded the return since Nyela's announcement. But here she was, in line behind Nyela and Ma-Mère again, her belly clenched.

"They got the air up high enough to freeze a firefish in here," Ma-Mère said, pushing through the heavy glass doors. "No wonder they're going out of business."

Copeland's Restaurant and Reliable Cafeteria was packed tight with Harlem's finest, the vestiges of a different time come to mourn the era's passing. The elaborate copper-colored hats, the prim summer dresses, the pastel pink and melon-green skirt suits all said Sunday, though it was a Thursday evening.

The smells of gravy, butter, and black-eyed peas danced thick in the entryway. Malaya's fear thickened with it. When she fell, weeks ago, she felt some final thing had fallen inside her. She had tried, and she had failed, and she had felt she would never return to the site of her failure again. But now here she was, plodding behind her mother and her grandmother, the big, unruly third in a trail of ducklings, bobbing back into the nightmare. Maybe that was it, she thought. Maybe life really was a series of spirals backward, false starts, hopes cut short at the stalk. This was how it had felt for her since girlhood: Saturday mornings of sterling resolve, Friday nights sloshed in failure.

Malaya lowered herself slowly to the booth seat and sucked in. She prayed the seat would hold her, that it was somehow stronger than all the others she'd broken. She held in her stomach, tensed her thighs, tried not to breathe. But there was no need. Her body slid into the seat in a quick, smooth motion. It felt easy, elegant. A rush.

She felt the absence of the table's press. There was space around her middle. Room. She looked down at the crest of her belly, a perfect half-moon of purple cotton sitting neatly at the lip of the table, as though leaning in for a kiss. There was not much space around it, just enough for a chuckle. She looked around the restaurant: same old booths as always, padded with the same foam cushions, draped in the same aged velour. Same bedraggled buttons, same cigarette burns. But as she looked down at her body again, there it was. Today, there was *room*. Today, she could move.

The sight was unreal. Stunned, she took a breath, and her chest filled with sudden air that came out in a strange sound, half-heave, half-snort.

When the waitress appeared, Nyela ordered with abandon: a large plate of oxtails with rice and gravy, candied yams, and cabbage with hush puppies, plus extra cornbread for the table. "And a side of collard greens," she added just before the waitress walked away. Malaya had not seen her mother eat like this in years, and to hear her declare so publicly her eating plans surprised her. "I worked straight through lunch today," Nyela said to no one in particular. She swirled her water, letting the ice cubes clink together like nickels.

"Nathallie!" Ma-Mère gave a sharp whisper, leaning across the table, her breasts flattening against the creased tablecloth. "You know that woman, don't you?"

She pointed her chin toward the front of the dining room, where a woman with a short halo of auburn curls was squirming out of a too-tight fall coat. She was of average height and plump, with thick hips and a round face. The most remarkable thing about her was the creamy purple of the scarf that seemed to glow around her neck once the coat was finally off.

"Oh. Oh, wow," Nyela said, shifting to get a better look. "That's Adelaide Price."

The woman looked up, alert to their eyes on her. She gave a panicked smile, which shifted into a forced grin. Once she had been shown to her table—a two-top with a single seat—the woman laid her coat down and came to their booth.

"Dr. Clondon," she said with a tentative smile. She stooped down to give Nyela a kiss, placing her hand around her own middle as though gathering her stomach in. "How you been?"

"Oh, I'm alright, Adelaide," Nyela said. "You know I always told you call me Nyela."

"Shoot," the woman said, shifting her weight awkwardly. "They don't give away those degrees for free. I'll keep calling you 'Dr.' if you don't mind. Now wait, is this Malaya? No! Girl, you have grown!"

She turned to face Malaya. It wasn't until Malaya looked her in her eyes, saw the smear of purple shadow and the watery eyeliner, the drawn-in eyebrows and the strawberry smudge of lipstick leaking past its lines, that she recognized her. Ms. Adelaide, the Meeting leader, minus the leanness and the stealthy, feline walk, minus the pie chart and plus a puff of flesh around her middle.

Malaya nodded. "Hi, Ms. Adelaide," she said. "It's nice to see you."

Malaya watched the women talk. They exchanged a few pleasantries,

Ms. Adelaide shifting and stuttering, Nyela exuding friendliness as if she hoped to smile the woman away. Their expressions went together, Malaya now saw, complementary hues on a color wheel: awkwardness and shame. *Oh, I'm fine, can't complain. Still trying to get this weight off . . . I hear you, I've been so bad lately . . . Have to get back on track. You know how it is! . . . I sure do . . . Have you seen so-and-so from the Meeting? She lost fifty pounds. A new woman now . . . Well, good for her. She's losing 'em and I'm finding 'em, I guess . . . Been so bad . . . You know how it is . . . I sure do.* Throughout the exchange, Ma-Mère sat stiff as a coatrack, her lips knitted into a smile that looked like it hurt.

Perhaps it was the unexpected space around her belly, or the wildness of mind that was starting to feel like a habit—but the leaden chitchat and guardrail spines now felt far from Malaya. She watched, thinking how like a game it was, and how unwinnable. Even your own face could turn on you, and your body already had. The best a woman could hope for was to be on her own side. The game made these women seem small, and that was something Malaya didn't want. Now there was space around her. If she tried, she could sit back, spread out, and take the women in like a familiar rhythm, like the drumbeats from African dance class, something in her, but separate from her.

"Well," Ma-Mère said once Ms. Adelaide was gone, "shut down the trough and the cows come a-runnin'." She followed Ms. Adelaide with her eyes and then smoothed down the bodice of her skirt suit. "But she's a nice woman. Shame to see her go downhill like that. She used to have quite a figure, remember?" She passed the question across the table on a sigh and slid her wedding rings up and down on her fingers.

"Of course I remember," Nyela said, looking suddenly fatigued. "Maybe something happened to her."

"Could be," Ma-Mère replied. "But something always happens in life, and even if other women lay down and die, that doesn't mean we can afford to." She looked at Nyela. "Your grandmother used to always say nothing like fat to make a woman's bad into worse. She wasn't more than a size ten, but even she knew. All these women in here stuffing their faces and pretending they're somebody's Jolly Auntie So-and-so, it's a lie. They smile at babies and they cook for their children and whoever else. Maybe they even have some scrap of man. But when they close their eyes at night, they're alone. They eat because it hurts, and the more they eat, the more it hurts, and the more alone they are, until a plate of food is the only company they can find. Then they come to places like this—the closing of a restaurant in a neighborhood that's slipping away like salt into water—and they act like the end of the restaurant is the end of the world."

Malaya waited for Nyela to say something, but she only sipped the water and looked around the room. Malaya had never seen photos of her great-grandmother, and she had always wondered what size she'd been. But now that she heard she wasn't surprised. A woman smaller than her, smaller than Nyela, smaller than Ma-Mère, who still hated herself for being fat. The conversation was timeless, and Malaya wondered how far back it began. These women didn't make up the world that boxed them in, Malaya now realized. They lived in it, just as she did, but it was made before and beyond them, by someone who cared less. She knew this world, understood its rules and melodies. But she didn't need it forever. She could suck out its comforts like sugar candy from a straw, and then say no. She could look at their universe of ravenous shame, hold it at a distance, and decide for herself.

When the food came, Nyela let her shoulders relax as she slid her plate toward her, the prickly sweet smell of the greens floating over the table. Ma-Mère's face was bright as she talked about the meal, how good the cornbread was and how she hadn't had hush puppies fried right since the Senior Sunbirds' last cruise, a two-week trip to Guyana.

"Nyela, do you ever think of traveling again?" she asked between bites. "You haven't left the country since . . . well, in a long time, seems to me. Might do you some good to move around, get out into a different place."

Nyela pushed a heap of greens around on her plate and pressed them into their juice. "No, not since our honeymoon," she said. She sighed and frowned. "But I have a full teaching load in the fall, and if I don't get this book written this year, I'm sunk."

Ma-Mère gave an imperious nod, making a show of holding her

tongue. Malaya looked down at her plate, at the whisper-thin space between her body and the table.

"I was thinking of going to the Dominican Republic," she said. It hadn't been true, but suddenly it was. "There's a summer program. Shaniece told me about it. She gave me a brochure. It looks pretty good. You study Spanish and work with artists. And you travel."

Nyela opened her mouth as though she wanted to say something. She sat there, her lips in the shape of an O. "Well, that sounds good, Malaya," she said finally. "Do you think they can accommodate you?"

Malaya frowned. "I don't know," she said. "I guess the deadline is soon. Actually it probably already passed." She picked up her fork and pushed it into a mound of rice.

"Oh, please," Ma-Mère said after a sip of water, swatting the idea away like a housefly. "You think they're gonna turn down your good green dollars because of a date somebody printed on a piece of paper? Rules ain't written in blood for everyone. Seem like all them years with those rich white children woulda taught you that. Sometimes you have to act like the world was made for you, even if all sense and signs say it's not. Go on and call 'em and you'll find out."

Then she added, "Anyway, that'd be better than sticking around here. When a place like this goes under"—she pointed at the restaurant's wood-paneled walls—"everything's up for grabs. Who knows what'll happen to Harlem. Lord knows this ain't no real fine dining, but if you put a gun to my head, I'd have to say it's the best y'all had."

Nyela pulled the basket of cornbread toward her. "Mom," she said finally, her voice quiet. "This place meant something to me."

Ma-Mère rested her fork on the plate. "I know, Nathallie," she said. She passed her the butter. "I know it did. Do you want dessert?"

The evening spun on from there, the three women eating and talking, their voices just a shade easier. But for the rest of the night, through the conversation and the paying of the check, the walk up the sweaty avenue back to the brownstone, Malaya found herself looking down. She had to check. She had done nothing to bring it on, for all her years of trying. She hadn't starved, she hadn't hurt, she hadn't nearly fainted. All she had done was make a habit of letting herself be. It was a total surprise, sudden and spontaneous as weather. But it was here, still, and no less true. She looked down at her belly, again and again. She felt the speed in her step. Today, there was room. Today, she could move.

THE NEXT NIGHT, after a day spent in her bedroom, Malaya put on her red EMCEE hoodie and her newest jeans. She braided Kool-Aid red into her hair—the first color since the funeral—and she went to see Shaniece.

She pressed the buzzer lightly and barely knocked on the door. When Shaniece opened it, she did not look surprised. Malaya had not seen the apartment before, but she felt she knew it. Small and crowded with stuff—empty bottles, old newspapers, ashtrays, and books. A labyrinth of piles leading to Shaniece's room, a neat yellow oasis. Her twin bed with its worn pink sheets. Like beats of breath at the end of a conversation, there was no telling, only having heard. They touched each other's faces. They kissed each other, grabbed each other's hair and bit. It was different from the first time. This was new, a weightier dance, with no bar and no men and no one watching. The music was their bodies, now, and they made it intently, like work, feeding each other muscled rhythms: slow, then fast, faster, slow again. Malaya let herself lead, holding her body over Shaniece on the narrow, rickety bed. She let her weight press on her—lightly, further, almost fully—then retreated. Shaniece held Malaya's hands to her face and closed her eyes. Squeezing each other's shoulders, they switched. Pressing each other's palms, they shifted. Grown and bucking and serious, they moved.

Neither said anything until afterward, when they lay on the bed, exhausted. At the end of several breaths, Shaniece turned onto her side and looked at Malaya, her face a question mark again.

"Did you get my note?" she said.

Another kiss, heavy, like pushing face-first through clouds.

Malaya nodded. "I sent in the application. I think I might go."

Soul Clap

THE NEXT DAY, Malaya started to clean. Not everything. Just her room was enough. She felt bigger and smaller at the same time, like a balloon filled with helium, thinning and stretching at once. As the feel of her body changed, the space around her seemed to change as well. Her room became a dizzy, headached place, full of trash and old air. It was a hiding place, fitted with its own cozy dangers, as most true hiding places are.

Shaniece had said she'd call, but she didn't. She didn't call the following night, but the cleaning kept Malaya busy. The wrappers and bottles and plastic utensils, slick and brown with weeks-old grease, had taken thorny root. Beneath each layer of the room's trash was more trash: half-finished collages of women torn from magazines, heads without bodies, bodies without heads, the stomach drawings she'd done after the visit to Dr. Sawyer, shaded in pastel and bisected with hard ink. Then, too, there were unused brushes, feather-soft and dry. The easel Percy had given her sat untouched, its palette stand holding oil sets still in their plastic, its base beams covered by blank canvases, yawning muted white.

So she cleaned. First to music from the radio, then to one of her father's funk CDs, then only to the sound of her feet moving quickly across the floorboards. She changed her sheets and breathed in the lemony cool. She folded her T-shirts, hung up her jeans, clipped the broad shoulders of her 5X hoodies to the too-narrow hangers with clothespins so they wouldn't fall off. She clapped the dust out of her curtains and watched it billow along the walls' coiled moldings like paisley print. She thought of the funeral. She wiped down the windows and paused for a minute to watch a group of girls jump double Dutch under the whirl of the streetlights, right in the middle of the street.

When the groan of hunger came, late that night, she went down to the kitchen. She was surprised to find the light on, the television chattering with static. Nyela sat at the table behind a row of Tupperware bowls and aluminum tins, a soup spoon in her hand. Malaya watched from the stairwell as her mother spooned cold food onto a paper plate, meats and pastas towering so high it seemed the plate might rip in two.

She was wearing the green nightgown she had worn years ago, but its lustre was gone. Now the fabric was worn in patches, and it clung to her breasts and stomach. Hunched over, Nyela shoveled spoonfuls of rice, greens, and pork into her mouth, her eyes fixed on the television's blizzard of black and white dots. Malaya pushed herself to the side of the stairway, trying not to breathe. When the food was finished, Nyela reached across the table, spoon in hand, and plunged into the cold lasagna for another helping. This time, she bypassed the plate, scooping glaciers of pasta and near-solid sauce into her mouth straight from the tin. She looked like a different person, the kind of woman she had warned Malaya never to become. She looked resigned, messy even, but also beautiful in her private freedom.

When a hunk of lasagna tumbled over Nyela's belly and into her lap, Malaya shifted, and the floorboards creaked beneath her.

"Malaya." Nyela looked up, startled. There was a dark red sauce stain in the middle of her nightgown, like a palm print. Malaya watched as she pulled in her stomach, edging up on the chair, stiffening, straightening, sucking in. She felt an urge to wrap her mother in something, to cover her up.

She walked toward the doorway. Nyela dropped the spoon in the tin and searched around the table for napkins, but there were none. She dabbed at the corners of her mouth with her fingertips.

"I just came down to put the food away," she said. She rolled the foil back over the lasagna tin, then snapped the lid on a Tupperware of cat-fish. "How are you doing?"

"I'm okay," Malaya said.

Nyela looked at the half-packed containers. "I'm just having a quick snack before I head to bed," she said. Then she looked at Malaya. She pulled a paper plate from the stack and pushed it across the table toward her. "Do you want something?"

It was a stunning offer. Malaya thought of apple pie à la mode, what a rare gift it had once been to eat with her mother, each time a Christmas. Eating, really *eating* with her mother had been the unimaginable height of living. But now Nyela's face looked dead, her eyes reaching out to speak beyond a frozen surface.

Malaya shook her head. "I'm okay," she said again.

Nyela looked at the table, drawing breath through her nose and straightening her back. She folded her greasy plate neatly and sat it beside her. She hesitated for a moment, then reached for the clean plate she had offered Malaya and pulled it back to her side of the table.

"They're doing a memorial dedication for him at the House of Worship on Sunday. Where your grandfather used to preach. They're building a computer room. They've been having trouble keeping their space, with rent going up. I made a hefty donation in his name. The Percy Clondon Center for Digital Technology. I thought he might like that." She pulled the lid off a bowl of potato salad and spooned some onto the clean plate. "I hope you come. But if you aren't feeling up to it, I understand."

"Okay," Malaya said. "I can go. I'm feeling alright. And anyway, Ma-Mère would have something to say about it if I didn't go." She tried a playful smile.

"Yeah, I know what you mean," Nyela said. She gave a small chuckle and pushed back from the table. "Your grandmother's a tough cookie. That's what your dad used to say. I never realized it till he said it. I spent most of my life taking everything that came out of her mouth so seriously, even when I told myself I wasn't listening." She looked up, her eyes warming. "Yesterday, she came to the room with a piece of carrot cake in one hand and a recipe for the new Celery Soup diet in the other. And she sat down on my bed just like you used to do. She gave me both of them at the same time, like it was nothing, and said, 'I brought you these. A woman's got to get out of her mess sooner or later. I figured if one of these didn't help you get started, the other would.' And then she walked away. And it was just so ridiculous, how earnest she was, even while being so mean. Like she just doesn't know any other way to be. And when she left, I don't know, I just started laughing. Your father always said it, and I never understood. All these years feeling hurt by the things she said. Now I realize—I should have been laughing the whole time."

"Yeah," Malaya said. She imagined the scene—Ma-Mère showing up, cruel and perplexing, Nyela letting herself laugh.

"She's tough," Nyela said again, "but there's something to her. She says what she thinks. And that's something. Half the battle, at least. Maybe more."

Malaya ran her fingers along the grooves of the door's wood paneling. She watched her mother's smile hang in midair, wondering when and how hard it would fall.

"I think he would like it," Malaya said finally. "The computer lab. I think it would really mean something to him."

Nyela looked up. "Yeah?" she said. "Okay, good. That's really good." She pulled the plate toward her, then paused. "Will you tell me something?"

"Okay," Malaya said.

"His book," she said, her eyes soft like custard. "Was there really a book?"

At first Malaya didn't understand; then suddenly she did.

"Yes," she said too loud, like a bark, like trying to save the day. "He worked on it all the time. In the family room, and around the neighborhood. He had filled up at least a few notebooks already. Maybe three. I don't know. They're probably in the family room. And he got all these old newspapers and magazines. Records, too. He would leave in the morning and walk around, collecting stuff and taking notes all day. It was pretty much all he did, I think."

"Yeah," she said. "I saw the books. But I wasn't sure if there was something else."

"I don't think so," was all Malaya could offer.

"What did he look like when he talked about it?" Nyela asked. "I mean, how was his face?"

"I don't know how to describe it," Malaya said. She felt the kitchen light on her as she searched for the words. "I've never really seen him look that way before. Like he felt powerful, I guess. But also kind of like a little boy."

Nyela nodded. Malaya let her body lean against the threshold. She felt she was helping in some way, though she wasn't sure how.

"You know," Nyela said, "when we bought this house, everyone thought we were crazy. Sometimes we thought so too. It was like crack moved in the day after we did, and here we were, this young couple with this kid and this mortgage we could barely afford, dodging bullets on the way to work. You couldn't play outside, and that was really serious to him."

She turned the plate around on the table. "We always used to talk about how we knew things in the neighborhood would change. Sometimes it felt like a lie we were telling ourselves, but we had to. We talked about it all the time. How the streets would spruce up and the trash would get collected more than once a week. How the new businesses would bring jobs and crime would go down. And the neighborhood would change for us—for black people. And we would be here, the three of us, with a gorgeous house in the middle of it all. This black family in Harlem." She looked at Malaya. "It's one of the funny things in life. No matter how grown you get, if you're a certain kind of person, you'll always hope. If you're a certain kind of person, you can always be naïve. Your father and I are both that way. I guess it's a good thing, in a sense. We saw all this change for the neighborhood, you couldn't have told us it wouldn't be for us. We never thought it would be for white folks moving in, as much as we know about the world. They don't even see it. They move in because they love Harlem—what they think Harlem is—and then they erase it. That's the story of black culture. We make magic, they consume it, make it theirs. We have to start over, and we do. Over and over again. It's hard on people."

She picked up the fork and traced a pattern on the grease-stained paper. Then she put it down. "Folks work and struggle and make do for years, longer, praying for things to get better. They hold on long enough, just long enough to see the change come, and as soon as change does come, they realize it's not for them. It's hard watching home unravel in your hands. It's like the minute home becomes what you dreamed of, it's not your home anymore. It makes for a kind of madness. Like there's no such thing as home."

Malaya looked past her mother, toward the kitchen window, at the plush, suede darkness of the backyard lit softly by the garden light. It looked like a theater set, fake and welcoming, thick enough to cover everything behind it, so that the space beyond could hold anything at all.

"He was right to want to write about it," Nyela said finally. "It was a good idea. One of his many." She pulled a tin of lamb chops toward her and rolled back its cover, cutting herself a chunk the size of her palm. It was cold, but Malaya could still smell the seasonings—thyme, mint, cool, gummy fat.

"And then there's me," Nyela said. She spooned a shimmering heap of onions onto the meat. "Here I am, looking for a book idea and can't find one to save my life. And so I guess I'm thinking, why not?" She paused with the spoon in her hand, swirling it slowly in the air. "What do you think your father would say to that?" she said to the space in front of her. "Me writing a book about Harlem changing. The psychology of his vanishing home."

Malaya looked at her mother and said nothing. Nyela pushed the fork into the meat, then put it down.

"Because I have no idea what he would say." She paused. "The old Pra would have loved it, I know that. But the new Percy was a stranger. But I tried. You try so hard to keep everything together. This is what it is to be a woman. Everything is your job. Your job is everything: to be attractive, successful, raise smart, healthy children who are ready for life. To be available to everything. To *be* everything. And you work hard at it, at everything, at doing all this everything right. And in the back of your mind you're holding your breath and waiting for someone to hand you a prize. Something that says, *You did a good job—You did good at everything—*

and *Someone appreciates it*. If you're lucky, you get little flashes here and there: a promotion at work, or someone notices you lost a few pounds. But you always hope for that one person who will look at you and see all the *everything* you do, and applaud."

Nyela picked up the fork, brought it to her mouth, then put it down again without biting. "But what kind of applause is thanks enough for *everything*? Who has those kinds of hands?" she said. "The everything of womanhood carries no reward at all. And yet, everything still has to get done. So you keep working and you stop waiting, but the hope is still there, tucked in a corner. Sometimes it's the only thing that keeps you going—the hope that that someone—that one person—will applaud." She picked the fork up for the third time, held it in front of her face, and inspected it, as though there were a story inside. Then she let it fall. "But now he's gone.

"I'm tired," she said, sitting up, straightening herself. "Grieving lets me be tired."

Malaya's throat felt full, as though she'd swallowed a bone. There were no words in her. But there was her mother, stained and wobbling, struggling to stay laced up—for her, she guessed, but also for herself, and for a mass of people that weren't even people at all, just the endless weave of rules and expectations that had always mattered, it seemed, more than people ever would.

"Are you okay?" Malaya said, finally. "I mean, do you need anything?"

Nyela sank into the chair, dissolving like a sand castle into a wave, her head lowering slowly and her back arching down until her cheek pressed flat against the table.

Malaya let go of the wall and went toward her. She perched on the rickety stool beside her mother and placed an arm on the back of Nyela's chair, resting her weight there to keep the stool from breaking. She felt her hand hover over Nyela's, felt it fall leaf-light on the cool skin. Then Nyela's head fell again, down like a sigh until it rested in the bend of Malaya's elbow. It was a feeling neither had felt in years: the prickle of one's hair on the other's cheek, one's skin so near the other's it stuck.

After a few seconds, Nyela inhaled deeply and propped herself up on her elbows.

"I'm sorry," she said, her face gathering slowly. "I'm really alright. Don't worry. This is just . . ." Then her face broke and she leaned forward, moaning into the containers in long, wordless syllables. Malaya reached out her arm again.

They stayed there for a while, time thinning down, until the noise stilled. "I'm okay," Nyela said. "I am. Are you okay?"

Malaya nodded. "Yeah," she said. She lifted herself up from the back of the chair. There was cool sweat on her arms where her mother's skin had been. Her throat was empty.

She looked at her mother, raised her eyebrows, and started to clap. It was a small, soundless gesture at first, a muted applause, like the kind people gave to show polite appreciation without taking up too much space. But then she opened her arms wide and sped them together, letting the sound grow loud and full, holding her hands up and clapping faster, an all-out soul clap, the way the choir at her father's church did when the music fell away and the voices and bodies took flight. She gave herself to the motion, laughing from her belly and adding a dance to the movement, jerking her shoulders like the leader of a choir, popping her hips out, dipping. Soon, Nyela was laughing too.

"I applaud you!" Malaya said. Her voice was big and unfamiliar, an echo of a voice she couldn't place, but one that delighted her.

"Well, thank you, Malaya," Nyela said, laughing again. She wiped her face, then kept laughing, her cheeks rounding and her eyes flickering with light as they had years ago. Nyela put her hands on her own cheeks and breathed. "I appreciate that."

"It's true," Malaya said. She placed her palms flat on the table next to her mother's, both still laughing, and she said it again.

Mz. Thang

No one seemed to notice the changes that mattered. The way Malaya cackled loudly now at chewing gum and concealer ads on the bus, sound pouring out bright and brassy from her mouth. The way she let her arms sway and her hips bop as she sped down Broadway, racing against her own breath. How she let herself crack jokes at dinner, no matter whether Ma-Mère would approve, no matter whether anyone would understand. Now she chose to go places if she wanted to, even if it meant requesting a seat that fit her. Now she talked about her father. Now she touched her mother. Now she let herself do the big, outrageous thing more often than not. But no one saw. What people noticed was the weight.

You slimming down, huh? . . . Looking good! What program you doing? . . . I was worried about you . . . How many pounds you lost so far? I know your mama's happy. Look at the new you! Just don't get too skinny now, ha-ha. A man likes some meat on his bones.

Shaniece still had not called, and the silence made Malaya feel jittery. Several times, she picked up the receiver just to make sure the phone was still working, which it was. She tried, at first, to calm herself with cheese puffs and chicken, but it didn't work. So she went out. She began prowling the blocks for images of bodies, ripping cardboard waists and shoulders from subway placards, snipping models' curved calves from the cognac ads plastered on the windows of Bee-Rite-Liquors, now out of business, and tearing glossy smiles from the tabloids at Mr. Gonzales's, the last remaining bodega on Broadway. She set aside painting and pastels in favor of street collage. She put the images together into caustic woman shapes, round here and here and narrow there, a roller coaster of bulges and lines. When each piece was done, she latticed it with words—chunky, mouthful phrases like FULL-FAT and NON-NEGOTIABLE and OCULAR COMBUSTION and GLEE, printed huge and black.

She hung the pieces up along the banisters in the house at first, but soon she ran out of space. So, again, she went outside. She taped the collages to the phone booths and streetlights, pasted them over the FOR SALE signs of the storefronts on Amsterdam, hung them like chandeliers from the bus stop shelters. Still, no one seemed to notice.

They only noticed the pounds.

"Damn, big girl," a young dreadlocked man on the corner said through a puff of weed smoke as she walked to the bodega. Malaya had seen him before, but he had never spoken to her. "You lookin' good. Whatever you doing, keep that shit up, yo." He eyed her belly as people always did, but now she felt his gaze on her hips, too.

"You look pretty, mami," Mr. Gonzales told her from behind the bodega counter as he passed her twenty cents' change for a bottle of water. "I don't mean to disrespect."

When men said these things to her, it produced an odd mix of anger and gratitude. Mr. Gonzales had known her since she was a child, had seen her spend a decade's worth of allowance on cheap cookies and pies, and yet he looked at her now as if he'd never seen her before—as if she were becoming a different person, a better person, before his eyes. And yet, it was nice to be told she was beautiful without caveat or reservation, and without having to offer anything in return.

Malaya nodded at these comments and sometimes even said "thank you," but she never smiled. Men's attention and approval were borrowed gifts she was no longer sure she wanted. If they were tied to weight—and it was clear they were—she would have to continue losing weight to keep them. She had no idea if that would happen, and for the first time, it didn't matter. Losing weight was not the point.

Eventually, a few Harlem women did pick up on this deeper change in her, and they commented as she walked down the avenue, enjoying the thrill of her new speed.

"Oh okay, I see you, Mz. Thang!" one sweet-faced neighbor chirped when she saw Malaya walking Broadway. "I know they can't tell you nuthin' now."

And it was true. Malaya had learned a kind of hearing that let her mute the taunts and turn up the praise and keep both at a volume just below her own quiet whisper: *Go ahead—Taste it. Say it. Do the outrageous thing.* She started to think of it as a sort of reverse-diet. Dieting meant you let go of pleasures and replaced them with work. If you were good at it, you soon convinced yourself that the work actually *was* pleasure, and that what you had once known as joy was really weakness, vice. Eventually, the goal was to come to see mashed potatoes and cookie dough as criminals—sinister, deceptive tricksters that robbed you of your perspective and your will—and to embrace StairMasters and celery as beacons of virtue and truth. The victory was to stop the indulgence and start the work and lay yourself down, a perpetual welcome mat for change. It was a nearly biblical narrative, one Malaya knew well.

But her new will to wildness flipped the script. Now, she did not stop indulging. She did not do anything that hurt. She committed only to doing exactly what she wanted to do at every moment possible. If she walked quicker and more often, it was because she was excited about where she was going. If she ate less, it was only because there were other things she wanted to do.

WHEN DR. WINDBORNE ASKED what she felt about how people were reacting to her weight loss, Malaya pulled her left leg up with her hands and crossed it over her right knee—something she hadn't known she could do until the moment she tried it. Sitting there feeling elegant if slightly confused, she smiled. "You mean when they say I'm beautiful?" she said. "Well, I'm glad someone finally noticed." And she gave a laugh so full it surprised her.

Dr. Windborne laughed with her, leaning her head back in her muffin seat and propping her elbows up on the cushioned arms. Then, without missing a beat, she asked, "Did anyone notice before?"

Malaya tugged on her crossed leg to keep it from sliding off its perch. She took a sip of her orange juice, then looked back at Dr. Windborne.

"My dad," she said.

She was surprised that she'd said "dad" instead of "father," as though she were eight years old again and he was right there at the windowsill. "He said things like that all the time. I hated it. I don't know if it was because I thought they weren't true, or because I wished he would say them to my mother instead. Maybe both."

Dr. Windborne nodded and scribbled on her notepad, her rings sparking under the light as her wrists shimmied across the paper. Malaya looked out the window. They were doing construction on the building across the street, and a maze of scaffolding covered the face of the structure, white tarps flapping like flags in front of the limestone. With every few beats of the wind, Malaya could see the gargoyles, exposed in flashes in their ridiculous poses, this one's teeth and claws bared, that one holding his cheeks, another's hands half covering his eyes as though playing peekaboo. On the roof of the building was another layer of scaffolding, covering an inset wall. It looked like they were adding something—a garden, or a pool. Whatever it was, the addition made the building look much bigger than it had been, and made the gargoyles small. Malaya thought of the flyer Shaniece had left her, the tiny spot of brown girl at the foot of a skyful of mountains that covered both pages with green.

"Can I ask you something?" Malaya said.

"Of course. Ask away."

"You like to travel a lot, right?"

Dr. Windborne made a panoramic gesture around the roomful of statues and figurines. "What gives you that idea?"

Malaya smiled. "Is it hard?" she asked. Her crossed left leg began to dislodge from its crook. She tugged it back into place. "I mean, getting around, you know? And not knowing, I don't know . . . how people see you."

Dr. Windborne nodded. "Sometimes it is hard," she said. "But then again, those things are hard anyway, whether you stay in one place or not."

"I guess that's true," Malaya said, holding her knee. "But so then why fly across the world to deal with the same old shit?"

"Well," Dr. Windborne said, "I'm someone who likes to learn about myself, so—"

"Does that make you a narcissist?" Malaya interrupted. If there was a line between outrageousness and obnoxiousness, she knew this was it. But it was something she really did want to know. Mail had come from the summer arts program, a thick envelope as long as her forearm. She had told no one, hadn't even opened it. Instead, she stuffed it in the shelf of her captain's bed, where the junkyard of candy wrappers used to be. But now, with Dr. Windborne, she found herself asking questions.

"No," Dr. Windborne shook her head, chuckling. "I would be a narcissist if I thought about myself all the time but never learned anything."

"So you travel because it teaches you about yourself? Isn't that kind of trite?" Malaya asked, her eyebrows arched. Part of her was having fun. "I think I heard that on a Peace Corps commercial."

Dr. Windborne gave a splashy laugh, like silver dollars tossed into water. "I guess that would be trite," she replied, "but that's not what I said. I don't travel because it teaches me about myself. I travel because I've been learning about myself for a while, and one thing I've learned is that I like surprises. Not a ton of people look like me, depending on where you go. Traveling lets me be the surprise, for them and for myself."

Malaya imagined Dr. Windborne out in the world, the spectacle of her. She pictured her showing up in places like Belgium or Sri Lanka or Basque Country, a thick smear of brown and blaring color, pushing through museums and subway tunnels and markets, curious in all ways. She thought of the eyes that must fall on her in these places, and all the things there were for her to see.

"I never thought of it that way," Malaya said, "but yeah, I guess I've always wanted to be a surprise, too."

Dr. Windborne nodded. "That sounds like the truth to me," she said, and she began to scribble again. Malaya wasn't sure what she was writing, but now it didn't worry her. She took a last swallow of her juice and listened to the dance of Dr. Windborne's bracelets against the clipboard, watching the gargoyles play their game beneath the billowing tarps outside.

MALAYA'S WEIGHT LOSS seemed to change the Clondon home, infusing it with an air of cautious excitement that made Malaya feel both proud and lonely. When the three women were all together, Nyela smiled and complimented Malaya. But then, when it was just her and Nyela crossing paths in the hallway, Malaya noticed her mother clasping her own hands together, gazing at her with the fidgety distance of a sister being left behind. Ma-Mère took a different approach. She treated Malaya's weight loss like a dream of a winning combination in the numbers—something to be seized on immediately and run with, all the way to the bank. As soon as Malaya cleared the 4X mark and could once again fit into clothes from Sizes Unlimited on 125th, Ma-Mère took the liberty of making her an appointment at an obesity surgery clinic she had seen on television.

"This doctor is very different from that quack your mother took you to," she said one afternoon. She and Malaya were going through Percy's closet, boxing his clothes to donate to the House of Worship. "It's a woman surgeon. She's smart and young and slim as a blade. Seems like just the kind of woman you'd want working on you. They said on the show her husband's a surgeon, too. Imagine that."

It was still early in the morning, too early for Malaya to try to figure out why anyone would connect a surgeon's marital status to the success of her practice, or how having surgery performed by a thin married woman would make a difference for her. In the past, she would've said nothing and kept on folding her father's dusty socks, but today, feeling free, she asked: "So you really think being thin makes people happy?"

Ma-Mère frowned, then sighed, and turned back to the wrinkled cuffs of Percy's pants.

"I think happiness comes in pieces, My Ly-Ly. Money, looks, a quiet mind that don't ask too many questions. Power. All those are pieces of what it takes to be happy. No exact science to it, but some things are just true: women are handed fewer pieces of happiness and pay more for 'em. Black women, that goes double. If you're fat, then double that again. You take a fat black woman with a smart mouth, strange habits, and no sense of shame, and she doesn't stand a chance, I can tell you." She looked at Malaya frankly. "Might as well cash in what little happiness she has, go to the buffet, and just stay there. Some women do."

She folded the pants, scrutinizing the crease. "But that's not what I want for you. Your mother and I have happiness in mind for you," she said. "And now you're on your way, finally, looking better than ever. You're going in the right direction, and this will make sure you don't swerve. Plus, you'll feel safer with this woman. Less to worry about." She gave a stiff, grammatical smile, like Nyela's. She held up another pair of pants and inspected the hem. "You'll see. If not now, then later, when you're dancing at your wedding. Course you'll have to put off your painting trip until next summer, but that's alright."

"I thought you wanted me to go," Malaya said. "You said it was important."

"It is," Ma-Mère said. "But ain't nothing as important as your future. The world will be there later. Think how much easier getting around will be when you're thin. Think how much easier everything will be. How all the boys will treat you." She laid the pants in an open box on the sofa, taped it shut, and bent slightly at the knee, lowering the box to the floor. Then she stood up straight, smoothed her neatly creased khakis, and brushed her hands against each other as though to wipe the work away. There had always been something elegant about Ma-Mère. It once bothered Malaya to notice it. But looking at her with more grown eyes, she saw that her grandmother had the learned grace of a woman who had been a fat girl in an era of black-and-white starlets, someone who knew she'd never be seen as beautiful, but who tried her best anyway, perhaps to prove the world wrong.

"You're on your way to changing things now, My Ly-Ly," she said, sliding another box toward her. "You don't want to go backward. This is your chance."

Watching Ma-Mère seal the boxes, Malaya felt several women's stories spread over her. She could see it—her grandmother's shame spilling heavy onto her mother, her mother's shame poured into her. For them, and for all the nameless women breathing in the shadows of the family line, having the right body meant freedom. But it was a freedom none of them ever seemed to attain.

In that moment, Malaya chose shamelessness. Sitting here amid her father's dusty things, she saw it clearly: unfreedom would be the biggest shame to bear. So, she decided. Surgery or no surgery, no matter what she ate or how she moved or what she did with her body, thinness would not be her goal. Thinness was small in an undazzling way, and it paled before the grander scales of size that called to her now—the smallness of a body against a broad scape of mountains. The smallness of a life in the big, busy world.

Talking about the surgery with Ma-Mère, Malaya thought, *No. Not now.* She didn't want to be stuck in bed, recovering. Not this summer. The choice rolled open before her: she could lie down or she could move. And the truth was, today, Malaya wanted to move.

"I think I see it differently," she said, nervous but firm. She raised herself up from the rickety stool.

Ma-Mère paused, a long teal necktie dangling loose in her hand. She turned her mouth down in a half-frown. "I can't tell if you take after your father, or if this is a part of your mother I never got to see," she said. "Either way, it's something to watch out for."

"Maybe," Malaya said, moving toward the doorway. She looked at Ma-Mère and tried a smile, hoping she would smile too. But Ma-Mère simply frowned again and smoothed her blouse over her the bulge of her stomach.

Malaya said, "I love you," and climbed the steps to her room quicker than she thought she could. She closed the door, opened the window. Then she reached under the bed for the acceptance packet, the brochure with the round girl skyed by mountains on the cover.

IF SHE HAD TO PUT money on it, Malaya would've bet Shaniece would show up at least once before she left. To say something about what had happened between them. To make a plan, or say goodbye. But as the weeks passed and Malaya made her preparations—as she spruced up her Spanish and figured out how to make international calls, as she researched how to purchase two plane seats and a buckle extender, as she shopped for things she'd never needed before, like bathing suits and shorts, and smiled for the man at the Cibao Pasaporte y Notary on Broadway, as Nyela made the program's tuition payment and, her eyes moist, said, "Your father would love this," Shaniece was nowhere to be found.

Malaya began to daydream. She imagined appearing at Shaniece's apartment as she had a few months ago to see if anything had changed. She imagined the space transformed, Jerome Armistice vanished or changed, the chaos of the apartment swooped into order, Shaniece sitting at the center of it all, calm and neat and in control of everything. She wondered how this Shaniece would look at her, whether they would touch again, and what it would mean if they did. Once, she even went to the new Pathmark with the discount flyer, hoping to see Shaniece there in a white manager's coat. Not finding her, Malaya strolled the aisles instead, admiring the bright marbled pinks of the meats, the reds and greens of the produce so rich they could have come from an oil set, so much brighter than anything at the old CTown. She had left the supermarket with several tomatoes, some ground lamb, and a bouquet of mysterious herbs she chose purely by smell, and went home to make dinner for Ma-Mère and her mother. It was the first time she had really tried to cook, and they all agreed it was good.

Two days before she left, Malaya packed a couple of dulce de coco candies in a paper bag and carried it along Amsterdam Avenue, to the crest of Sugar Hill. It was a Sunday, and she had been roped into an afternoon of last-minute shopping at Lord & Taylor with her mother and Ma-Mère, both of whom seemed thrilled at the prospect of being able to dress Malaya in regular plus-size women's clothes, right off the rack. The trip was to be a mending of fences. After Malaya's uncharacteristic back talk, Ma-Mère had complained to Nyela, instructing her to tell Malaya that the surgery was the best thing for her, pushing her to put her foot down about the trip. But Nyela had surprised them both. "Mom," she said simply, "let her go."

It was hot out, and crowds of sticky-faced children gathered around the Coco Helado carts that stood on every corner. As Malaya walked, she thought about the children and their games, how different they seemed from the games she and Shaniece had played, but how similar, too. A hydrant was open across the street on Amsterdam, and children took turns running into the water, shrieking and splashing one another, then yelping and pulling each other back to the pavement as cars rolled past. A group of girls jumped double Dutch beside the rushing water, singing a song about boyfriend love, their hips rolling to their own rhythm.

Malaya moved to cross the street, toward Shaniece's building, but as she felt the spray of water on her face, something stopped her. It wasn't fear—it was something else, fear's opposite. It was knowing, and it calmed her. Shaniece was never one to be found; she always did the finding. It was a skill Malaya hadn't known to admire until now. Tentative and uncertain as she might have seemed, Shaniece always found her way to what she needed. And if she couldn't find it, she made it up herself. It had been the base of their friendship since back in the school bus days—the gifts of bodega candy and cake that made the secret gobbling of their fantasy lives possible. It was what kept them going, separate and together, through the stories of Clarence and Patricia Guzmán. Shaniece had even found herself safety at Galton—a family and a mission, something to be part of and to protect—and she had shared it with Malaya. Since then, she had found so much more. Shaniece never wanted anyone to find her, to save her. Successfully or not, she made it her business to look out for herself.

As she paused on the corner, Malaya listened to the girls' voices, a light but insistent tap from this childhood game she'd never had the chance to play. She let the package slip from her hand and watched the candies fall, dappled with sun, into a black stream of water rolling down Sugar Hill. Then she turned to the hydrant, to the game of double Dutch in the middle of the street, and jumped in. While the girls chanted their rope-twirling song, Malaya sang with them.

She had once thought she needed to pack herself with all the easy feeling she could find, to save her from the heavy press of the world. Closeness, safe and thick. But now she saw that wasn't the whole story.

Closeness also needed a limit: a point where a woman could be a woman and not somebody's mother; where a man could wonder without wandering away. A place where a girl could forget she was somebody's daughter, and could grow into a woman who was no one's but her own.

What Malaya needed was space, and the freedom to move through it. She felt it now, her teal braids wet and flapping in the air while the girls sang and laughed, clapping as she whirled through the rope to the rhythm. Space—*movement*—was the thrill. And Malaya had a right to be thrilled. She knew it like the taste of her tongue. The hugeness of living was not just for rich or wispy or butter-colored girls. It was not just for thin, white women, or the men who made the rules. The spark, the speed, the bigness of living was for Malaya, too. Hers as much as anyone's. And anything that wanted to stop her from gulping the hugeness of life had to be stepped on, stepped over, or kissed carefully and left behind.

Turning back up Broadway, she passed more hydrants, more children, women catching shade at bus stops and old men hopping out of the mouths of corner stores, twisting the caps off soda bottles, their faces wide with smiles. She walked uptown, past Chinese food stores and construction sites, bakeries gone out of business and mysterious new storefronts with bright colored signs that read COMING SOON. Hip-hop beats gave way to merengue horns and old soul bass lines as she walked, past teenagers sitting on cars and grandmothers sitting on stoops, past empty lots turned into health food stores and newly repointed brownstones, their windows plastered with realtors' crests, past the smells of food and smoke and broken concrete.

Damp with water and sweat, she moved past places she knew like blood and places she had never noticed, colors she could not be sure had ever existed before. She watched them, moving, moving, until home was in view.

She felt her legs beneath her, their fat and their muscle, and she opened her mouth. She looked at the house, the block, the sky, the hungry world around her. Then she closed her eyes, breathed deep, and opened them again, awake to the possibilities of the day.

ACKNOWLEDGMENTS

I have been imagining this book since the moment I discovered that a big black girl's life could be something to write about. I am fortunate to have learned that lesson early, and to have been supported by extraordinary family, friends, teachers, and loves along the way.

My father, James Sullivan, is one of the most special people I know. Thank you, Dad, for exemplifying wonder and the power of imagination. To my little brother, Malik Kahlil Sullivan, witness to so many stories, thank you for all the worlds we created back in the Family Room days. (Remember: "Kick! Punch! It's all in the mind!") And to my mother, Dr. Martha Adams Sullivan, you are a standard and an inspiration. Thank you for encouraging my work and nourishing my vision always. I love and appreciate you.

When I first shared news of the book's publication with a dear friend, she said, "That's Audre Lorde's publisher. You're in excellent company." And it's true—the book has been in spectacular hands from the start. I could not be more grateful to my phenomenal editor, Gina Iaquinta. Thank you for the talent, thoughtfulness, magic, and heart you've brought to this novel. Learning from you has been a true pleasure. Cordelia Calvert, Zeba Arora, and the rest of the rock-star team at Liveright, thank you for your truly brilliant work. Janet Silver, your eye and your vision have helped make this novel what it is. Thank you for believing in Malaya's story since those early days on the mountain years ago.

I am grateful to the many teachers who have helped this novel along its way: Samuel R. Delany, Darryl Pinckney, Joan Mellen, your imprints on this book are deep. Thank you for all the time and care you've offered over the years. Percival Everett, Howard Norman, Jonathan Lethem, Elizabeth Nunez, Noreen Tomassi, Patricia O'Toole, Jim Sheppard, Ibrahim Ahmad, and especially Arthur Flowers, I'm grateful for your feedback and your wisdom. Thadious Davis, Herman Beavers, Heather Love, Salamishah Tillet, thank you for supporting all the parts of my work. Kevin Quashie, Amy Kissel, Nancy Gannon, Daniel Rous, Anne Rosenthal, Ginger Leigh, thank you for showing me what inspired teaching can do. I am grateful beyond words to the late Randall Kenan and Richard McCann, and the inimitable Ntozake Shange. Your ever-presence is our fortune. It was a gift to have learned from you.

Thank you to all the mentors, colleagues, and friends who have helped shape my writing life, including Tiphanie Yanique, Evie Shockley, Kaitlyn Greenidge, Ivelisse Rodriguez, Rion Amilcar Scott, Natashia Déon, Nicole Dennis-Benn, Sheila Sundar, Marie-Hélène Bertino, Kristin Henley, Harriet Clarke, Sarah Mantilla Griffin, Isabel Geathers, and Colleen Kinder. I'm grateful to the Temple crew, especially Smriti Jaiswal, Andrea Lawlor, M. Milks, Sarah Dowling, Shinelle Espaillat, Joel Nichols, Amanda Lisle, and Adrian Khactu for the feedback and the fun. Abigail Baumann, thank you for new language in a tough time. Natalie Diaz, thank you for being a friend. Julie Enszer, thank you for your generosity, and for all the incredible work you do. Big love to my SPACE fam: Darius Bost, Marlo David, Treva B. Lindsey, Angelique V. Nixon, and Marlon "Big TX" Moore (who requested this shout-out specifically). This Harlem shake's for y'all.

This novel has had many homes, and has been fed by many families. I am grateful to the Department of English and Creative Writing at Temple University, the Bread Loaf Writers' Conference, the NYC Emerging Writer Fellowship at the Center for Fiction, the Yaddo artists' retreat, the National Endowment for the Arts residency at the Hambidge Center for Creative Arts, the New York State Summer Writers Institute, the Key West Literary Seminar, the Hedgebrook writers' retreat, and the Pan-African Literary Forum in Ghana. I'm also grateful for support from the Institute for Citizens and Scholars, the Mellon Foundation, the Social Science Research Council, the American Association for University Women, and the Gaius Charles Bolin Fellowship, each of which helped make this book possible. Thank you to the many colleagues, past and present, who have supported me as a writer and a scholar, especially those at the University of Pennsylvania, Williams College, Rutgers University, the University of Massachusetts, Duke University, Bryn Mawr College, and Georgetown University. Thank you to the Claw, Tree House Books, and the New City Writing Program in Philadelphia. Shout-out to my Hunter College High School peoples, especially the AGC: Christian Pierre, Eric Prengel, Elizabeth Adams, Jamal Jimoh, Brian Goetz, Larcenia Cooper, Adrienne Ford, Karnellia Brake, Candace Holmes, Joy-Anne Mitchell, and La Marr Jurelle Bruce. Thank you for the luv, 93 till infinity.

I'm grateful to the village of Harlem, New York, whose complexity and beauty define home for me, and to the many aunties, uncles, cousins, godparents, and more who have shaped my understanding of family.

To my friends and my loves: Effie Richardson, Erica Locke, Keisha Warner-LoSasso, Nicole Shawan Junior, Connie Utada, Kieu Smith, Quincy Scott Jones, and Marci Blackman, thank you for showing me the many gorgeous faces of community. I'm honored to call y'all my fam. Rachel Brown, Julia Jarcho, and Ásta Bennie Hostetter, early companions of my imagination, thanks for all the cool stuff we made together. Kalika Fail, thank you for showing me that new friends can be true friends. Finger tassels and typewriter fires all the way down! Cheryl Clarke, genius and muse, *merci pour tout*. Kamilah Aisha Moon, eternal starshine, you are in these pages. I am grateful for you. Hanifah Walidah, thank you for being my family, and for riding it out with me and Malaya all these years. Lecynia Marie Swire and C. Riley Snorton, you are friends of my mind. Thank you for gathering me in all the ways. L. H. Stallings, you already know.

Nina Sharma, you are this novel's fairy godmother. Thank you for reading, for listening, for wondering, and for caring about these characters. I couldn't have dreamed up a truer friend than you.

Jeanette Aycock, keeper of my words, you are in every part of this story. All I can say is thank you. And I love you.

And to all the students, readers, friends, and others I haven't named who've helped along the way, big, big thanks.